Thus Bound

The story of Tadziu and Marysza

TO JANET
MERRY CHRISTMAS
ALL THE BEST IN
THE NEW YEAR
12/26/09
Gerry

Geraldine Wierzbicki-Roach

First published by Dog Ear Publishing
4010 W. 86th Street, Ste H
Indianapolis, IN 46268
www.dogearpublishing.net

ISBN: 978-159858-877-4

This book is printed on acid-free paper.
This book is a work of Fiction. Places, events, and situations in this book are purely fictional and any resemblance to actual persons, living or dead, is coincidental.

Printed in the United States of America

Acknowledgments:

The completion of this book would not have been possible without the assistance of many people.

Thanks to my husband Robert whose love and patience I felt every step of the way.

To my immediate family: my father Jerome, my mother Tillie, my brother John and my sisters Christine and Nanette, for their encouragement and enthusiasm.

To my children: Robert, Mary and Timothy, for tasks as diverse as reading the first draft, providing critical commentary and keeping my computer in operation.

To Col. George Navadel USMC (Ret.) who served two tours of duty in Vietnam, for hours of technical assistance in the portion of the novel that deals with the Vietnam War. Any errors occurring therein can be attributed only to myself. Incidents portrayed involving the corps are purely fictional.

To my uncle Anthony Burakowski, a World War II veteran who fought with the marines in the island campaigns, for sharing his Marine Corps experiences with me.

To all other friends and relatives who cheered me on.

For Mama

Prologue

1938

An Ending

Darkness surrounds us all, especially me. I am hunted, will be found. Red lights on the roofs of police cars, revolving eyes trying to see. Men huddle, speak in hushed tones. I'm not to know. I shrink into myself, no longer solid, never again solid, forever a mass of holes with everything falling through. I watch it beginning to fall—our bed, the new sheets, the pillowcases, the baby's crib—and I'm afraid. The red lights turn. A siren wails, then fades, like a child told to stop crying. My baby cries, but Ma comes from someplace behind and takes her. The red lights turn.

I see this morning. My breasts are sore. The boy who is the man sucks hard but he is gentle, claims my breasts with his mouth, his tongue, his hands. He calls them flowers, sometimes plucks them from behind. Then I am lost. Hold my breasts out for him. We laugh in secret and slide down further into the bed.

He can't reach me now. We're not in the bed, in the room with faded paper on the walls, lace curtains with holes and puffs of pierzyna,[1] *with quills poking out to scratch us. Now it will all be gone, I know.*

The darkness was our darkness. I opened for him until the night was gone. When he left, I carried him inside myself and waited, heard only the baby, the girl-child. He returned at night to find the place between my legs. He knew that I waited, that I gave my breasts to the child who nibbled and made me ready.

Sirens grow louder. Men carry other men on stretchers and lay them on the ground. He carries one: the ropes of vein in his arms inflate under the stretcher's weight. He turns and our eyes meet. I will be waiting.

Voices and movement grow. Fear inches through me, drags itself outside and wraps me in a scream that will not sound.

"They were fumigating the mill for rats. The gas masks weren't enough, didn't work or some God-damned thing. They started dropping like flies. Joe saw it first."

Hours, years pass, my fear growing, eating me into pieces. Ambulances begin to move, shouting their right-of-way. I hold part of myself. Ma holds another part. The men won't look at me, turn their eyes away. He's gone, not behind the lights or the men sweating, wiping their foreheads on their arms or the women crying into their hands.

"They're bringing him now. He dragged out every man. Then collapsed. Just collapsed."

I see them thrust him into the open mouth of an ambulance. He won't hitch-hike from the mill tonight to get home fast so we can start. It won't be that he kisses me, unable to break from my mouth as we move into our room when no one is home and the baby is sleeping. Buttons will not tear from my blouse, the part covering my milk-swollen breasts, a corner of the cloth caught in his mouth. His bird teeth won't forget, won't bite so I cry out, and he's sorry and tries to be slow.

I stand in the darkness and the red lights. Stretchers are taken away. I can't count them. Eyes I don't want to see confront me, drown me in their sorrow. Ma tries to drag me away. I won't go. In a dream, the cars and trucks and ambulances pass. Tires grind the stones like flour in the mill. Women cry around me, wave their bodies, come together like a wall. O Jezu, O Jezu,[2] *one moans, looking around with empty eyes, as if watching for someone to approach. No sound leaves me. I know I'm not forgiven, that he will never be allowed to return. My knowing rises like a stone with wings and blocks the scream now tearing at my throat, still wanting to rip itself free.*

"Elizabeth," says a man with a paper mask on his face, "we don't know how he is. He'll be at the hospital." But they don't know how to leave, how to stop looking at me. They're ashamed for being grateful they're the lucky ones, the ones not punished.

"I'm sorry," I say to God if He is there but I haven't made Him be there, have let Him leave. Shaking a fist at me.

"I won't do it again. Just let him be alive. I won't do it again. Won't do anything ever. Just let him be alive."

But I know he's gone. I can't pull him from what I always knew could take him—our sin, God's envy of our joy. My body knows, the shrinking breasts, the dryness climbing my legs, entering, spreading. My body knows. There is no "we", only me. Forever.

They tell us at the hospital that Joe died on the way there. They were testing a new gas to kill rats in the flour mill. He is the only one who dies because he went back in so many times. The men he helped to escape will all survive.

He lies for three days in the living room in a satin-lined box, an expensive box because all the men from Pillsbury give money, but it's not him. His face is pale, his hair pasted. Hands that will not touch me again are crossed on his chest. People come and go. His mother cannot talk to them. She starts to cry, loud, hysterical. I don't cry, don't unleash what sits within. It is useless to challenge this blow, dangerous to tempt this God. And so I talk to people.

"Yes, it's a terrible thing," or "yes, he was a good man," or "yes, Marysza and I will manage," or "yes, he loved his baby girl so much." I think of the days that will come, empty days, dry, with no milk for the baby. I don't want milk for the baby, don't want to hold her to my breast again.

The church is full. The men, dressed in dark suits, carry a coffin draped in black cloth, the huge white cross at its center lost in folds that fall to the wooden floor. Joe's father and brothers are first, then Pa and Ben. They place the box on four tall posts. He is still on display, still staring beneath the wood and the black cloth.

The priest says prayers, many prayers, long prayers, walks around the black box, sprinkling it with holy water and swinging something on a chain that releases sweetness into the air. Each time he faces the altar, he bows low.

There is Mass. In the sermon the priest speaks of Joe's unselfishness toward his fellow workers. He speaks of Joe's parents and his brothers and sisters. He speaks of me and Marysza. He tells us that we must be brave and trust in God for what we can't understand. Everyone cries but I turn away from their tears and don't cry because tears can't pay for what God has done to punish Joe. And me.

After the Mass, a long procession of cars rides to the cemetery. People stand around the open grave. The priest recites more prayers, long prayers, a litany of saints. The people reply Ora pro nobis [3] *after the priest says the name of each saint but the names are all in Latin, so except for names like* Sancta Maria *for the Blessed Virgin Mary and* Sancta Elzbieta *for the Blessed Virgin's cousin and me, I don't understand them*

Joe never said this many prayers in his life. I did but I won't anymore. At the end, the priest throws some dirt on the coffin which isn't in the ground yet but rests on a piece of white canvas that is becoming dirty. We leave him there.

The people sing a song in Polish that sounds like the entry of death.

Serdeczna Matko, opiekunko ludzi[4] *The crying grows louder, turns into what are not human cries but the cries of injured animals. When I was small and the song frightened me, Ma told me the English words. Something about our beautiful mother hearing us cry and protecting us*

I cry a little because of the song but mostly because of Joe's mother who stands small and gray. She was always nice to me, tried to put her Polish talk into English so I could understand. Sometimes the words came out funny.

"You get married, yes. Baby needs father."

And then I stop crying and feel cold. Thinking of Joe's mother's funny English. And our wedding.

I wore white. No one cared. They saw, knew about me and Joe and smiled as they shook their fingers. Even the priest lost his mean face when he married us. There were cakes and pies more than anyone could count and a band playing polkas and obereks[5] *all night long. We greeted relatives and friends and I felt sad at the looks some had. Even men. Sadness for themselves, because Joe and I made their eyes see what was far away and gone. Like the memory of sun when there is only rain and crops turn brown and rot in the fields.*

But after eating and drinking and dancing, their eyes turned happy. Because they remembered they once knew what Joe and I knew. And they saw it was a wheel that turned for everyone. For three days after the wedding, people returned to eat leftover food. Pa kept saying it was a wonderful wedding,

"Jakie to ladne wesele*".*[6]

Joe and I don't come back after the wedding. We stay in my aunt's house for our honeymoon. She is a widow and comes to stay with ma and pa until Joe and I come back. We'll live with ma and pa while Joe looks for work. There is more room for Joe on our farm because he still has younger brothers and sisters at home. I only have one brother, Ben.

Joe tries and tries but there are no jobs. Someone will try to get him into Bethlehem Steel. He helps Pa with the heavy work. I help Ma pick beans and dig potatoes until I'm too big to bend over and Ma says no more. The miracle happens just when I'm about to go into the hospital. A job opens at the Pillsbury flour mill, except for Bethlehem, the best place for a man to work around here. Joe's friend works there and gets Joe in.

My happiness. My happiness. Each day Joe returns from work, I smell the wonderful smell, the oily smell of the water down at the pier where the silos are located. I see the pride in his face, his feeling he is taking care of us. He starts work as a sweeper, the job every man starts at. I look at his arms and his hands, their black hair now covered with the white dust that travels through the air when flour is ground.

"There's no way to stop it," Joe says. "It gets into your eyes, your nose, through your pants and into your crotch." He tells me that heat from the machines makes the flour dust pasty. I see that it sticks in the grooves of Joe's hands but I can't look at his hands without thinking of night and wishing it would hurry and get dark.

We stay at Ma's because Joe wants to save money for us to get started on our own. He gives Pa money each week and Pa doesn't want to take it but Joe tells him we can't live there without paying our way. Ma is quiet but tells pa that if we leave, the baby will be gone. Pa rocks Marysza each day when he is finished with the farm work, holds her in his strong arms and tries to sing her songs he must remember from his childhood, like Goralu, czy ci nie zal.[7] *Some of them are not really songs. Pa just puts words to music, most of them to the tune of Christmas carols like* Cicha Noc [8] or Lulajze Jezuniu[9]

He sings the same words over and over again. The baby seems to be listening because she starts to cry when Pa stops. We are all used to his rocking and singing and wait for it because it makes us happy. If Pa knew we were listening, he wouldn't sing anymore. So we are just quiet, go about our business as if we're not paying attention and listen.

Joe puts money on the table for Pa each payday and the pile grows bigger. After a while, Pa takes it. I know Ma is happy about the money even though she doesn't say it. When he's not at the mill, Joe keeps on helping Pa and Ben with the farm work, especially big chores like cutting down the hay. He is never tired, loves to work. I know it's because he knows how proud of him it makes me and how it shows ma and pa and grandpa and grandma on the other farm how smart I was to marry him. I always knew he was the best man there could be and that everyone else would see it too.

After we leave the cemetery, people eat again, just like at our wedding, but now everyone is quiet and people don't stay long.

The days after the funeral bring darkness but the darkness is a relief because it covers everything and I don't have to talk, don't have to think. I lose days and then weeks. Ma stops trying to make me talk, settles into something she has inside that I don't have. My breasts are dry. Marysza sleeps. And cries. I hear her crying but don't have strength to pick her up. Ma buys bottles and takes care of her. I watch her sleep and I love her. But he is gone and love is hard. We should all dry up and blow away, like leftover leaves before winter.

When canning season comes, I tell ma I'm not going to do it. Each day I see more the way we are pitiful——ma and pa and Ben and me. We're worse than grandma an' grandpa because they have three sons who work on the farm and the two with families have jobs besides. Grandma an' Grandpa bring stuff here so we have enough. I see that things will never change and that I'll be canning tomatoes or milking cows forever, that one summer will lead to another and another, so many that I can't see them all. He wanted something better for us. I heard him telling his friends that farming in Angola was too hard a life and he had other plans. I don't know what the plans were but I know it was only a matter of time.

Time passes but I can't wake up, can't leave the nightmare behind. Tomatoes and beans still grow. Ma says it's time to harvest.

I don't hear you, Ma, except from far away, can't take the baskets and follow you into the bright July sun. I don't want to see sun, don't want to leave the darkness of our bedroom, Joe's bedroom and mine.

There's nothing here. Won't be anything here. Only tomatoes and peaches and hands burning from tomatoes that spit their juice as you touch them, hands covered with red and yellow skins. The cut-off ends of beans sticking to the floor. Steam making Ma's face red, making the kitchen too hot for the baby, too hot for any of us.

I won't do this again. I can't do this again. There's nothing here. Joe knew there was nothing here. When there was enough money, he was going to take us away from Angola and into the city. Joe and me and Marysza would be gone. Gone from the heavy blue kettle filled with water boiling around glass jars in a wire rack. Gone from Ma lifting the heavy rack onto the table. From Ma wiping the water around her eyes with the white towel on her shoulder. From the fatigue that pushes in and stays through summer light and winter darkness. That slithers and crawls like a worm through every season, fastens itself with teeth on everyone's heart, impossible to loosen, to shake away.

"At least we're eating," Pa is always saying and Ma nods in agreement.

But Joe knew. He'd look at them with a quiet smile. Then he settled his look on me and I was lifted high by happiness that curled itself around me like a cat, stirring, waking my desire. We would be gone.

Now he's gone and I can't do this. Can't do this.

Ma looks long at me. She knows, holds the baby close.

I'm sorry Ma. I can't do this anymore.

Chapter One

Happiness

When her mother left, Marysza's grandmother cared for her. Her grandma had loved her.

"Marysza," she would say, half-talking, half-singing, holding Marysza on her lap when she was small enough to be held and even when she was bigger and they were together in the small flat that was home, "Marysza is my girl." Or sometimes, it was "Marysza is my princess."

Marysza remembered the bedroom she and her grandma shared, remembered the chest of drawers, the crucifix that sat atop the chest on a crocheted doily and the assortment of holy pictures on the walls. One of the pictures was draped with the rosary grandma reached for when she woke up in the morning and before she went to bed at night, the long string of beads moving through her grandmother's fingers while her lips formed the words. Marysza could tell what prayer she was on even though her grandmother prayed silently. She would look up to smile at Marysza lying in bed.

Ojcze Nasz, Zdrowasz Marja, Chwala Bogu [10]

Marysza knew those prayers in Polish from hearing her grandma say them but her grandma spoke English for everyday talk.

Marysza knew her grandma was not religious in the way some of her lady-friends were religious. She didn't look up to heaven as if she expected someone to descend at any moment. She swore sometimes and complained about things when she was mad, but with determination in her eyes, she would say, "God knows how hard things are. He still loves me," then laugh as if she if she were a child caught cheating.

Grandma's eyes were blue, deep-set and piercing, beacons that illuminated the world and revealed her. When sorrow sat in her eyes, it did not triumph. Behind the sadness, Marysza could glimpse the stubborn happiness, the quiet laughter that always remained. The hair that framed her grandma's face was gray. Her skin, crisscrossed with lines, was pink and soft when you touched it. In winter, or when she was excited about something, her grandma's cheeks turned red, and though she didn't act excited, Marysza knew a battle raged inside her, a battle of which the outcome was uncertain. After a period of quiet, her grandma said to herself or Marysza, or both of them, "never min", words that were a signal that a decision had been made, so Marysza could turn back to what she had been doing.

Marysza remembered that her love for her grandma had filled the small bedroom and overflowed, washing over the dresser and bed and the picture of Jesus with the rays of light coming from His heart, then floated through the door and into the living room where it settled on the knitted black- and- red afghan that covered the cushions on the couch. She could still see the heavy brown television Uncle Ben had bought for grandma. It sat on a tall table so you had to look up to see it, just like watching a movie. Every night after she did her homework, she and grandma watched their favorite shows until bedtime. In summer, Marysza could watch television as late as she wanted and grandma would send her to buy a pint of ice cream and a big bottle of soda pop at the delicatessen down the street. Marysza made ice-cream sodas to drink while they watched television. On winter nights, Marysza would always fall asleep thinking about summer.

In the mornings, when Marysza went to school, her grandmother went to work. Marysza couldn't remember a time when her grandma didn't go to her job cleaning offices. In the evenings she sat with her legs on the plastic footstool in the living room. The legs were circled and crossed by purple veins so large they looked as if they were pushing to break free.

Someday, I'll marry a rich man and buy grandma a house. She can rest her legs on the stool all day if she wants.

Marysza had been too little to remember much about her mother. Her grandma did not talk about Elzbieta and said "never min'" when Marysza asked about her, so that Marysza thought about her mother less and less, though she never forgot her completely. From a part of herself that was almost closed, she remembered when her mother lived with them and slept in a bed next to grandma. She remembered listening silently, enraptured by *The Three Bears*, a book her mother read while holding Marysza on her lap, and looking up at her mother with wonder because she looked like a princess and her skin smelled like flowers. When Marysza reached up and touched her hair, it felt like the inside of a cloud.

The memory she recalled most clearly was the night a man had come to take Marysza and her mother. The man was big and loud and had a beard like the devil. He said that now Marysza would be raised right and not by a couple of stupid women. He tried to take Marysza, picking her up like a piece of baggage to be thrown into the back of the truck waiting outside, its motor rumbling like a hungry dinosaur. Marysza was frozen with terror, so that she couldn't even cry.

Grandma had raised her arms, arms that were outlined against the light like the thin girders of an old bridge. Her small voice became thunder, spewing words that cracked through the room like lightning.

"You get out, both of you. Marysza stays with me!" The man's power had collapsed, disappearing like a burst of wind that whips across a street before a storm, then turns the corner and is lost. He dropped Marysza and climbed into the truck reaching out his hand impatiently for Marysza's mother. In a moment that wouldn't end, Marysza heard grandma breathing hard and saw her mother's eyes looking back, as if making a final plea, then turning away as she followed the man into the truck. When they were gone, grandma took down her rosary and Marysza watched the beads fly through her fingers. She hadn't seen her mother since.

When Marysza was six or seven, she looked at pictures of grandma when she lived in what she called "the country", where you could see trees and grass and flowers.

This is my grandma in this faded picture, this thin girl who is pretty, who looks shy and turns away from the camera, whose hair falls around her shoulders like a scarf.

"Grandma, why'd you come to the city, to Buffalo, when you were young?"

"To find work," grandma answered, and sighed. "The same old story. We thought it would be better here than on the farm in Angola. They were bad years. Hardly enough for all of us to eat, and your gran'pa was gettin' more and more belligeren', you know, because there wasn't enuf' for everyone." Marysza's grandma liked the word "belligerent", and used it often to emphasize someone's bad behavior.

"It wasn' his fault. There just wasn' enuf. It made him feel bad, real bad. He was a good man. I left with your gran'pa, an' Uncle Ben and your mother so's it'd be easier, so's your gran'pa could find a job an' not have to work so hard on the farm anymore. An' for my ma an' pa too. So's there'd just be less mouths to feed all the way roun'"– here her grandma's voice would grow sad–"even though your great gran'pa, my pa, wanted me to stay. I was special to him, you know. He died when I was gone." Her grandma said this without emphasis. It was simply a fact that her father loved her, his only daughter of four children.

"We all came here with ol' suitcases holdin' everythin' we owned." She stopped and her eyes traveled to someplace Marysza couldn't see.

"Your gran'pa was a good worker but it was even hard for young men to find jobs. The only work was for me in the laundry or cleanin'. Then your gran'pa kind of gave up, didn' try no more. He didn' last long after that. I was 'shamed to go back home, to say I couldn' make it an' was bringin' my kids an' my gran'baby back. Anyhow, there was nothin' much more for us there than was here, only dependin' on others. So I jus' kep' on workin' in the laundry when they needed me, an' cleanin' houses an' offices. Your uncle Ben was good, came back even after he left, to make sure I had ennuf money for the rent and the doctor when I hadda go." She stopped and sighed again.

"But your mother was hard, real hard. She believed all that stuff she read in them magazines an' thought if she was real pretty, everythin' would come to her. An' she was real pretty. It was okay with your father 'cause he was a good man. But somethin' happened to her after she lost him. You was maybe a month old when he died. She went kinda crazy. Then in the city here she got in with a man, Irish he was, who was no good and lef' with him. It was no sense talkin' to her so I didn'. You were the only blessin' from it all."

Here grandma would stop and run her hand over Marysza's hair, and Marysza would curl into the crook of grandma's thin arm, waiting for the story of herself to continue.

"They wanted to take you, you know, but I said no, 'cause I knew what I knew. So I kep' you and here we are. That man was bad, *Niedobry*, *zabrany*. Marysza knew those words meant "no good" and "shitty", a word she wasn't allowed to use. Grandma's eyes filled with water so that the blue pupils began to swim.

"But it wasn' no surprise she lef' with him and ain't come home since. God knows what he tol' her. They say he was killed in a truck acciden'. Drinkin' an' goin' off the road. Your mama prob'ly saw what he was when it was too late. She wasn' dumb. Only in certain ways. Jus' remember Marysza, women get crazy sometime when they get mixed up by a man. Don' you do it. You take care of yourself firs'. An' don' be too hard in thinkin' on your mama. Because she'll be hurtin', real hurtin', in the end."

With this pronouncement, Grandma took the rosary down and began passing the beads through her fingers.

Grandma's praying for my mother. For me too. So I don't fall into the arms of a bad man.

Marysza was silent. She knew when the story was ended and she couldn't ask any more questions.

Grandma gave Marysza old magazines she found in the offices and houses she cleaned. There were pictures of flowers in the magazines and on the stamps Sister Edwina put on her school papers. Marysza lay on the floor and propped herself on her elbows when grandma looked at the pictures with her..

"There was always daisies in the woods on the farm when spring came. The kids use ta' string them together ta' make necklaces an' bracelets. My father had an orchard wif apple an' plum an' peach trees. Before fruit came, the flowers were beautiful. That was all gone once your gran'pa an' me moved to the city here." Her eyes took on their faraway look, like the look they had when she talked about Elzbieta, Marysza's mother.

There was no grass or flowers outside the house where Marysza and grandma lived. Hard black dirt covered the ground like asphalt covered the street. She remembered the day grandma decided they should plant a tree near the front door, a spring day that announced winter was leaving but could return unexpectedly.

"Here, Marysza." Grandma handed her a large spoon and pointed to a space close to the front window. Marysza began digging a hole. Her grandma dug also. As if revealing a secret, the ground became soft when you reached beneath its hard crust, exciting Marysza as the dirt flew in all directions. The excitement became stillness, a stillness whispering words only Marysza could hear, words that spoke of the good things waiting for her, words that spoke of her taking her place in the large and beautiful world.

I feel my strength. I know all the things I can do with my life.

Grandma was quiet. The black dirt flew from the hole as if it were alive. The hole grew bigger and bigger. Marysza began to laugh at the game she and grandma were playing. When the hole was large enough, grandma placed the small tree within its dark and protective walls and Marysza filled the hole back up with dirt. Grandma told Marysza to get the pail used to mop the floor, fill it with water and bring it outside. Marysza hurried, trailing a stream of water all the way from the door and down the steps.

"Pour it on, water it good," grandma instructed as Marysza dragged the bucket around the tree. "You'll have to do that everyday."

Marysza did. She hurried home from school, watered and examined the tree to see if it had grown. "It'll grow slow," grandma said but Marysza was impatient. She wanted it to soar to the sky.

When summer and fall were gone and the sky began to look more gray than blue, her grandma took a paper box, cut away the bottom and the top and told Marysza to find as many dry leaves as she could. Marysza ran up and down the street, stopping wherever there was a tree and collecting leaves that crinkled like paper. She crumpled them until an odor like dry spice filled the air, and except for the bits and pieces that clung to her hands, she dropped the shredded leaves into the paper box.

When winter came, Marysza continued to look at the tree each day. When the blanket of leaves in the box began to sink, Marysza's grandma told her she could use torn newspapers to build it up again. Marysza tended the tree through the winter, brushed the snow from its small circle and covered it with her jacket until grandma told her that might hurt it. She pretended the tree watched for her, knew when she was coming and whispered words to her, even though she knew that was silly.

I know the other side of things, that winter is cold, that wind and snow can hurt the tree and make it stop growing. But those things won't happen. Now is the time when everything is right. I can feel it.

On a cold winter evening, Marysza stood at the window watching the snow cover her tree and turn the dark houses into white castles. She turned to see Grandma holding a small box covered with what looked like blue-and-white patterned wallpaper, paper torn where it had been folded to cover the corners.

"When I'm gone, this is yours. You can open it."

The box gave off the faint odor of chocolate like the candy boxes Marysza saw in the window of one of the stores on the main street of the neighborhood. Grandma called the store the "candy kitchen." and took Marysza there for ice cream sodas

Marysza always had trouble deciding on the flavor she wanted. Her grandma and she sat across from each other on soft seats in a little wooden booth as if they were sitting in a boat or a plane. A man in a white apron set two napkins and two small glasses of water before them, then ice cream sodas in tall glasses that had round pedestals and sides with grooves running down them like roads. The glasses contained spoons longer than any they had at home and were capped with froth and bubbles that began to disappear as Marysza began to stir. When they had ice cream sodas at home, they were made in their usual glasses, most of which were jars that had been saved and washed after the jelly was gone. Marysza tried to make her soda last as long as possible. When they were finished and grandma paid for the sodas, the man put the money into a cash register which rang when the drawer popped out. Marysza liked everything about the candy kitchen.

"What's in the box, grandma?" Marysza knew she couldn't open the box, because grandma meant what she said, but the words, "when I am gone," were meaningless then, were brushed from Marysza's mind as soon as her grandma spoke them.

Grandma didn't answer. Her forehead was curled with wrinkles, her mouth set in a line. She replaced the box as if she didn't wish to part with it.

"It 's in this drawer in my dresser here."

Marysza had seen the pictures of her grandma as a little girl but she wondered what else the box could contain. It must be important. Grandma's eyes were filled with a look different than the looks Marysza knew. She didn't ask again.

There were other places besides the candy kitchen on the avenue: a store grandma called the junk store, filled with piles of clothing and fabric on tables, piles you could rummage through in the hope of finding something you wanted and had enough money to buy. Assorted figurines, white and colored, some with cracks or chips, sat on shelves behind the counter. Grandma bought a radio from the junk store. It was a brown wooden box about two feet tall, rounded at the top with little windows of brown mesh across the front. One of the knobs was missing but there was a metal rod that stuck out from the hole where the knob had been. You could turn the rod to find the stations and the knob on the other side made the sound loud or quiet.

"Two dollars," the man told Grandma.

Nie, zbyt duzo,[11]grandma told him. The man said a dollar would be okay. Grandma gave him fifty cents and told him she would bring the other fifty cents next week. The radio was heavy so the man told grandma she could take it home in his red wagon and bring the wagon back the next day. As Marysza pulled the wagon she could feel grandma's happiness. Grandma found the Polish station and Marysza heard polkas whenever grandma played the radio that week except when grandma listened very hard to President Roosevelt talking as people cheered loudly in the background. Marysza listened also and tried to understand. The next week, grandma gave Marysza two quarters

"Marysza, take this to Mr. Weinstein. And the wagon too."

Marysza's grandmother watched through the wundow as Marysza ran with the wagon clattering behind her and watched for her return, moving her head so Marysza wouldn't see.

Here she comes, prettier than other pretty chil'ren. My Marysza. Curly hair. Large eyes that see everythin' around her, and growin' wide when somethin' on the ground catches her attention. She stops to examine it closely. When she's satisfied, continues on her way, skippin', hair flyin', brushin' it from her face, lookln' up and concentratin' on the sky, almost walkin' into someone ahead on the sidewalk. Her eyes show no shyness, her lips form the words " 'scuse me" and seein' our buildin' over that person's shoulder, she begins to run home, hair still flyin' behind her like a sail on a boat.

Grandma's lady friends bought duck feathers from the butcher at the Broadway market or collected the feathers when they bought ducks to make *czarnina*[12] When they had enough feathers, they met to separate the fluffy part from the little stick so they could make comforters and pillows from the down. Marysza always knew when the ladies were there because their talking was so loud, little clouds of down floated in the air and the kitchen smelled like sewing machine oil.

Grandma showed Marysza how the pierzynas had to be sewn into squares so the down wouldn't bunch up in one place. Marysza loved her pierzyna because it was so warm and soft but sometimes she got pricked by a little stick that worked its way through the material.

This time the ladies met, Marysza heard one of grandma's lady-friends say something in a snotty voice about grandma buying things from Mr. Weinstein. She used the word *Zyd*[13]. Grandma became angry and said things in Polish that Marysza didn't understand except for the words *Pan Jezus*[14] and *kazdy*[15].

The lady became quiet and lowered her head to concentrate on her feathers. The next week Grandma went back to the junk store and bought the red wagon from Mr. Weinstein because she said they needed one of their own. It was a pretty good wagon with no broken parts and only a little rust. It cost fifty cents and they kept it in the outside hallway.

Past the junk store was a dark and noisy place her grandma called a saloon. The windows were streaked. Brown and beige checked curtains with threads so far apart in the material that you could see through to the dusty brown sills on the other side, hung limply on the windows' lower halves. Inside, Marysza saw the faces of men lined up in a row as if they were sitting at tall desks in school.

A man wearing a green shirt and pants, his sleeves rolled up as if he were working, his pant-legs dragging on the sidewalk, came out from the darkness without bothering to close the door behind him, spat on the ground and wiped his mouth with his hand. He swayed back and forth like a puppet, kept his head lowered and his eyes on the ground while he talked to someone who wasn't there. When he saw Marysza, he smiled at her, but when he saw grandma, he looked embarrassed and turned away. Marysza recognized the smell of beer, a smell that sometimes trailed after Martha's father like smoke from a train.

Martha's father is happier when he smells of beer, laughs and jokes more than ever but something must be connected to drinking that makes grandma angry.

Marysza started to ask but grandma dragged her away from the saloon with her usual "never min' ", muttering something about those "damn eye-rysh-key", her grandma's Polish for "damn Irishmen". Marysza saw that the sign above the saloon said *Mazurek's*. which was a Polish name, so she knew it couldn't only be Irishmen who drank.

Grandma must have reasons for saying what she says. Maybe Irish men drink more than Polish men.

Then she remmbeed that her mother ran away with an Irish man who drank.

Past the saloon and almost at the end of the street, a big red sign shaped into an arrow stood like a king high over the other buildings. The sign was outlined with light bulbs, some broken, and read *The Masque.* More bulbs framed the metal canopy that displayed large black letters announcing : *Sun & Mon—Casablanca—Hit of the Year—Kids show on Saturday.* When Marysza asked her grandma when she could go to the show on Saturday, her grandma answered "pretty soon." She told grandma she wanted to go with Martha and grandma said "all right then." They continued to walk, passed a shoe store, a clothing store and the A & P, a grocery store with a wooden floor that made a hollow sound when you walked on it, its aisles lined with rows of shelves stacked with cans, and a big refrigerator in the back for milk and pop. Sometimes her grandmother stopped there if they needed bread or milk. Marysza was always glad when her grandmother took her to the candy kitchen and they walked home on South Park Avenue.

1943

Children

Marysza was washing the blackboards for Sister Edwina when the new boy came. She could tell there was something different about Tadziu Wreblewski and not just because he was older than the other kids. She kept washing the boards and wiping away the chalk, only looking at him from the corner of her eyes, until she reached the last row and the blackboards were all wet and black with no lines showing between the rows. She wanted the boy to see how important she was, to know she had the best job. She could feel him looking at her back and knew he wanted to call her "teacher's pet."

Sister Edwina saw where the new boy directed his look. She turned and saw the lowered eyes of the child who was the object of that look. From the beginning, Sister had acknowledged her partiality toward the girl who was the brightest of her students.

The curiosity, the eagerness to understand that fills her eyes disguises a love for everyone and everything. She possesses a self-esteem rooted in her belief that the world is good. Her empathy for everyone betrays that belief. I've never seen malice or jealousy in those eyes, always the confidence that she is loved. Amazing, when one thinks of her history. Her grandmother has done well.

"Sister, should I empty the water in the bathroom?"

"Yes, Marysza. Tadziu, could you come to the desk to fill out these papers?"

Marysza looked straight ahead, not paying the least bit of attention to the boy as she walked past him, but from the corner of her eye she saw he was skinny and his bones moved when he walked. He wore a red-and-white checked flannel shirt that was too small with buttons that strained across his chest and made him look even skinnier. The shirt was clean but his pants were torn and dirty as if they had been worn longer than the shirt.

Marysza was sure the boy had cut his own hair. He made her think of the time she had gone with grandma to the farm at harvest time. Like the leftovers in the field after the farmer's machines had passed, blonde stubble stuck up from his head except around his ears where it was longer and fell in short waves. .

He probably had trouble reaching there to cut it.

The boy's lips were pressed together tightly until he laughed and they opened into a large grin. His large blue eyes were framed in long blonde lashes. Marysza saw that the look in his eyes had two meanings. One of the meanings, the meaning that all the kids would see, said, "Keep out of my way or you'll be sorry." The kids wouldn't notice the other meaning, the one that said, "I'm scared." If they did notice that meaning, they'd think it was because the boy was new. Marysza knew it was more than being new, that the boy was new and alone everywhere.

When she left to dump the water in the girl's lavatory, Marysza knew the boy was waiting for her return. He was fooling and laughing with the other boys but a part of him was locked into her and wouldn't leave. Marysza's face turned red and burned like a fever when she was sick. That happened whenever she was excited just like it happened to her grandmother. She imagined water flowing over her, surrounding her, washing away the redness and filling her with a happiness that kept growing. She closed her eyes and pushed her face into her book. No one would see her happiness.

When she closed her eyes, Sister Edwina and the other kids disappeared. She was alone with Tadziu. Alone with this boy whom she sensed needed and claimed her, a claim she knew would be a bother, alone with his large eyes and his skinny arms, alone with her happiness and an unfamiliar resentment. She tried to write but her hands refused. This stupid boy was interfering with her thoughts. She stopped trying. She wanted only to return to the water, to be lost in the waves. Tadziu was laughing with hysterics as he and Daniel Wojciechowski punched each other in the arm. Even the girls laughed, covering their mouths and hiding their faces from Sister Edwina's eyes until she turned and glared at everyone. In the instant silence, Marysza looked at Tadziu.

He doesn't know he's caught in the current also.

During recess, the voice of Marysza's friend Martha interrupted the waves and took them away. For some reason she did not understand, Marysza felt shy.

"What's wrong with you?" Martha asked. "You sick or somethin? You look funny." Marysza pulled herself back to her ordinary life.

"I'm okay."

"C'mon, we've got time for hopscotch."

Marysza linked arms with her friend. Tadziu's face disappeared and the waves fell away.

Marysza's grandmother gave her six pennies each day for bus fare, three cents to get there and three cents to get home. The big red and yellow bus came and waited at the corner. The driver, wearing a uniform like a policeman, always looked tired and in a hurry. He mumbled "hello", and tried to smile. Martha was already on the bus because she lived further away. They talked until the bus pulled up to the curb in front of a brown brick building.

"Did you listen to the radio last night?"

"Did you do your homework?"

Marysza had loved Martha since the first day of kindergarten when her grandmother had brought her to school, told her to be good and learn everythin', then hugged and kissed her goodbye. Marysza was a little afraid but mostly excited. All the kids looked at her but mostly Marysza felt Martha's eyes. It was hard to miss Martha's eyes. They were brown like the brown of some gentle animal, but that was only when the thick lenses of her glasses dragged them down her nose. When the glasses were up, her eyes were magnified into what looked like the eyes of a giant frog. Both sets of eyes told Marysza that Martha liked her.

In her seat with her hands folded and her arms outstretched before her on the desk, Martha looked like a square with a large head and long arms. Her hair was brown, straight and thick, came out of the many barrettes on her head and fell across her face. When she smiled—-and she smiled a lot, wide and full—her two front teeth seemed too big.

Martha was constantly brushing the hair from her face while pushing the sliding glasses up the hill of her nose. This automatic movement arrested Marysza. She saw that one of Martha's large brown eyes crossed into the corner and seemed to rest there until it found its place again. At recess, she heard kids call Martha "four-eyes" and "cross-eyes" but Martha hid her hurt and was not afraid. She threatened to punch a repeated offender, a boy who was taller than Martha but so thin and clumsy he made Marysza think of a rag doll that had lost its stuffing.

"You bag-of-bones," Martha called, "I'll knock the shit out of you", and the boy ran.

Marysza was impressed by Martha's fearlessness and by the language she used, language Marysza's grandmother would frown upon, not because she could not see its necessity, but because, as she would say, "You're not big enuf' for such language yet."

"Just let me know if any a' them bothers you," Martha told Marysza. Almost no one did because Marysza was smart and pretty, smarter than Martha in things that concerned learning.

Martha had three older brothers. She said that her oldest brother, who was fourteen and in his first year of high school, thought he was hot stuf. So she made fun of him. He called Marysza and Martha little brats, looked at them as if he could not be bothered, and closed his door when they were around. He played loud music in his room until Martha's father hollered and he had to turn it down. Then he got mad, especially when Martha laughed. If Martha could not move fast enough, he hit her, but Marysza knew Martha never squealed on him.

Martha's father was a tall man with long legs that made him take big steps so he always seemed to be running, eyes that held laughter and a face that always wore a smile. He carried a metal lunchbox with a thermos botttle and made an elaborate curtsy to Marysza whenever he came home from work and saw her with Martha. He called them little ladies and never yelled at Martha although he yelled at the boys a lot. Martha told Marysza that was because she was the only girl.

Martha's parents treated Marysza as if she belonged to their family. Marysza could tell they were happy because Martha had such a smart friend. Marysza knew they didn't know why she lived with her grandmother but they never asked questions.

Marysza kept begging her grandmother to let Martha sleep overnight. Knowing her grandmother was thinking she never did such things when she was a girl, Marysza persisted, told her grandmother that Martha was her best friend, that Martha's mother said it was okay and that she, Marysza, would never ask for anything again.

"All right then," her grandmother said.

That night, Marysza put Martha's hair into curlers. The next day, she combed and fussed over Martha's hair and they looked into the mirror. Two faces grinned back, Martha's lit with disbelief.

"It looks just like yours."

Happiness settled into Marysza like a warm blanket. The two friends talked in bed until Marysza's grandmother told them to go to sleep, then whispered until they were exhausted and fell asleep without noticing.

Marysza and Martha took their lunches to school—bread and jelly sandwiches wrapped in old plastic from something bought at the store. Milk was three cents but the kids who didn't have three cents still got the little paper carton to drink with their lunch. Some of the kids had more things than she and Martha like cookies or an orange but she and Martha didn't care because they had cookies or an orange sometime and then the other kids looked at them. One boy always brought things to school and showed them secretly to the other kids, expensive things that Marysza looked at and told her grandmother about.

"Billy had three new watches in school today," Marysza said one evening. "He was showing them off." Grandma was cleaning the floor. Her long mop stick stopped its dance.

"Never min' that," she said, "Billy doesn' need them and you don' neither. And that's not sayin' nothin' 'bout how he got them. You jus' need to pay attention to your homework." That was all the answer there was going to be. Grandma resumed her mopping and Marysza was satisfied. If grandma said it, it must be right. She turned back to the homework she liked, practicing the curves and loops of penmanship on the blue-lined paper Sister had given out to everybody. She didn't look at Billy's things anymore and never thought about what she didn't have, because life with grandma was complete and safe.

Sometimes the kindergarten kids had nothing to do because kindergarten was in the same room as the first grade and Sister Edwina concentrated on teaching first grade. The two rows of kindergarten desks were separated from the six rows of the first grade by an empty aisle and were closer to the windows. Sister Edwina gave paper and crayons to the kindergarten kids but that was not enough to keep the boys quiet. They didn't pay attention like Marysza did.

I can learn everything Sister teaches the first graders.

She went home and showed grandma that she could read. She knew all her arithmetic and learned to write carefully-formed letters when sister taught penmanship to the first grade. Sister trusted her with many jobs, like delivering messages to other classrooms, cleaning the erasers and washing the blackboards.

While she did these tasks, Tadziu whispered, "Hey Marysza, sister's pet", left notes on her desk or threw notes at her, none of which she could read because they were scribbles. Because he had come into the class half-way through the year, Tadziu was behind everyone else especially in penmanship. He made spitballs and threw them at Marysza, then grinned when she turned to look at him

He's trying to pretend he knows as much as the other kids.

Martha called him a smartass.

Tadziu was almost invisible because he sat in the back row with the other kindergarten boys but he made loud comments about everything, so he was always in trouble. His clothes were old and sometimes torn but it didn't matter because everyone wore clothes that were old and had passed through numerous brothers, sisters and cousins.

Tadziu was not as smart as Marysza. Sometimes Marysza gave him her homework to copy because he never did his own.

I don't know why I help him. He never says thank-you.

One day Sister hollered at Marysza for giving him her work. It was the only time Sister ever scolded her for anything. Marysza felt her face turning red. Tadziu had to stay after school again. "Teacher's pet!" he muttered under his breath as Marysza left the room.

At the end of kindergarten, Tadziu was kept back and Maryszas moved ahead to second grade so she didn't see him in school anymore. He started to wait for her after school, trailed along behind her and Martha, and threw things into the air as if he was not interested in the girls. At first Martha was jealous but when she saw that Marysza was not going to stop being her friend, it was okay.

Tadziu didn't have gloves in winter but he still thrust his hands into the snow and made snowballs which he threw at Marysza and the other girls. Marysza pretended to be mad. Martha didn't pretend. She **was** mad and threw snowballs back.

When it was cold and Marysza saw Tadziu through the window, grandma told Marysza to "call that boy inside." His ears and his hands were always red. Sometimes he carried a baloney sandwich in his pocket, the bread all mushed and stuck together. He was good in grandma's house, acting as if he were in an important place and grandma was an important person. He and Marysza played cards with an old deck of cards grandma found, Tadziu became mad if he lost but when he won, he jumped up and down and slapped the cards hard on the table.

Why does he think it's so important to win such a silly game?

Tadziu never talked about his family. When grandma met with her lady-friends to pull chicken-feathers, she found out that Tadziu's mother and father came from Poland, but all the children were born in America. Marysza never understood anything the women said because they spoke in Polish, but they were loud and sounded angry talking about Tadziu's family. Later, grandma told Marysza they called Tadziu's father a lousy Polak.[16] She heard her grandmother swear under her breath. Whenever grandma was angry enough to swear, it had something to do with people, like the reason why Tadziu's father was a lousy Polak. Marysza would never know the reason because grandma would say "never min' " if she asked.

Marysza remembered the day in first grade when her grandmother came to school.

"Grandma, you have to come to see how I'm doing. Sister says all the parents should come. I asked her if that meant my grandma too. And she said yes. You have to come, grandma!" Marysza was so excited she couldn't keep from jumping up and down. All her papers were good, the best in the class, Sister said, and she couldn't wait for grandma to see them.

"All right then."

Most of the kids had at least one parent in attendance so the classroom was busy that night. When grandma walked in the door, for a moment Sister Albert and other people turned to look, until Sister returned to the papers on her desk and the woman she was talking to. Marysza's grandmother stood in the door and looked around. When she saw people standing in line before Sister's desk, she went to the end.

Grandma wore a dress Marysza had never seen, a dress whose folds did not fall smoothly from the waist but stood as stiff as soldiers and whose black background blazed with large blue flowers like a garden growing out of control. She had on her black work shoes with the thick heels and the ties, but Marysza had never seen the purse that hung from the elbow of her arm. Her grandmother's gray hair was worked into a fresh bun with no loose strands creeping out as they usually did until her grandmother fastened them with large hairpins. Her grandmother's hands were crossed over her stomach, folded neatly and tucked under the belt of her dress.

"Grandma, Grandma," Marysza called in excitement. "Look at my papers!" Her grandmother stepped out of line, came to look at the white papers that hung from yellow push tacks on a corkboard and turned them in her reddened hands until she saw the colored sticker each of them carried.

"Oh my, oh my." When she was finished, she stepped to the back of the line again but people moved aside to let her take her former place. When she reached the teacher's desk, Sister smiled and held out her hand. Marysza heard her say, "Hello, Mrs. Jargosz," in her best voice, a voice she never used with the kids.

"How nice to see you." Then the talk became quieter as Marysza's grandmother bent and examined the papers Sister was showing her. Grandma paid close attention to Sister's words.

Marysza stood at the blackboard, trying to control her excitement, making small jumps from one foot to the other. She watched grandma nod her head as Sister Albert talked, then turn to look at Marysza. Her grandmother's eyes had grown large. Marysza thought a mist had settled in them or that grandma was crying. She realized she had seen the look before but never this strong, that it came from inside her grandma, that it made her eyes shine and caress Marysza as she stood and absorbed their light. The eyes said to everyone, "This is what I knew, what I saw in her. I don't love anyone else this way, not my own children. This girl is special to me." Marysza didn't hear those words out loud. She only understood them, the way in which one understands that it is warm or cold.

Her grandmother didn't speak as they walked home. She didn't say how proud she was, how good the papers were or how Sister had told her that Marysza was her best pupil. But Marysza knew these things. She jumped over the cracks in the ground, then came to walk next to her grandmother, then jumped again.

"Grandma, where'd you get this purse?" she asked as she held, half-swinging, onto its strap.

"It was time for a new one," her grandmother said, and Marysza knew her grandmother had bought the purse to go to school.

"And the dress, grandma, where'd you get the dress?"

"It was time for that too."

Marysza jumped over another crack. It seemed that she could never stop jumping.

A Winter Stroll

Marysza was in third grade. On a sunny but cold winter day—the kind of cold which made you notice it was harder than usual to breathe—Grandma sent her to the fish market. She wore a jacket with a sweater underneath, and snow pants and boots because even though she protested vigorously, her grandmother said, "Never min', lady. it might start snowin' again," and made her wear the snow pants. She put a scarf over the hood of Marysza's jacket and around her neck so that all Marysza could see of herself were her eyes and nose.

Tadziu was outside, sliding on the ice in the street.

"Where you going?" You look funny, like somethin' from outer space."

Marysza's voice was muffled by her scarf and Tadziu thought this was even funnier. Holding his stomach, he laughed boisterously and fell to the ground.

"What'd you say? To get a dish, oh, fish, fish. Where you gonna catch a fish today?" When he realized the words made a rhyme, he improvised more.

"The fish is on the dish. The dish is on the fish. Fish wish he not on dish!" Marysza thought he was too silly to be bothered with so she stepped over him and walked past. He scrambled to his feet and walked alongside her. Marysza felt her warm hands and moved her fingers inside her gloves.

Tadziu has no hat or gloves. He never has a hat or gloves.

She took off her scarf but he wouldn't take it so she had to struggle to get it back on. After they walked for a time, he said, "Okay, I'll take it," and Marysza pulled the scarf off again. Tadziu wrapped it around his head like a turban.

"Eh, eh, eh, I'm an old lady. Could you help me, ma'am." His voice was feeble and he pretended to have trouble walking.

"My grandma doesn't sound like that. She doesn't walk like that either."

"Then I'm a man from India, and you're my slave." The voice was as deep as he could make it. "You have to do whatever I say, or I'll put you in a round dish with a snake."

"Baloney."

"Not baloney, Marysza. That's not what you say." He shook a finger at her. "Bull-shit, Marysza. Bullshit. That's what you say."

It's useless to talk to him.

The cold air was beginning to creep into Marysza's gloves. Tadziu's nose was red sticking out from the scarf. He kept his hands in his pockets. Marysza gave him one of her gloves, so they would each have one warm hand. He didn't object. When they crossed the street, leaving behind the silent square buildings where people worked, and passed the railroad tracks, Tadziu began jumping along the ladder of wooden ties that lay buried in the weeds joining the rails together, and frightening Marysza because grandma said she could never go near the railroad tracks.

"Tadziu, come back! It's dangerous!" He didn't listen. Large pieces of concrete sidewalk lay in piles on the ground. Marysza was glad because it made Tadziu forget about the tracks. They played Jungle and King and hollered loud noises even though it was hard for Marysza to climb with all the clothes she was wearing. Tadziu found a dirty shoe filled with snow and mud, some empty cans and cigarette butts.

"People live here Marysza, under the stones. They come out only at night." The sound of his voice turned to surprise. "Hey, I can live here." He began to run and holler monster noises. Marysza ran too. Tadziu's scarf traveled up over his nose and covered one eye but he wouldn't let Marysza fix it. They ran until they were tired. Marysza's skin started to sweat and prickle beneath her clothes. Tadziu took the scarf off his head again and they both walked slower. Marysza looked up to see the sun beginning to lose its light and moving down the sky.

The fish market was long and black, a chain of stores that ran along a platform located above a flight of stairs. Trucks were pulled up to the platform and men pushed ladders on wheels with boxes leaning against the ladders. Marysza and Tadziu walked around the platform to the other side, and went into a store with white counters, a big window and a silver scale hanging on chains.

"The window is for the fish, Marysza, so they can look at people." Marysza ignored him and held her nose with her free hand. -

"Smells like shit in here," Tadziu said and the man behind the counter looked up.

He's going to tell us to go away because of Tadziu's language.

Marysza told the man she wanted a pound of yellow pike. He weighed the fish on the big scale, wrapped it in white paper and fastened it with a rubber band. The man was big and red and looked as if he did not like anyone, especially kids, so Marysza took the package without saying thank you. She and Tadziu went into another room and looked at black lobsters crawling over each other in a big tank. Their hands had big teeth that opened and closed. Marysza did not like watching them so they went to look at clams in big barrels. The clams looked like stones and Tadziu said they were not much fun to watch, that lobsters were better.

"But clams have something inside."

"Yeah, how dyoo know? You ever see their insides?"

"No, but I read about it in a book." Marysza watched the clams to see if one might move by accident when she remembered pearls and told Tadziu about pearls. He listened but said he didn't believe her.

He always says he doesn't believe me but I know he does.

By the time they reached home, it was getting dark. Grandma asked Marysza what took so long.

"Oh, we were just looking at things," Marysza answered, her nose pressed against the glass, as she watched Tadziu sliding on the ice again. After a while, he was gone. Marysza didn't know where he lived. She asked him but he never told her.

That night Marysza told Grandma how Tadziu never had a warm hat and gloves outside and how she shared her gloves with him when they walked to the fish market. Grandma was quiet. The next week when her lady friends came they brought different sizes of children's jackets and hats and gloves, even boots, all used but clean. Grandma told Tadziu to take them home but he said he was afraid his father wouldn't like it. Grandma put them into a bushel basket and put the bushel into their red wagon. She and Marysza walked and pulled the wagon past the church, the school and houses with brightly-lit windows until they came to a house that was darker than the others on the block. There were two doors but only the one going upstairs had any light.

Grandma knocked and a lady came down the stairs so quietly that Marysza didn't hear her until she was there. The gray hair that reached her shoulders looked wrong on the face that resembled a child's but Marysza could make out nothing else in the dim light. The lady and grandma talked in Polish and the lady had tears in her eyes when grandma showed her the clothes. Marysza helped and together they carried the clothes up the stairs. Marysza thought she saw a girl her age come and stand behind her mother but she couldn't be sure.

Takie ladny[17], the lady said, holding Marysza's face in her hands. *Bog zaplac*[18] she told Grandma. *Idz z bogiem, idz z bogiem*[19] they waved to each other as Marysza and Grandma went back down the stairs. So now Marysza knew where Tadziu lived. The lady was nice but she liked Grandma's and her house better.

The next time they walked to the fish market, Tadziu had a warm jacket and hat. The hat was leather and all cushiony inside. It had furry ear flaps, a visor and a strap that was supposed to snap under his chin but Tadziu ran with the ears flapping in the wind. It looked funny but Tadziu liked it because it was an airplane hat from the war. He jumped from the highest stones to the ground making a machine gun noise as he pointed sticks at what he called en-i-mee planes.

"Look, Marysza, look," he hollered again and again, "I got it" or "I got another one", or "dyd za see that one hit the ground?" Marysza smiled and answered as she kept walking.

"Yes, I saw, I saw."

He quieted down as their walk was ending.

Another Home

Tadziu had forgotten about time. It was very late. He ran all the way home, then up the stairs. He could hear his heart thudding in his ears and in his chest as if it was banging on a door to get out. He would have to walk in after his father was home. He knew as soon as he opened the door that he was in for it. He felt the force of his father's hand across his face and heard his angry voice.

Czy byl? Na strycze? [20] His father's face was twisted into a mask with no face, only huge eyes behind his glasses, the worst mask he wore, the one Tadziu hated the most. The blows fell on Tadziu's head and his back like stones someone was throwing at him. If he was quiet, they would stop. He heard his mother screaming for his father to leave him alone. His father turned and screamed at her so she became quiet except for the sound of crying. When his father turned from him, Tadziu ran into the bedroom. His father forgot him, as he usually did after his anger was empty. His sister Helcia came in, put her arms around his shoulders and cried. Everyone was always crying. Tadziu did not cry. He never cried. His mother's crying and his sister's arms around him only made him feel bad.

Helcza's just a year younger than me. They'll make her go to school next.

Tadziu sat in his room. The shadows on the wall grew larger. Night was coming. He didn't want to fall asleep. He had nightmares, nightmares in which his father always appeared, always wanted to kill him, and Tadziu could never escape. Only once or twice was he able to kill his father first. The nightmares scared him..

I don't want to kill him. I want his face to change, to turn into a face like Joe's. I want to laugh, to run through the street with him, playing ball or kicking cans.

He woke from those dreams crying. That was the only time he ever cried.

Tadziu stayed away from home as much as he could when his father was there, stayed outside playing with other kids even when it was freezing. His father went to sleep early so Tadziu knew when he could come back. His mother never said anything when he came in late, only kissed him and brought him leftovers from the supper she had cooked for his father. The next day his father never remembered that Tadziu was not there the night before, or if he remembered, he didn't care. His father's anger didn't have a plan Tadziu could count on.

Sometimes Tadziu thought about things. He knew he was not bad. Other people liked him even though his father didn't. Joe liked him. Kids in school liked him. He could make them laugh. Even Sister liked him, he could tell. He could make her laugh too. Marysza liked him. Marysza's grandmother liked him. So he didn't think his father was right.

Shopping

Tadziu came home from school. He went to his mother and put his hand on her shoulder, his body trembling because of his love for her and because of his hatred of her. He knew she was sick but he couldn't remember when she became sick. It just happened and was there like your blanket falling off at night and you're suddenly cold. He couldn't stand that her body was thin, as if it would break when he touched it, or that her hair fell in tangled strands around her face and down her neck. He remembered, or thought he remembered, when her hair shined, with light bouncing from it like pieces of sun. Now she wore old cotton dresses that never looked like anything. The patterns in the dresses, flowers mostly, were so faded they were almost gone.

Tadziu was almost seven now. He had never been to school or known Marysza until he met Joe.

There were four children younger than Tadziu, two girls and two boys. Janek and Tomasz, the twins, were the youngest, babies who mostly nursed at his mother's breast but looked for other things besides. Tadziu watched as his mother brought them bowls of milky soup with pieces of egg floating in them. He remembered days when this soup, *kluski z mlekiem*[21] had been good, but now it was watery and had no taste. His two sisters ate the soup in the bowls, spilling half of it on themselves and the floor. Sometimes Helcza, the older sister, stuck out her lower lip and called their father bad names. Janina was closer in age to the twins. She didn't make a sound, drank the soup quietly and stood trembling when their father went crazy.

Tadziu knew the soup wasn't enough and tried to find other things for his brothers and sisters to eat. His mother didn't always have money but when she did, she took some from her purse and sent him to the store, as if he would know what to buy. He was afraid.

I can't do this, mama. I don't know how.

The man behind the counter in the meat store was big like his father. He smiled when he saw Tadziu.

"What's your order, young fella?" Tadziu pointed to something in the window he thought his mother had given them before.

"How much, sir?" the man boomed and Tadziu was frightened again. He couldn't answer, could only open his hand and show the man his money. The man scratched his head and began slicing the meat. He handed Tadziu the package but wouldn't take his money. Tadziu grasped the package tightly and then, a thought entered his silence, came into his head like a leaf settling on the ground after a storm. The fear left. He ran to the bread counter and took a loaf of bread, one that was already sliced. This time the man took some coins. Tadziu ran home, his heart beating in his chest all the way. He had something to give them, something that would take the empty look from their eyes. He put the bread around slices of the meat. His sisters ate greedily, traces of smiles on their faces. Even his mother took some and told him how well he had done.

I can make my mother talk. The sun will shine in her hair again.

He had to shop all the time now because his mother would never go, would never leave the house. He always ordered the same thing. The butcher looked puzzled.

"Don't you ever get tired of baloney?" he asked. Tadziu was surprised at the sound of his own voice, because no one in his house talked very much, only cried or made noises that didn't mean anything. His mother and father spoke in Polish. Tadziu knew Polish but he also knew that most of the people he met didn't. So he began to speak the world's language, slowly at first, then easier. He told the butcher yes, they were tired of bah-low-ney but he didn't know how to make anything else. He could not tell the man that his mother only cooked once during the day and that was supper for his father. The man looked at him as if he suddenly understood. He took Tadziu to the shelves and showed him jars of brown stuff which didn't look like anything Tadziu wanted to eat. The man laughed.

"I know what it looks like." He opened the jar, put some on a spoon and offered it to Tadziu.

I'll do it. I have to do it. I'll close my eyes and maybe it won't taste so bad.

The brown stuff was good. The man spread some on a slice of bread and folded the bread in half.

"There, that's easy to make." The butcher-man put the jar of brown stuff into a bag with some other things. One was a package of cookies. "How many in your house?" Tadziu held up six fingers. He wouldn't count his father. The man threw another package of cookies into the bag. Then he added two quarts of milk and told Tadziu to be careful he didn't fall.

"Okay," Tadziu said and hunted in his mind for something to call the man.

As if reading Tadziu's mind, the man said, "Joe, young fellow. I'm Joe," and held out his hand for Tadziu to shake.

"Okay, Joe. Thanks, Joe."

Tadziu wasn't afraid to go shopping anymore. He ran there eagerly because Joe always gave him some candy. And his mother was always pleased, even though she didn't understand all the things Tadziu brought home. Sometimes Joe took money and sometimes he didn't. When Tadziu brought money back, his mother was frightened because she thought Tadziu stole the food. He told her over and over again that he didn't. After a while, she believed him. Each time he came home, his brothers and sisters followed him with big eyes, waiting to see what he would take from the bag. Mostly they liked everything, but once one of his brothers made a face and spit out some licorice candy.

He had long forgiven Joe for betraying him, for the day the priest came to the house and talked to Tadziu's mother. The priest didn't have a face as nice as Joe's. He looked around their flat and got a funny look on his face. They all stood quietly in the living room with his sisters under the spot where the ceiling leaked and the wallpaper was falling.

They're afraid of him. They're afraid of everything.

Tomasz didn't want to stand anymore so he plopped down and started to cry. The priest talked to Tadziu's mother in a muffled voice, as if Tadziu couldn't understand important things. Tadziu didn't like that.

I know about the world. I know how to take care of us.

After the priest was gone, his mother said he would have to go to school. He was already a year older than the other children in his class. Tadziu was frightened again. And angry at Joe. He knew Joe had something to do with him going to school. Because once when Joe told him not to look so sad, that nothing could be that bad, not even school, Tadziu told him he didn't go to school. The next time he went to the store, he stared at Joe, but couldn't speak bad words to his friend, could only think them.

Why did you do this to me? You were my friend.

But school wasn't so bad. There were other boys. There were stupid girls. Even though you were supposed to learn things, at least he was away from home. He didn't have to look at his mother's sad eyes, didn't have to see his brothers and sisters, didn't have to feel bad inside every time he thought of them. He met Marysza. She was a stupid girl but he liked her anyway. She had a nice grandmother, an old lady who looked tough. He was behind Marysza in school now but her grandma still let Marysza bring him in for supper sometimes. They ate things he never had at home, things his mother only gave his father. Tadziu forgot about home when he was in Marysza's house.

Very Good Food

Tadziu's mother sent him to Church on the Saturday before Easter with the *swiecone*[22], a basket of food the priest would bless. His basket contained hard-boiled eggs and bread. Other people's baskets had things like ham and sausage, butter in the shape of a little lamb and pierogi, the traditional Polish food for Easter and Christmas, but Tadziu's basket didn't have any of those things. He didn't care. Marysza always went with him, carrying the basket her grandmother made, its contents covered by a clean white cloth. They both acted very solemn when the priest walked down the aisle scattering holy water into the air from a small thing he held in his hand that looked like a microphone.

After his mother got sick, she never made a basket again. One day when he and Marysza were playing cards her grandmother came over to the table and asked Tadziu if he was strong.

"Oh yeah." His mind searched for a way to demonstrate his strength before Marysza.

"Good," said Marysza's grandmother, "because I need someone to help roll the dough for pterogi. It's hard and my arms get tired."

"No problem. Mrs. Jargosz." Tadziu said this in as deep a voice as he could.

That Saturday, he and Marysza wore big white dish towels Marysa's grandmother had pinned to their clothes. She began rolling a round ball of white dough she had made the day before and kept rubbing her rolling pin with flour so the dough wouldn't stick to the metal table. Sometimes it stuck anyway and she had to start all over again. She told Tadziu to watch how thick the dough should be before rolling it and after a while she turned the rolling pin over to him. Tadziu looked at the small white mountain, took a deep breath and started to roll. His first two tries were bad but Marysza's grandmother said nothing and he kept rolling. Flour traveled through the air like white dust, settling a fine misty powder on all of them. Globs of dough were stuck to Marysza's chin.

I wonder if I look as funny as she does. Boy, the old lady wasn't kidding. This stuff is tough

When Tadziu rolled a good piece, Marysza's grandmother used a glass to cut circles and placed a spoonful of stuffing she had also made the night before —-cheese or raisins or potatoes—-in the center of the circle. Then she folded the circle into a half-moon so the stuffing was covered, lifted the half-moon carefully with a pancake turner and pinched the edges shut with her fingers. She slid the pockets of dough into a big kettle of boiling water and boiled them until they rose to the surface like little boats. The boats were lifted just as carefully from the boiling water so they wouldn't break, then lined up on the floured counter to dry so they wouldn't stick together when they were stacked on plates. If one broke while it was boiling, the filling rolled through the water like snowflakes.

"That's why they have to be pinched tight," Marysza's grandmother instructed Marysza who now had the cutting and pinching job. "The ones that break are lost, gone. All the work and all the expensive ingredients." Marysza's tongue stuck out from the corner of her mouth as she concentrated.

"We need to sample these and make sure everything's okay," Marysza's grandmother said. She took six of the stacked-up pierogi, put a little bit of butter in a frying pan, very little, because she said it was so expensive, and fried the pierogi in the melted butter. Tadziu watched the slow crackle of the bubbles that surrounded the pierogi as they fried, that turned the edges of the white dough into a crisp brown and filled the kitchen with a smell that was better than anything he had ever smelled, that made him want to cry because he couldn't wait to eat them. Maryszas's grandmother turned the pierogi over with a clean pancake turner and fried the other side until it was just brown enough to make a hollow little cave which she pressed with her finger, fast, without burning herself.

"To make sure they're hot inside," she said. On her good blue-chipped plates, she gave two to Tadziu, two to herself and two to Marysza. Tadziu cut his carefully with his fork—it was cheese—-and ate it slowly so that it would last. Marysza was not as excited as he was because she had eaten them before.

"Mine is raisin," she said. "Want to trade half"? Tadziu cut his pierogi carefully into two pieces, kept the larger half and put the smaller one on Marysza's plate.

"I have here a potato one," said Marysza's grandmother and without even asking to trade, she gave half to Tadziu and half to Marysza, then gave Tadziu two more. Tadziu had all three kinds on his plate, ate one small piece and sat so quiet that Marysza asked him if something was wrong. Tadziu didn't want to talk but he answered no. He was still eating slowly when Marysza and her grandmother began washing the dishes. Marysza made fun of him but her grandmother spoke again.

"We need a man to wash these big pots."

"I'm comin'," Tadziu said, and hurried to clean his plate.

Marysza's grandmother gave him a heaping plate of pierogi to take home, placing a white dish towel on top so they would stay clean.

"They're cool now. If your mama can fry them, it's better, but if she can't, it's all right. They won't hurt your brothers and sisters." Tadziu thought about eating one of the pierogi on his way home, but knew he would feel guilty if he did. He showed the pierogi to his mother and couldn't understand why her eyes became sad. He lied and told her Marysza's grandmother said they were only for her and the children, and put them in the back of the refrigerator. His father never went in there, just waited for Tadziu's mother to wait on him.

The next day, without Tadziu telling her, his mother fried them, but only in a little bit of water because they never had butter. They were still the best food Tadziu ever knew. When they were cool, the babies picked them up like little pies and took big bites. Raisins or cheese or mashed potatoes dribbled down their chins and they used their fists to stick the potatoes back into their mouths. Janina and Helcza used a plate and a spoon. Tadziu realized his mother didn't eat any.

"No, just the children," she said.

"No, mama, no," Tadziu cried. "Mrs. Jargosz said you too." But his mother wouldn't eat any and Tadziu knew it was because Tadziu didn't want his father to have any. That made Tadziu feel bad but he still couldn't stop eating. When Marysza's grandmother asked if the children liked the pierogi, he told her how they ate all fourteen of them in one day. Mrs. Jargosz gave Tadziu another dozen to take home. After that, he always helped her roll the dough and she always sent his mother a plate piled high with pierogi at Christmas and Easter. Tadziu never had any to take to church to be blessed because his sisters and brothers ate them as soon as he brought them home

Character Development

After Tadziu made his First Holy Communion, Sister had the bright idea that his behavior would improve if he was an altar boy, that it would "occupy him in a constructive manner" even though most of the altar boys were older. So he and Henry Lukasik, another boy who needed improvement, had to go to Sister Beatrice two days a week to practice Latin. After school even. They had to learn all the answers, sister called them "responses" to the prayers the priest said. Sister made them say the words over and over and it was hard because the words were funny.

The first response was easy, just an amen. But the second was harder: Ad dayum kwee lay tee fee cot yooven tootem meyoom.[23] And they kept getting trickier, some lines repeating themselves, and some parts pretty long, like "see koot ehrat een preen cheepee oh at noonk at sem pear at een say koo la say koo lo room. Amen[24]." and "kuhn fee tee or day oh uhm nee poh ten tee".[25] Sister didn't care. You just had to keep saying them and she said that after about a year you would know them by heart.

Oh yeah.

Then you had to practice kneeling, je nju flek ting [26] sister called it. And carrying the flasks of water and wine up the altar steps without tripping over your long dress that was called a kasik.[27] On top of all that, you had to go to whatever Mass Sister assigned you, some of them pretty early, before school even.

Only he and Henry, out of all the other boys in his class, were bad enough to be altar boys. But Sister was kind of right. Once you memorized the answers they never changed and you could almost say them in your sleep which was pretty much what Tadziu was doing when he had to serve an early Mass on Saturdays.

Tadziu and Henry studied a long time, and Sister kept testing them, a hundred times. They had white cards with all the answers on them but Sister didn't want you to look at them unless you had to. And she thought you never had to. Tadziu could never figure out how she knew when they were reading off the cards but she could. Like she had another set of eyes on the back of her black hood.

Even with the cards in front of them they got mixed up a lot, especially Henry and when Henry got mixed up, he mixed up Tadziu and they were like two trains going in opposite directions on a track with neither of them knowing how to stop. Father Zielasko, with his eyelids like window shades too heavy to stay up, just kept racing on no matter what they answered and Tadziu knew that if you were a hundred years old, which Father Zielasko probably was, you couldn't hear good. So it was okay. And Father Mikolajczak went slow so they could look at the cards. Father Mikolajczyk was young and not so bad. Most of the kids liked him. He was the one they went to for their first confession.[28]

Tadziu remembered his first confession. His biggest sin—outside of the things he did to the girls in his class like throwing spitballs and snowballs at them, lying on the floor close to the door outside the girl's lavatory with Henry Lukasik so the girls couldn't see and would trip over them when they came out, or making the girls scream in disgust when he picked his nose and ran after them so they thought he was going to wipe the booger on them—was making his father mad.

I told Father Mike about the girls first. I knew it must be my fault that my father hated me even though I didn't know why. I didn't know then that I hated him and I wouldn't confess it anyway because that was too terrible a sin. So I told Father Mike I made my father mad. Almost every day. And I just said I didn't like my father. **At all.** *Father Mike asked me why I made my father mad and I told him I didn't know why or even what I did that made him mad and hit me all the time. Father Mike was quiet for a little while. Then he told me it wasn't my fault, that I was good and Jesus loved me. He said my penance was to pray six Hail Marys for my father. I asked him if I should say them in English or Polish. He said I could say them either way. Then I said my act of contrition and Father Mike blessed me and took away all my sins. It felt pretty good. I didn't feel like praying for the old man. But I didn't want to go to hell. Going to confession means you have to try not to do your sins again. Maybe my penance did some good with God because my father doesn't hit me so much anymore, just looks at me with real mad eyes. That's almost worse.*

Tadziu left the girls alone for a few days until he forgot.

One part of being an altar boy made him glad. .It made his mother leave the house. She went to church and took his brothers and sisters with her because she was so proud of Tadziu. She sat in the pew never taking her eyes off him even when the babies cried and she had to move one of them in her arms or hand them to Helcza or Janina. His sisters sat on either side of his mother and shifted the babies in their arms or jiggled them up and down so they wouldn't cry. The first time his sisters saw him at the altar, their eyes got big as if they had just seen a movie star and it was only him, Tadziu. Helcia always told him how handsome he looked in his white blouse and long black kasik, but as usual, Janina was too shy to say anything.

He remembered the Sunday Joe came to church with his family and how Joe's kids all waved to him until Joe told them to stop. Tadziu tried to pretend he didn't notice their wild waving and said his prayers louder than usual so they could all hear him. He could just see Joe after Mass telling his kids that altar boys were not allowed to look around because their job was too important.

After his mother got sick and didn't go to church anymore, Helcia and he washed his white blouse called a surplus [29] like they had seen his mother do when she had enough energy to wash clothes. She didn't wash it with all the other clothes in the bathtub and the machine with the big rollers—rollers that frightened Tadziu when he was small because his mother had warned them never to go near them or it would catch their hands—but separate, all by itself in the sink. It was a good thing the kasik he wore underneath the blouse never got washed, just hung on a hanger behind the door in the rectory.

Janina tried to iron the blouse after it was dry the way she had seen their mother do it with the big metal iron you plugged in the wall. He remembered how Janina carefully spread the blouse on a towel she placed on the table, how hard she concentrated and how long it took her. Helcia told her it was good enough and Janina finally finished. She did a pretty good job too, because no one ever noticed or said it looked different.

Tadziu tried telling sister, because she was the boss of all the altar boys, that he couldn't come anymore after his mother got sick but she wouldn't let him quit. So Helcia, Janina and he had to keep washing and ironing the blouse. He thought of just never showing up anymore and then he saw that Marysza was proud of him, just like his mother, so he kept going. And it was the truth, even though he didn't want to admit it, that it made him feel special, different than most of the other boys in his class and was the only thing he could really be proud of.

If Tadziu had to serve a wedding or a funeral the people gave the altar boys money. Tadziu gave the money to his mother but she always gave him back a little for himself. He liked weddings because the people were happy but not funerals because everybody cried. The crying got louder when the people went to the cemetery and sang what he called the funeral song after the Mass was over. *Serdeczna Matko, opiekunko ludzi Nie cie placz sierot Do litosci wzbudzi Wygnancy Ewy do Ciebie wolamy Zmilujsie zmiluj niech sie nie tulamy*, and then after other parts, the chorus again, louder. *Wygnancy Ewy……*[30]..He remembered watching while the people threw dirt into the grave and feeling his body turning weak, into someone that was not him anymore but someone he only watched from far away because if it was him he might run away from the singing and the crying and never come back.

Tadziu's mother didn't go to church on Saturdays so he didn't have to worry whether he made her embarrassed on the Saturday he and Henry got into trouble. Tadziu was lucky his father didn't find out. After he and Henry confessed, Sister never even told his mother. Tadziu told Marysza about it later, making it sound bigger than it really was. The basic facts were pretty simple.

It was seven o'clock mass on Saturday. He and Henry were kneeling on the altar steps waiting for the time to carry up the flasks of water and wine. Their most important job was pouring the water and the wine into the chalice[31] so the priest could change it into Jesus' blood at the kon se krey shun, [32]Sister called it, and then water over the priest's hands when he washed the chalice.

Henry's head was bobbing and Tadziu could see he was almost asleep. So Tadziu stayed awake. He and Henry had this agreement that one of them would stay awake and pay attention so they didn't get into trouble for being late with what they were supposed to do. Father Zielasko was crabby a lot, especially with boys and especially at early Masses.

Tadziu was paying attention so he could poke Henry in the ribs when it was time to go up to the altar stairs. He heard an unmistakable sound, once and then again, the second time louder. Father Zielasko was farting. Tadziu started to laugh and poked Henry, who was kind of irritable because it wasn't time to go up yet, until he heard the noise himself and his eyes opened as wide as if Tadziu had thrown water at him.

Tadziu looked at Henry triumphantly. His friend sure knew this was important enough to wake up for. The farts came in rapid succession now, like small rifle shots. Tadziu and Henry started to laugh, quietly at first, with their hands over their mouths, but then, unable to control themselves, louder and louder. Father Zielasko didn't even know he was farting and was unaware of the boys' laughter. He went through the Mass kind of on automatic pilot, more asleep than the boys. But then it was time for Tadziu and Henry to go up the altar steps and hand the flasks to Father, which they did, trying not to laugh, and not to trip over their long black gowns.

It was no use. Father Zielasko reached for the flasks just as a louder burst of gas left him. He lifted his eyelids to look directly into the face of the two boys who were laughing uncontrollably and trying not to fall backwards down the steps. Father Zielasko glared at them with a look that was enough to stop an elephant in his tracks, but the spurts he emitted did not cease, only grew less in volume, petering out slowly but unable to exhaust themselves. No matter how hard they tried or how frightened they became, Tadziu and Henry could not control their laughter. Each time they stopped laughing, a new spurting sound made them start again. They were helpless, their situation growing worse by the minute, so they gave up trying and surrendered, pretty much doubling over and falling down the steps as soon as Father Zielasko had washed his hands and their official duties were over.

Tadziu understood Sister Beatrice's reaction. She was dumbfounded, always knowing they were bad but not this stupid.

"Why, why," she kept repeating, her face as close to theirs as it could get, "why did you act so disrespectful, so blasphemous, in Mass?" Both boys were tight-lipped, silent. "All right, I'll have to tell your parents and suspend you from school for awhile." Tadziu didn't think that was such a bad deal because he knew that telling his parents meant Sister would tell his mother and Tadziu was safe with her, but Henry started to cry.

"It was Father Zielasko," he blubbered, and Sister could make no sense of Henry's incoherent sobbing. Tadziu knew he had to step in.

"It was Father Zielasko's fault," he said. "He was farting all through Mass and wouldn't stop." As if he were a turtle, Henry was trying to disappear by pulling his head into some non-existent shell. At the same time, his eyes became wide with admiration for Tadziu, for his telling, his using the unspeakable word "fart" in front of Sister, who stared at the two boys as if she had been hit by a sledgehammer. Her eyes were wide with disbelief and surprise and she seemed unable to talk. Then the tiniest flicker of a smile crossed her face.

"Go to your seats," she said, and write one hundred times, "I will not laugh during Mass." I'll tell Father Zielasko you've been punished," and then, for good measure, added, "don't ever do that again." Tadziu thought she should be saying that to Father Zielasko and telling him to write "I will not fart during Mass" one hundred times but of course, he kept his mouth shut. Henry was still sniveling so Tadziu spoke for both of them.

"Yes Sister," he said, and pulled Henry to his seat. He knew Sister was really the boss around here and he now had the great feeling that she wouldn't tell their parents, and would satisfy Father Zielasko by telling him she had personally punished them.

It wasn't exactly the best penmanship but it took Tadziu a half-hour to write his hundred sentences. Henry was still writing at the end of the day.

"You can finish tomorrow," Sister snapped. She didn't say another word to Tadziu.

He had a good time telling that story to Marysza. Her grandmother walked in and heard them laughing. He even told it to her. The three of them laughed long and hard as if they had caught the same laughing bug and couldn't stop.

Chapter Two

1950

Change

Grandma became sick. Marysza was frightened. After a week had passed, Marysza knew grandma wasn't getting better, even though she said she was. She lay in bed covered to her chin with her crocheted bedspread because she was cold and asked Marysza to bring her tea. Marysza ran the water in the hot water faucet just as grandma had taught her and put some over a teabag in a cup. Then she put in a little milk and a teaspoon of sugar. Grandma murmured "thank you" and Marysza put the cup on the dresser, close to the edge so grandma could reach it.

"I should be better soon," grandma said, "able to go back to work nex' week", but Marysza knew grandma was saying that to keep her from being frightened. She knew grandma wouldn't get better, although she couldn't form the thought that she could die. A world without grandma wasn't possible.

Friday was always a good day for Marysza because there was no school the next day. When she came home this Friday, grandma wasn't there. Dread settled in Marysza's stomach and kept climbing, growing bigger until it reached her throat and kept her from talking. She tried to tell herself grandma had felt better and gone to work for the day but she knew that wasn't true.

Grandma didn't come home at the usual time. Someone knocked at the door. When Marysza opened it, the dread rushed from her throat to her insides so she thought she might wet her pants. Two strangers, a man and a woman dressed in clothes that made Marysza think of uniforms, looked at her as if she were something in the window of a store.

"Marysza?" they asked. She heard herself answering "yes", knowing she was in a place and time where she didn't want to be, hearing words that marched toward her like ugly creatures she wanted to push away, words telling her that grandma had been taken to the hospital and died.

Maybe me and Martha were eating lunch. Maybe my grandma died while we were eating lunch.

Marysza's Uncle Ben came and cried because he hadn't known grandma was sick. He tried to find something in Grandma's things that would tell him how to find Marysza's mother but he couldn't. Marysza could tell he wasn't sure what to do with her, or what to do with all the things she and Grandma had. She watched in alarm as Uncle Ben began packing things.

"Look, Marysza," her uncle said, "the things can't stay here. They'll go with you, wherever you go." He looked away.

"Where will I go?" Marysza waited for his answer.

"I'm not sure yet," he mumbled somewhere into his shoulder. As he walked through the rooms, picking up things and throwing them into boxes, Marysza looked around, her frantic eyes knowing the importance of holding the picture of the rooms as they were.

He'll disturb them. He'll change them forever.

Like water, she drank in the pictures, tried to hide them inside herself so they'd be safe. She couldn't tell Uncle Ben about the importance of the red-and-black afghan or the blue bedspread grandma had crocheted.

She saw the big television with the word Motorola under its small round screen. She saw the table that held grandma's Infant of Prague statue with the two fingers on its right hand raised, a statue that had clothes for every season the Church celebrated, clothes that Grandma made out of pretty scraps of material, some bought in the junk store on South Park, the table with legs shaped like ropes twisting around each other, legs that wobbled if you walked into them. Marysza knew she'd remember the way pieces of black paint lifted themselves from the top of the table like bubbles showing the older brown paint underneath. Her eyes moved to the red clock shaped like an apple that hung on the kitchen wall, to the shiny white table where grandma and she ate, with its patches of black where the enamel was chipped, to the gray- and-blue linoleum with black islands at its edges where it had begun to tear.

She thought of how Grandma mopped the linoleum every week and how Marysza's job was to wash the table with a sponge that made soap bubbles each time she squeezed it. Sometimes Grandma would say "hey lady, quiccher playin' and finish washin' that table," but Marysza knew she never meant it. Marysza just kept on playing, dipping the sponge into the pail, squeezing it in the water and watching the soap suds grow, then squeezing the soap suds from the sponge onto the table until the bubbles disappeared.

Marysza knew she couldn't look long enough before it would be time to leave, couldn't see everything the way she wanted to see it so she could take it with her, and hold it inside her forever. She looked at the kitchen sink, hanging from the wall like a crooked boat, at the plastic stool beneath the sink that she used so she could reach the faucets. She looked at the stove with its silver tea kettle and the red potholders she made for Grandma in school last Christmas so they would match the clock. Then she looked hard at the bird on the calendar which hung beside the stove, the bird Grandma called a goose. All around the bird were words, messages scrawled in Grandma's writing, big writing with tall loops and full round moons because Grandma always wrote big.

Uncle Ben and Aunt Irene

Marysza went with Uncle Ben and stayed in his home with his wife and two children. Her cousins did not speak much to her at first, but Marysza didn't care. The thought that grandma was gone filled all of her so that she couldn't talk if they spoke to her except for short answers like "yes" and "no". She thought maybe Uncle Ben was trying to find another place for her. He was on the phone a lot and covered the talking part with his hand when he knew she was around. He talked to people whose names Marysza thought she recognized from sometime when her grandma had talked about them, but she didn't care about that either.

He's trying to find someone to take me. No one wants me.

If this was another time she'd tell them out loud that she didn't care. But it was a time when she couldn't run to the person who loved her, the person who would click her teeth and say none of them mattered so that Marysza would forget about caring. Now she began to care, began to think that it did matter, that something was wrong with her because no one wanted her.

In the end, she stayed at Uncle Ben's. Her aunt and uncle were kind to her, but Marysza saw that her uncle was the boss and had a different kind of kindness than the kindness Marysza had known with her grandma, a kindness meant only for her. Her uncle's kindness was thrown into the air in a general way and loosely, so that, like birds hunting for seeds in winter, the one who got there first was the one who got the most. Her aunt was quiet when she looked at Marysza as if she wanted to talk but couldn't.

Marysza knew her two cousins thought of her as someone who had fallen into their lives and they didn't know how to fit her in. Jimmy was a child, too small and shy to understand anything. Her cousin Barbara, who was her age, didn't talk to her because she resented having to share her room.

At night, Barbara turned on her pillow away from Marysza and went to sleep. Marysza told herself she didn't care. She wanted to spend the time before falling asleep thinking of grandma, of how she was the only one in her grandma's eyes. When her grandma and she had seen her cousins at Christmas or other holidays, Marysza knew her grandma didn't think they were as smart or as good as Marysza.

Thinking of grandma filled her with pain, but Marysza was afraid that if she didn't think of her, grandma would be lost forever. She thought about Martha and Tadziu and whether she'd ever see them again. She couldn't talk about them to Aunt Irene or Uncle Ben because her missing them might seem ungrateful.

One night Barbara broke her silence. "Do you like our school?" she asked. Marysza lifted herself from her thoughts and replied, "It's okay." Barbara began to giggle.

"What about Billy? Isn't he cute?"

"He's okay, but not as cute as Donald." Her cousin shrieked in disbelief.

As if their talk had escaped from chains, Barbara and Marysza talked without stopping, about the different boys in the class, about the teachers, about what they wanted to be. They even talked about Marysza's aunt and uncle. Barbara told Marysza her mother embarrassed her but Marysza told Barbara her mother loved her and Jimmy very much and Barbara was lucky because Marysza's mother had gone away and left her. Marysza was surprised by her own words. Like a giant hand that reached down and covered their mouths, that made Barbara quiet and it made Marysza quiet too.

Marysza knew they had crossed a bridge. They became friends and began to share secrets. They did their homework together and went to the movies together. Marysza tried not to think of Martha because Martha lived far away and belonged to her other life and that life would never return. When she did think of her, it was the same wound that opened when she thought of her grandma.

At first, Marysza's days were filled with the thought that this wasn't her real home, that her home was gone.

Something they call the center has been taken from me and my life will never be the same.

After more time had passed, she began to think of her aunt and uncle's house as home, although she never jumped onto her uncle's lap the way her cousins did, because it would embarrass her. In her secret self, she kept the storm that had filled her since her grandma died and tried to settle into her new family, to fit into the pattern of their life. There were times she felt herself standing aside and watching the life of the house. Marysza saw her uncle watching her observe them but her aunt didn't notice.

Uncle Ben didn't often holler at his kids and never at Marysza but she knew when he was angry or impatient. He was quiet but his silence was heavy. Marysza remembered her grandma talking about all the good things Uncle Ben did. Marysza had thought then that her uncle was rich because he bought her grandma a television set and other things, but now she learned this wasn't true. Uncle Ben's and Aunt Irene's house was small and looked as if it had been pressed from a giant cookie-cutter so it was identical to every other house on the block. The living room held a couch, two chairs and a television set. The seams of the couch were splitting along the back and the arms like a chicken or a turkey with too much stuffing. Everything looked old and worn, just as it had at grandma's house, but the floors, windows and whatever you could see, smelled of soap, even more than in grandma's house, as if it had just been scrubbed.

Marysza's Aunt Irene was pretty, with wavy blonde hair cut short so that the waves fit close and neat around her head like a cap. Like her house, she smelled of soap, but a lighter and prettier kind. In the bathrooms and the kitchen, her aunt had dolls with wide skirts and things hidden in the skirts that smelled like flowers. When Uncle Ben brought Marysza home, her aunt put her arms around her and said "poor baby, it will be all right."

Aunt Irene talked most of the time—to her husband, her children, and now Marysza. Usually it was about the children's activities or cooking or something a neighbor had said. Now and then something important stood out from her talk but you could never be sure when that would be. Marysza saw that her uncle and her cousins didn't listen to her aunt very much, but sensed when something important was going to emerge and turned their faces toward her, waiting expectantly...

Aunt Irene looked for happiness and found it without effort. She smiled a lot, admired things like the pattern in a new tablecloth, thought that Barbara's s accomplishments in school were magnificent and that Jimmy's would be also. The pictures Jimmy drew with his crayons were all on display, pinned to the curtains with silver straight pins or hanging from the windowsills with tiny pieces of scotch tape. She sang as she washed dishes, or when she put supper on the table. Her voice was delicate and filled with a quiet astonishment.

My aunt has a light inside, a light different than grandma's but still a light.

Marysza knew her aunt's light depended on her husband and her children, that it would disappear without them, just as something inside Marysza had disappeared when her grandma left her. One night after Aunt Irene had made a good dinner, everyone complimented her. Later, she motioned to Marysza from the kitchen and spoke in a hushed voice, as if she were divulging a secret.

"I try to limit myself to two dollars per meal for meat" she said, as if Marysza was grown-up, although Marysza and Barbara were the same age. Marysza began to look for her Aunt Irene after school, to sit at the table while her aunt fussed with bringing cookies and milk, talking about her day and asking Marysza about hers.

A Small Friend

Uncle Ben worked in a factory and when he came home at night, he was tired and dirty, wanted only to eat supper and lie down on the couch to watch television. Sometimes he didn't bother to change his clothes.

"Jimmy, bring me a beer," he'd say, and Marysza's younger cousin would run to the refrigerator as if he'd been chosen for something special. If she was around, Barbara rolled her eyes and looked up at the ceiling, as if to say, "isn't he dumb?" Then they'd all laugh, including her uncle.

"Leave him alone, you guys," her uncle would say, "Jimmy's my guy!" Jimmy would beam proudly, and Barbara would look up at the ceiling again.

Marysza liked Jimmy. He was four years old. Even though his father and mother treated him special because he was the baby, he needed more of something, something he seemed to think Marysza had. He followed her faithfully, if not with his feet, with his eyes, and acted as if she was very important. He brought her toys, his eyes speaking his hope that she would play with him. When he bothered his sister, she became impatient but Marysza never did, so Jimmy tagged after Marysza more and more. He sat next to her on the couch in the living room where she studied because if she studied in Barbara's room, they'd talk too much.

Today, Jimmy sat as close to her as he could, looking at the pages in her book and asking what the book was about. Marysza was studying her history, a subject which she liked but the book was an old one and not interesting. She tried to make it appealing to Jimmy.

"It's about America," she said, "and how we came to be a country." She told him about King George and the first colonists, how they objected to unfair taxes and threw the tea into the Boston harbor. Jimmy listened to every word, his eyes glued to Marysza's face. Marysza had other assignments, felt harried and, for a moment, resentful. Jimmy was taking her time and she felt that, against her will, part of herself was being removed. But the joy in his eyes changed her perception. She saw her foolishness, understood that this child made her more whole, and willed her consciousness into being with him. He liked the story of the tea and she showed him the picture of the event that led to the Revolutionary War. The picture was not very good, but he examined it carefully. He looked spell-bound when she told him that was what Fourth of July was all about.

"Wow!" he exclaimed, again and again, "wow!" and would have stayed next to Marysza and the book all evening, but she told him she had to answer some questions and moved to the dining room table. She heard him talking to himself about nasty King George and the Fourth of July. His talk was mixed with something about a big pot of tea and his eyes were seeing something far away that only he could see. Remembering such visionary moments from her own childhood, Marysza ran her pencil through her hair. As she listened to Jimmy, his happiness became her own.

Aunt Irene was always telling Uncle Ben she wanted to go to work and earn extra money. Marysza could tell her words were half-hearted, that she was afraid and didn't really want a job, that she was grateful when Uncle Ben said "no" as if he were insulted and told her the kids needed her at home.

"They're not babies anymore, for heaven's sake," Marysza's aunt would protest but her uncle didn't pay attention, as if this was an empty ritual. Sometimes he kissed his wife on the forehead as if she were a child. At the same time, his own forehead became furrowed and he looked worried. Marysza knew he was thinking that he didn't earn enough money. No one ever mentioned Marysza's name because they were kind, but she held a part of herself away from them. She knew she didn't belong, that she was an additional strain on their already-tight budget.

"My mother and father are talking about the summer, about whether we can afford to go to a cottage for a week," Barbara said one night. Marysza heard something almost-not-there in her voice, something which said, "Now they have to pay for you too." She didn't know if her aunt and uncle said that to themselves. They never talked about money when they thought the kids could hear them but she knew they needed more money because of her.

She stayed with her aunt and uncle and cousins until she was eighteen and finished high school. She graduated at the top of the class. Her aunt and uncle went to her graduation, had a small party for her friends and gave her a wrist watch. They said they were proud of her but it wasn't the same.

No one understands my accomplishment the way grandma would have.

Marysza knew she had to look for a job. At first, she worked in a store downtown. That was where she saw Martha again and was able to ask about Tadziu. Martha scrunched her face and said she hadn't seen him since they finished grade school.

"I don't know if he went to high school or not. He kind of disappeared." Marysza smiled to herself.

And you're probably glad he did.

She and Martha resumed their friendship as if it had never been interrupted. Marysza brought her home to meet Aunt Irene and Uncle Ben but was careful not to make too much of Martha so that Barbara wouldn't be jealous. Martha worked at Howard Johnson's restaurant and told Marysza she could make more money as a waitress because of tips.

Since grandma's death, Marysza had feelings that were new to her, feelings that suggested she wasn't as smart or as good as grandma or she herself had thought. Now, as she heard Martha's words, the unwanted feelings returned. She hesitated, knowing she was afraid to apply for the waitress job, afraid she would be turned down because she wasn't like Martha, because she didn't have enough of whatever it was a waitress needed.

She got the job but she was still afraid. She began in the back of the restaurant where it was less busy because she wasn't as fast as the other girls. They were glad she wasn't fast and leaned against the counter staring at her when business was slow, waiting for her to make a mistake. When Martha was there, it was different. Her eyes crossed when she looked at the other girls because she was angry. They made fun of Martha's eyes and sneered when she tried to help Marysza, but Martha told them to "kiss her ass" and began to teach Marysza what she needed to know.

Martha was a demanding teacher but Marysza encountered little difficulty in following her friend's instructions until they reached the most important lesson—-the facility to carry several full plates at a time. Marysza's eyes grew wide as Martha loaded plates into a bag to take home so they could practice away from the gaze of the other girls. Marysza thought she could never master this skill her friend performed so effortlessly.

They had their first try. Marysza struggled until beads of sweat broke out on her face. Martha's voice began to sound like the voices of the other waitresses.

"You have to balance the plates on your arm like this. No, not like that!" You'll drop them all!" Martha screeched as the plates teetered like a listing ship, then clattered to the ground and broke into large puzzle pieces. Marysza'a eyes filled with tears.

"I can't do this. These aren't ordinary dishes. They're heavy as hell!"

"Of course they are. They're restaurant china, not wimpy stuff. You'll get it, believe me." Her voice softened. "I broke my share when I started."

Martha came to Marysza's aunt and uncle's house and with Jimmy watching in silence as if he were holding his breath, practiced with her each day. She became more patient as Marysza improved and taught her all she needed to know to be as fast as the other girls. Before long, Marysza was earning as much in tips as anyone, but despite this success and the fact that no other picture presented itself, she couldn't think of herself as a waitress and her job remained nothing more than a way to get the money she needed.

Her grandma's picture had faded in her mind, but when she lay in bed at night Marysza concentrated on that picture despite the sadness it brought. She thought of how her grandma had worked until she died, how she had never complained of her legs when Marysza knew they hurt her, how she would say, "The Lord means us to earn our way into the next life." When Marysza was small, she had believed that whatever her grandma said was true, and that belief had not changed. Things were as they were because God meant them that way.

Her job was something she had to do even though it was difficult and boring. Other people did easier or more interesting things, but they lived in a different world than she did. Her world was filled with girls who wore their hair in hairnets, took their uniforms home each night to wash them, and were mean to anyone who was new or whom they didn't like. The reasons they didn't like other girls—and it was hard to keep track of who didn't like who at what time, it changed so often—-were difficult to understand. After a while, Marysza just stopped caring, feeling it was better to be alone with Martha than to keep switching to the side of whoever was on top at the moment.

Marysza became a good waitress. When she and Martha saw an ad in the paper for jobs at an exclusive country club, they went together to apply. Marysza was hired but didn't want to take the job because Martha wasn't.

"Don't be silly," Martha told her. "You'll make more money. You can buy me a better Christmas present."

1957

Old Friends

On summer weekends, Marysza and Martha frequented **The Pier**, a bar on the lake filled with young people seeking each other in the romantic setting of the lake after their week of work in the hot city. Some of them set up tents on the beach and stayed there for the night or weekend. If you got there early enough and were lucky, you could sit at a table instead of standing in the crowd that pressed on you from every side. A wall of bodies was made exotic by the cloud of cigarette smoke that spiraled upward in the dim light, its aroma mingling with the smell of beer, alcohol and the scent of sweet perfume, then settling like a cover on the heated air. Inching your way to the bar and back to your table gave you the chance to check out the crowd, for girls to bump against guys with their boobs and say "excuse me", for guys to say "sure baby", then wander over to your table if they were interested. Couples then made their way to a wooden dance floor that waited like an island in the sea, to dance to rock and roll singers like Elvis Presley and Bill Haley and the Comets.

Marysza did not like beer, so she drank coca-cola but Martha was a beer person. They watched the crowd and the kids dancing and listened to juke-box music blare from huge speakers that made conversation almost impossible. Marysza, who was always asked to dance, didn't accept when Martha wasn't asked because she didn't want to leave her alone.

"Go on, dance," Martha urged as she saw a good-looking guy heading for their table. Marysza could tell he was from one of the local colleges. His swagger and the look on his face gave him away; his khaki pants, white buck shoes and white wool socks making it certain. Marysza watched his approach.

I know my face reveals my uncertainty but I can attract any boy here. My sweater and pants fit well. My lipstick and nail polish are too bright but they're the latest fashion. I can fool these guys into thinking I'm a college girl, a student like they are.

"Hiya, hon," the boy smiled, leaning over Marysza's shoulder, beer in hand, "here I am," and began laughing at himself, an easy laugh that infected Marysza and Martha and persuaded Marysza to dance with him. He asked Marysza where she went to school, but she evaded the question. When he asked for her phone number, she evaded that too, and he began singing into her ear about how much he loved her. She told him she didn't have a phone, that she lived alone and couldn't afford one. Even though he was half drunk, the boy looked at Marysza in surprise.

"No phone, okay. Then where do you live? How can I get there? Do I have to send a letter?"

Trying to explain anything or trying to lie required an effort Marysza didn't have. The boy brought her unwanted thoughts. There was nothing about her life she wanted to tell him, nothing he could understand. Something that wasn't his fault, that was part of what he was, made her ashamed of what she was. He continued to sing as his hand drew strands of her hair between his teeth. The colored lights edging the wooden platform blinked as Elvis Presley's voice intoned "Heartbreak Hotel", and the moon watching the dark water dropped long ribbons of light that shimmered and unrolled, appeared and disappeared. Over the boy's shoulder, Marysza watched the waves and heard their barely perceptible sound as they ended their journey and crept back and forth between the water and the sand.

The afternoon she recognized Tadziu, the owners of the club were sponsoring a picnic for patrons. He stared at her for a long time, his eyes revealing his reticence. Marysza turned to Martha who said nothing but rolled her eyes and threw up her hands.

He's afraid. I know about feeling afraid.

She smiled to give him courage. He came over and sat on the ground next to her.

"Is it ok?" he asked, and she answered "sure", then "how've you been?"because it was so natural, because she couldn't think of anything else to say and because she was impressed by his manners, manners which told her he wasn't one of the college boys, young men so sure of themselves they thought manners were unnecessary. He wore his hair short and neat, combed away from his eyes, in contrast to the college guys who acted uninterested, above caring about such trivialities and wore their hair as messy as they could, believing they looked original though they all looked the same. His shirt was clean and he carried glasses in a leather case in the pocket. She knew he was like she was in the way he behaved and in the things he didn't have, that he probably worked in a factory like Uncle Ben.

"Okay. How 'bout you?"

"Okay."

Martha looked at him and said "Long time no see," and Tadziu laughed at the tone in her voice which clearly said it had not been long enough for her. He turned back to Marysza and said something about her being the prettiest girl he ever saw, a mistake, he knew, and drew Martha's utter disgust.

"You new here?" Marysza could tell he was trying to make conversation. She wanted to reach out and touch him.

He knows he's not good at small talk. His voice almost trembles like Jimmy's does when he's frightened or afraid.

"No, I've been here before," she answered, realizing she felt as anxious as he did.

They talked on the small plot of grass beneath the trees, slowly, haltingly. Marysza felt Tadziu's gratitude floating over them like the dandelion spores in the air.

"This is life in the country," she said, knowing he understood her meaning, that, like her, knew their freedom was only momentary, a short respite from the real life waiting to reclaim them. They ate hamburgers and hot dogs and as Marysza alternated between Martha and Tadziu as a partner, played picnic games, one in which Taziu and Marysza threw an egg back and forth to each other, caught it each time without breaking it, and won a prize. As night approached, a live band played music while the crowd, with heads jerking and hips swaying in time to the rhythm, sang the words. Tadziu held Marysza close in a slow ballad and refused to let any of the other guys dance with her. Marysza felt herself moving back in time, returning to her childhood, when she was seven years old and Tadziu sat behind her in class, throwing notes to her when Sister turned to the blackboard.

Is this what was never finished? Will it be finished? I feel his words, words he doesn't speak, can't speak. A secret hides behind his sad eyes, sadness that leaves when his face becomes glad because of me. Can I hold him, make him safe from things I don't know, don't understand? I feel his claim, the bond that travels through the years to find me, the tie that joins me to him. "Do you remember", he asks me again and again, and I answer "yes", because I remember it all, have never forgotten.

After she told him about her grandma's death, she was quiet, not wanting to say any more words, knowing he would know that saying more words would somehow dishonor her grandma. He knew.

"She was the nicest lady," he said quietly and the knot that sat within her since her grandma's death loosened slightly, because someone remembered her grandma as she remembered her, knew and understood the hurt, the emptiness she felt inside. But what was the hurt, the anger she had sensed in him when they were children? Her grandma once said his father was a *diabel* which meant a devil. Tadziu didn't talk about it then and he didn't talk about it now. Something in his silence frightened her but she didn't ask questions.

He rubbed her back, and without words, she knew what finding her meant to him. He asked if he could drive her home and she knew he meant not only to take her home but to be part of her life. She hid from the look in Martha's eyes when she told her she wanted to leave, flinched when Martha said to go ahead, that she would be fine, then submitted to the silence that reminded her Martha still thought Tadziu was a jerk.

"Some things never change," he said to Martha and she answered, "boy, if that ain't the truth," which made Tadziu laugh again. "I'll drive you home too," he said. Martha just looked at him as if he was crazy and muttered "no thanks." Marysza couldn't persuade herself to stay with her friend.

Something I don't understand, have never understood, pulls me, something as strong as the tide rising and creeping on the sand.

He took her to his car, which was parked on the grass with a hundred others, but she saw that it was nicer looking than most of them, not a chip in the blue and white paint, the chrome polished until it shone like a mirror—and that he was proud of it. He held the door open for her and she saw the interior was attractive. The seats were dark brown and looked like leather. The floor was spotless, as if it had been vacuumed, the windshield so clean it seemed not to be there. The little white lights on the dials glowed in the dark as if announcing they were all on the job and working perfectly. Tadziu closed the door carefully and turned the radio on. She was surrounded by soft music and couldn't tell where the speakers were located, so smoothly and evenly did the music fill the air.

"Your car is beautiful."

He smiled with pleasure.

She couldn't focus her thoughts, couldn't keep her mind on what was in front of her. For a moment, pictures of the other guys, the college guys, flashed before her eyes, and a hidden part of her admitted she had found several of them attractive. Martha was always squealing about one or another of them when they approached saying, "oh

Marysza, he's cute, you should go out with him, you lucky dog." Nor could she deny she liked the effortless way they laughed and made fun of things, the way they disregarded anything that seemed serious or sad. But she couldn't think of going out with any of them, couldn't believe she could fit into the bright and expensive worlds she thought they inhabited, a world that seemed lifted from a television or movie screen. It didn't occur to her that some of the college boys weren't rich, that some of them might even be poor.

Tadziu's car was a lifeboat appearing on the horizon of a dark sea, a lifeboat which would take her to an unknown and exciting destination. The hidden part of herself again emerged and she saw that stepping inside would have consequences neither she nor Tadziu could understand or control. She didn't want to know, pushed that knowledge away.

I'm having a romance. Tadziu needs me and wants me.

"Yes," she said to him when he asked if he could kiss her and leaned over to cover her mouth with his and slowly run his hands over her sweater. She repeated that "yes", each time he took her to his room and reached for her in bed. He was her first experience of a man's love.

Her uncle looked pained after she told him she'd marry Tadziu. He'd met him and Marysza knew he didn't like him. Tadziu turned into someone different around other men, especially older men or men with some authority over him. He didn't look at them as they spoke nor acknowledge what they said, responding only with a look of animosity. Marysza tried talking to him about his manner but he shrugged his shoulders and stopped talking to her. She told herself they would discuss it another time, that he'd see how unreasonable he was and would change.

"I've tried with him, Marysza," her uncle said and she knew it was true. Her uncle was a good man, a fair man. "I don't know what the hell his problem is. It's like he's hiding something." Her uncle looked away from Marysza, his hands thrust so deep into his pockets that his pants appeared to be falling down.

"Marysza, you're not my daughter and I can't tell you what to do. But you're blood"—-he stumbled, hunting for words—"you're family, and I want to protect you."

It's hard for him to say this to me. I love you, Uncle Ben.

"I just don't feel good about this," he continued, halting again and rubbing the back of his head, "not good at all." His face told her this was his last word and should be sufficient to make her reconsider. Marysza felt herself tightening.

It's as if I'm my aunt and he can dismiss me

The thought made her angry with herself. Her uncle did not dismiss Aunt Irene. She knew the depth of his feeling for her and knew that though he feigned impatience, he treasured her innocence, and knew that, to the detriment of neither of them, he didn't think she and Aunt Irene were similar, but he had difficulty explaining his thoughts, and that, above all, he didn't want Marysza to feel he was bossing her around. She knew his unspoken words. "If you were my daughter, I'd have the right to absolutely forbid you to do this. But you're not my daughter and I can't.

"You're awful young," he said with conviction, and then quickly, as if he had struck on something important, something that had not occurred to him before, "you can stay here as long as you want. We love you."

Her uncle shifted from one foot to another and put his arms around her carefully, as if she were made of something that could break.

"It'll be okay, Uncle Ben," she said and put her arms around him too. Her uncle left the room with sad eyes.

A short time later, Aunt Irene came into the living room. Marysza knew Uncle Ben had sent her, that he was making a last desperate effort, thinking that maybe a woman could do better. Her aunt smiled her patient smile, her eyes wandering around the room like a lost sheep. Then her smile left, as if a signal had been sounded, and she had to put on a serious mask. She began to talk slowly as if she were reciting a speech in school and couldn't remember all the words.

"Marysza, I know you think your uncle and I didn't want you to live with us. I saw you watching him on the phone when you first came. It's not true, Marysza. Other family people wanted to take you but your uncle said no. He thought you belonged with us, that you knew things here better." Both Marysza and her aunt became quiet. A sudden sense of relief overtook Marysza, as if she were freed, as if Uncle Ben's and Aunt Irene's words allowed her to escape approaching danger. She felt something touch her, something that felt like Grandma's hand on her forehead when she was small and had a fever. She knew her uncle would never tell her what her aunt had, that he probably didn't realize what she was thinking when she heard him on the phone that day. But somehow Aunt Irene knew. Her aunt took a deep breath and began again.

"Sometimes a person doesn't know what to do." She paused, then continued. "And it's not always easy for a person to know what to do." Marysza wanted to laugh and cry at the same time.

My dear aunt, I know what you're trying to say. I know the cost of this effort for you and the depth of your sincerity. I know you respect me, that in some crazy way we've become equals.

"But sometimes a person does know," her aunt blurted out suddenly, positively. "There'll be more men to marry. We know you shouldn't do this!" This was said with such emphasis and conviction that Marysza knew her aunt's speech was ended. She didn't answer but felt something within her grow large as she realized what she had never been sure of, as she saw the reality of her aunt and uncle's love for her. Heaviness dissolved; the light-headed feeling of freedom descended on her again.

She thought of Tadziu, of his mouth, his body, fitting into her, possessing her. The moment created by her aunt and uncle passed and the force reappeared, the force driving her to do what part of her knew was not good.

Marysza knew her silence told her aunt she was defeated, that there was something in Marysza which she could not understand. Marysza didn't understand it herself.

1957

Tadziu

Tadziu stood before the mirror combing his hair. He walked to the chest of drawers, opened the bottom drawer and surveyed its contents. The clothes were laid in neat piles: socks, undershirts and white shorts smelling of bleach. He washed all his clothes at a laundromat where the machines and the dryers were clean and in good shape He didn't mind soap spilled on the tables or the floor but he didn't like pieces of dirty clothing left behind. He kept his weekend clothes, the ones that were stiff with grease from working on his car, in a pile on the closet floor and washed them in the machines used for rags.

He was ready to leave. He heard noises in the hall outside his bedroom door, the bump and thud of something being dragged down the stairs. He opened the door and saw Jim—the guy who lived across the hall and woke up the whole house when he stumbled into his room on Friday and Saturday nights—-dragging his suitcases down the stairs. Tadziu wasn't surprised.

Serves you right, you smartass.

Mrs. Jablonski, the landlady, had warned the guy a couple times, had stood on the landing with her hands on her hips, her apron spread across her large stomach like a tablecloth, as she shook her finger at him.

"Vun morr taym, Jeem," she said, "vun more taym," her voice rising on the word "vun" like a shot being fired.

Mrs. Jablonski never complained about Tadziu. He kept his room clean, paid his rent on time and did his damndest not to make noise. It was the smart thing to do.

I won't be here forever. Might as well keep the old lady off my ass.

He had a stereo system but he kept the sound low, just loud enough so he could hear. The times he was drunk, the guys got him back into his room quietly or, if he was impossible, one of them took him home. The one time he made noise because of his excitement over a close football game, Mrs. Jablonski only told him to "vach it1" She didn't even shake her finger at him. Tadziu did watch it. Now he saw Jim struggling with his suitcases, his shoulders hunched low like a dog that had been kicked. For a minute, he wanted to help the guy with his shit but he didn't want him to know someone was watching and embarrass him.

You dumb bastard. Did you think the old lady was kiddin'?

He'd have to leave later so he wouldn't pass the guy on the stairs and embarrass him more. He turned and went back into his room.

It was Friday. He was on his way to meet the guys in the bar. His friends were mostly all 21. He wasn't but the bartender wasn't very strict. They would shoot some pool, play pinball, and look for girls. Just general fooling around. His friends were guys who worked with him in the factory, joked with each other, and told lies about the things they did. They weren't exactly lies, just a kind of bragging, trying to top each other's stories, whether it was about their cars or their experiences with girls. Tadziu didn't date girls much because he didn't know how to talk to them and he didn't want to look stupid if he said something dumb. But he knew cars.

The guys come to me. They know I'm better than any of them at keepin' cars runnin' no matter how many miles the clock says.

When he took off his jacket, the guys were already having a great time. Until he had enough booze in him, being in a bar and drinking always made Tadziu think about things he avoided thinking about when he was sober. He didn't have enough in him yet.

It had been four years since he left home. He was fifteen when he ran away and knocked on Joe's door.

"I can't keep you here, young fella," Joe said.

He wanted to keep me. I know he wanted to keep me. He just couldn't.

Joe helped Tadziu find the room at Mrs. Jablonski's and paid his room and board. Then he found Tadziu a job delivering vegetables and eggs for the farmer who brought his stuff to the store. It wasn't a hard job. The main requirement seemed to be keeping quiet.

The farmer never talked. He wore a tattered black cap with a torn visor and one ear flap missing, looked straight ahead and drove his truck, a vehicle that seemed, like him, to be slowly falling apart. Tadziu carried the bushels into the stores. When they were finished, the farmer drove Tadziu to Mrs. Jablonski's and before driving away, silently tipped his hat in Tadziu's direction. One weekend the farmer said *mie brzuch boli* which were the first words Tadziu had ever heard him say, and meant that his stomach hurt. He asked Tadziu if he knew how to drive. Tadziu said yes so the farmer told him to take the truck and do the deliveries.

Tadziu sat behind the wheel and tried to look sure of himself, for a moment felt proud, despite the truck's advanced state of disrepair. He did everything he remembered the farmer doing–turned the key in the ignition, pulled back the clutch and yanked the motor into gear. The truck bolted like a horse, and yelling in surprise, Tadziu almost went through the roof. Somehow he managed to move the truck into second and then third gear. Now he laughed out loud at the memory of himself hanging onto the truck as it zigzagged up the street with a mind of its own. He laughed out loud, remembering how he couldn't turn to look back, could only hold on and try to get the truck to go straight. Thinking they had missed a joke, Tadziu's friends laughed with him.

He thought of how he moved from store to store like a drunken sailor.

After each stop his driving got better.

By the time I finished that route, I had the old rattletrap moving smoother than that farmer ever could.

The truck was like a girl in his arms, a girl who responded to every touch.

That was how Tadziu learned to drive and how he learned to love cars. He saved enough money to buy an old rattletrap of his own and put money into it each week. He didn't have to stay at the boarding house anymore in his free time. He could go to Joe's house and eat Sunday dinner with Joe and his wife and kids. He always remembered that silent farmer, how he tipped his hat to Tadziu at the end of their work day and felt sad when Joe told him he had died.

After a while, he decided not to go to Joe's on Sundays anymore.

"I can take care of myself now," he told Joe. He couldn't tell him about how he looked around the table one Sunday and knew he didn't belong.

They were just being nice. I didn't want them to be nice.

Tadziu still missed his mother and his brothers and sisters. He thought a lot about Marysza. After he left home, he never went to her grandma's again because he didn't want them to know about his life. He went home only once, a couple years ago. He knew his old man didn't like seeing him and Tadziu didn't like seeing his mother because she looked like she was dying of some awful disease. His sisters were gone but his brothers looked okay.

Maybe it's easier for Ma with only two kids left. She was ashamed to tell me about Helcza and Janina, that they lived with Aunt Leona now. She turned her face away and spoke so quiet I almost couldn't hear.

"They wanted to go, Tadziu. They wanted to go," she kept saying, like she was begging Tadziu to believe her.

"It's okay, Ma," he said. "It wasn't your fault." But he knew she thought it was. His old man had filled her with bad things. Her eyes burned with the look of a hurt animal looking for a place to hide. She whispered that she missed Tadziu and that he was a good boy.

Ma doesn't feel good. She's sick. Hell, who'm I kidding? It's more than that, but I don't know what it is.

If Tadziu just got drunk enough, he could stop going over all these things again, wouldn't be pulled back to what he didn't want to remember. He went once to see Helcza and Janina. They'd changed their names from Polish to American, they told him. Helcza was Helen and Janina was Jeannette, or Gina for short. He laughed and told them he'd try to remember but he wasn't making any guaranties. His mind was stuck in that place where his brothers and sisters were Helcza and Janina and Janek and Tomasz.

"How about the twins? What are they now?" Even Helen laughed.

"We're trying to tell them they're John and Tommy, but they have trouble remembering." He wanted to show off his car, the '40 Desoto that looked like new, to his sisters, Helen and Jeannette, whatever the hell their names were. He also wanted them to see he was okay, so they wouldn't worry. He and Helcza—or Helen—laughed about things he didn't know they had to laugh about. Janina—-Jeannette—Gina—was quiet, just looked at Tadziu and Helcza like she didn't understand.

When he kissed Helcza and Janina goodbye, he felt the same sadness he saw in Janina's eyes. The sadness stayed with him for a long time after he left his sisters. He felt it more when he was alone in his room or like now, in a bar before he got tanked up. After that one time, he didn't go to see his sisters again. He couldn't remember to call them Helen and Jeannette anyway. But Helcza wrote to him, letters he never answered but carried in his wallet all the time.

He tried to stop thinking of all those things but he couldn't stop thinking of his mother and his brothers and sisters and he couldn't curse the old man unless he was real drunk.

It's like I'm still afraid of him, like he can hear me.

On the day Tadziu had visited, his father sat on a chair in the kitchen, his small eyes watching intently from behind his glasses. The old man was still a bull, his veins traveling through the muscles of his arms like thick rope. He didn't like Tadziu's mother making a fuss over Tadziu.

"Enough already," he said in Polish, *dosycz, dosycz*, [33] in the same angry voice Tadziu remembered. There was no point in sticking around because his father never said good-bye. As he left, Tadziu felt his father's eyes on his back. He heard the footsteps of his childhood pursuing him, and tried to move faster down the stairs. He heard all the times the old man called him a bum, never believing he would be anything good.

He didn't remember what time the guys broke up on Friday night but on Saturday morning Tadziu looked at himself in the mirror.

Holy shit. What a mess. I drank too much. I do that a lot lately. But what the hell. You only go around once. Might as well enjoy yourself.

The problem was that if he stopped to think about it, Tadziu wasn't sure he was enjoying himself. More and more, his drinking seemed to be something he did because he always did it, because it was a habit.

One of these days, I'll stop. I'll just say "no more", and that'll be it. The guys won't understand. They'll think I'm a chicken, but so what? They can't lead me around by the nose.

He opened a bottle of beer and drank it down.

No sense leaving this when I'm going to quit. Besides, I don't always drink as much as I did yesterday. No need to blow the whole thing out of proportion.

The hangover brought back his worse thoughts. They wouldn't stop, kept going around in circles.

Yeah, the old man was something else. I can't count the number of times the bastard knocked the shit out of me. Well, better me than one of the younger ones. Or ma. The old lady must have been plenty scared of the old man because she sure as hell never did anything to stop him. C'mon, what could she do? It wasn't like she was anywhere near his size. All she did was keep out of his way. I don't blame her. Don't blame anyone. Whose fault is it my old man hated me?

He laughed.

God's. Because he made me born into the family I was. And not another one.

He picked up another bottle, drained it, and rubbed his eyes. He must have a piece of dirt or something in them. Something that made them water.

God-damn!

He wiped his eyes with his shirt and hit the table with his fist. His old man had smiled at the other kids once in a while, especially the twins. He remembered one Christmas when the old man actually held his younger brother on his knee, looked at the kid as if he was proud, and said words to him in Polish that sounded nice like *Ja cie kocham* [34]or *moj anioleczek*[35] or something like that.

It would be a cold day in hell before I'd ever hear that from him.

He picked up another bottle.

Who cares anyway? The old man can rot in hell as far as I'm concerned. Bet your ass I'll never do a thing to help him. I didn't want much. Just for the old man to be a little like Joe.

He was on his third or fourth beer. Maybe fifth.

Joe was good to me. Liked me.

It embarrassed Tadiu to remember how he always pretended he was one of Joe's kids. The next bottle went down in one long swallow. Things were becoming less painful to think about.

Maybe ma's happy in some way I don't know. Maybe sometime I'll understand the old man. Nah, that's stupid. I'll never understand either of them.

Morning light lost itself in gray fog. Tadziu's thoughts were blurred, like the outlines of the buildings outside the window. Only one thought stood out from the deepening fog in his brain.

I don't care whether the old man lives or dies. That's the truth I can't do anything about it. I don't know why that makes me feel guilty but it does.

He drank until the last bottle was gone. The room began to wave. Like water in a lake.

His eyes wouldn't focus. He wanted to get to his bed but his legs were unsteady. He got up carefully and held on to the table like a kid learning to walk. When he reached the bed, he fell face down and lost consciousness. His sleep had no thoughts, no dreams.

He told himself he was trying to watch the drinking but he had more nights like that.

In the summer, Tadziu and his buddies went to a place on the lake called **The Pier.** Your chances of meeting a girl there were good, even picking one up if you wanted, although none of his buddies ever took a girl home. They just claimed they did. Except for Tadziu, they all lived at home and had no place except the back seat of a car to make out.

It was Saturday, July 4, 1957. He knew he would never forget the date. His eyes were checking out the crowd and he suddenly felt as if a slab of concrete had been dropped on his head.

There she is, standing in front of me like it was planned or somethin'. I must look like a jerk standing here and staring. The guys are laughing.

"You see a ghost or somethin', Tadziu?"

"Yeah, a ghost. A girl I used to know."

"Yeah, uh-huh, sure, a girl he used to know."

"Shut up, you jerks, it's true. We used to go to school together."

There's no way she'll remember me. Why should she? She was smart and pretty. All the kids knew it.

He had to work up his courage because the guys were watching. When he walked over to her, they shut up, all right. He was jealous, because of the way they looked at her, and a lot of other guys too, the smart-asses in the preppy crowd.

She was just as pretty as he remembered, her long hair kind of surrounding her, making her look old-fashioned, like a girl on a Valentine or something. She didn't throw her head back so her hair got thrown over her shoulders the way some girls did just to attract attention. She just sat quiet and thoughtful, not posing at all. He thought of the ducks gliding on the lake when he went fishing, how he was amazed each time he saw their perfect formation, that they made no sound, looked straight ahead like they belonged to a royal family or something, had no protection and no fear, just floated easy past everything around them, their eyes shining like brown marbles. Marysza was something like that.

Tadziu watched her smile and laugh, like he was laughing with her. One of the smart-ass groups of guys approached her. Tadziu's jealousy turned to anger.

Can't the jackass see she's mine from a long time ago?

Marysza sat with another girl whose back was turned to him. Something about the girl seemed familiar. She turned and he caught a glimpse of Martha, Marysza's old girlfriend. Martha turned around and saw him. He almost laughed at the look on her face. The years that had gone by were nothing.

It was unreal—him coming here on the same night as her. It seemed more unreal when he first talked to her and saw she was glad to see him. Martha mumbled some kind of greeting and he replied but he was so slaphappy he didn't hear much of what she said after that. Only when they all talked about where they worked. He sat on the grass with the two girls, happiness just traveling through him. It was like he was the only guy in the place and she was the only girl. Like they stood in some kind of spotlight, with all the other people outside the edge of the light so you couldn't see or hear them.

"You're the prettiest girl I ever saw," he said and knew right away it was a dumb thing to say. He knew better. Guys didn't say that kind of thing. But he just forgot. Standing next to Marysza made him forget what he knew. Martha muttered, "oh brother," under her breath but Marysza smiled in a shy kind of way. They said the usual things, like "how've you been?" and both of them said "okay". Then when they sat on the ground, he lost a lot of it, because of the noise and laughter around them and him just trying to act casual and not show how excited he was. He remembered Marysza asking, "What have you been doing?" like it was only last week they had seen each other and he answered, "Oh nothing much. Just hanging around. And working over at Jones-Courtney making machine parts."

"I'm a waitress at the country club," she said. "I worked at Howard Johnson's for a while but this job's a lot better. A Cadillac place for waitresses." Her laugh sounded a little nervous.

"I'm still at Howard Johnson's," Martha said, in a voice that sounded like he always felt. "It's a shit place to work."

"I know what you mean," he said, and felt Martha's eyes on him, looking at him with a sudden spark of interest, then moving away, so he wouldn't see her look.

He turned back to Marysza. "How's your grandma?"

Marysza's face lost its smile. "She died."

"She was the nicest lady," he said, and stayed quiet. Her grandma was real nice, even to him. Always nice. They sat for a while without talking, just listening to the music with Martha drumming her fingers on the hard ground in time to the beat. He brought beers for the three of them. And was so nervous he almost spilled one on Martha. She glared at him again. But he didn't care. All he could think of was Marysza.

After they played picnic games and danced, he was still in a kind of daze

Can I ask her to go out? She might think I'm dumb. C'mon, this is Marysza. She always liked me.

He said it quick when Martha wasn't listening and braced himself.

"D'you wanna go out sometime?" He couldn't believe it when she said "sure." Martha refused a ride but he drove Marysza home, lost his head, even kissed and touched her and when he got home got as drunk as he could remember. He knew he'd have to watch himself on their date but he told himself he was celebrating.

They started dating, doing things like going to the movies or the bowling alley. Once they went to the zoo. They laughed a lot. And talked about all kinds of things. Sometimes she asked him questions he couldn't answer, like what did he want to do with his life?

Well, what the hell. How do I know? Just work and stay alive. Maybe get married. I'm nobody special.

She asked if he was going to stay at the factory. He told her he didn't know. They talked about the television shows they watched. He didn't have a television. He had to go down to Mrs. Jablonski's living room to watch it so he didn't watch much because he didn't like to sit with her. She wore a hairnet held on by a band that crossed the top of her head and came down behind her ears so that she looked like her head was divided into two pieces. She wore white shoes, like a nurse, and rolled her stockings down so they looked like sausages around her ankles. Her eyes were red and puffy and looked straight at you like she was daring you to say you didn't like the way she looked. His mother never looked like that even when she was sick. His mother wore long cotton dresses so her legs never showed and she never really looked straight at anyone, just kind of down.

But he always sat with Mrs. Jablonski to watch *I Love Lucy*. The show made her laugh a lot and her false teeth clicked when she laughed. That made him think about his mother's straight white teeth, and how he never really thought about it, about teeth at all, until he was around Mrs. Jablonski. He sat with her to watch the Lucy show because that gave him and Marysza more to laugh about.

It's all a dream. I'll wake up and there'll be a "dear john" letter in the mailbox from Marysza telling me she's made a mistake and I should get lost.

The first time they slept together, she clung to him as if she was drowning and he was a life-jacket. He wanted to make her feel safe. After that first time, he knew again what he always knew when he was a kid, even though he couldn't explain it. Marysza held some kind of key to the things locked inside him, things he himself didn't know. He knew she wouldn't date anyone else. Some kind of honor system she had inside. He worked up his courage again. This time it wasn't so hard. He didn't get down on his knees but he would've if she wanted him to.

"I guess you know I love you," he said. A look of self-consciousness mixed with certainty filled her eyes, like she always knew she had him.

Well, what the hell, she did. He'd never want anyone else, not ever.

The silence became alarming. She whispered and he leaned over to hear, lightly brushing his head against her breast, the touch of a wing and feathers against the air. He'd already slept with her but it never changed. Longing rushed over him like water falling over a precipice, crashing against rock and fragmenting into a million drops. He always wanted to know the coolness of her bare skin, place his hand between her outstretched legs and travel her body like water over hills and mountains. Pieces of himself rested against her, and waited. After a thousand long minutes, she said yes, she would marry him.

Chapter Three

1957

A Home

Tadziu found a flat on the top floor of an older home where the rent was cheap. Marysza was overwhelmed with excitement.

A home. A place of my own. Our own. As they drove, she heard the swagger in Tadziu's voice.

He's trying to be proud.

I'll love what he's found.

They reached the flat by climbing a long flight of wooden stairs in a dim hallway. Marysza saw the dirt embedded in the grain of the wood, and the dust balls collected in the corners of the stairs. She tripped on he loose rubber treads beneath her feet. The stairs ended and Tadziu opened the door. Marysza's eyes traveled around the room. She saw painted woodwork that was once white but now yellowed with age and chipped in so many places that the brown spots formed a kind of crazy pattern. Red linoleum covered the floor, its gloss hurting Marysza's eye, its sworn spots resembling islands of various sizes and shapes floating in a red sea. A small refrigerator and stove coated with layers of grease stared at her from the corner where they huddled like old people, poverty-stricken, ashamed of their age and the neglect they had endured. Gray light entered through windows coated with grime.

Grandma's house was poor. And old. But not filthy.

She thought of the small bedroom grandma had used as a sewing room, of the way the sewing machine was piled with clean clothes grandma would mend, of the way the painted wooden floor smelled of grandma's soap.

I'll mend our clothes with a needle and thread. Until we buy a machine.

She thought of her aunt's small but spotless kitchen, of the way her uncle kept everything in good repair.

Something in her stomach tightened. Her thoughts wound themselves around each other. Words repeated themselves.

Until we buy a machine.

"Not much, huh?" said Tadziu, looking around, then walking into another room. "The rest ain't much better." Marysza saw he was trying to be casual. She said nothing. Trying to control the bitterness of her thoughts and to sound cheerful, she told Tadziu it wouldn't be so bad when it was cleaned up. And tried to believe it herself.

And so she prepared for battle. She went to the library and borrowed the maximum number of books she was allowed, all having to do with home repairs, books

Tadziu and she both read and took turns explaining to each other. Marysza washed the windows three times, rubbing the dirt from them like poison she was scrubbing from herself and Tadziu. They asked the landlord, a tall thin man who smoked incessantly as they talked, and stared at them with narrow, lifeless eyes, if they could paint.

"You kin paint whatever ya want," he told them, looking as if he was silently laughing, "as long as ya buy the paint."

Each week when they were paid, they bought paint.. They tackled the kitchen woodwork first. Tadziu sanded all the chipped spots and created a fine dust which traveled through all the rooms, settling on everything, even though Marysza closed the kitchen doors and stuffed any open spaces with plastic bags. Each time they worked, she vacuumed up the dust and blessed Martha for giving them a vacuum cleaner as a wedding gift. When they finished the kitchen, they were encouraged. The woodwork was a soft blue-grey, smooth, and no longer spattered with ugly brown spots.

They planned to finish a room each week but saw they would need more time because of tasks that needed to be done before and after they painted, like patching cracks in the walls and sanding and varnishing woodwork. Marysza's hands and fingers grew red and sore because she used her fingers to plug the cracks and holes with putty. Tadziu's hands were too big to do that as well as she could. When they finished a room, they stood together and admired it, as if they were seeing something that had been dead come alive. For Marysza, each chore they completed acted like a drug. The depression she had experienced seemed no more substantial than the fine dust that floated through the air when Tadziu sanded.

They bought used furniture and refinished it. Marysza bought pale yellow curtains for the kitchen at Woolworth's and dark gold drapes she thought looked like satin to hang in the living room when it was finished. She indulged in a bouquet of artificial peonies for the middle of the kitchen table, flowers arranged in a white milk vase and so intensely blue they seemed black. She walked around the room admiring the flowers from every angle, allowing their loveliness to banish the unease at the edge of her consciousness. She scrubbed the kitchen linoleum until it looked as near to a new floor as she could manage.

I'll never like the red color but at least it's clean.

She watched the newspapers for sales and bought new sheets for the bed and a pillow edged with ruffles that she would lean against a new white bedspread.

The bedroom must be the prettiest room, because it's the place of our honeymoon.

Pleasure filled her as she looked at her purchases.

As long as some things are beautiful, I can close my eyes to what can't be changed.

Tadziu worked on the flat every day after his usual work hours. He read the books less. Marysza saw that once he understood the task, he seemed to find some instinctive knowledge and worked with a zeal that resembled fury, taking the worst jobs, not letting her do anything he thought was too strenuous "for a woman." As if it had a spirit, the flat touched and united them, imprisoning them like a jailer as they viewed its mutation. Marysza's happiness grew, uncertainty slipping from her shoulders like a heavy weight. It made her proud of how much better Tadziu was at doing these things than she was, at how quickly he learned, at how he devised better methods than the ones in the books. But the end was far from sight. Finishing one task made them aware of what remained to be done. On a Friday night, Marysza was kneeling on the floor scrubbing the insides of the cupboards. She turned to see Tadziu scraping solidified grease off the bathroom floor with a chisel.

The muscles in his arms tense and relax like moving stone. I feel the moisture between my legs, like an animal in heat, drawn, held by the sight of him.

She went to him, kissed the back of his neck, saw his eyes surrender their absorption in his work as they filled with desire, then heard the clank of the chisel as it fell from his hand. He walked to the bathtub, removed his clothes and dropped them to the floor in a heap.

He sprayed water over his head with the rubber hose, lathered himself with the soap that lay in a wire basket hanging on the tub, and holding the hose over his head again, rinsed himself.

He has no shyness, abandons himself to my eyes. He carries me to the white bed. His hands shake as he unbuttons my blouse. My breasts harden when he holds them. We move through fits and starts, begin, climb, fall. He travels faster, then waits, leads me through that narrow passage where I disappear, am consumed, left empty and exhausted. We do not talk. He looks at me with adoration and I know I will always own him.

Marysza was sorry when the flat was finished, so happy had she been as they worked together. Their happiness stayed. With Tadziu's job at the factory and her job at the restaurant, they could pay the rent and the bills and have something left to go to the movies on weekends. For special times, they went to a neighborhood bar that had a live band on Saturday nights. Tadziu liked drinking beer. Marysza liked the dancing, being held close and looking up at Tadziu's face as they swayed to romantic songs. When the band took an intermission, Tadziu gave her the dimes he had saved all week for the jukebox. They sat close together at the small table and talked about things that were unimportant, things that neither of them cared about or would remember, and listened to the jukebox play popular songs like Elvis Presley's *Love me Tender* or the Platters' *My Prayer.*

As Tadziu held her hands and moved his fingers along her arm, Marysza felt the urgency of his longing and her own, knew that he wanted to place his hands into her blouse and fondle her. Feeling loved and cherished, she abandoned all thought, as immersed in her love as she was in the music and the lights, until Tadziu would say heavily from deep inside, "Let's go home." They waited for the waitress to bring their bill, and Marysza felt her breasts become firm with anticipation. She looked away, feeling that the waitress could see what she was feeling, what she was thinking.

Our love will never change. We'll belong to each other forever.

Marysza Alone

They bought a second-hand television set. Sometimes Marysza felt envious of the things she saw on television shows and commercials—- homes and cars, glamorous clothes, vacations and travel—things which the people in the shows took for granted and which were far above any expectations she dared to have. These people were not real, she knew, but people like this did exist, did inhabit the kind of world she saw depicted. She remembered the words her grandmother said when Marysza envied other kids, and said the words to herself.

Never mind. Never mind.

When Tadziu was working and she was alone, she realized how much she missed her aunt and uncle and her cousins, especially Jimmy. She thought of her uncle's ready smile and wrinkled forehead, the worry his face sometimes revealed, of her aunt with her patient face and bewildered eyes, eyes which said, despite the strange and silent knowledge they held at other times, that she did not want to understand the complications of the world, that she wished the world were made only of her husband and her children. Thinking of Jimmy was the most painful

She remembered her wedding day, how her aunt had pinned white bows at the ends of the few pews they occupied, how Jimmy had held on to her hand after the ceremony and began to cry as they left the Church, sobs that echoed like small birds hitting themselves against the high ceilings of the huge stone structure. His mother tried to comfort him.

"Jimmy, Marysza still loves you. She has a husband now." Jimmy looked stricken, unable to believe Marysza's betrayal.

"I want Marysza to come home," he sobbed and pointing at Tadziu, said, "he can come too." These last words were a question as well as a statement. In desperation, he pulled Marysza in the direction of their car. Marysza knelt to hold him. He opened his fists, revealing his favorite toys, two small soldiers in combat gear. "Here Marysza, here," he said, as he dropped them into her open hand. She took the plastic soldiers, feeling guilty over her deception when she said, "I'm coming home for a party now," and he smiled. Marysza was glad he fell asleep before the party was over so he didn't have to see her leave.

Signs of change

On workdays, when Tadziu walked in the door at four o'clock, he took a paper bag containing brown or clear liquor from his back pocket and, pouring the bottle into two glasses, gave more to himself than he did to Marysza. The drink was so strong, Marysza couldn't drink it and threw it down the sink when Tadziu wasn't looking. Tadziu didn't notice anything except that his own glass was empty and had to be refilled. Nor did he seem to mind when she told him she didn't want anymore to drink. Marysza said words she hated to say.

"Tadziu, you're drinking too much." Tadziu said nothing but Marysza felt her safe world begin to break apart when he first glared at her with anger in his face. The next night, he did not have liquor in his pocket, but carried two paper cartons of beer. She had no answer when he said, "Well, are you satisfied now?" and dropped the cartons onto the table. By the end of the evening, the beer was gone.

News

Her period stopped and Marysza understood why she'd been tired and found herself sleeping more. When she looked into the mirror, she saw heightened color illuminating her face and imagined that her abdomen was expanding.

I'm something I haven't been. Like the baby, I'll be new.

She felt a secret happiness, an emotion as strong as her love for Tadziu.

This child growing inside my body needs me more than Tadziu needs me. It's helpless, dependent on my body, will remain dependent on me when it leaves my body.

She thought of families, of her mother and father, of her mother's leaving her. She thought that she would care for this child with all her strength, would be to this child what her grandmother had been to her.

She didn't become disturbed at the nausea, the "morning sickness" which arrived each day as soon as she awoke. She often felt giddy, laughed at herself, and enjoyed everything about this new experience. When she felt the first kick, she danced around the floor on her toes, like a ballet dancer.

I'm beautiful. I'm a movie star because of my baby. I'll never be as alone as I was when grandma died.

The sadness that filled her whenever she thought of grandma had lost its first intensity, now lived inside her like a slow-burning fire, warm and comforting, shielding her against the cold.

Fear

Anxieties drifted into Marysza's life stealthily, like strange creatures flying in the air, impossible to see, until they sank to earth, settled in, and would not leave. It angered her that thoughts of money intruded into her happiness. She told Tadziu she'd return to work as soon as the baby was born. He shrugged his shoulders and said nothing. He was the same person he'd been when they were children yet she didn't know who he was. She hated the way he drank. She pushed into hiding, wouldn't allow the thought that festered within her like a wound—that Tadziu wouldn't love the baby—to enter her consciousness. And always there was the feeling that lay buried under all the other feelings—the feeling that her life was not under her control, was slipping through her fingers and running away like a crazed and frightened animal.

How can you do this to me, Tadziu? I'm lost, wandering aimlessly, tryng to put together a puzzle for which I don't have all the pieces. No one can help. Not even Martha.

Martha had been one of the witnesses to their marriage but she didn't say much to Tadziu and he reciprocated by ignoring her. That wasn't unusual. Marysza tried not to think of it. There were more important things that Tadziu ignored. Like the baby. She put her head into her arms.

Birth

It was time for the baby to be born. The initial pains were mild but after Marysza's water broke, their intensity increased until she felt she was drowning in waves of pain. She lost the veneer that covered her so deceptively, no longer knew who she was and became ashamed to hear herself scream like an animal as she heard the doctor and nurses encouraging her to push—-"Marysza. C'mon honey. Last time"—-and she pushed as hard as she could, feeling herself splitting open, breaking into jagged bloody pieces that would fall to the floor, leaving parts of her behind. The pain began to subside as somebody said, "time for ether" and they placed a mask on her face.

Oh lovely people, lovely nurses, lovely doctor, I am filled with gratitude for the darkness beginning to descend. I hear you say "It's a boy." I hear his cry. But I move ever downward and deeper, become lost, wander through white corridors, endless white corridors with flowers blooming in the walls. Only loveliness here.

In the recovery room, a young black girl in a crisp yellow uniform touched her with the gentlest hands, washed her wounded areas and her face with cool water and asked if she was hungry.

How can I be hungry after the pain I've lived? But I am. How can this girl, this child with an angel's face know what it has been? But she does. Her smile tells me she knows, tells me I'll be strong again, that I've earned the right to be strong again. Exhilaration fills me.

The girl brought her an egg-salad sandwich because regular meal hours were over.

"I found these," she said, taking some plastic-wrapped cookies from her pocket like a conspirator.

I want to kiss her.

The baby was sleeping when they brought him into Marysza's room. She examined his face, uncovered his hands and his feet, and then covered them again, knowing, as she drank in his perfection, that her life would never be the same. Attendants wheeled a woman into the room. The woman moaned as they lifted her from the gurney and onto the bed.

She's not a woman. A girl.

The girl switched on her light but there was no response. Marysza thought she heard the girl crying. She switched on her light also.

"What is it?" the nurse asked, through lips that looked like a downward slash in her face and glaring at Marysza from beneath eyebrows with frown lines like large quotation marks. Marysza swallowed hard and said, "I'm fine. The girl needs help." The nurse looked angry, went to the other bed, looked at the girl without speaking, and walked out of the room. Another nurse came.

"There, there, honey," she said, in a voice that soothed Marysza as well as the girl. The nurse helped the girl drink water through a straw and gave her a pain shot. After the girl fell asleep, they came to take Marysza's baby and Marysza slept.

Tadziu Visits

Marysza's bed was next to the window. Through the winter twilight, she watched the moon climb. Snowflakes swirled downward, then up again, stopping along the way like friends greeting each other. The flakes drifted into small piles on the sill outside the window as Marysza drifted in and out of sleep. She woke to see Tadziu in the chair next to her bed, his hands held together, his elbows resting on his knees and his head hanging down as if he was deep in thought. Without speaking, she watched him, felt her longing begin to stir, then reclaim her. He was dressed in a white shirt and tie.

He thinks I'm asleep, waits for me to wake. How beautiful he looks, this man I married, his strong profile outlined in the bright hospital light, the large hands that know my body so well huddled in each other as if uncertain of me as well as himself. He doesn't own a white shirt or a tie. He bought them for me, for the baby. Don't be uncertain, Tadziu, never uncertain of me.

He raised his eyes and seeing she was awake, read the words in hers. Neither of them spoke, neither able to say the words floating in the air before them. And so she waited to say what it was possible to say and asked if he had seen the baby and if he wasn't beautiful.

"Yeah, sure," Tadziu said, and dropped a box of candy on the bed. He had remembered her favorite, chocolate-covered cherries.

"Thanks. I love these," she said, watching his pleasure at her words.

I won't tell you I can't eat these. They're on the list of things to avoid because I'm going to nurse the baby.

Tadziu walked in and out of her room several times, looking at the clock in the hallway each time. A clattering noise told Marysza the aides were bringing dinner. She knew she could make Tadziu laugh by lifting the silver dome and showing him the entrée which looked like yellow glue covering nondescript white lumps.

"Macaroni and cheese," she told him. "I'll share it with you." He did laugh.

"No thanks. Even my cooking looks better than that."

They brought the baby into the room, Tadziu looked at him and said, "He's nice," but didn't ask to hold him.

He must be feeling what I'm feeling, that we've accomplished something of great importance.

Marysza held the baby to her breast and followed the nurse's instructions but the baby couldn't suck and she was frightened.

Something's wrong. Why can't I do this right?".

The baby cried. Marysza held him to her chest and spoke softly.

"My darling, we have to try. The more you pull, the better it will be, I promise." She tried again and felt a tiny nibbling at her breast but was tense because Tadziu was watching, and she knew it wouldn't go right. And it didn't go right. She continued to soothe the small body with her caresses. The baby's eyes widened and, as if he recognized her voice, his crying ceased. She rejoiced in his life and forgot her own, until she was brought back to thoughts of Tadziu, to the silent protest she felt in him, a protest she knew was at war with her need to protect this child, to make the world right for him. Certainty filled her.

Because of this child, my own life has been made stronger. Tadziu must accept this.

The nurse told Tadziu it was time to leave. She smiled at Marysza.

"Don't worry. Nothing unusual. It happened with my first baby. We'll try again later." Marysza looked at the nurse's graying hair and felt united with her and all the women who had preceded her and experienced this profound alteration in their lives. She kissed Tadziu good-bye, reluctant to admit she was glad to see him leave. As soon as he was gone, she was overtaken by sleep.

On the day she was leaving the hospital, her wheelchair was parked next to an older woman sitting on a couch in the lobby. The woman's white hair was shaped into a bun sitting beneath a black hat larger than her head. Her legs were sticks planted in black Enna Jettick shoes, their laces tied in symmetrical bows. As Marysza saw the woman's gnarled fingers and the wrist that turned under like a claw and watched her overly white false teeth break into a wide smile, she knew she was in the presence of one of those people who managed, despite their circumstances, to find life an ongoing delight. It seemed the most natural thing in the world for the woman to talk to Marysza, to tell her and the people passing by that the baby was beautiful..

"Look at him, just look at him," she exclaimed, the smile lines crinkling at the corners of her eyes. "Doesn't he look at least two months old? He was eight pounds, three ounces, you know." She proclaimed this fact with amazement in her voice, then turned her wheelchair toward the small audience that had gathered, and, as if making an important announcement, said, in a voice it seemed natural should contain love and praise, "This is his mother, you know." Lowering her voice to a level meant to be private, she asked Marysza how she felt, if the delivery had been difficult, and, with the back of her twisted hand, brushed the hair from Marysza's forehead, as if Marysza were a little girl.

"It's never easy, poor baby." Marysza's eyes filled with tears. Before her feelings could clothe themselves in words, they floated somewhere, like parts of herself she had lost and could not retrieve.

Is it grandma she reminds me of? Or my mother?

The attendant who had brought Marysza to the lobby kept looking at her watch. Marysza was glad when the elderly woman saw another woman beckoning to her from outside the door. She rose and hobbled away, never to wonder where Marysza's husband was.

Tadziu arrived. Marysza saw the fear in his face when he looked at the baby but he said nothing. Marysza was happy to see he was wearing a clean white shirt and a tie again and tried to ignore the smell of liquor on his breath. For a moment, it was attractive, masculine.

The line of cars moved slowly as they left the parking lot and Marysza lost track of what was happening. Tadziu jumped from the car and shook his fist at a man in a car that Marysza thought had moved from another line and snaked in front of them.

"My wife and my kid are in here, you asshole," Tadziu screamed, eyes bulging and voice shaking. The man rolled down his window and threw up his arms.

"Okay buddy, sorry, sorry." Marysza was frightened.

I'm afraid to ask why you're so angry. I should probably know. You try too hard. To prove you love us. I know you do. You do things like this because anger is all you know.

She touched Tadziu's hand but he didn't look at her. When they reached home, she put her hand in Tadziu's and drew him to the crib. He looked at the baby because she wanted him to look but after a short time, moved away, continuing to mutter about the asshole who cut him off. Something within Marysza sank. And became filled with sadness. When Martha, her arms loaded with gifts, came to see the baby, Tadziu, with eyes cast down and holding a bottle of beer, sat across the room and said nothing. Marysza was ashamed.

That night Marysza dreamed of a woman with a young face and long tangles of dark hair that fell across her breasts like cloth. The woman turned and began to walk away. Marysza could see only her back, and was overwhelmed by feeling small and helpless. She tried to cry out, to tell the woman to wait but no sound came from her throat. She tried to run, to catch the woman but her feet were attached to the ground and she could not move.

"Mama, mama," she called but the woman moved further away. Marysza knew the woman was ignoring her screams: she didn't want to hear. Marysza desired to reach out and touch the woman's hair, to feel its softness between her fingers, to hold the strands to her face and smell its fragrance, to know if it smelled like crushed autumn leaves. When she awoke, Marysza's face was wet. She became angry with herself.

This is crazy. I never knew my mother. She didn't care about me, left me with grandma and never came back.

The dream didn't leave. Its memory stayed with Marysza, returning each time she looked at Jimmy.

At home

Days passed like questions without answers. Marysza's inner voice lost its certainty. She remembered the gaiety she'd felt before the baby was born, but that memory deepened her despondency. She told herself that Tadziu liked the baby, that he would grow to like him more and no longer used the word "love" in thinking about them. Tadziu did begin to pay more attention to Jimmy, always after work, when he had a drink in his hand.

"Hi fella, how are you?" he would ask, with exaggerated jocularity, but that soon began to sound like a broken record, and Marysza found herself picking Jimmy up whenever Tadziu began to say "hi fella", because she thought the baby didn't like it and because Tadziu's voice gave her an uneasy feeling. She tried to forget her apprehension, to think of her own delight in the baby, of holding, bathing and feeding him, of the way she lost herself in the rise and fall of happiness each time he emptied her heavy breast. She was glad when Tadziu stopped paying attention to him.

Martha often came to see Marysza and the baby. Marysza luxuriated in her pride, felt her son's life close any distance that existed between herself and her friend. Each of them watched his face for an expression they could interpret as recognition of themselves.

"Oh, Marysza, look, look, he's laughing. I'm te-e-e-lling you, it's for me."

"You're probably right. He knows who brings him all the nice stuff." Marysza wrapped the baby in his towel and handed him to Martha. Martha didn't look confident, fumbled as she tried to put the hood over the baby's head, her eyes beseeching Marysza, who, from her superior status as the baby's mother, laughed.

"He won't break," she assured Martha. "After a while, it's easy." Martha managed to get the hood on, and carried the baby from the bathroom.

"I'll clean up," Marysza called. "You can dress him for me."

She's happy but he'll set up a racket. He doesn't like being taken out of his bath and he's hungry.

She pretended to be cleaning the bathroom so Martha could hold Jimmy longer but he began his protest. The wails stopped short when he began to nurse, as if a plug had been inserted into his mouth. They laughed.

"Thanks for dressing him," Marysza said, and smiled at Martha's attempt to sound nonchalant.

"Sure." She rested her head on Marysza's shoulder and watched the baby's contentment.

Marysza loved her time alone with the baby, especially during the night when she rose to feed him. She sat in the rocker, watching the night through the window—points of light like watchmen in the darkness—and pushed away the fears that grew larger at night. The baby pulled at her breast, then paused for breath, sometimes falling into sleep for short moments before waking to pull again, drawing, taking life from Marysza's body, a taking that made Marysza stronger and increased her own life. Sometimes his eyes were wide and focused on her, as small streams of milk ran from the corners of his mouth. When she lifted him to her shoulder and patted his back, the silk of his hair brushed her cheek. A rhythm of pleasure took hold and spread through Marysza, locking her child and herself together.

Sometimes she sang to him as they rocked, sometimes she held him quietly, feeling another presence watching with them, a presence that enveloped, filled the room like warm air. Though they were alone, and sharing private moments, the baby and she were not only a part of each other but also of something larger, something that filled Marysza with peace and well-being. Tadziu never noticed or cared when she returned to their room. Like a child himself, he slept on his side of the bed curled into a tight ball, protecting himself against the darkness, not wanting to be a part of the night, not knowing, as she did, how beautiful it could be.

The Christening

Marysza decided to name the baby after her young cousin. She asked Jimmy to be his godfather and Martha to be his godmother. Jimmy pretended to know what godfather meant but his eyes betrayed his uncertainty. Aunt Irene explained that he was promising to help the baby grow as a good Catholic especially if Marysza and Tadziu died. Uncle Ben put his hand on his boy's shoulders and said, "congratulations buddy." Jimmy stood tall as Martha squeezed his hand. Tadziu was indifferent.

At the ceremony, Jimmy's hair was flat and shiny, as if pasted, except for the strands that broke free and stuck up in the back. He wore new shoes that looked bigger than his feet and a new suit which must have been uncomfortable because he kept scratching his neck and his crotch until his mother quietly told him to stop. With great solemnity, he answered yes when the priest asked the official questions, emphasizing his yes when the priest asked if he renounced the devil and all his works. He watched closely as the priest poured water over the baby's head and automatically blessed himself when the priest pronounced, "in the name of the Father and of the Son and of the Holy Ghost." [36] Marysza thought of her mother, that, though she didn't know it, she was a grandmother now. It was difficult for Marysza not to think of her mother, that she was unaware she was a grandmother.

Marysza's aunt and uncle gave a christening party. Marysza asked her Uncle Ben whether he remembered when she was christened, whether he remembered her mother. Her uncle scrunched his lips into a frown and shook his head. His pained face contained sadness and anger.

I don't care about her. Why am I upsettiing Uncle Ben? She's not only my mother, but also his sister. But no one ever speaks of her. Silence surrounds her like a wall.

"It would've been nice if she could see her grandson," Marysza said. She thought that remark would serve to cover the awkward silence between her uncle and herself, the break in the regularity of their landscape. Her uncle's face remained unchanged

What've I done? We're standing at the edge of a hole into which either of us can fall at any moment.

She heard her aunt behind her, turned to see her rocking baby Jimmy in her arms, his long white dress moving to the cadence of her aunt's sing-song voice.

"And such a handsome grand-nephew! Such a handsome, handsome boy. We all love him so." Her aunt's voice changed to one of mock distress as the white cap the baby wore moved and covered his eyes. "Oh dear, oh dear." Marysza and her uncle looked at each other, pretending to shake their heads and look up at the sky. Marysza was filled with profound gratitude. Because it was all right. The breach that threatened to open between her and her uncle had been dissipated by Aunt Irene, by her obvious attempt to show everyone the beautiful christening dress Jimmy wore, by her hope that she would be asked and could tell everyone that Jimmy wore the same gown her children had worn when they were christened. When Marysza asked her aunt whether the dress, so delicate and finely made, was an heirloom, her aunt answered that she didn't think so because she had sewn it herself from the material in her own wedding gown. Marysza continued to admire the dress and soon everyone was commenting on its beauty and its excellent workmanship. Aunt Irene beamed with pleasure.

"Well then, it will be an heirloom now, Aunt Irene. It's being passed from your children to Jimmy. From Jimmy, it will be passed to your children's children, and my children's children." Then Marysza became quiet.

Jimmy wears this christening gown because Tadziu and I couldn't afford to buy one. I don't know when things will be different. But something else is true. The gown gives Jimmy his place in the family. His family is Aunt Irene and Uncle Ben and their children. And Martha, of course. And the memory of grandma. I'll tell him about his great-grandma and my mother when he's old enough to understand. As much as I can tell him. Because I don't know my mother's story, a story that seems important today, my child's christening day. I thought she was gone, forgotten. That I didn't care. Because she doesn't deserve it. Now I'm not sure of anything.

Aunt Irene's face was flushed with excitement. She had baked a cake, covered it with white frosting and traced Jimmy's name on it with blue candies, candies that formed perfect writing, not one out of place.

"Please help yourself," her aunt kept saying to the guests, which included Martha's parents and some of her aunt's neighbors. "You can put the baby in our room on the bed, Marysza. It will be quiet in there." When Marysza carried Jimmy to the bed, she saw that her aunt had put a clean cover on it. Jimmy looked lost in a sea of white.

Marysza heard people congratulating Tadziu, heard him saying "thanks" but not much more. She saw the look on Martha's face but her uncle extended his hand to Tadziu.

His hand goes out so easily. For my sake. But also because he's a kind man. They forgive me even though they don't understand why I married him."

Aunt Irene was undisturbed by anything Tadziu did or didn't say and smiled at him in the way she smiled at everyone else. She moved back and forth between people, carrying slices of cake, cups of coffee, and small glasses of pink punch with white froth floating on the surface.

"Would you like cream or sugar?" she asked Tadziu, and when he nodded, Aunt Irene brought him the tray with the pitcher and the bowl. Marysza saw how good Aunt Irene was to Tadziu, and how sullen and ungrateful he remained. Large pieces of anger filled her, would not be stilled by the usual things she told herself. When Aunt Irene came to Martha, she said, "This is the first time I tried this recipe," as if she were confiding a secret.

"Everything you make is good, Aunt Irene," Martha said.. Aunt Irene saw Uncle Ben smile at Martha's praise.

"Aw go on, Martha," she said, happiness in her voice. Marysza was not sure how long Tadziu would last. She tried to forget her anxiety.

If this is the way it's going to be, I'll get used to it. He's Jimmy's father.

Then she began to feel angry again, an anger that was directed at the very people she loved.

None of the people here understand Tadziu as I do, how much he needs me, or how much I love him. I'll always stick by him. Isn't that what marriage is supposed to be? Or is it that I'll stick by him because I have nothing else?

She wanted this thought to disappear but like a parasite, it attached itself, grew and would not be ignored. The look on Tadziu's face told her it was time to leave.

"I don't like parties", he said, then, as a kind of apology, "I don't like people sizing me up." Marysza's voice lacked conviction.

"I don't think they do that."

"Aw c'mon Marysza, you know better. None of them gives a shit about me." She saw the pain in his face. He didn't like being what he was. She looked into his eyes.

"I love you. I don't care what they think of you."

"Yeah, sure," he replied, but the tone of his voice changed, lost part of the anger that always simmered beneath his surface. The baby began to cry in the bedroom. Tadziu followed her. They sat on the edge of the bed and she opened her blouse.

I sit here with this child. And with him. With his dark brows and his frown. All the things I can't reach.

"Look Tadziu, how he holds onto my finger. Give me your hand."

"Yeah," he murmured, but she could see he wasn't interested. She convinced him to stay a while longer. He began drinking beer and things went better. They stayed until the end of the party. Marysza was relieved when it was over, saw clearly that her life with Tadziu would be one relief after another and that it was becoming difficult for her to understand what her feelings were.

Problems Continue

Tadziu drank more each day and Marysza knew he was not growing closer to Jimmy. He was interested only in her and the sex they shared each night, as if the drinking and the sex gave him a refuge from his pain, pain he didn't understand and couldn't share. His passion was clumsy, but he never left her behind, brought her to where she was made free, where she could know again the strange, seething tenderness they had known together from the beginning. She sensed it was different for him, that he reached a place of inner violence, violence which excited her further. She didn't know there was another way to love.

I can't live without him, without this. I'll wither and die.

Her only certainty was that she was a woman important to the man she loved. Each time they made love her hope that his love would come to include his son was renewed.

"We'll be all right," she told him in those moments, believed it herself, that this passion could hold them, could bind them all together.

Problems Multiply

Marysza could not work for six weeks. Their budget was limited to what Tadziu earned at the factory. There was barely enough to pay the bills but she avoided thoughts of returning to work. That would mean Tadziu would have to stay with Jimmy and that thought added to her growing desperation.

"I have to go to the doctor's this week," she told Tadziu.

"You sick?"

"No, it's called a six-week check-up, after a baby. The baby too. The baby has to go."

"I can't take off from work."

"I know. You'll have to take the bus that day. I can drive myself and the baby. Okay?"

"Yeah, yeah, okay." Tadziu pushed himself from the table and went into the living room to watch television. Several six-packs of beer leaned against the side of the chair.

By the end of the evening, the beer was always gone. Some nights, he went out for more. Usually he fell asleep in the chair. If he didn't, he went to bed without saying anything. He slept heavily and never heard the baby's cries.

The realization that Tadziu and she lived most of their life in silence frightened Marysza. She tried to make him talk but stopped when he became irritated. Tonight, she looked at him sitting in his chair and saw the forsaken look in his eyes. She was moved with pity and touched his hair. He turned, reached for her hand and looked intently into her face.

"I miss you," he said, "I mean us, at night, the way it was before."

So this is all it is. He's going through a husband's impatience after the birth of a baby. He misses our sex life. I miss it too. This must be normal. Everything will be all right after I see the doctor. Am I comforting myself, reaching for straws?

But even in bed at night, life didn't return to normal. Changes had occurred. Marysza was watchful for the baby's cries.

I know Tadziu feels I'm withdrawing. I don't care. The baby is part of us, both of us. Why doesn't he feel that? Will he ever?

Marysza knew the answers to these questions. Her resentment began to grow.

There was something else which dampened her sexual responses to Tadziu. Even though Tadziu always kept himself clean, his breath and his clothes had the unappealing smell of beer, a smell Marysza had never been around except for Martha's father. When she told him she didn't like it, Tadziu complained.

"Jeez, what's wrong with you? You're changed." She tried to recapture her former behavior because she didn't want him to blame the baby and because she knew, despite her reluctance to admit it, she'd miss Tadziu's paycheck, was afraid to be without Tadziu. She thought of how he brought home his paycheck, gave her most of the money and after she divided it into separate envelopes to pay each of the bills, took what she gave him, whatever was left. She was sure it went for beer. There was nothing for her but when she shopped for food, she sometimes managed to sneak in a lipstick or socks or underwear when she needed them. She listened again to her inner voice.

I don't care that I can't buy much for myself. I want to be with Jimmy. Tadziu never bothers me about going back to work. And we have a car. Those beautiful hands of his keep our junker going, that old junker he had before we were married. He always gets up to go to work, no matter how hung over he is. And the health insurance. His job has insurance decent enough so we only had to pay a small amount after Jimmy was born. I need Tadziu. I can't manage without him.

Tonight she sat before the television watching the stock-car races with him, trying to be interested, to keep her attention from wandering. Tadziu held a beer in one hand, hit his knees triumphantly with the other each time one of the cars crossed the finish line. "Damn, damn, that was a good race." He opened the bottles of beer more quickly than usual. His laughter had a reckless quality but Marysza's hopelessness forced her to laugh with him. Empty bottles collected on the side of his chair.

"Tadziu," she said, trembling with fear and anger as she took an almost empty bottle from his hand, "that's enough." He didn't seem to hear. His eyes were on the television, one arm stroking the back of his head. Now and then he jumped up, shouted at the television and hitched up his pants, then walked around the room in a frenzy of excitement. When he reached to the floor for his beer, and saw that Marysza had taken it, he became livid with rage.

"Damn you, Marysza," he screamed, "damn you, don't ever do that, you hear!" He lifted his arm to strike her, then, as if awakening from a dream, realized what was happening and stared at her as if he were more frightened than she was.

She lay in bed that night, trying not to think of his raised arm, of the way his face had been distorted with rage, of the emptiness inside her and the emptiness next to her now where Tadziu should've been.

He's gone to a bar. I know he's in a bar. It's useless for me to try to sleep. I'm filled with fear. It controls me, spins inside me like a wheel, catches me in its spokes and drags me along the ground. I'm powerless, unable to help myself, unable to change anything. He doesn't know what's happening to him. The baby's in the next room. I'm responsible for him. Will Tadziu return? Will things change? I'm angry, angry because of my fear and everything he's doing to us. I never thought I could be angry with Tadziu.

Aloneness loomed over Marysza like a cold shadow, a death from which there was no escape.

Tadziu came in very late, very drunk. Her anger and fear dissolved when she heard him. She suppressed the inner voice which told her there would be no relief, that, like a terrified animal, she was caught in a trap.

Tadziu sobbed uncontrollably. He became a child with glassy eyes, snuffling and wiping his nose in the sleeve of his shirt, reaching his arms out to her, saying over and over again, "I'm sorry, Marysza, I'm sorry." She was accustomed to his emotional displays when drunk, but she took his distress seriously and held him while he sobbed.

He needs me. I need him. We're together.

The next day, Marysza didn't know how he did it but Tadziu got up and went to work. She was tired all day, felt lost in a fog, a fog that protected her from what she knew was there, prevented her from seeing what she didn't want to see. Tadziu had come home. He had gone to work. Everything was going to be all right. That week, he gave her all the money and took nothing for himself.

Trying to Hope

Like a sickness that had been in remission, Marysza's despair returned. Her self-deception became a floating face that laughed at her, a face she knew was her own.

. *How long can this last? How long? My aloneness drapes itself around me like a shroud. I want to be close to Tadziu in more than the physical moments, to talk with him about his life, the things he's never told me, the missing years since childhood when we separated.*

She knew Tadziu carried some great hurt and it was because of that unknown hurt, she told herself, that she always forgave him. Once, when he was drunk, he had said, "my father beat me", but didn't elaborate, and when she asked, he answered "aw, it was just the way he was, thassal." When she pressed it, he became angry. "I don' wanna talk about it, Marysza. Don' ass me, fer Chrissake." He wouldn't, or couldn't, say more.

She sensed this matter was important to their survival and brought it up again when he was sober.

"I want to tell you my thoughts and my feelings," she told him. "To know yours. I never know what you're thinking. What do you think about, Tadziu"? Her voice was a plea. He answered that he was thinking about money, always about money.

"We haven't got enough anymore, ever since the kid came."

"Did you think it would never happen, that I wouldn't get pregnant"?

"You shoulda been more careful. You're smart."

She had no answer, knew this was only another revelation of what lay beneath the surface of their lives, though she pretended it wasn't there. Tadziu didn't want Jimmy, had never wanted him. All the other questions were wiped away. He wouldn't understand if she told him about her fears, of not wanting their marriage to end, of not wanting to be alone. And she would never know the secrets that lay inside him. Knowing they would never be close was the saddest thing of all.

Her life with Tadziu was like shifting sand beneath her feet, ground that was not solid, threatened to disappear at any moment. It couldn't continue as it was and she was afraid of how it would end.

"I'm sorry," Tadziu said to her one night, "sorry for all of this," but he was drunk and when he started to walk toward Jimmy's room, muttering almost unintelligibly, "I'm sorry about him too. I'm a lousy father. I'm no good," she was startled because she had never heard him use the word "father" before, but also frightened, so she ran ahead and took Jimmy before Tadziu reached him. Sorrow flashed across Tadziu's's face, and sat there until it became rage..

"You think I need you," he screamed. "I don't need you." He stumbled into their room and she heard him collapse on the bed. She slept on the couch that night which, she realized, had become a habit.

Their sex decreased as Tadziu's drinking increased. Marysza was imprisoned by feelings that vacillated between love and dependency and anger mixed with something that felt like hatred. On days when Tadziu came home from work quiet and apologetic and looked at her with shame in his eyes, her original feeling for him returned. She did not doubt the love that swept through her. She saw again that he looked beautiful, that he was a handsome man, that he took good care of the way he looked and when he wasn't drinking, was always clean and well groomed. On those days, she once again said to herself, "It will be all right."

Health Problems

Marysza had trouble sleeping at night. She had no appetite and the fit of her clothes told her she was losing weight. She knew she didn't look well. She avoided looking in the mirror, realized again that personal beauty was important to her, that this sense of herself as pleasing to others was a trait so much a part of herself she didn't stop to think about it. Now, as she looked at herself and saw that her face had lost its color and her eyes, as if they had lost interest in the world around them, no longer held their liveliness, she thought about it. How strange that vanity still surfaced in the midst of pain.

Was it always that way? Would she think about how she looked when she was dying?

She posed the question to Martha who looked perplexed and didn't answer. She thought of Grandma's words when she told Marysza her mother thought everything would come to her if she was "real pretty".

Martha came to visit Marysza regularly, did errands Marysza couldn't do, even brought her books from the library. Marysza didn't talk to Martha about her life, because she didn't want to betray Tadziu and because she was ashamed to admit her unhappiness. As Marysza looked at Martha, she thought how good a friend Martha was.

She never asks me difficult questions. She knows the answers, I'm sure.

Today, Martha looked ready to break her silence.

"You don't look good", she said. "Something's wrong. Are you feeling okay?"

"Sure. Nothing's wrong. Really."

Martha's mouth became a tight line. She came closer to Marysza, stared into her face with such concentration that Marysza laughed.

"Are you going to look down my throat?" Martha didn't laugh.

"Nobody should stay cooped up all the time like you do. Even working in the restaurant would get you out a little. You'd see some people."

"Well, just what am I supposed to do about it?" Marysza asked, in a tone she knew Martha didn't deserve. Martha shrunk visibly at Marysza's words but she said nothing.

"I wouldn't mind going back to the club, but I can't leave the baby." She forgot she hadn't spoken to Martha about her fear of leaving Jimmy with Tadziu.

Martha seemed to notice neither Marysza's irritability nor her silent remorse.

"What if we worked different shifts and I watched Jimmy while you worked?"

Marysza couldn't answer.

I know how you feel, how you've always felt about Tadziu. We've never discussed it. Even now, you don't pry. If you did, where would I start? How could I explain this mess? You're a rare friend. But you can't help me. Nothing can help me, dear Martha.

"Geez, you've got dark circles under your eyes. You never had those before." Marysza looked into the mirror.

"Yeah, I know." Her sleeplessness was not because of Jimmy. He was a good baby. It was her life, her marriage. Tadziu was drinking more, barely spoke to her and was sullen most of the time. Marysza's unhappiness pursued her like a grotesque monster that grew bigger each day. Tadziu had bursts of his passionate need, and in those moments, she felt that need could assuage her fear, could make her believe what her rational mind knew was an illusion. She was divided, cut in two, had no center. Living with him was unmanageable, but she couldn't envision herself without him. Her life stretched before her like a canvas covered with pictures of failure. Even her despair frightened her, made her feel guilty.

I must stay strong for Jimmy's sake. He has no one but me. But how can I? Where is the end, the end? Where am I going?

She'd made a mistake, deserved what was happening to her but she couldn't pronounce the word "mistake", couldn't give up the last shred of a hope that she'd wake up and the nightmare would be gone.

"Martha, I get up a lot at night with the baby," she lied, trying to sound convincing.

Martha looked at her, began to say something, then stopped. Anger filled her large brown eyes. In bad moments, Martha still had to push her glasses up her nose. She pushed them up now and said good-bye. Marysza was filled with more regret, more guilt.

Moments of Peace

It was summer and hot in the flat. Marysza spent a half-day scrubbing generations of dirt from the porch outside the back door. She carried out the small plastic pool she had bought for Jimmy and filled it with water heated in the tea kettle. She dragged out a kitchen chair and sat next to him, watching him laugh and splash as she trickled water through her fingers onto his legs, his arms, his chest and his head. Drops of water hung from his eyelashes, then a cascade ran over his face. He didn't cry, only paused for a moment, looking confused, and when the water stopped, sharply drew in his breath.

"Oh Mommy's sorry," Marysza said. Her voice drew a wide smile from behind the water still rolling down Jimmy's face, as if he was telling her he knew she played a trick on him but it was okay. Marysza knew this would relieve the heat and help him sleep well. She looked up at the night sky, a sky which had always seemed friendly, had always spoken to her in a language she understood. Tonight the sky was silent, provided no comfort, no reassurance. The chirping of the crickets was a monotonous drone. The faint fragrance of some unknown flower growing nearby seemed a pitiful effort at beauty and only made Marysza think of something that couldn't bloom. Her despair grew. She thought of the tree she and her grandmother had planted many summers ago, of the happiness she had felt then, a happiness that no longer existed for her, would never exist again.

Turmoil

Marysza could not interpret Tadziu's face when he walked in the door after work. His expresson was so agonized she thought he might have been hurt by a machine. He said nothing but that meant little because he was often silent when he walked in the door. He sat down, rubbed his hand through his hair and remained in the chair without any sign of the usual things he did. He seemed to have forgotten about cleaning up, just stared into space like an animal that had been wounded and was in shock.

Is he drunk already? Before coming home. He's never done that. Besides, he wouldn't have had time. Has he had bad news? His parents, his brothers and sisters? Do I dare to ask him? I must dare. He may need me.

As if determined that everything should proceed as normal, Tadziu rose from his chair and went to the bathroom to wash and change his clothes. When he came out, Marysza asked what was wrong.

"Nothing," he said sullenly and was silent for the remainder of the meal. Then came the sound Marysza detested, the usual clinking of beer bottles as Tadziu sat in his chair and stared vacantly at the television screen.

Marysza couldn't stand his silence or her inaction. While knowing the futility of her hope, she hoped his mood augured a turning point of some kind, a realization he'd, had that would change the desperation in which she lived. And because she retained her love for him, because it had never left her, she sought to comfort him and placed her hand on his head. It was then that she felt the red ball of the sun falling into her black night and the earth opening and swallowing her whole, then that she felt the slashing of her insides into pieces of blood and flesh to be scattered like refuse, trampled upon and ground into disintegration, then that she felt Tadziu's hand across her face, his arms pushing her out of his way.

An Ending

She began to rehearse what she would say if she had the courage to leave Tadziu, arranged and rearranged the words, put them from her mind, then took them back, like some impossible poem or song she was trying to write. She thought of Tadziu needing her, looking for her out of frightened eyes like a child who had no mother. In the next moment, she thought of that child punishing her because of what she'd failed to give him. How could she find that thing he needed? Jimmy looked at her from his baby seat on the floor, the seat Martha had brought for him. After a while, his eyes began to close. Marysza lifted him and buried her face in his warmth. Tears of anger, sorrow and frustration filled her eyes, rolled down her face and onto his. He raised his hand, rubbed his face and promptly fell asleep.

Marysza lost track of the hours. Tadziu had struck her. Her life was crumbling. She began to berate herself for her mistake in marrying Tadziu, then told herself it was natural they were together, that it could have been predicted . She couldn't admit she was glad her marriage was degenerating so quickly, that the worse it became, the closer it was to ending. Yet fear remained her constant companion. When she turned her face, it turned around and faced her from another direction. She and Jimmy couldn't survive on the money she made. She had betrayed her aunt and uncle and Martha, couldn't ask them for help, couldn't even tell them what was happening. She'd be alone.

Marysza had paid the heat and the electric bill for the month but there wasn't enough to pay the rent. She wasn't sure how the money had been spent. She heard Tadziu come in.

"We had money in the envelopes, but it's gone," she said to him, surprised at her question, but worried that she might not have watched expenditures carefully enough.

What, am I stupid?

She stared at him as if she were seeing him for the first time–at his shirt, which was clean, as it usually was, at his neatly-combed hair, as if he carried a comb in his back pocket like a teen-age boy, at his carefully polished shoes. "Where is it all?" she asked, her voice less of a plea, more of a demand. Because it came to her that she should be afraid, she scooped Jimmy up from his seat on the floor, but she could tell by the look in Tadziu's eyes that the baby was safe.

"There's no money left," he answered, turning his eyes from her like a child who couldn't think of an excuse. He had the look of a cornered animal and she saw he was afraid of her, knew again there was something terrible in his life she didn't know, and filled with pity, wanted to tell him he needn't be afraid, that it was she, Marysza, and to forget about the money. "I needed it," he cried quietly into his sleeve, as if he didn't want to say the words, then louder, "I needed it," and disappeared into the bedroom where her eyes couldn't reach him. Jimmy began to cry small cries that promised to grow bigger..

"I'm not angry with you Tadziu," she called, following him, carrying Jimmy in her arms.

Tadziu went out that night. Because it was hot and Jimmy was fussy, she soothed him with a bath, becoming lost in his delight so that, for a moment, she could smile. She pulled the clean shirt and nightgown over his body and tied the strings at the bottom into a bow. After she nursed him, she wrapped him in a light blanket and carefully walked down the steep hallway stairs, carrying him into the night air as if he was a prince. The night air was cooler than their flat upstairs. She walked beneath a black sky strewn with hundreds of flickering lights, felt the strands of hair which stuck to the wet skin on the back of her neck, not noticing the effort it took to breathe as she walked in the still, oppressive heat. She forced herself to forget the facts of her life. For that moment with her baby, all things were as they were intended to be, and were good.

She returned to the flat and placed Jimmy, now sleeping peacefully, into his basket. As she struggled to open the old windows in the bedrooms, she heard Tadziu come in and knew, when she entered the living room and saw his face, that it wouldn't be an easy night. Her body stiffened, moving into a state of alert. Tadziu's voice was loud, almost a scream.

"Listen Marysza," he stammered, then, for one moment, was uncertain and hesitated. "I know you have money. You put it someplace. I want it." His eyes were red and shot through with blue veins. Marysza thought she had never seen those eyes. This was a stranger. Tadziu was gone, gone forever. The man behind those eyes could hurt Jimmy. She heard her heart pounding in her ears. Fear spilled over as if she was a cup which could hold no more.

The light from the lamp on the living room table made a circle against the wall. A shadow moved in the circle, turning itself into a form Marysza didn't recognize. But it became clearer until she knew it was grandma. She was filled with comfort, wanted to reach out and hide her face in her grandmother's shoulder, but she knew that would cause her to disappear. The face moved closer, looked at Marysza as if to say "never min'. you know what to do." Marysza saw that this wouldn't be easy, that her grandmother couldn't save her. But she would help. Marysza heard herself say no to Tadziu.

"What do you mean NO," he bellowed as he came toward her with his fists clenched. "I want the money."

Marysza listened to a voice that sounded strange, then recognized it as her own. "I'm not giving money to you for booze, ever again. I want you to get out. If you hit me, I'll go to the police and have you locked up." The calmness with which she said this astonished her.

Tadziu's eyes grew large, then larger, glared at her like the eyes of a fierce animal, contracted into slits, half-open windows. They opened again, this time appearing surprised. Something resembling heat grew and spread inside Marysza. Her own strength appeared before her like a long-lost friend. Absorbed in what she was experiencing, for a moment she forgot about Tadziu, then became aware of him again and realized she didn't fear him, but was filled with pity. He raised his fist to strike and she thought she would feel the blow, but she ducked and his fist flew into the air and crashed against the wall, causing him to lose his balance and fall in a heap at her feet.

She didn't run but stood there, again feeling the strength that had, at first, seemed new to her, that she saw now was not really new but the return of something she owned and had placed behind her for a while, something she remembered as part of herself and was now reclaiming, a strength that mingled with the pity that caused her to stare at Tadziu, even at the cost of his rising and becoming a threat again. He tried to lift himself, fell back again and gave up, his eyes no longer fierce but filled with a new look she couldn't name. She thought it was fear. He was afraid, she was not sure of what, then realized with a start that it was of losing her, of her meaning what she said, of his being left alone. Marysza knew she meant what she said. And that he knew it also.

When it was over and Tadziu was gone, when he'd taken his things and moved out, Marysza was calm. She knew her actions toward him were the right ones. But she thought of him with sorrow, remembered there were parts of him she didn't understand, things he'd never told her. She remembered the tenderness he'd been capable of and had shown her, how, like a child, he'd clung to her beneath his anger. She stood at the window watching the birds in the tree outside, the way they pecked at the ground hunting for a tiny morsel of food. Tadziu had been like that, like a hungry bird. In the next few days, her feelings struggled to define themselves, to declare themselves clearly. At the last, she knew their name was forgiveness. She told herself she'd already forgiven Tadziu. And believed it

Martha helped her find free legal services. The divorce was an easy one and didn't take long. She asked for nothing from Tadziu because he had nothing. He gave her the car. The judge set a fee for child support. In the same breath he told her about family court where she'd have to go in order to sue for payment. As if he already knew the payments wouldn't come. Martha helped her file the papers to change her name. She took back her grandmother's name, was no longer Mrs. Tadziu Wreblewski but Marysza Jargosz again.

Chapter Four

Tadziu stood at a bar. He lived alone now. It wasn't exactly a flophouse but not much better. It made him think of the days when he lived with Mrs. Jablonski. He was back in a hole again. He deserved it. His father was right. He had messed up everything. He'd never be anything but a bum. Worse, a creep. A mean and nasty creep.

All he had now was thinking. Even when he was loaded which he was a lot because it didn't matter much anymore. He lived over again every minute he had been with her, every day he was her husband and even the kid's father. He had it all down pat, from beginning to end. He thought about the other things in his life. It didn't matter. Everything was connected to her. All the parts of him, everything that ever happened to him was connected to her.

When they were just married, "newlyweds", he thought you called it, he watched Marysza try to make their apartment nice. She called it an apartment but it was just the upper floor of a two-story house and he called it a flat. He knew he was the bum his father always said he was, because he couldn't give her more, because she had to work in order for them to pay all their bills. It did no good for him to pretend things would get better. He was just a worker in a second-rate factory.

He'd tried to get into the bigger places, went to the steel plants and the car factories, places where guys made big money and had all kinds of benefits. But he never got a phone call.

I knew I'd never get a better job. You needed pull to get those jobs. I sure as hell didn't have any.

He never knew it was so easy to make babies. He remembered how scared he got when he heard Marysza throwing up one morning. She could be sick with something bad. She could die. He watched from the bathroom door, not knowing what to do, his own stomach hurting each time she retched.

"I'm pregnant," she said, happiness and nervousness mixed together on her face.

"How do you know?" He still felt how his thoughts tied themselves into knots.

"I haven't had my period in a while," she said, looking guilty. He didn't say anything. He knew she was thinking the same thing he was, that she would have to quit work. Some weeks the money she collected in tips was more than his pay. Without her working, they couldn't make it.

We'd be tighter than ever. Fuck, I couldn't blame her. It was my fault we didn't have enough money. I was a failure. Even for Marysza.

"I'll figure out something," she said. "Maybe my aunt will watch the baby". Even now, he felt the panic that had scrambled inside him, like an insect desperate to find its way out.

She'll leave me. I can't take care of her and a baby.

He turned to leave and remembered how he walked into the bathroom door. Neither of them laughed.

She had to go to the doctor a lot. The health insurance from the factory paid some of the bills. Marysza was good with money and they managed but right away he could see this baby wasn't going to stop costing money. There was all that excitement over painting a crib and buying things to put in it. Blankets and something called bumpers.

Bumpers. Was it a crib or a car?

Then baby clothes. A party at Martha's house where everyone brought something for the baby.

At first, Marysza wore his old shirts but then she had to buy some clothes. He didn't notice her stomach growing until one day it was big, like a balloon that had filled overnight. But she was prettier than ever. Men still turned to look at her.

She told Tadziu she could feel the baby move inside her. She wanted him to feel her stomach. He didn't like the idea but he said okay.

"Here, Tadziu, right here." She put his hand on the spot. He was afraid to press too hard.

"You see, did you feel that?"

He told her he did but he wasn't sure.

Anyway, what was the big deal? She acted as if this kid was going to be some kind of king or something. Not just an ordinary kid.

Adjustments

Their life changed. Marysza started to move away from him. In small ways. It wasn't the two of them anymore. The kid was always there. One night in bed, she acted as if Tadziu was a pain in the ass.

"C'mon Tadziu. You know what the doctor said. No sex for six weeks before and after the baby comes." So he turned away. She touched his shoulder.

"It's okay, it's okay. Forget it."

He still heard the anger in his voice, and felt his stomach tighten.

Each day when I looked in the mirror to shave or comb my hair, I saw my father's face. The eyes held anger that could break out any minute without warning.

He was filled with shame.

His friend Jerry, who was older, and married with a couple kids, had told him what to expect when it was time for the baby to come. He tried to memorize everything but his fright or resentment or something made things fall out of his head as fast as he put them in. On the night Marysza's water broke, she was calm. He tried to help her put her coat on because it was cold but she only wanted it thrown over her shoulders. He ran around looking for the little bag she had packed.

"Under the bed," she said, the sound of pain growing in her voice.

He dragged out the bag and then dropped it, scattering its contents in different directions. He was grateful when Marysza started to laugh. It made him forget his clumsiness and he started to laugh too until she said , "you'd better hurry," her laughter turning into a small scream, and as if awakening from a dream, he remembered what was happening.

They got to the hospital, and he sat in the room Jerry had told him about, the father's waiting room, and thought he would choke from the smoke. The doctor came out.

It's a boy," he announced, and shook Tadziu's hand.

When Tadziu got home, he remembered the guy who said, "Nice going. I've got three girls," as he held up his crossed fingers. Tadziu couldn't even remember what the guy looked like, or what his name was, but he remembered he tried to look serious and said "good luck" to the guy, as if he knew what it must be like to have three girls.

He was scared when he went to pick up Marysza at the hospital, scared he wouldn't look right. He wore a white shirt and tie because he thought that was probably what you should wear for your wife and new kid. Before he reached the hospital, he stopped for a couple drinks, just a couple so he'd stop feeling scared.

He remembered how he stood at the bar alone that night thinking of the days when it was only him and Marysza, the days after they were first married and even further back. Thinking of how he used to eat supper with Marysza in her grandmother's house and how the chairs for the table were all different. One had wooden arms at the sides, arms you could stretch your own arms out on and pretend you were a king. Marysza and he both tried to get that chair first, pushing and pulling it until her grandmother told them to stop. Then they sat across the table from each other, laughing and swinging their legs against the wooden chair rungs. They were always laughing, even when no sound came out.

Yeah, supper at Marysza's grandmother's house. He could still see it —the bright light overhead, the shiny white table with the black edges, both the black edges and the white center chipped like the inside of a pot when it was used a lot, and the two endpieces that went up or down so the table could be made bigger or smaller and pushed into the corner after supper when Marysza or her grandmother swept the floor. Sometimes they prayed before they ate. It depended on whether Marysza's grandmother thought of it. They folded their hands and blessed themselves by touching their foreheads, their chests and their shoulders in the form of a cross while Marysza's grandmother said

W'imie Ojca i Syna i Ducha Swietego. Amen [37] . He remembered the words because he'd heard his mother praying a lot. Probably for the old man to drop dead.

'*Naw, she wouldn't do that. I would.*

He laughed out loud. The other guys at the bar turned and looked at him.

Tough shit.

Marysza's grandmother always wore an apron and her hands would hold the wet cloth from the sink to wipe her mouth with when she finished eating. She was a nice old lady. Marysza and he giggled a lot, even during the praying, but the old lady never said anything. Those times at Marysza's grandmother's house were his best times. He thought of the winters when Marysza's house was a shelter from the cold. He thought of summers when he and Marysza went swimming in the city pool. Marysza always told him to wash his feet good, especially between the toes. She said they checked between your toes to make sure you didn't have athlete's foot before they'd let you in the pool. He always listened to her even though he pretended he didn't.

Then all of a sudden it wasn't just the two of them anymore. Just after he'd found her again.

He didn't stay long in the bar that night on his way to the hospital because he didn't want to smell like beer. He worked up the nerve and left.

When he got to the hospital, Marysza was waiting for him, all excited about the baby. He pretended to be excited too, looked at the kid's face, and said he was nice-looking so that Marysza would be happy. He saw how she looked at the kid with a special thing in her eyes, how she pretended to listen to what Tadziu was saying when she really wasn't.

She paid more attention to that baby than she did to me.

He knew right off he'd never get used to it. He was really a creep.

`The New Arrival

It stayed that way. He went to the hospital each day until it was time for Marysza to come home. She talked mostly about the baby and wanted Tadziu to be just as goofy over him as she was. One day they laughed together when she offered Tadziu some of her hospital food. Those were her only words for him alone. Everything else was the baby, the baby, the baby. It didn't change when they got home. She kept asking him to look at every damn thing the baby was doing, most of which he knew she imagined and didn't happen at all.

How many things could the kid do anyway, except eat, sleep, cry and shit. Oh Christ, I was more and more like my father. Joe wouldn't have been that way about his own kid.

So he had promised himself to try. To be like Joe. When Marysza called him, he went and watched whatever it was she wanted him to see. Sometime it really was something, like the way the kid followed your finger with his eyes. Once the kid got a funny look on his face and Marysza said he was smiling at Tadziu. Tadziu never believed that. It was just a funny look.

He thought Marysza must have something built into her head, an antenna that picked up every movement the kid was going to make. She always knew when he was going to cry. Even at night she ran to him before he started. Then she opened her nightgown and placed her swollen breast, like an overripe fruit about to burst its skin, into his mouth. Tadziu didn't watch the kid eat, but he heard the pull of his mouth, heard him stop to breathe, take gulps of air, as if he was drowning.

I should've been the one sucking her nipple, my tongue making it grow hard. It was going to be a long time before things were the way they were before. If they ever would be.

Sometimes he watched the way Marysza did things. Like she enjoyed everything, even the shit things. She went from scrubbing the floor on her hands and knees to taking a shower and making herself look pretty, then washing the baby in that little plastic tub, feeding him, dressing him and playing with him, then cooking dinner. When the baby fell asleep, she tucked all the blankets around him. Before she sat down on the couch next to Tadziu to talk or watch television, she washed the dishes or did some other thing that must have needed doing because she did it. She seemed to like everything, even working.

At night when she sat down, Tadziu held her hand. He had always known he was luckier than other guys.

She was the best thing I had. I didn't deserve her. I couldn't give her more than that dump. I figured she'd get tired of it all and leave me.

He remembered how each day at work he thought of how crummy his job was, that he was a bum, and his father was right.

One night he laid awake, unable to stop thinking about his job, how he watched the men on his floor, the men who worked next to him. Some of them didn't seem to mind the work. Others were too dumb to do anything else.

Tadziu hated the work, doing the same thing over and over, sweating his balls off in the summer when the only air they had came through one narrow door at the end of the floor. Some guys brought fans. He didn't. Because Marysza and he didn't have one.

Marysza had spoken to him that night from her side of the bed but he pretended to be asleep. He listened to the tac-tac of raindrops hitting the windows like some kid playing drums and kept thinking about his lousy job. When he felt the slow breathing that told him she was asleep, he got out of bed and walked to the crib. Just stood there. And looked.

Light came through the window as if the moon was right outside the glass, filling the crib in the corner of the room and making the skin on the kid's head look thin, so that Tadziu thought he could see the veins underneath. The kid slept on his stomach, wrapped in a blanket like some kind of papoose. The way the blanket raised and lowered itself must have been his breathing. His mouth was open and pressed into a small V against the sheet, his eyes tightly shut as if he was dreaming of another place and wasn't completely here yet. Marysza had folded the sleeves back from his hands because the pajamas, the gown, whatever it was, was too big. The hands made small fists that opened and closed so Tadziu saw all the fingers.

He remembered how startled he was when the kid moved and turned his head to the other side.

Jesus, I didn't think babies could turn their heads like that.

The kid moved his lips slightly and made a noise like a sigh. That small movement changed the look on the side of his face that Tadziu could see.

I wondered if the kid really looked like me or if people always said that.

A strange feeling had filled him and thinking of it now filled him again. He didn't know what the feeling was but it was okay. The kid sank back into sleep. Tadziu had walked out quietly and crept back into bed.

One night when Marysza went to the grocery store, he was supposed to watch the kid. He fell asleep in his chair in front of the television. The kid was screaming his head off when Marysza rushed in the door. She glared at him, as if he had committed murder. The kid was fine, just yelling in his basket. But Marysza wouldn't leave the kid again, Tadziu knew, not with his old man. He sat alone and drank beer the rest of the night. Marysza never came near him, only looked at him when she had to. Her voice was like acid.

Advice

"Hey Tadziu," his friend Jerry said to him back then on a Friday night. "how about comin' with us for a couple. Maybe play some pool. The old lady got the ball and chain too tight?"

Jerry was three or four years older than Tadziu. He'd been in the Marines toward the end of the Korean War, and seen combat. So nobody ever fooled with him. Listened to everything he said. But he never said much about the war, only "Hey, I got back, back to the wife and kids. My buddies weren't all so lucky." Then everyone got quiet and Jerry would change the subject to something you could laugh about

Everything about Jerry was oversized. His shoulders were bigger than a quarterback's. His head and face were big with heavy eyebrows, a large nose and a wide mouth jammed with big teeth that poked out like bricks that weren't laid straight. His hair stood out from his head like he was frightened. Tadziu always asked him if he'd lost a fight with a porcupine. What everyone liked best about him—something Tadziu thought maybe came from the war—was his easy friendliness, his willingness to concentrate on whatever you were saying, like you were important. Then he had that shit-eatin' grin that was always waiting for a reason to break out, a grin that didn't exactly come from happiness, but was a kind of spitting at all the shit in life that was comin' at you. He told awful jokes, jokes that made everyone groan just so he could laugh at himself and pretty soon everyone else was laughing too.

Jerry worked part-time on a construction crew besides his job in the factory. He was going to tell his boss about Tadziu as soon as he saw an opening. Then Tadziu could've worked two jobs and been able to take care of Marysza and the baby. There was nothing at that time but Jerry said something had to turn up sooner or later. He was a good friend. Smart too. He was the union steward and had plans to go back to school and study electronics on something called the G.I. Bill that he'd get because he'd been in Korea.

"Electronics. Tadz-boy. Television, radio!" he'd say, punching Tadziu playfully on the arm, "electronics is the way to go."

Tadziu knew if he went out with the guys, he'd have to listen to Jerry's electronics talk all night long. Jerry would try to convince him to go down to the community college and apply. Once Tadziu told Jerry he didn't have a high school diploma but that didn't shut him up.

"You can get one, man, I'm telling you. It's called a GED and they'll help you get it. All you have to do is go to some classes to get ready for the exam. I know guys who did it. It's not hard and even if you fail, you can take it again."

Tadziu got tired of listening. He had pushed away thoughts of going to school. He never liked school. He'd have to study. Other people there would know he wasn't smart. He would've had to do things he didn't feel like doing, things that scared him.

"I can't, Jer." He bet Jerry heard how hot and bothered he was when he added, "shut up already. I don't want to."

Jerry should've been talking to Marysza. She's the smart one, not me.

So Tadziu didn't go out with the guys that night.

"Naw, I don't feel like it", he said. He bought beer and drank at home.

After that Friday, he said "no" so many times the guys stopped asking him. No one seemed to notice but Jerry.

"Jeez, Tadz, jeez", he said, always punching him on the arm. "we miss you. The old lady must really be tough, huh?"

Tadziu missed going out with the guys, especially Jerry. But he couldn't listen to Jerry's talk, couldn't watch his face get excited about electronics anymore.

Some guys were just lucky. Lucky to be born smart.

Remembering Home Life

Tadziu remembered sitting at the table one Friday night, his six-pack already gone. But it was okay. He had two. And wondering where Marysza'd gone. Probably outside with the kid, walking him in that buggy her aunt and uncle bought. Marysza and Tadziu couldn't buy extra things like that. Not without giving up something else. Marysza kept telling him not to worry, that she'd figure out a way to go back to work soon.

I didn't know how the hell she was gonna do that. Without me helping with the kid, watching him when she worked. I didn't want to do that.

Marysza was still trying to teach him things. So he wouldn't let the kid holler like he did that time she was gone.

She brought the kid to him one night and put him into his arms. Tadziu could still see it.

I guess he was cute. Everyone said he was cute. He was okay when he wasn't yelling. I still didn't know what I'd do if he started his yelling again when Marysza wasn't there.

Tadziu put the kid over his shoulder, struggled to fit him there until it felt right and patted his back the way Marysza told him. The bundle made small movements on his chest, curled its arms and buried its head in him as if looking for safety. It felt sort of nice, like Marysza when she moved close to him at night.

A kid needed someone's protection all the time. I didn't know if I wanted to do it all the time. What if I dropped him?

He'd heard a noise in his ear. Marysza said it was a burp.

He'd brought the kid down slowly and put him back into Marysza's arms where he settled and looked right, like a screw that perfectly fit its threads. The kid was happier with Marysza, but holding him hadn't been too bad. If he hollered, Tadziu supposed he could've walked with him the way Marysza did, rocking him in his arms and singing silly songs. Once Tadziu had seen one of his married friends change his kid's diaper when the old lady was gone. He could see by the look on his face, by the way he tried to be casual, that the guy wasn't thrilled. Still, he didn't seem ashamed or nervous. Tadziu admired it but he never could've pictured himself in the guy's shoes.

The next Friday, Tadziu went out with his friends. He didn't want to hear any more wisecracks about his ball and chain.

"Holy shit. You got away, huh? What time you gotta be home?"

They punched him in the arm and slapped him on the back. They played pinball and pool, and drank. He probably drank the most, because Jerry said to him, "Hey take it easy, slow down." That had pissed Tadziu bad.

When Tadziu drank enough, he could almost forget his boyhood, could almost erase the memories of his father coming home after his work-day. But he could never forget the thing that wasn't really a memory but a feeling, a sinking into the blackness of terror, a dryness that suddenly crept into his throat so he couldn't swallow, could barely speak.

His father was a big man, so thick around that he looked like the trunk of a short but large tree. He had fat hands and fat fingers, wore overalls and heavy boots that clumped as he walked up the stairs to the flat so everyone knew he was coming. His small eyes peered out at the world from glasses with black frames and thick lenses. Black hairs protruded from the nostrils of his large nose, as if they'd jumped from his black mustache. Tadziu always thought his father's sloppy mustache hid the crumbs and scraps of old meals. He remembered how different it was at Marysza's grandmother's house, how everything had been so clean and orderly.

His father never talked much, except to yell orders or insults to Tadziu's mother. He never spoke to the kids, as if he didn't know they were there. Tadziu understood his father's Polish, remembered him telling Tadziu's mother that he didn't understand the difficulty of life in this country where everything was supposed to be so easy, all the while shouting at her as if she were personally responsible, blaming her for the five children who had to eat, who made his life so hard.

Once when the old man came home from work and was yelling at Tadziu's mother, he'd threatened to hit her. When Tadziu clenched his fists and raised them against his father, his father grabbed Tadziu by the back of his neck like a dog, pinching the skin between his fat fingers until Tadziu couldn't feel the pain any more, felt nothing except the room beginning to spin. The old man threw Tadziu into a corner of the kitchen where he landed against the rubber boots and the papers stacked there.

Tadziu stayed on the floor in the papers and the boots, pretending to be away from it all, vowing to himself that he'd find a way to leave, knowing he couldn't help his mother, knowing his sisters and his brothers would have to find their own way of leaving. His father's eyes had glared at Tadziu huddled in the corner, peered at him as if he couldn't see well, which he couldn't, Tadziu knew, so if he was still, his father would lose interest in him. Tadziu didn't move, made himself stiff and listened to the crying of his mother, his brothers and his sisters. Each day after his father came home, there'd always been crying in his house.

His mother never did anything, except come to him after his father was gone, reach down and stroke his head, brushing his hair back with the palm of her hand.

Mojego synka, [38] she would cry, with a voice like a feeble and broken bird, *mojego synka*, again and again while she continued to stroke his hair. That was all his mother ever did. That was all she could do. The day after that time, she told Tadziu it was one of God's commandments never to raise a hand against your father.

"Aw shit, Jer, leave me alone," he'd told his friend and pulled himself from thoughts of his old man. He was hung over all the next day, even had trouble driving Marysza and the baby to the doctor. She knew but she said nothing. It pissed him off more when she was quiet, when she didn't complain.

On weeknights, he used to spend his hours after supper watching television. And drinking. When he wasn't drinking, his mind worked constantly. Sometimes he felt like an overheated engine about to blow.

He remembered thinking of Jerry and how he went to class each night instead of sitting in front of the television. And thinking how shitty that would be. Going to a place where you didn't know anyone, where you'd have to find some office and let somebody know how dumb you were, that you didn't even graduate from high school. All the faces in the class would stare at you when you walked in and sat down.

I always hated being stared at. A lot of them would've been kids younger than me, real smartasses.

He remembered the turnaround—his thoughts stopping and changing, as if a hand had been raised to halt them. For a moment, he saw himself as a child with a child's fears.

So what if someone stared at him? So what if they were pissy smartasses? Hadn't he been one? Joining the kids who laughed so he wouldn't be the one laughed at. How could he stop being afraid? Maybe by just doing the thing. Going down to the goddamn school and seeing what he could find out.

In the next moment, he had brushed the thoughts away, like pesky bugs.

Who was I kidding? Why the hell did I think such dumb things? Who the hell wanted to go to school? Only wimps like Jerry.

Struggles

That thought had been trouble—the idea that he could do something about himself. He didn't want to struggle with it or try coming up with an answer. The only way he could forget the thought was by drinking.

It was only gonna be a couple beers, just enough to take the edge off his nerves.

Whenever he opened a beer, Marysza's face got that look he hated. He told her to relax, that he was only having a couple. He meant what he said but then he lost track. Marysza started to yap about his smoking, about the holes his ashes were making in the rug. He told her to leave him alone. He heard himself, knew what a shit-head he was. From the corner of his eye, he saw her changing and feeding the kid.

God, what a good mother she was. What a lousy father I was. I'd never be anything but a jackass, just like my father said.

The bottle he'd lifted to his mouth began its work. Things wouldn't be what they were. He wouldn't be stuck in a crummy job, wouldn't be a bad husband to the girl he loved, wouldn't be a crummy father, a father afraid to hold his kid. When the beer began to have its effect, he felt himself grow. He became a man who'd go back to school and learn something. Something that would get him a decent job. He'd buy Marysza and his kid all the nice things they wanted. He'd buy his mother nice things and take them to her. Things that would take the sad look from her eyes. He'd buy his sister something nice and send it to her. She was a good kid. A smart kid. Hell, they were from the same family. He must be smart too. Joe had told him he was smart when he used to shop for his mother.

"You a good kid," he'd say, in his funny English. "And a smart kid. Takin' care of yer mama and yer brothers and sisters like dat."

If he took nice things to his mother, he'd have to move her from that crummy place she lived in. Hell, he'd do that too. All he needed was a better job so he could earn more money than his ol' man ever did. The thought came back.

I'd do it. I'd go back to school. I was going to tell Jerry the next day.

The next day, he had a hangover. He laughed at what he'd thought the day before. It was only the beer talking. He was a jerk, a loser. Each time he got drunk, he hated himself more. Hopeless. Hopeless. Hopeless. .

"Marysza, Marysza," he said to her one night when he was drunk by eight o'clock, "get yourself outta this while you can. You're better off without me."

That scared her. He could tell. He laughed. It was easy to scare her. He wanted her to be scared, to be afraid of something happening to him. He wanted somebody to care if something happened to him.

Another night he sat watching the wrestling matches on television. Those guys were paid for what they were doing, for making assholes of themselves. Were paid a lot. He was an asshole too. Just didn't get paid for it. Marysza came up the stairs from outside with the baby.

"Oh Tadziu, it's such a beautiful night."

It was summer. He looked out the window. The sky held hundreds of stars. The broken glass in the alley behind their house reflected light from a window somewhere, making it seem like more than just broken glass, like diamonds or something. The way the night was pretty had excited Marysza.

"Let's go out on the porch with Jimmy."

She went out on the porch a lot. It was the only half-way decent thing about this place. After she cleaned it all up, scrubbed off years of dirt. Made it nice. She always made things nice. Didn't care how much work it took.

"Naw, I don't feel like it."

"C'mon Tadziu, please."

Then he had screamed. "I said no!"

She started backing away with that look in her eyes. That same look my mother always had. I'd hurt her again. God-damn-it, why'd she nag me so much? When I said no, it meant no.

He remembered how hard it'd been to stand, get up out of that damn chair and head for the door.

"Tadziu, don't drive,." she'd begged, a frightened look in her eyes.

"Marysza, don't you ever shut up?" he said, because something made him say it. He slammed the door behind him.

The next day he was filled with remorse. He remembered nothing about his drive. He put his arms around Marysza. She was quiet.

"I love you. You know it," he said. He buried his face in the front of her nightgown, felt the curve of her breast against his hand and ached. It wasn't just her body he craved, but all of her, her life, her thoughts, her existence, so he'd never be alone, so he could live, so he'd have a chance. He cried into her shoulder while she stroked his head.

"I'm no good, Marysza, I'm no good. Get yourself outta this."

"Yes you are, Tadziu. I love you."

He wanted to make love to her. Because of the booze, it wouldn't have done him any good but he could show her how much he cared, could show her he'd do anything she wanted. He'd felt her resistance, her drawing away.

"I'm tired Tadziu."

I didn't notice because I was too dumb. She'd lost weight. She was pale. I was hurting her. I told myself I'd never have a drink again. Other thoughts came, flew around my head, dug into my brain. That I couldn't stop. That thought went deeper than the one that said I could stop whenever I wanted. It made me afraid.

The next night he'd sat on the porch with Marysza. He remembered how the sun found a place in her hair. Just like it used to do with his mother. Then traveled to her arms and her shoulders, making the skin glow softly, sort of like the sky at the end of a summer day. Her breasts, separated by a small canyon, swelled on the front of her dress. He felt his sorrow like a huge stone he dragged behind him. The baby laughed as he approached. His sorrow became heavier, turned to dread. He wanted Marysza and the baby to be with him always. He didn't know how it would all end. Marysza looked at him, her eyes trembling like moving water. Tadziu realized she was afraid. Afraid of him. That made him angry.

I'd never hurt her, or the kid. She should've known that.

His anger was replaced by pain. He felt the fear he felt when he was a kid, when his father was about to come home, about to burst through the door, the way he became paralyzed, couldn't run, couldn't hide, could only stay rooted to the spot, waiting for what was coming. Until later, when he was accustomed to his life, when he learned how not to feel anymore, how to travel to different places in his mind. But he never travelled far enough, never knew how to stop the tears he didn't cry, the tears that stayed inside him. And Marysza felt that way about him. Was afraid of him. He remembered how he'd looked down at himself, expecting to see ugly growths covering his body and his skin.

He heard his father's words, heard his father's thoughts. That he would never be any good. He saw his mother's face. He remembered how he'd begun to cry.

"It's not true, mama", he said to her invisible presence, "I'm good. I'll stop. You know I'm good."

Marysza had been alarmed. He realized he was talking out loud and shut his mouth. He looked at the beer in his hand, walked from the porch to the kitchen sink and poured it down the drain. That was enough remembering for one night. The beer didn't work so good anymore, He didn't have anything to drink for the rest of the week.

Days passed. Tadziu remembered some and some were lost. One night he fell asleep in the chair. He didn't know what time it was when he awoke but Marysza and the baby were asleep in the bedroom. Two opened beer-bottles, half-gone, stood on the table next to him. A third one, empty, lay on the floor next to a damp circle on the rug. Empty six-packs were stacked next to his chair. He looked out the window. It was almost light. He knew what he'd see when he looked into the mirror. A bum. With bloodshot eyes and stringy hair, his clothes rumpled and dingy-looking.

God, the taste in my mouth was horrible. The room smelled like beer. Even after I took a shower and cleaned myself up. Marysza would probably never get that smell out of the rug, no matter how hard she scrubbed. I didn't want to get up. Just wanted to sit in my stink and punish myself. But what good would that've done? I'd only do it again. I thought I should die. I didn't want to die.

The thought of death made him think of what he always thought of when the wind howled and the snow fell–of cemeteries and how cold it must be beneath the ground.

How stupid. Dead people didn't feel anything.

But he was wrapped in cold, felt the chill of the grave. He looked out the window again. The light grew but he was immersed in blackness, held by hands that were choking him. He couldn't free himself. He'd begun to sob, great wracking sobs.

Light began to fill the room, the start of a day. From somewhere inside himself, he knew it could be a different day, a day that moved in a new direction. As light poured into the farthest corners of the room, he knew this. But he turned away. Light settled on the threadbare arms of the sofa, on the red linoleum in the kitchen, on all the things he couldn't stand to see. He turned away, chose to drown himself—in disgust at the way he'd lost himself in beer, chose to lose himself in thoughts of what a lousy husband and father he was. Some voice within him made him know that didn't have to be true. He wouldn't listen to the voice. He turned away.

Children Again

Now they were gone. Tadziu lived in his own apartment, if you could call it that. And had only memories. He laughed, tasted his bitterness and tried not to think. It was easy not to think about Jimmy. Marysza, he knew, thought about the kid enough for three people. But he couldn't stop thinking about her.

At work, when he did the monotonous operations of his job, he had to think of something. He filled his mind with thinking back to the first days he and Marysza lived together, before the baby was born and they were alone. He thought of how they hurried home from their jobs to work together on the flat, working until they couldn't work anymore, then falling into bed exhausted but never too exhausted for love, the way Tadziu had always known love with her would be—- joyful, like an arrival home after being lost and wandering aimlessly. But he remembered his fear that he couldn't absorb enough of her life before he was forced into sleep, the dread that she wouldn't be there when he awoke.

He thought about their night out, the Friday nights they went to the neighborhood bar for a fish fry and beer, a "date" that served as a prelude to their love-making at home. After Jimmy was born, they only went when Martha or Barbara could watch him because they couldn't afford a baby sitter. Once when they did hire a neighborhood kid, Marysza had to call home practically every five minutes and their "date" wasn't the same, was wasted and he felt robbed.

I complained about that but she never complained about anything, not about the stinkin' amount of money I earned, or that a lousy fish fry was our biggest night out. Not about the hard work we were doin' or the old furniture we had to take from her aunt and uncle and Martha's parents. Only about my drinking toward the end. Never about anything else.

He remembered how she moved over Jimmy, touching him in that way she had, that way of speaking her love with no words, only the movement of her hands and the lowering of her face to his.

Maybe my mother did that for me. Or Helcza. Maybe. But not the others. There wasn't enough life left in her for that. No life for cleaning the house, for making herself pretty, for anything. Only for crying, and holding me after my father beat me.

Tadziu sighed. His thoughts became more painful, a knife cutting into his skin. He remembered everything about those last days with Marysza. The last memories were the worst.

Snapping

He remembered his habit of cleaning up after he came home from work and how he combed his hair carefully, looking at it several times in the mirror before he was satisfied. His thoughts were always the same.

It's important. I gotta be different from the guys who remind me of my father. I laugh and swear with them all day. But I gotta clean up. The factory's hot and dirty. You get hot and dirty fast. I wash up as soon as I get home. Put on a clean shirt and pants.

His old man had always been dirty, never bothered to clean up after work, only to wash his hands a little before he ate. Tadziu never saw him comb his hair. The greasy hair had stuck together in patches, forming stiff clots that framed his face and stood out from his head like swamp grass.

Tadziu also combed his hair at work, depending on how hot it was and how much he perspired. So he remembered that on his last day with Marysza, the day she threw him out, he'd done all the ordinary things, at least at first, and all those things had come together in a kind of hurricane that picked him up and sucked him into its violence.

It was a very hot and sweaty day at the factory. He'd gone to the john to throw cold water on his face and comb his hair. When he was returning to his station, one of the guys began to taunt him. Separating his fingers with mock delicacy, the guy ran his hand through his hair, as if he were combing it, then tossed his head and twisted his body into an indecent pose.

"Sweetheart", and "darling", he sighed, as he fluttered his eyebrows and walked across the floor in a twisted dance that was meant to be feminine, but became something neither male nor female. Tadziu always knew this guy hated him. That day his disdain was open. Most of the other guys ignored him and turned back to their work, but a few laughed.

"Knock it off Charlie, "someone said, but Charlie, who was known in the plant as a troublemaker and an instigator, continued his crazy dance, trying to draw as many as he could into his audience.

"Oh my, ain't I pretty?" he jeered again and again, "oh my, ain't I Just so cute!"

Tadziu kept at his work and struggled to keep his hands from encircling the man's throat. Like a deadly acid, rage filled him. He felt his insides being dissolved, felt the pain of his own disappearance. His eyes and his ears burned. He no longer saw or heard the life before him. Like a film that had been halted, figures and objects had no motion or sound, stood suspended in time, trapped in a dream, a nightmare from which Tadziu couldn't awake.

When the guy saw he was no longer attracting attention, he came to Tadziu's station and stood there, curled his mouth into a final "sweetheart" and as if, like Tadziu's father, he couldn't see well, pushed his face into Tadziu's so closely that Tadziu felt the spit hit his eye. Tadziu felt himself transformed into a man driven by the need to destroy. He attacked Charlie with hate packed hard in his stomach, hit him again and again, like he would hit a rat that needed to be exterminated.

There was silence, a pause before his actions registered in astounded eyes, then men running, shouts of "What the hell you doin'? You nuts or somethin? and you stupid sonofabitch", all of which mingled and became one voice.

Tadziu remembered men pulling him, trying to restrain his arms. He felt one of his wild punches sail into someone's stomach and heard the guy yell "Jesus Christ", as he fell back. Two or three men took the fallen guy's place. Tadziu was pinned back, stood panting, trying to get air into lungs that had forgotten how to breathe. He saw Charlie on the floor beneath them, blood running from his nose, crying like a kid as two men tried to help him stand. One of the men looked at Tadziu and said, in an exasperated voice "for Chrissake", and sounding like a kid whining, "aw, now look what you've done."

That was the only reproach Tadziu received. He didn't know how, but the guys must have convinced the bosses of something. A while later, he was called to the office and told it better not happen again. Nothing ever came of it, except that Charlie was transferred to another department on another floor.

That night Marysza knew something was wrong. She asked Tadziu what was bothering him. He couldn't tell her.

"Poor Tadziu", she said, as if in mourning, sympathizing with him over whatever had hurt him. She tried to place her hand on his head. The look on her face reminded Tadziu of his mother, when she'd done nothing except cry and stroke his hair after his father was gone.

"Marysza, god-damn-it, don't bother me", he snarled, pouring himself another drink and reaching to adjust the television set he was pretending to watch. The baby began to cry in that helpless way his brothers and sisters had cried all the time. Marysza began to say something and he struck her, struck her because she didn't deserve to be struck, because she was quiet and suffered quietly like his mother, because he knew he did nothing for her, probably not even when they made love, because he was usually drunk. Marysza said nothing, only looked at him with large eyes. He pushed her away.

Now he wanted to close his mind, to drag a curtain across its screen but the thoughts wouldn't go away. He could never stand it—-all that goodness—-all that suffering. In a crazy way he loved Marysza more after she told him to get out. That's all he wanted his mother to do, to tell his old man to hit the road. Yet he was angry at Marysza for what she did to him, wanted her to be more like his mother. It was all too complicated for him to understand.

He wasn't big in the understanding department. He saw what she tried to do and wouldn't let it happen, didn't want it to happen. Some things pissed him off more than others. Like the way she kept pushing the kid at him. Trying to make a perfect little home.

Jesus. She didn't get it. I'm like my old man. Wouldn't recognize what was good for me if it hit me in the face. Kids are a pain in the ass to me. Not only cost money. They do other things too. Like take all their mother's time. Take her away from you. Really away. Because she didn't think of you first anymore. Jesus. I wonder if my old man felt that way. If he got jealous after I was born.

He was getting a headache, wasn't used to thinking this much. Thinking like a woman. They were always looking to see what was at the bottom or behind things. Always the reason. Could never see that things were just what they were. Maybe Charlie was right. He was turning into a queer. He laughed. Well, that was Marysza's fault. Trying so hard to understand her made him this way.

He'd never understand her. He didn't care. All he wanted was to be in her life. He thought of Jimmy's birth. She made him lose all sense, even when he saw her in that white hospital gown, made him want to take her again the way he had before the baby stopped it all. Instead he went home from the hospital and drank, tried not to admit how scared he was, how he knew, somewhere inside himself, that things were never going to be the way they were.

He always knew it wouldn't be long before he was out on his ass. But he wished it could have happened in a different way. Wished he had told her what was going on with him so she'd know it wasn't anything she'd done, wasn't anything she could do anything about. But he couldn't. Never knew how to say things in words. Only felt them like big dumb things eating away at his insides. So he said words he knew how to say. Like showing her he'd hit her again if she didn't give him the money. He was just like his old man, good at threatening. Then she called his bluff, said she would call the police, and it was over. He never tried going back. Knew he wouldn't make it if he told her he was going to quit drinking. Wouldn't make it if he tried to be a good father to Jimmy. Would never make anything of himself.

I miss the kid? How can I miss the kid? All that pulin' and bawlin'. Still, sometimes it was okay knowin' he was around.

I miss her bad. Feeling her head on my shoulder, the way it was when I climbed into bed at night, feeling like a homing pigeon returning after a long journey. Returning to where I belonged.

But this is the way I always knew it would be. She'll make it. Her and the kid will be fine without me. I live in a flophouse but I don't have any money to send her. I must be spending it somewhere but I sure as hell don't know where. I can't be drinking that much booze, can I? I don't know how she did it, how she paid all the bills. I wonder if she's happy with me gone? If her days are quiet, if they move slow? Mine are quiet and ugly, never move enough to make a difference, never change, just sit like the mud beneath a still pond. I go from the factory to my room and back again. With my beer. They don't care what you do in the place I live in. Just take your money and ask no questions. No one cares. Maybe Jerry but he's a pain in the ass. Never shuts up. Always tellin' me to watch my drinking." Let him watch his own ass. I don't need him. Or any-one else. They all screw you in one way or another. What's she anyway besides a crack between the legs? Not hard to find another one. Okay, that's a dumb thought, you dumb ass.

In a kind of crazy fight, the thoughts in his head became pictures, and the pictures became thoughts until they turned into each other and couldn't be separated. He saw himself going to the hospital the day Jimmy was born and remembered how he didn't know what he was supposed to wear so he played it safe and wore his suit from the wedding with the white shirt and the tie. He'd show her he wasn't completely dumb, that he knew she had done something important. He sat and talked with her most of the time he was there and they let him stay longer because he was her husband. No one else was allowed to visit yet. Her aunt and Barbara and Martha would probably be there the next day. They kept you in the hospital about ten days.

Children Again

She'd looked like a little kid in the hospital bed, small and pale, covered in white up to her chin, dressed in a white hospital gown, and holding the baby wrapped tightly in a white blanket like a hot dog. He remembered that whiteness exploding like a flash-bulb and carrying him back to their childhood.

To the third grade when they made their first Holy Communion and she was dressed in a flowery white dress covered with ruffles. All the girls wore veils like they were getting married. He remembered he wore a white suit that someone had given his mother for him. It was tight and the sleeves too short so they rubbed against his skin and he had to keep pulling at them all through the Mass. When they knelt at the altar rail he kept looking back to see Marysza and that got him in trouble with Sister. She told his mother and his mother cried because Tadziu didn't behave in church but she never told his father. That was one thing he could say. His mother never told his father anything he did in school and she sure as hell got plenty of complaints from the sisters. His old man never cared about church anyway but it would've given him a good excuse to beat Tadziu.

The kids marched into Church before the First Communion mass like a white army and walked in a procession through all the aisles and all around the church. They even went before the priest and the altar boys who walked at the priest's side swinging their long chains with the things like gold balls on the end that sister said was a sen-ser.[39] The air in the church became filled with the sweet-smelling smoke, called in-sens that came from the balls. One of the altar boys tripped over the black gown he was wearing and almost fell. The boy's job was to go before the priest and kind of announce him, Tadziu guessed, as he thought back, by swinging the sen-ser.

The priest wore a huge fancy cape with a smaller cape around his shoulders that was long enough for him to wrap around his hands so he didn't touch the round gold house that held Jesus and make it less holy. The gold house had rays like the sun and a handle so the priest could carry it. And right in the center was a round glass that Tadziu always thought, when he was a boy before he knew better, must be a window for Jesus to look through. When he marched in procession, the thought of the window did make him think twice before he did anything he wasn't supposed to do.

When they came back from the altar rail with Jesus in their mouths, Sister told them they should keep their head down and their eyes closed for at least five minutes. Tadziu talked to Jesus about all the things he could, mostly asking him to help his mother get better and change his father so he'd leave him alone. He didn't know when five minutes was up because he didn't have a watch. He saw the other boys didn't know either because they were peeking through their hands or smiling at each other. The girls were the only ones who didn't cheat but Tadziu remembered looking through his fingers one time and seeing Marysza looking back at him. She closed her eyes again fast but he knew she cheated and later he threatened to tell sister. She just laughed and told him he was lying. She knew he'd never tell on her.

They had to wear their white Holy Communion outfits each time there were processions in Church for big holidays like Easter when Jesus came up from the dead. Tadziu remembered thinking he was kind of glad he wasn't there because it could've been a little spooky, even though the Roman soldiers deserved it. He also remembered his suit was tighter each time he wore it.

Easter was even whiter than First Holy Communion, the altar a mountain of Easter lilies with petals like white arms. Each kid carried his own lily in a pot as he walked in the procession. Some of the boys' Holy Communion suits and the girls' dresses already had smudges of dirt. Tadziu's had a lot. Communion clothes were not the kind of clothes your mother could wash and it was expensive to take them to the place where they were cleaned. Tadziu had wanted to throw his away anyway.

The priest's white was very clean. Tadziu had always thought he looked like a king, with his big white cape swishing around and the smaller cape on top making big folds on his chest and his arms. All the priest's white had some kind of gold thread in it somewhere. Tadziu remembered how all the white stood against the blackness outside the windows and how sometimes everything began to swim in his head. Because he was always tired. The procession Mass was the first Easter Mass and was at six o'clock in the morning. Sister told the kids they had to be there by quarter to six and Tadziu's mother always got him up at five o'clock.

But once he was in church, Marysza always woke him up. At Easter, it was easy for Tadziu to exchange glances with her. All the people stood and sang as the priest, the altar boys and the children marched through the church so no one paid any attention to him. The church was always cold and Tadziu remembered that one year after the procession was over and all the children knelt at the altar rail before returning to their seats, a woman left her seat, went to the railing and put one of those knitted shawls around Marysza's shoulders. He laughed now as he remembered thinking that he was cold too but boys didn't get scarves around their shoulders. His arms were in a stupid suit so everyone thought he was warm.

Memories brought on by thinking of Marysza in the hospital in her white gown. They make me smile, even laugh. I forget the pain of my aloneness, think that somehow it might change, that somehow I might change.

Another memory entered and overthrew the others. Tadziu remembered how Jerry and the guys came over that night the baby was born, Jerry with a box of cigars and a bottle of whiskey. They kept slapping Tadziu on the back and asking him how it felt to have a son. He kept drinking because he couldn't answer, couldn't tell them he didn't know but if he had to guess, he didn't like it. And of course Jerry wouldn't shut up, kept talking about his boys and the things they could already do. The oldest one was going to kindergarten in the fall. Jerry had choked up, just talking about it, how it was just yesterday the kid had been born and now he was going to school. Tadziu remembered how he felt listening to Jerry. He remembered his thoughts.

Shut up, Jer. Shut up. I don't care about your boys. I don't care about mine. Can't you see something's wrong, wrong with me? I'm not like you.

He wanted to throw them all out, wanted to be left alone, but he kept quiet. By the time they left he was drunk enough to fall into bed and shut it all out.

Tadziu remembered that night as if it were yesterday.

And I'm not changed. I'll never change.

The smiling and the laughter were gone. Once again, he was alone. He threw a cigarette butt against the wall and laid his head into his arms. He could see spots of dried food on the table. He could hear the ticking of the huge brown clock that must have once hung in a school or a bank. It was the first thing he'd seen when the landlord showed him the place. It was the first thing that greeted him when he walked into the door each day.

All the memories were gone. There was only the ticking of the clock.

Chapter Five

1958

Public Assistance

Marysza sat in the waiting room holding Jimmy. She saw rows of wooden chairs joined at the backs, their armrests faded and worn into hollows, their empty seats holding discarded newspapers and magazines. Smoke streamed up to large windows plastered shut by years of paint. Metal ash trays stood in the aisles, their overflow littering the floor and saturating the air.

Marysza wanted to run home, to sit at her kitchen table with Martha.

I can't believe I'm here. How did this happen? There are other women, none dressed well, some with babies. My jeans have a hole beginning to wear through the knee. I fit right in.

She saw clients who wore better, more fashionable clothes. A woman who had skin the color of chestnuts and deep auburn hair wore tall leather boots and tight jeans. Head high, she walked like a sleek horse, buttocks trembling as she took long strides from her chair to the ladies' room and back. Several men turned to look but most sat with their arms folded and their eyes cast down. A woman with a small boy and girl tried to keep them quiet but like children on a holiday they ran through empty rows of chairs playing games. Some people smiled at their antics with tolerance. Others showed irritation and glared at the children's mother.

"I'll get you," the boy hollered at the girl whose face was a mirror-image of his own. The girl squealed and ran, turning periodically to hurl threats of "I'm gonna tell on you." Marysza wanted to laugh but the children's happiness seemed unreal, a thing apart from herself and unfitting in this atmosphere heavy with despair. She looked around at people who were not people, but shadows.

I have the same look. I'm becoming part of an army. We wear the same uniform.

A Member of the Club

In the ladies' room, Marysza looked in the mirror. She wore no lipstick and her hair was gathered into a pony tail fastened with a wide rubber band. Her pale face apologized for her life, for herself. She thought of her days of happiness, the days at her grandmother's house, when she had existed in another world. She thought of Tadziu, knew he would suffer, and felt guilty for leaving him. Along with the guilt existed a feeling of freedom, and the hope that she would be a person again, a different person, she knew, but one who would feel again the power she had felt as a child in her grandmother's house.

What crazy thoughts. I'm sitting here in this office, in the bottom of the barrel, thinking I can climb out. Not just climb out, but climb out and be someone, do something, be myself again.

She looked down at the bundle in her arms, and, in the instant of her seeing knew it was nonsense to feel guilt over leaving Tadziu. She had acted for the baby and herself. There was nothing else she could have done. She lifted her eyes, looked at the children making the racket, and tried to smile.

A Meeting

At the front of the waiting room, an attractively-dressed black woman stood behind a desk that resembled a podium. Marysza rose when the woman called the name "Jargosz". The woman motioned for Marysza to follow, walked through the swinging doors down a long corridor, the click of her heels muffled by the rubber floor, entered an office and stopped at the desk of a harassed looking middle-aged woman. The woman peered at Marysza through spectacles attached to the collar of her flowered dress by a long gold chain.

"Marysza Jargosz," the woman said, glaring at the new set of papers the other woman dropped onto the mountain of papers on the desk. The black woman smiled and left. For a moment, Marysza wanted to call her back. Beneath the mountain, she could see a small black nameplate bearing the name, "*Mrs. Hoggenkamp*".

"Yes," she replied.

"And a child, James, your son, three months old," the woman continued, without raising her head, Marysza nodded, then murmured "yes."

"Do you have identification?"

As the woman checked boxes on the papers before her, Marysza held out the social security card she had been instructed to bring when she called on the phone, then took the card back when the woman didn't reach for it.

"You reside at 54 Harvest St. with your son"?

Marysza nodded.

"Does anyone else reside there, anyone who contributes to the support of the household?

"No. Not anymore." Mrs. Hoggenkamp continued her writing as if she didn't hear this, didn't want to lift her head or look at the person before her. The baby began to whimper but Mrs. Hoggenkamp ignored it. Marysza began rocking him in her arms.

"May I see your social security card please. And the baby's birth certificate." These were not questions, but statements, tired commands. Marysza took the card out again.

"Now Ms. Jargosz, you are aware that your eligibility for public assistance is contingent upon your enrollment in a job-training program, that is, upon your willingness to take a job if the county finds one for you." Marysza nodded yes to each question. Like the impact of a bullet came a sudden boldness, then embarrassment at what she heard herself saying.

"Miss uh Mrs. Hoggenkamp, I just left my husband, I mean made him leave me and I wouldn't be here if it weren't for Jimmy."

Mrs. Hoggenkamp lifted her head for the first time, peered from behind the spectacles that now perched atop her head. Saying nothing, she continued her questions. Part of Marysza feared Mrs. Hoggenkamp and recognized her position of power. Another part of her disliked the woman because she didn't lift her eyes, because she didn't see Marysza when she did lift them.

"Do you own a car?"

She continued to write, her face once again buried in her papers. Marysza replied that she owned a 1956 Chevrolet that Tadziu had left behind, knowing, as she answered, that Tadziu had left the car because that was all he had, all he could give her. Mrs. Hoggenkamp took a blue book from somewhere beneath her papers and leafed through its pages.

"The market value of that is below the line," she said to herself, and then to Marysza. "You won't have to sell it."

I don't know whether to be grateful. I didn't know I might have to sell the car. I don't know anything about this process. I only know that the baby and I have no money, no way to pay bills or buy food.

After Tadziu left, Martha had helped Marysza, staying with Jimmy as much as she could while Marysza waited on tables, but it didn't work. Marysza couldn't work enough hours. It was difficult to coordinate her work schedule with Martha's and impossible to design one that allowed her to nurse Jimmy. She waited as long as she could before coming here but as the days passed, her panic grew and she gave up.

Looking at Mrs. Hoggenkamp, Marysza felt as if she were suffocating. The feeling of optimism she had felt in the waiting room vanished. She felt her face burn with the shame of being here, shame at her helplessness. Shame and helplessness fed her growing resentment. She turned her eyes away from Mrs. Hoggenkamp and concentrated on the framed pictures she saw on the bookshelf behind her. She could make out the picture of a girl and a boy in their teens, then the girl at an older age, wearing a cap and gown. A college graduation perhaps.

Marysza felt the stir of envy, not because college was something she had never thought of, but because it was so far beyond her reach. Envy turned her resentment into anger.

I could do as well as anyone. I know I could. I didn't have their chances.

If Mrs. Hoggenkamp saw her staring at the picture, she said nothing.

Marysza thought of the first school days she could remember, carefree days when she lived with her grandmother. She saw herself rushing off the school bus with the other kids, stopping on the way home, throwing her schoolbag to the ground so she could play hopscotch on squares drawn in colored chalk on the sidewalk. She saw Martha and herself talking each day about the things they wished for, the things they wanted to be someday. She heard herself saying she wanted to be a movie star, heard Martha saying, "Oh you will. You're so pretty," then thought of the last grade she had spent at her old school before her grandmother's death, of Sister telling her how well she read, singling her out from the other girls and boys and asking her, Marysza, to read aloud.

She remembered her favorite dress—the blue and red plaid with the white yoke—that her grandmother bought at Woolworth's downtown and washed in the sink each night so Marysza could wear it as often as she liked. She wore the dress the day she read in class, the day she told Martha she wanted to go to college.

Mrs. Hoggenkamp interrupted her thoughts.

"Now Mrs. Jargosz, you will be eligible for a subsistence allowance of one hundred dollars per month for you and your son. That includes rent and utilities. Of course, you're also eligible to apply for food stamps." She said these words without expression, hastily, as if she said them a hundred times a day. Her large bosom heaved with a sigh expressing tenuous regret for the small allowance she was telling Marysza she would receive but there was nothing she could do. Marysza understood that this faint sympathy was meant to ward off any comments.

She hadn't expected it would be this bad, the money so little. She chewed at the inside of her cheek and looked again at the name plate on Mrs. Hoggenkamp's desk.

"How do I apply for food stamps, Mrs. Uh…Mrs. Hoggenkamp?"

"I can make an appointment for you on the thirteenth.

The thirteenth was two weeks away. Marysza was not sure she had enough food at home until then.

"Please," she began, then stopped her question in midair, frightened by the rush of anger she felt.

How can I manage on so little? Nobody can live on that.

Mrs. Hoggenkamp stared at the wall as she handed Marysza a pen.

"Sign here please."

Marysza was quiet. The baby started to fuss and like an automatic machine, Marysza resumed rocking him in her arms. Mrs. Hoggenkamp looked over the papers she had filled out and threw them into the pile on the side of her desk. She stared at the girl who sat before her. Marysza felt her scorn, saw the thoughts mirrored in Mrs. Hogenkamp's face, felt them burning a hole in her consciousness. The thoughts hardened into a question Marysza could almost read in Mrs. Hoggenkamp's eyes.

What gives these people the right to present their problems, self-made problems, to someone else and expect them to be solved?

But Marysza couldn't read Mrs. Hoggenkamp's other thoughts, couldn't know that she floated in a sea of indecision.

It's been so long since I can recall having the instinct I have at this moment. There's something different about this girl. I don't know what it is. Still, every single one of them is diifferent. Each has their own story to tell. This girl has the same signs in her face that marks them all —-depression, loss of hope, feelings that make her look straight ahead as if she's afraid to look either way. But the girl has an innocence, not only surprise at the disappearance of her foolish dreams, but the belief that she must and would help herself if she knew how. Perhaps I should examine the case again. Perhaps this is one of those rare clients for whom the effort would not be wasted.

"Mrs. Jargosz," she said, as Marysza got up to leave, holding Jimmy tightly in her arms, "there are two emergency programs which will get you food vouchers for the baby immediately. Take this slip and go to Room 116. Tell the girl at the desk that Mrs. Hoggenkamp has your case." And then, "I'd give some thought to changing my name to Mary."

Marysza's anger began to burn again but it was transformed into gratitude. She turned to say something to the woman. behind her, the woman whose manner was so ambiguous but, as if she had no more time to spare, Mrs. Hoggenkamp waved her away. Marysza mumbled as quick and fervent a "thank you" as she could before leaving the room. She also whispered a fervent "thank you" to God. She would be able to get food for Jimmy.

The New Reality

Marysza came home. The house was cold and she knew the pilot in the furnace had gone out. The landlord said he would be there as soon as possible. She wrapped Jimmy in as many blankets as she could find and wore her coat. The landlord didn't come until the next day. She told him there had been no heat all night. He was terse.

"I'm sorry, lady," he said, looking at her in a way that made her feel naked and exposed, so that she wanted to run and hide, " but I kin only answer one call at a time."

She wanted to tell him there was a baby here and heat was more important to them, but she did not have the courage and he continued in an even voice, telling her that every person had a complaint and he was doing the best he could. She thought of how Tadziu would have yelled at the landlord last night and the landlord would have yelled back in the way that men had of dealing with each other. But after the yelling, they would have had heat. And he wouldn't dare look at her in the way he did now if Tadziu were in the room. But Tadziu was gone

The man revolted her, with his unwashed hands, his filthy clothes and the odor of old perspiration that enveloped him. She remembered Tadziu's cleanliness, how he had showered the minute he came home from work. How he protected her from whatever was vile, because he thought she was refined and he cherished that in her.

It doesn't matter what good things I remember. I'm alone. Afraid in the apartment with Jimmy at night. I check the locks. An empty bed waits. No one holds me. Pictures of our childhood, our meeting again at The Pier, our marriage, our short life together, roll before me like a movie, one that plays over and over, filling my days and haunting my dreams. But the pictures have lost their color. I'm absorbed in gray, non-color, non-life.

In the weeks that followed, Marysza's despair grew, tightening itself like fingers around her throat. She lost that ability she'd inherited from her grandmother to find happiness in the things she must do, to feel the value of work, the innate and characteristic joy that lay in the most ordinary tasks. Now nothing seemed worth doing. Only thoughts of Jimmy could lift her from the darkness where she lived and force her to do essential chores.

Anger

Martha repeated words she had spoken more times than Marysza cared to remember.

"Geez, Marysza, you look terrible. You gotta snap out of this. The guy wasn't worth it."

Marysza couldn't admit this was true—-that Tadziu "wasn't worth it" and clung to whatever good she could find in her memory of their life together.

She was ruled by contradiction and blamed herself for failing to think clearly. The grain of happiness for the freedom she now possessed struggled with her picture of that last scene with Tadziu. Perhaps if she had done this or that, had not done this or that, things would have turned out differently. When she voiced these thoughts to Martha, her friend became impatient.

"That's bullshit, Marysza, plain bullshit. You did the best you could. It didn't work. Forget it."

Marysza knew that Martha was right but she didn't have the ability to let things go, to peel dead things from herself like old skin. She'd left Tadziu. But mourned ever since. So that she had never left at all. She didn't admit this to her friend, instead became angry with her for being right, and heard her own voice filling with sarcasm, as she retorted—helplessly, she later told herself, and unable to stop the words—"I can't just forget it!" At Martha, whom she was hurting for some reason she didn't understand.

She tried to explain her behavior. Truth stood at the fringes of her consciousness and came to her in pieces.

Martha, the friend I've always loved, who has always loved me. I'm no longer sure of myself, will never be sure in the way I was as a child, in the way I was before my marriage to Tadziu. But I'm sure of Martha, of her always loving me.

She saw that in some terribly convoluted way, she blamed Martha for her failure at the same time that she feared the loss of their friendship.

I'm using Martha, who loves me, as the target of my anger, the anger I feel toward myself, the failure I've turned out to be.

As it happened in the story of the blind man in the Gospel— a story her grandmother had told again and again when Marysza was a child and begged long enough, the story in which her grandmother became dramatic, reaching out her hands, looking up to heaven and telling how the blind man cried out with joy, "I can see. I can see!" so that Marysza, holding her breath, saw through the blind man's eyes as the world exploded into color and light, so now did a revelation come to Marysza, and she saw that in order to love Martha or anyone, she must first love herself. She saw that love toward one's self and others demanded forgiveness, always forgiveness, that without forgiveness, life could not proceed. She saw that in order to free herself, she had to leave the past, forgive Tadziu and forgive herself.

As clearly as she saw, she then refused to see, turning away from her thoughts as if they were obscene pictures.

I can't, I can't. I'll never forgive myself or him.

She held her hands to her head, covered her eyes and walked to the cupboard for the bottle of aspirin, in an automatic exercise, ran the water and tested it with her finger for coldness, not dead to feeling, and seeing, seeing, all the while seeing what she didn't want to see, coming face to face with her own unwillingness to see. Despite the clarity of her thoughts and her certainty of their truth, once again she pushed them away, allowed them to escape, and knew she wanted them to escape, to be forgotten.

I'm tired of thinking. None of this matters. Martha has always been here. Martha will always be here.

Another Meeting

On her next visit to the welfare building to get her food stamps, Marysza sat next to a young woman her own age who was there to be re-certified, which Marysza knew, from Mrs. Hoggenkamp, she would also have to do every three months. The young woman resembled any one of a hundred others except for her eyes, eyes that made Marysza think of Spanish dancers, senoritas with luminous blue-black hair hiding their faces behind fans. A child wearing a thin blue cotton dress and white sandals with no socks stood next to the young woman, quietly sucking her thumb. The woman began talking and Marysza listened as words rushed from her like water from a dam that had suddenly burst.

Her name was Nancy. She told Marysza she'd dropped out of school to live with her boyfriend who didn't work but hung around with other guys he brought home to drink beer and play cards. Nancy couldn't keep up with working and cleaning up their mess. She worried about leaving her daughter with them and when one of the guys tried to "hit on" her, she found the strength to throw them all out.

"I'll tell ya, Marysza, I was scared to do it. I didn't know if he'd leave even though I paid the rent, or if he'd hit me or something. He wasn't happy with me, I'll tell ya. I thought about it and thought about it. Things got worse all the time. Finally, I just did it." Nancy's hands shook as she lit a cigarette. "I have no regrets. I should've done it sooner. The S.O.B. promised me all kinds of things. A house. A car. I believed that shit."

She laughed a bitter laugh, then her black pupils grew larger, filled with what Marysza at first thought was fear, then recognized as sadness.

"My Ma can't do any work any more, can't watch Jennie. So I gotta get this welfare. Hopefully not for long."

Marysza turned the pages of a book Nancy had brought for Jennie

Nancy's embarrassed. Doesn't want to be here. I don't know why that makes me feel better but it does.

"My story's similar."

Surprising herself, she told Nancy about her life with Tadziu, that he **had** hit her and that was why she finally left him, and surprised again, saw that the talking helped, that it gave her comfort .

Maybe Martha's right. Maybe Tadziu isn't any good.

Nancy knew about some of the other clients waiting to be re-certified. Hilda, a middle-aged woman whose husband had died without insurance, who'd never worked and was not old enough to collect Social Security. Hilda had a deeply-lined face and stooped shoulders like a nest into which she seemed to draw herself. Ed, a younger man who leaned on a cane although he seemed able to walk without it.

"He claims he can't work." Nancy jeered, but Social Security seems to think he can."

The man smiled and waved to Nancy, then turned solemn, as if suddenly struck by pain. Nancy didn't bother to wave back. She motioned toward a woman who sat in a corner crying softly and wiping her face with a crumpled Kleenex she clutched in her hand. Marysza couldn't see the woman's face because she looked only at the wall, never turned her head to see or speak to anyone.

"She has a husband and a family," Nancy said with sympathy, "and a nice home," emphasizing the word "nice". She told Marysza she overheard the woman in the caseworker's office. Her husband was a salesman who worked on some kind of commission basis. She thought their life was fine but her husband had not been doing well and was drawing something called "advances" from the company so they could pay their bills. When the company refused to issue him any more, the woman found out. There was nothing to live on and they were greatly in debt. The woman would have to sell her home, and take her children from the private schools they attended. Nancy heard her tell the caseworker she couldn't look for a job. "All she does is cry." Nancy said. "She wouldn't even talk when I went and asked her if I could help."

There were others whose stories Nancy only knew from what other clients had told her—-those who were alcoholics or drug addicts or had mental problems, people no one would hire even if they wanted to work. In a kind of crazy circle, the employment service sent them here because they were considered unemployable but they had to return to the employment office regularly to be pronounced unemployable in order for their welfare benefits to continue.

Nancy looked at Marysza with despair in her eyes. "I don't know," she said. "Maybe he'll change. Maybe we can get back together", then looked away, as if she knew she was slipping into something bad. Marysza knew she was guilty of wishing the same thing about Tadziu but she forced herself to turn and stand away, to see Nancy and the other clients through Mrs. Hoggenkamp's eyes.

This is crazy. It's useless to feel sorry for these people. They don't know they have to help themselves. I'm different. Somehow, I'll climb out of this mess. I'll find a way out.

The System

Marysza didn't see Nancy after that. She thought of Nancy doing the same thing she was, kept busy trying to comply with all the rules of "the Department", Nancy's term for the Social Services Unit. Marysza was required to submit a certain number of job applications each week. The process depressed her.

I go to factories, other places for the unskilled, climb dreary stairs, ride old elevators and hunt for personnel offices. Then I lie. I ask for applications, fill them out and hand them in. I don't want them to have any jobs, breathe a sigh of relief when they say they have no openings and ask them to sign a card saying I've been there, so I can take the card back to the welfare office. The personnel people sign the cards without looking at me. Some are curt, act contemptuous. I don't blame then. I have contempt for myself. I'm wasting their time. They know how the system works. Now I know too.

This empty exercise spoke of her inadequacy, of how unprepared she was to take care of Jimmy and herself. There were no jobs for which she qualified except factory jobs and those frightened her. She remembered what Tadziu had been like when he came home. Other low skill jobs would not pay enough for them to survive. Except for a small amount designed to act as an incentive, any money she did earn would be deducted from her welfare check. Even if they located Tadziu and forced him to pay child support, which was unlikely, that money would also be deducted from her check.

If she worked, her financial situation wouldn't improve much and she'd have to take Jimmy to day care, sometimes very early in the morning. Jimmy was less than six months old and still nursing. The welfare department would pay for child-care as soon as she went to work, but could offer no help in locating what they termed a "provider". Mrs. Hoggenkamp gave her a list of day-care centers the social service department would subsidize. Marysza could visit these and choose. The two Marysza tried were filled to capacity and not taking any more children. She was glad.

Her thoughts ran in circles. Sometimes she thought the best plan was to wait until Jimmy was old enough to begin school. Then she wouldn't have to worry about paying someone to watch him and could perhaps survive on the money she was able to make. But that was a long time away and Marysza wasn't sure she could exist in this system for that long, that something in her might not die if she did. She needed further training, more education in order to get a better job but she didn't know how to accomplish that.

In her next visit to the welfare office, she asked. Mrs. Hoggenkamp told her there were no vocational training programs at the present time but that she would refer her to a program which provided training in job skills. Marysza was indignant.

I don't need that. I know how to report to a job on time, how to do what I have to do. Mrs. Hoggenkamp is trying to keep me quiet, so she can forget me.

She told Mrs. Hoggenkamp the program was not for her. Mrs. Hoggenkamp raised her eyebrows. The eyes behind her glasses looked at something on the wall behind Marysza.

"You know, Mrs. Jargosz, you are endangering your grant by not cooperating with the intent of the department. You must either accept employment, or enter into a program to prepare yourself for employment." Marysza felt her stomach knot itself into a ball.

Does she enjoy this, this woman who brushes me aside like a fly that irritates her? The look on her face tells me that I'm not worth her time, that I'm lazy.

She knew she was defeated. She murmured that she'd comply, she'd attend the job skills program.

Unsolicited Advice

When she came out of the room, a girl with fiery red hair and two missing front teeth said loudly, "Don't let the old bag scare you honey. They can't do nothin' while you have a baby, while you nursin'." Another girl laughed raucously.

"Yeh, that's why so many big babies are still nursin'."

Marysza felt her dismay sharply, in that moment, saw before her, the contents of Mrs. Hoggenkamp's days.

Why are they cruel? I hope she didn't hear. Not so much the nursing remark but the" old bag" remark. I think she heard. Who are these people? Different from Nancy and the others. Not despairing. Hating. She turned away, hurrying past what she wished she hadn't heard, filled with the desire to separate herself from these women, to find a way to show

Mrs. Hoggenkamp wasn't lazy. The familiar merry- go-round of her thoughts returned.

Being lazy is a part of what's happening to me. The world knows I'm lazy, that I've failed. I feel it each time I walk into these offices, each time I walk out. Mrs. Hogenkamp will never see me, will always look straight past me. I'm of no importance to her, of no importance to anyone.

She wanted to throw her thoughts against the wall like something hard and watch them shatter into thousands of pieces, wanted to remember, to regain whom she had been.

I am Marysza, my grandmother's Marysza.

When she looked down at her worn sneakers, at the socks that were losing their color from so many washings, when she looked at her face in the hallway mirror as she left, she saw that something in her eyes was gone. Neither sorrow nor anger could bring it back.

Friction between Friends

Marysza's behavior confused her more each day, as if she had no control over her actions, as if they came from a stranger who lived inside her. She felt a growing tension between herself and Martha, remembered her anger when Martha told her to forget Tadziu. Now, Martha was often impatient with her. As she was today, Marysza knew, from a certain abrupt tone in her usual cheerfulness, from the way she spoke carefully, as if it were an effort. Marysza felt the cold at her neck, like an icy hand.

I'm afraid, afraid of losing Martha, of losing the only friend I have.

Martha reached for Jimmy, took him into her arms, and began to make sounds and words that belonged to no language at all.

"Oh, how is him today?" then as the baby yawned, "is him tired, the little sweet-ums?"

Marysza began to laugh at the absurdity of Martha's talk. Martha looked at her and laughed also. Their laughter broke the ice in the air, cracked it into a thousand pieces.

Abruptly, without warning, without thinking, Marysza snatched Jimmy back and felt the ice inside herself return.

He belongs to me. I've done something she can't deny, no one can deny is good. She's jealous.

She looked at Martha silently.

I won't say she's right. I always end by feeling she's right, telling myself she's right.

Knowing it was a futile gesture, she asked Martha if she wanted coffee and in Martha's refusal, felt her friend pull away, felt, like the ripping of flesh, Martha separating herself from her, and because of her, from Jimmy.

"I can't stay," Martha said, pretending to look at her watch so she could avoid looking into Marysza's eyes. And Marysza responded "okay" because she didn't want to reveal her resentment, resentment that was growing, she suddenly knew, because she no longer felt superior, because in some way she didn't understand, Martha had something she didn't.

Something has changed between us. I no longer stand in the place I stood. She wants it this way. Wants me to feel that I'm foolish. And that she isn't.

Marysza held Jimmy's hand to her mouth and kissed it so that Martha could see.

Rock Bottom

Marysza went to bed struggling with the thought of her behavior toward Martha, with the certainty that she'd hurt her best friend, then rose and walked into the kitchen to sit at the table, pulling at the strings on the edge of the tablecloth as images and thoughts filled her mind,. Martha, Jimmy, her life, Tadziu—all became entangled, inseparable.

I'm not responsible for any of it. It all just happened.

She looked around the kitchen, the kitchen that she and Tadziu had painted, saw that their efforts had been like putting makeup on a deteriorating face. She saw tile that had long ago lost its shine, that was ripped in spots so that black rubber or bare wood showed, windows that didn't meet their sashes, rattled in the winter and one so tilted it couldn't close at all.

We didn't even make a dent in the ugliness, only made things clean and livable. If Tadziu were here, at least the sash would be fixed.

She looked into the living room at the couch, the arms worn to a smoothness she tried to hide by covering them with white doilies. Her eyes travelled over wallpaper that no longer had a recognizable color and was coming loose at all the corners. In one glance she saw her own attempts to make the flat prettier: the lace curtains at the kitchen windows, the live flowers on a table in the living room, flowers she could not afford but bought at the supermarket anyway, and the imitation milk-glass vase which held them. As she looked at them, these attempts, which now seemed pitiful, stared back and mocked her efforts.

She longed for more, so much more. It was not the lack of possessions which hung in the air like gray smoke and caused her despair, but the longing, the need, to be in contact with beauty, with things in her everyday life which could take her beyond that life. She would never escape. She thought of Jimmy, knew that his need for her enabled her to walk through the ugliness of her existence. She felt tears that were dry and wouldn't fall.

I <u>am</u> responsible. I'm the reason for all the ugliness which surrounds me. I've done everything I shouldn't have done, nothing I should have done.

She laid her head in her arms. There was no light.

A Dream

Marysza's sleep that night was uneasy. Her mind, immersed in a nightmare that wouldn't end, sank into a dark pool while her body tossed and turned. She saw a light that grew as it approached, touching and warming her cold and shrunken self.

She was a child in second grade. Her grandmother, wearing a blue-flowered dress and holding her shiny black purse, stood in the doorway of her and Tauzin's kitchen. She looked at Marysza, her eyes filled with the fire Marysza knew, the look that could only be grandma's, eyes holding light that grew until it filled the kitchen and the rest of the flat. A hint of something else lay in her eyes, something that appeared and disappeared quickly, a question that bordered on being a reprimand. Marysza remembered that half-questioning, half-scolding look .

In her sleep, Marysza was ashamed of the blackness that filled her. Her tears were no longer dry.

Grandma loved me. Was proud of me.

The light faded, then disappeared. Marysza heard herself repeating the words.

She loved me.

She awoke and lay thinking of her grandmother, thought of the way her grandmother would say "never min' " when some dilemma presented itself, and after thinking deeply, a thinking Marysza would never dare interrupt, would wipe her hands on her apron, as if she had neatly disposed of some trouble, and tell Marysza to get on with her work.

Marysza rose from her bed and walked toward Jimmy's bedroom.

"Never mind," she said to herself, "never mind."

Reconciliation

Martha didn't come again that week, nor did she call. Marysza tried to tell herself it was just as well. In the next moment, she saw she was lying to herself and that she missed Martha. Fear traveled through her body like pain, threatening to paralyze her arms and her legs, to snap the muscles in her shoulders and her back.

Martha must be tired of me, must wonder how I can think and act the way I do. She sees things directly, never obsesses.

Marysza knew she didn't possess that quality. She saw how much she had always envied Martha without being able to admit it, how that secret envy turned into anger and caused her to turn, unfairly, against her friend.

Guilt eats at me like acid. Because of the way I've treated her. Martha, my friend for as long as I can remember, Martha, whom I've loved as long as Tadziu. Almost as long as my grandmother. I don't know where love for a friend stands, if It's as strong as other loves or if it can replace other loves. I know that she fills part of my grandmother's place and part of Tadziu's place. I've been arrogant, spiteful, and childish. Admitting the truth, if only to myself, is cleansing, like going to confession.

On Thursday, she sat Jimmy in the back seat and listened to the familiar churning of the motor as the car's transmission struggled to kick in. After it finished groaning, she and Jimmy were on their way to Martha's home. She hadn't visited Martha's family in a long time, or even thought of them, but had surrendered to the chaos of her recent life.

Maybe you shouldn't forget friends, even in chaos.

"Marysza! How 'bout that!" Martha's s mother said, dropping her dish towel, and hurrying to hug Marysza and the baby. Marysza saw that she looked older.

H*ow can she have aged so? I just saw Martha's parents at Jimmy's christening. Or did I see them at all? Was my fear, my unhappiness, a selfish thing? Locking me inside myself? Closing off everything around me? Making me blind?*

Martha's mother asked why they hadn't seen Marysza lately, then, as if she'd had a list she'd been preparing for a long time, asked questions faster than Marysza could answer. Martha's father, who was sitting before the television in his slippers and robe, rose to greet her, a smile of surprise on his face.

For the remainder of the morning, Marysza talked with them about the usual subjects, found herself enjoying the chatter and felt something within her returning, washing away the darkness that had become her companion.

How strange that I like myself more as I move away from the problems that have possessed me and pay attention to others, to these people I didn't realize were so important and necessary to me.

With surprise, she suddenly knew that Martha had been expecting her. She watched her friend as she took Jimmy and carried him to her mother. As if nothing had changed between them. As if everything was the same.

"What'd I tell you, Ma, isn't he getting cuter all the time?"

Marysza wrapped herself in the peace that settled on her like a blanket.

I can't forget the people I love. I'll go see Aunt Irene and Uncle Ben. I've been foolish.

She didn't know what to say to Martha but she knew her coming was right. Unspoken words floated in the air between them until it was time for Marysza to leave. When she began dressing the baby, Martha's mother came and sat next to her, shifting her weight from one foot to the other and pulling at her apron nervously.

"You know, we feel so bad about what's been with you. The divorce."

She stopped and looked at Marysza, uncertainty filling her eyes. Marysza was moved with sadness for this woman's discomfort and gratitude for her kindness.

W*ords don't come easy to these people, the kind who will give you anything and never talk about it.*

"I know you do," Marysza said, knowing her words reassured Martha's mother and helped her continue.

"It's hard for you now, I know. Martha tells us how bad you feel, how you're struggling. I'm an old lady, Marysza, but I know more than you think. You're young. This will pass. Life will get on before you know it."

Marysza was quiet.

I can't tell her how much her words mean to me. I can't say how much I love her.

Martha's mother knew. She patted Marysza's shoulder, then turned away, trying to hide the tears that filled her eyes.

Martha walked to the car with Marysza, helped her place Jimmy in the back seat and then spoke without meeting Marysza's eyes.

"Thanks for bringing him. My Mom asks about him all the time." Marysza answered that she would try to come more often, that it was getting easier with Jimmy each day. So the subject of the baby lay between them, became a safe place, the place where they could shed the animosity that had come between them like an unexpected detour, a space in which to nurse wounds and reclaim the friendship neither could bear to lose. Marysza knew she must speak first. She looked into Martha's eyes, silently acknowledging her fault, then spoke.

"I'm sorry." She knew there were other words she must say, but right now, she didn't know what they were or how to say them.

A New Understanding

In the days that followed, a change occurred in the tone of Marysza's words to Martha. She began to understand the not-so-subtle demarcation of high and low, superior and inferior which had lain between them, undermining their friendship. Martha continued visiting Jimmy. On one of these visits, Marysza spoke the words whose meaning she had unraveled like a code hidden in the depths of her awareness, words she had extricated slowly, painfully, even rehearsed.

"I know I act superior. I know I'm not," she began.

"You are," Martha insisted, "in so many ways you are."

Marysza understood Martha's feeling because it had always been that way between them, but she had no right to rebuke her friend. Their manner of relating had originated in Marysza herself and become a pattern sustained by both of them.

Part of us is not good, sort of like a bad spot in a good apple. *We can't go back to that place. We've passed through it. I love her too much.*

"And in so many ways I'm not," she said aloud, careful that her voice didn't sound as if she were instructing her friend. "No Martha, we're just different."

"Yeah, like Beauty and the beast," Martha began, in her old self-mocking voice. Marysza stopped her..

"You can't talk like that anymore. It hurts you and it hurts me too." And Martha, with eyes like burning embers, was quiet.

Gestures

The memory of their conflict began to fade.

"C'mon Marysza," Martha said on a Saturday about three weeks later. "You go out. I'll watch Jimmy. Go to the show or something, my treat." Marysza looked at the money her friend took from her purse and turned her face to the wall. Martha was quiet, bit her lip. Marysza saw her eyes begin to cross. She put her arm around her friend and rested her head on Martha's shoulder.

"It's o.k. Mar," she said, "I just don't feel like a show tonight."

Marysza's television was broken. The next night Martha knocked on the door, lugging a set she had rented, then ran back to her car to fetch the gigantic metal rabbit ears that served as an antenna.

"In case we have trouble with the picture, the man said this is easy to connect." Marysza looked at the antenna dubiously and hoped the picture was good because she knew neither Martha nor she were mechanically adept. They turned the set on to a dismal display of horizontal lines accompanied by snow and static. Martha lifted the antenna. Marysza read the manual attached to one of the wire ears and handed it to Martha.

"C'mon now, Marysza, this can't be that hard." Martha pressed her lips together in concentration as she read aloud, several times, directions neither of them understood, directions that seemed written in a foreign tongue. Martha decided they should just go ahead and try their hand at the little wires and screws, a process complicated by the fear that they would be electrocuted. Marysza thought to pull the plug. After struggling for half an hour, they managed to complete the connection.

"Nothin' to it," Martha said. "That was easy." Getting the television to work was not as easy. They sat on the floor flipping the pages of the manual, and holding their breath as they fiddled with the control knobs and the stiff antenna wires.

"Maybe they mean this," Martha said each time she moved the antenna in a different direction.

Marysza began to laugh. She lay on the floor beneath the small hinged door housing the control knobs of the small wooden box, tossed away the instruction booklet that defied all logic she and Martha could apply, and laughed the cleansing laughter that only occurs with someone one loves. Somewhere behind the laughter, she heard her thoughts.

I'm so lucky to have a friend like Martha, someone who cares about what happens to me.

Martha joined in the laughter. They rolled on the floor and laughed until their eyes began to stream. As if by magic, they heard the comforting sound of a voice emanating from the television and like the world when God created light, the screen turned bright and a picture emerged.

"Hooray," Martha shouted. Fresh peals of laughter burst from them when Marysza said they'd better hurry and watch something before they lost the picture again. They watched *Your Show of Shows* with Sid Caesar and Imogene Coca and laughed at that too. In the large cooking pot Aunt Irene had given her, Marysza made popcorn and they sat together watching television the rest of the evening. They were still laughing when Marysza helped her friend carry the television down the long flight of stairs. She stood on the curb and waved as Martha's car disappeared into the night.

Good-bye, Martha. I can never repay your generosity. Yes, I can. I will. When I land on my feet. But friendship is not about repaying. What Martha and I have can't be paid for, can't be purchased anywhere.

Multiplication

Marysza sat looking out the window, thinking of Martha, glad that things were good between them again, and, she knew, stronger. Blue sky was fading into the gray of early evening. Jimmy was playing on the floor, surrounded by toys—small cars and trucks and a set of wooden blocks. Marysza smiled. It could just as easily have been a hundred or a thousand toys instead of the ten or so which represented his entire supply. He was content.

The resolution of her conflict with Martha filled Marysza with a sense of well-being but another concern struggled to break into her consciousness, something that, like a pebble in a shoe, brought on a nagging pain. She looked at Jimmy again, watched him in his world. A child's world.

My childhood was filled with contentment. I didn't know there were other things to want, didn't think my grandmother and I lacked anything.

This happiness was lost, became replaced by the longing for other things. It had been a gradual loss, one that grew as the years passed and childhood turned into adulthood, as her life with Tadziu disappointed her, as she began to feel disappointment and doubt in herself. She was absorbed in these thoughts, felt Jimmy pulling at her hand, pushing the red fire truck he was holding into her face, so he could gain her attention.

"Look," he said, "look how this truck can go." He made a siren sound. "It's going to put out a fire. And save the dogs, mama." Her attention was captured.

Dogs? Yes. Dogs lived in houses. With families. Mothers and fathers, brothers and sisters. What does Jimmy feel about his own family, about me and a father he never sees? He's bright. He watches television. I read books to him. He knows what families are made of. I see he's happy. Will it stay that way? Children adjust, accept things. She had, hadn't she?

"I hope you save the people, too," she said, and Jimmy answered "oh mama" in an exasperated tone, a grown-up voice that said he knew she was teasing him. She laughed at him but couldn't laugh away her thoughts.

He's being raised by only his mother. Will he remain intact? Will he be angry? Like I feel angry at the mother who deserted me, anger that becomes confusing, can turn around and direct itself at me. As if I'm the one at fault.

Thoughts of her mother came at times like this as she looked at her child. She didn't know how to rid herself of this anger, or, if she was honest with herself, whether she wanted to. Her mother deserved the resentment she felt. It was easy for others to preach forviveness, especially those who had little or nothing to forgive. The sky became darker. The last remnants of light fell across Jimmy's face, illuminating his eyes, his almost translucent skin, until the shadows deepened, and it was night

A Visit

She was washing dishes and felt his presence before she saw him. He stood in the doorway, looking unsure, reluctant to enter. A sense of dread seized Marysza, held her until she remembered she didn't have to be afraid, that they were no longer married.

"I thought maybe I could see Jimmy," he mumbled. She saw the look she could identify when they were married, a look that told her he was afraid, afraid and envious of something in her, something he thought he didn't have.

"I'm sorry, Tadziu, Jimmy's not here," she said. "He's with Martha today, because I have to go to the welfare office. It's too hard to take him with me. I never know how long it will take."

She heard her words and reminded herself that she didn't have to explain anything anymore, then shrugged.

What difference does it make what he knows? Maybe he'll leave. Maybe I should ask him to leave.

But it was hard, too hard to move away from what they had once been to each other.

"You can come in," she said, moving a kitchen chair so he could sit down.

"Maybe I could see him sometime," he said, avoiding her eyes. "I could pay towards him too." Remembering his antagonism toward Jimmy while they were married, she was unable to reply,

"I go to AA now," he said. His head had been hanging limply on his chest. He raised it and continued.

"I should pay for Jimmy and you," he muttered, emphasizing the word "should," letting her know he was aware of his failure. She saw that his eyes were pleading, asking for help with this thing he didn't know how to do and she felt her love and her need returning. She stopped herself.

"Maybe I could come once in a while to see you," he said, and she knew that was wrong, would pull her into the place where she couldn't be again. She shook her head.

"But you can see Jimmy," she said, her love and her need turning into pity. She tried to make her voice sound bright.

"Whenever you want. Just let me know ahead of time." Sitting next to the window with the broken sash and looking like a child who didn't want to go to bed, he drank coffee and talked frantically, feverishly, about all that had happened since their parting, as if she needed to know it all. She couldn't answer and as he became louder, felt herself pulling away. Her unhappiness was too new, too fresh. Then it came. She felt a bitterness standing beside the bitterness she felt toward her mother, bitterness toward him and what he had caused.

He rose from the chair and asked where he should send the money. For a moment, she thought of how she would have to tell Mrs. Hoggenkamp about whatever she received, then relaxed, because she knew that nothing would come. She answered that he should send it here, listened to the fear in his voice when he said that he was glad because he thought she might move away.

No money came.

An Experiment

Marysza went to the welfare office at the appointed time to report on her job-seeking efforts. She had placed applications in four places, the minimum number for the month. She sat in the same chair she always sat in, across from Mrs. Hoggenkamp, and hoped Mrs. Hoggenkamp would be satisfied. Mrs. Hoggenkamp did not look at her. She was quiet and preoccupied, as if she were thinking about a difficult subject and, as Marysza remembered her grandmother, carrying on a debate in her head, a debate in which she held both sides. Finally she spoke.

"Marysza, there is a new program which I think will be good for you." Marysza knew that her eyes and her face betrayed her thoughts, her fear that Mrs. Hoggenkamp had more regulations for her to follow or another required program she didn't want to be in. "This is not like the other programs. It's experimental." Marysza tried to look interested as she heard the next words. "Only three people from this district can be in this program. I thought you should be one of them. The program is designed to send participants back to school for more than the usual training."

Marysza was confused. She looked at Mrs. Hoggenkamp's face and tried to decipher the ordinary words which she suddenly had trouble understanding.

"The county will pay for you to attend classes at State to receive college credits. There is an on-site day-care center for students at State. You can be near Jimmy and see him during your breaks. The program lasts ten months, the time period required to complete an academic year." She paused, Marysza thought, to see if she registered any reaction, and seeing none, because Marysza was uncertain, continued.

"The hope is that academic exposure will act as an incentive for clients to continue on their way toward a degree. A certain calibre of client, that is." Mrs. Hoggenkamp hesitated slightly at these last words, as if she was dubious, as if she feared, Marysza knew, that whatever this program was, Marysza would only be another disappointment, another failure. "After the year, if you wish to continue the pursuit of a degree, and (she emphasized this and as if she had memorized the program's guidelines) apply for the various sources of state and federal aid, the county will continue your welfare grant and supportive services." She looked up at Marysza. "That means child care".

Marysza heard the words but still did not understand, did not connect the words degree and program. Her only understanding of the word "program" was as something she must do in order to keep her welfare grant, whether or not it made sense. She didn't know she was going to college.

An Unexpected Return

Uncle Ben walked through Marysza's door with a look of pain on his face.

"I had no right to do this," he said. "I should've given it to you right away. As soon as Ma died."

He placed a box on the table, a box that looked strangely familiar to Marysza. Her uncle continued. Quietly. As if his voice didn't want to leave his throat.

"I read the things in there, Marysza. I didn't want you to be hurt. I thought a right time would come."

Marysza said nothing. Her mouth was dry, her hands damp. This had to do with her mother.

How could I have forgotten. After what Grandma told me? I should've asked. I assumed it was lost.

"She called and wanted to see you, wanted to know where you lived. So I told her. I had to tell her, you know?" Marysza's eyes couldn't meet his.

I should be glad to hear of my mother. Shouldn't I?

"It's your business Marysza. But ma wanted you to have these. I know she did."

Marysza knew Uncle Ben. He was wrestling a demon, fighting a battle he'd probably faced before. Elzbieta, her mother, was, after all, his sister. "It's okay, Uncle Ben. I forgot about it anyway."

His eyes looked grateful. He ran his fingers through his hair. Marysza understood. A man at home with the things he understood—-his job, his house, his wife—whose eyes betrayed his inability to comprehend Marysza, and his knowledge that he must oversee and protect her.

"I'm sorry." he said, "call if you need me." There was no sound as he shut the door.

Marysza stared at the box without moving, seeing the candy kitchen and her grandmother sitting across from her. The box still smelled of chocolate. The blue flowers in the paper were as faded as she remembered. Her hands shook as she opened it and saw the picture she knew so well, her grandmother as a girl.

There was an envelope in the box—big, white, and stuffed. Grandma was gone. She could open the envelope. There was a picture of Elzbieta as a girl. She didn't look as pretty as Marysza's grandmother, didn't smile like Marysza's grandmother did.

What keeps her from being pretty? Her hair is straight, her teeth big and her arms and legs shapeless. But it's more than adolescent awkwardness. She's poor. Her clothes show it. Her eyes show it. More than one would expect. Because many people weren't aware of their poverty. Were happy despite it. But this girl's aware. There's resentment in her.

Other pictures——the girl grown, her beauty and radiance beyond belief, enveloped in the white and lace of her wedding gown, arm linked with the man at her side —-Marysza's father, handsome, tall, his face filled with pride and confidence, looking into the camera, straight at attention but for the slight turn of his face toward the woman at his side.

A picture of her father alone, the muscles in his bare arms relaxed, holding a baby wrapped in blankets, gazing at the small face, astonishment and unbelief in his eyes. Marysza held the picture close. There were no more.

He loved me. My father loved me. There are no pictures of my mother and me. I can't see her holding me, looking at my face. I can't know what she felt. The way I always knew with Grandma. The way I can see with my father

There was a red ribbon edged in gold, a Christmas adornment, the size that would fit into a little girl's hair. Someone had bent a hairpin—the kind her grandmother had always used—and attached it to the ribbon at its center. A child's dresser set, comb, hairbrush and mirror, painted in silver and tied together with a pink ribbon lay on the floor of the box. A plastic ring, crackerjack treasure, rolled against its paper walls. Then something expensive, incongruous with the other trinkets—-a gold locket, heart shaped, framed in studs of shimmering light, a jeweler's monogram etched onto its back.

Letters were stacked neatly, fastened with a rubber band and tucked into an opening cut into the bottom of the box.

Marysza removed the first letter. She could discern the postmark on the envelope, even though it was faded— New York, New York. Not that far from Buffalo. But a universe away.

She unfolded the letter, written in a woman's delicate handwriting.

Dear Mama,

I am sorry for all the stupid things I did. Mike drank too much and killed himself in the car. I do not think I should say it but I do not miss him. He kept trying to find me but then he was killed. I work in a night club taking people's coats. I can not come home because I am ashamed of what I have done. I am going to work hard and come home when I have a better life and more money. Please take care of my baby. I know no one will love her like you will. Please do not try to find me but forget about me for now. You were right with everything you told me. I didn't listen. Please forgive me. I am sending some money so you can buy some things you and Marysza need. I will send more. Elzbieta.

Marysza thought of her grandmother—that the memory of her father's objections when she left kept her from returning to her family when life in the city failed. Marysza knew grandma's father forgave her even as she walked out the door. But grandma never knew. Because her pride wouldn't let her return before her father died. And Elzbieta didn't know of her mother's forgiveness. Because she did not return. And Grandma died.

There was a change in the sound of the letters.

Dear mama,

A man with lots of money has been taking me out. He is older than I am but I do not mind. He wants to marry me. I will live in a big house and have pretty clothes. I have not told him about Marysza yet. I wish I could talk with you and ask you what to do. He is really a nice man. But nothing like Joe. There will never be another Joe for me. Elzbieta

Dear mama,

I am afraid, just afraid, to tell Henry about Marysza and that I want to bring her here. I have told myself over and over again what a bad mother I am. I remember how beautiful my baby girl was. Maybe you should tell her I died or something. I am sending a gold locket and chain for her. You can give it to her for Christmas or her birthday. Just don't tell her about me. It's probably better if she never knows me. I have a new baby now, a boy and he is very sweet. But Marysza was special, always special, the child of the man I will always love. Please forgive me mama but I can not come home. I love you. I love Marysza. Elzbieta

Dear mama,

I have another baby boy and my husband loves his sons very much. I can't tell him about Mike and the crazy life I had with him. I can't tell him about Joe and how much I loved him. He thinks he is the only man who was in my life, the only man I ever loved. I do love him and I love my sons but it's different. I live in another world when I am alone, a world where I am with Joe and Marysza and you. Forgive me, mama. If I pray for courage, maybe I can tell him about Marysza. But I don't think so because I am afraid. I am not sure of what. Sometimes at night I think Marysza is still a baby and I can hold her. Elzbieta

There were no more. Marysza held the letters, wanting there to be more yet not wanting there to be any at all.

My mother was Elzbieta. Elizabeth. I remember the way Grandma said her name. With longing. And love.

The lady in the hospital, after I had Jimmy. I can't forget her. My mother wasn't there. My mother never saw my baby.

She heard the words she'd said to Uncle Ben. "You did the right thing. I'd forgotten about the box." And then words she couldn't believe she'd said. "You can tell her to call me." But she couldn't take the words back. She felt a tightening in her chest and fear, like a lump, caught in her throat.

If her mother did come, she could be disappointed in Marysza, in something about her. Or Jimmy.

Why should I care? That a mother who never loved me might not like me now.

She ran her fingers through her hair, walked to the window and looked out at the street.

*G*randma kept the box and didn't tell me because I was a child. She wanted to protect me

She didn't trust her daughter to return, loved her despite that, loved her no matter what. Because she was her child. And told me to forgive her.

A Winter Stroll

She did not see Tadziu again until the winter. It happened by accident. On a clear and cold evening, when the snow banks were piled high on each side of the street, she was walking to the supermarket and saw Tadziu walking in the same direction. She realized he must be living somewhere in the neighborhood and was astounded by the way her heart skipped at that realization.

Why should that make me glad? Why should I care?

It was a night for children. School had been closed that day because of the snow. Boys and girls were out, sledding on the streets and throwing snowballs at each other. Ordinary life was suspended, the air filled with the feeling of holiday and play. She saw a group of kids trying to push a boy through the opening of a gigantic mound of snow she guessed was supposed to be an igloo. She laughed easily, spontaneously, when she reached Tadziu.

"What are you doing out on a night like this?" He laughed back as she knew he would, and answered, "The same thing you're doing, hunting for food, before everything's gone." They walked together, smiling at the excited children they passed.

"I didn't send money," he said, "I lost my job." She ignored that, asked no questions, and he said no more. She knew that neither of them wanted to lose the feeling of the night.

"It's good to be inside," he said, instinctively reaching for her hands and rubbing them in his own as they entered the supermarket.

"I don't know how those kids can do it." She was moved by his attempt to warm her hands, gave herself to the arousal of his touch. "It's because they work up such a sweat with their playing," he continued. "I was the same way. Never wanted to come in, stayed out in the cold playing until my fingers wouldn't work anymore."

They walked up and down the aisles together. She thought of him as a child in the snow, knew he stayed outside because he didn't want to go in when his father was home. He'd never told her this when they were children, never told her the details of his life, as if he were ashamed that she was loved and he was not, as if he felt he deserved whatever happened to him. But she'd thought of it many times after they parted and somehow she knew. Her grandmother had also known although she never said anything directly, just swore a few times when she mentioned Tadziu's father, more after she met his mother and always after she met with her lady friends and exchanged neighborhood gossip. She said Tadziu's father had not treated his wife well, but gave the details in Polish so that Marysza couldn't understand.

Tadziu followed behind her now, throwing the same things into his cart that she did.

"I figger you know better than me."

"Are you going to make soup?" she asked, unable to suppress her laughter, the mirth that filled her, filled the night, the children, and the sky.

"Because that's what the bone is for." Then he laughed too and silver mountains of snow reflected their laughter into the night and she felt her love, his love, the love neither of them would ever again say.

"Sure, if you tell me how. I like soup."

For those moments, the facts of their existence were forgotten, didn't intrude. They played a game, a children's game in which they put aside those facts as something the world had imposed and from which they were momentarily free. They became two people talking, entering each other as they walked, living in the present with no thought of yesterday, innocent of what each had been. When they emerged from the supermarket, fresh snowflakes swirled around the lights of the street lamps.

"We better hurry," Tadziu yelled, turning up the collar of his jacket. In the lights of the store window, she saw that his face was handsome, saw him look back at her and knew he thought she was pretty. She thought of being in their bed together, of lying in his arms under mounds of blankets. She wondered if that would break any rules. She shook the thought away like she shook the snowflakes from her hair.

Memories of what had been began to cover the words and the laughter, and like the snow covering the ground, crept into everything. She knew he had been in the hospital, that his drinking had landed him there and that he had no money. She didn't know how he lived. But she and Jimmy were separate from him now. She didn't have to think of what happened to him, could keep unwanted thoughts away, just as their gloves and jackets kept away the cold.

They parted at the corner. Marysza watched Tadziu disappear into the blue night, watched his back until she could no longer see

Chapter Six

A Meeting

Tadziu stared at the man sitting across from him, a man he wanted to kill. The man knew.

"Look, kid. For a while, it's gonna be real hard."

Tadziu laughed. The thoughts whirling in his brain felt like acid he had swallowed, acid that moved through his body burning holes along the way.

Hard? What does this guy know about hard that I don't know. So he's stopped drinking. So what? Now he can look down on guys like me. Can feel superior. What, because he wears a tie? He's nuthin' but an alky like me. Except my hands are dirty, the nails black underneath and dirt ground into the skin.

He worked construction now. Jerry had finally managed to get him in and he had no problem leaving the factory. He would've kept both jobs but the construction job demanded long hours and paid much better wages.

That last job was a pisser. I like hauling lumber and mixing cement. A hammer in my hand feels good. Holding nails in my teeth feels good. But that guy thought he was a big shit. Never said anything to us except in that lousy voice. "Hey you. Do this or do that." Called the kid stupid when he made a mistake on that window. The kid looked scared. That asshole loved it. Making people scared. He never said anything to me. He knew better. Probably opened that construction company a month ago. It won't last long. Because of the lousy way he does things, cutting corners wherever he can. We never even had time to sweep up the nails or pieces of wood off the floors. That really bothered me. He said it would all be covered with rugs anyway. So what? The SOB. Were rugs going to make the floors beneath them any better? I would've done it differently. Would've done a good job.

Why should I care anyway? What the hell's the matter with me? I collected my day's pay, right? Since when have I got such a conscience? But people were paying for that house. Maybe young people. Like Marysza & me. Maybe it was their first house.

I'll never have a house.

He was talking to Steve, Steve Kopniecki. Or a name something like that. After an AA meeting. A guy supposed to be his sponsor.

The last time he passed out he was on a bus. Because he didn't have a car for a while. The police took him to jail. The judge said he had to go to AA or be locked up. Not much of a choice. So he went. Sat there and listened to all those guys talking about themselves, about all the things that happened to them because of drinking. He'd be damned if he was going to do that. Tell a roomful of people about his life. About his drinking. He was only there because the judge said he had to go. Now this guy was beginning to irritate him. Wouldn't leave him alone.

Get lost, Steve Kopniecki, or whatever your name is. Get lost. I'm gonna do what I want to. Drink when I want to. Not drink when I want to. Nobody's going to tell me what to do. Not even if they follow me around like a shadow. This guy does. A shadow. That's what he is, all right. A fuckin' shadow.

They were drinking coffee in a diner. The guy had a kind of washed-out face that made you think of nothing. Just red and kind of swollen. Thin yellow hair plastered across his head as if he did it with his hands. Not enough to comb. Tadziu tried to look interested in what the guy was saying.

"You know, young fella, you're lucky. A lot of us didn't get into the program as young as you. You can lick this sooner, before you lose more. Some of us lost everything, were crawling on our bellies before we found the program. You know that. You heard them. Lost wives and families and careers. Everything. You don't have to sink that low. You're getting another chance, young fella. Another chance."

What a jerk the guy was. As if he knew something Tadziu didn't know.

What about my wife and kid? I lost Marysza and Jimmy, didn't I?

But he wasn't going to tell the man that. Wasn't going to whine like all those other guys.

They lost their careers. Yeah, I had a career all right. Workin' my ass off. That was my career. Aw, so what.

Lots of those guys in there looked like they couldn't even hold jobs. This guy would never know what a jerk he was.

When I have to talk at a meeting, I'll talk. Won't whine though.

He felt something running around inside him like a bowling ball, hitting the inside of his chest, bouncing off and slamming against his back. He didn't know what it was. But he knew he wanted to get away from this guy and he couldn't. The guy kept talking, low and friendly-like. The pain in Tadziu's chest continued. Getting no booze when you were used to it, stopping so suddenly, did all kinds of bad things to you.

That's all right. I've been here before. Even in shittin' hospitals a couple times. It'll pass. It'll pass. I just gotta hang on. I wish this guy would shut up. He's got the most God-awful voice. His smile ain't exactly charmin' either.

The guy just kept calling him "young fella". Then Tadziu remembered something. And got a warm feeling, a nice feeling inside. He knew what it was. He saw Joe's face. Heard his voice. Joe used to call him "young fella".

I never forgot you, Joe. I never saw you again but I never forgot you.

Memories Again

That night in the bar, he was still thinking about Joe. He talked about him to the guy on the next stool. They started buying each other drinks.

"Ya know what I mean buddy? You know how you remember people who do things for you? Even though you forget about them for a while. It comes back, comes back later an' you never really know it until then. That they did this thing for you. Ya know what I mean, buddy?"

"Sure I do. Sure I know what ya mean. Yeah, I knew someone like that. A kid who lived near me. We didn't even go to the same school. He was older, too. A coupla yearz oldern'me. He always helped me when I was in a jam."

The guy told his story—about a kid who helped him learn to play baseball the right way. So that other guys didn't laugh at the way he struck out all the time.

"I was swingin' at everythin', at anythin', cuz I wuz scared and dint' know what I waz doin'."

Tadziu nodded his head. Tears filled his eyes, huge tears he thought would spill over onto the bar. But he forgot about being ashamed. How come he only cried when he was drunk? He saw Joe as clear as if they were sitting next to each other. He remembered how he wished Joe was his father, how it made him angry because it was pitiful he was jealous of Joe's kids. So he never said anything to him. That he loved him.

The tears came faster, dripped from his eyes and his nose, turned into huge globs in his throat, globs he could not gulp down. He was glad the bar was filled with noise so no one paid any attention to him. The other guy kept patting him on the back, squeezing his shoulder.

"I like ya, buddy," he heard himself saying, as if he was another person, far away.

"Me too, pal, me too. C'mon, quit that, pal. No more cryin'." The guy took a white rag off the bar and wiped Tadziu's face. "Iss okay," he said, "Iss okay. C'mon, les have another round." The bartender came over and looked at them. He shrugged his shoulders and poured the drinks.

A Rescue

The sky was a huge and beautiful place, so beautiful it made Tadziu cry more. Somebody had an arm around him, was opening a car door. He thought it was the AA guy but he couldn't be sure. How the hell would the AA guy know where to find him? He looked at the guy's face under a street light. It was him.

"Where th'hell dzoo cum frum?" he demanded. The guy didn't answer, just kept moving him along. Got him into a car and up the stairs to his room.

"C'mon, young fellow," he kept saying, "c'mon young fellow." He was a jerk, had a jerk's face. Because Tadziu didn't want to go home. Didn't want to go to sleep and wake up again. To face another day. He felt thrown into a sea that was not water but some thick and ugly thing through which he had to swim upstream all the way. If he wanted to make it. But why should he want to make it? To where? It would be easy to just let go, to sink into darkness. But someone else would not let him sink, would not release his hold. Someone who kept calling him "young fella." He couldn't free himself from that voice, that face.

"You son-of-a-bitch." He struck out but could not feel his fists strike anything. Something like lightning lit the sky. He saw Joe's face, knew it was Joe he was trying to punch.

"It's all right, young fella," Joe said. "You'll be okay." Then Tadziu lost consciousness.

He awoke because an ax was trying to split his head in two. When he could stand the light, could focus his eyes, he saw the man from AA asleep in a chair next to the bed, the only other piece of furniture in the room. The man looked like an angel now. An angel with a balding head covered with strands of thin hair and a nose like a red bulb.

Steve

They were drinking coffee in the diner after another AA meeting. Next week Steve was going to call on him to talk. Steve was telling him not to be nervous, just honest.

"I'll never know how you slept in that damn chair all night," Tadziu said. "I sat in it once when I first moved in. It was the most uncomfortable piece of shit."

"Yeah, it was," Steve agreed, and Tadziu was quiet.

Damn. The only other guy who ever did anything for me was Joe, and he never did anything like this guy. Sits over me like a damn father. Sponsors are supposed to do things for their guys but Steve's not real. He tells me over and over again that the way he stays sober is by helping other guys, guys like me who can't control their drinking. That's bullshit anyway. I can control it if I make up my mind.

He heard the word "father" in his thoughts. He was beginning to think of Steve as a father, leaning on him, listening to him. Even now, even when Steve talked about all the things he didn't want to hear.

"You can't blame your wife for your behavior," he told Tadziu. "Every alcoholic does that. If not his wife, then somebody else. Just never himself."

But she shouldn't have given up on me like she did.

Tadziu didn't bother saying it. He knew it was useless. Steve would just say he was whining. Steve talked about Jimmy and the support Tadziu was supposed to pay, then went into how Tadziu had to be careful with his friends.

"I'll pay for Jimmy," Tadziu said, waving his hand impatiently. "I'll catch up." Then he added, "I don't have any friends left. The guys dropped me when I started going under."

"They're still your friends," Steve told him. "You'll see. But you can't go to bars with them." Tadziu thought about Jerry and the guys. He told Steve how they liked to play basketball and volleyball. Steve told him to call Jerry and get on one of the teams.

"They go out afterwards and it would be hard to order coke or ginger ale. I'm not strong enough for that." Steve's answers were starting to sound alike.

"You aren't the same as everybody else and the sooner you get used to that the better. They can drink. You can't. You have a disease. And none of us are strong enough. Remember, a stronger being will do it for you. Don't think about it. Don't waste time worrying. One day at a time, young fellow. One day at a time. And you're going to have lots of new friends, guys who know exactly what you're going through."

Steve told him that talking to other guys like himself would help him. Tadziu wasn't sure. He didn't really want to talk to them. He was no prize, but still, some of them were real losers. He liked Steve all right but he was sick of hearing him talk.

"A broken record. You're a broken record," he told Steve after he went on another binge and got drunk. Steve said nothing. Just picked him up again. Tadziu remembered the way he felt for the couple months he didn't drink. At first, it was hell, didn't seem as if it would ever stop being hell. But after the couple months, each day was a little easier. Now, he'd messed up again. Would be back in hell. And he was afraid Steve would give up on him.

When he said that, Steve laughed. Then became serious. "You know how many times they picked me up? I owe a lot, young fella, a lot. I have to pay back. It keeps me straight, remember? I'm no better than you. A lot worse, young fellow, a lot worse." Tadziu looked at Steve's face, saw that it was cast down in a way he didn't like. Panic entered his thoughts.

I never really believed this higher being crap. I believe in you. I thought you were strong. C'mon man, I've listened to you a hundred times. Yeah, I know you owned a business and made lots of money. Lost it all, even your family. But still. You got yourself out of it. I need you, man. What is it I need? I don't know, but something you have.

He punched Steve on the side of his arm. Steve didn't notice, just kept talking.

"I let everyone down. The guys who worked for me got nothin'. Nobody got nothin'. Except my shit. My son wants nothin' to do with me. I never even get a Christmas card." Tadziu was silent. This kind of talk was bad. He could take it from other guys in the meetings. But not Steve. "I'm tellin' you, young fellow. Don't forget your boy. Because he'll forget you." Tadziu didn't want to listen anymore.

At the meeting, he went up to talk when Steve called him. Talked about his mother. How she had never been able to do anything. She just wasn't strong. He talked about Marysza. That he never thought she would leave. Would stick around like his mother. But she fooled him. He didn't tell them that part of him was pissed at her for that. Or that another part of him could never stop loving her. That was too hard.

He didn't tell them that sometimes he dreamed of Marysza and him playing cards in her grandmother's house. Or dancing at The Pier. Fixing up the flat. Screwing around in the bed with all those damn ruffles she made. Sometimes on the couch. He didn't tell them he could never wait to get inside her, to own her, to know how he pleased her. He didn't tell them he got hard just thinking about her.

He couldn't tell them he never thought of Jimmy. That he kept himself from thinking about him. Because he knew his real feeling. Jimmy had messed it all up.

Steve's kid hated him. Just like Tadziu hated his old man. What would Jimmy think about him? It was all too complicated to think about, ran around in his head until he pushed it out. Maybe he would tell the AA guys all that stuff another time. He knew he'd have to. Steve said so. If you wanted to start healing.

A Job

This time he stayed drunk a week. He kept telling Steve to go away, to kiss his ass. But Steve wouldn't go.

When he came out of it and went back to the job, the guy told him not to come back anymore. He looked straight past Tadziu, the S.O.B., and said he had new contracts coming in and he needed guys he could depend on to show up and work. Tadziu couldn't believe it. The guy never cared before. He looked straight into the guy's eyes.

"You're an asshole. I'm one of the best workers you got." He was. He never goofed off on the job. He did things right too. Kind of a matter of pride. But that probably didn't matter to the guy anyway. He liked fast better than right. Now he just repeated himself.

"I got to have my crew show up every day."

When Tadziu told Steve about it, Steve shrugged. "You asked for it. You can't expect anything different. The world runs that way. People have to show up for work. What do you want the guy to do? Hold your job until you're ready?" Those were the hardest words he had heard from Steve. He knew Steve was right but that just made him angrier.

"Up yours. I don't need him. The world's full of jobs. And I don't need you either." Then he did something he couldn't believe. He threw Steve's jacket at him. He was sorry immediately, sorry for saying the words, sorry for throwing the jacket. But he couldn't say so. Steve got up. The lights blinked in the window of the diner. Steve's face was orange, then green.

"All right, young fellow," he said, "You know where to find me." Waitresses shuffled around tables. Forks and knives clanged. Words stood out, were almost heard, spilled into each other and were lost in the blanket of sound that covered the room.

Tadziu watched Steve, watched him walk to the door and outside. He started to run after him. Then he stopped.

I don't need him. Not him or anyone else.

The Whole Thing

He couldn't stop thinking of Steve's face. Problem was a lot of other things went along with thinking of Steve. That "higher being" crap was one. Tadziu had never seen that God did anything for him. His mother prayed all the time and nothing good ever happened for her. Or any of them. Well, that wasn't really true. His brothers and sisters had made out all right. As soon as they got away from home and the old man. That had nothing to do with God, did it? They were just strong, that's all. Not losers, like he was.

Aw shaddup already. I'm getting tired of the sound of my own voice. Saying the same things over and over. I hate pa. Pa hates me. God Himself could never change that. But this crazy program expects you to make peace with all those you owe. Marysza. Okay. His mother. Okay. Jimmy. Okay. His father. Not okay. I never did anything to the old man. Even Steve admits it. And then the next word out of Steve's mouth is to forgive him anyway.

That was asking too much. He just couldn't do it. But unless you put your faith in this "higher power", this God, you couldn't make it. Couldn't forgive, couldn't stop being a boozehound, couldn't stop killing yourself slowly.

There was one thing that kept at him, though. Steve always said "God as you understand him." That was a little different. Maybe the God he always thought was God wasn't really who he thought. Wasn't like his father putting people in hell all the time.

Maybe he was some kind of good guy who put Marysza into his life. And Joe. And Steve. Even though Steve was a pain in the ass. Steve said you had to trust this higher being. That was harder. And admit your own faults. Take inventory of yourself, for Christ's sake. And try to make "restitution" wherever you could. Even harder. Why should he? Why should he listen to any of that crap?

Alone

Jobs were not easy to find. Tadziu drifted from one dead-end job to another—drove a delivery truck for a furniture store, and stripped roofs for a roofing company. Nothing lasted. Either they didn't need him anymore or he drank too much and was fired.

He began to have dreams, dreams filled with faces—Steve, or Joe or Marysza and Jimmy. Sometimes he was a boy again. He saw his mother, her hands covering her face as she screamed for his father to stop beating him. One night he saw his youngest brother, the way he held his hands out when Tadziu returned from Joe's store with a bag of groceries. His brother's face turned into Jimmy's face, the face in the crib he had once secretly watched. He woke from that dream in a cold sweat, and drank a glass of whiskey. But he couldn't forget. He wanted to touch his son's face that time he went into his room but he was scared. And the feeling disappeared whenever Marysza pestered him about Jimmy. Until the kid turned into a wall that separated him from Marysza.

One night he had a nightmare. He saw the flat and the inside of Jimmy's room, looked through Jimmy's window to the bare stone wall of the building next door. He didn't know why Jimmy came through the door, wrapped in his baby clothes, some kind of knitted cap and a sweater rolled up at the sleeves. He saw someone jump from behind the door and, terrified, heard himself scream "Stop!"

The man began beating Jimmy's face. Tadziu felt the pounding of the man's arms, arms as strong as tree limbs and covered with dark hair. He saw Jimmy's pink skin turning red, his tiny face covered with blood.

The dream went on. His screams mingled with Jimmy's cries. He saw his reflection in the mirror of the cracked blue dresser. Greasy clumps of hair hung from the man's head and fell across his face.

He wanted to hold Jimmy, to shield him from the blows, to absorb them himself. But he couldn't move, was rooted to the ground, held by the arm that forced his eyes to remain open, forced him to watch. He heard himself screaming "no" again and again. The baby turned into a mass of red meat that grew smaller and smaller, then began to disappear.

I'm suffocating. Can't breathe. The am hammers my chest. I know this is a dream. I can't wake up. I'm limp, drowning in my own sweat, my, own heat.

He exerted his last ounce of strength, fought for wakefulness, almost reached the surface, then descended again. The disembodied black-haired arm was alive, played with him, threw him back and forth between sleep and consciousness.

I'm awake. Am I awake? The blood's gone. My dead son's gone. Will my breathing return?

He lay in his bed, breathing hard, trying to tell himself the dream was only a nightmare, that it was the result of his drinking.

Jimmy's fine. He's with Marysza, right? She takes care of him, won't let anything hurt him, right?

It was no use. He couldn't escape the dream and the belief that his son was in danger, stalked by a monster with huge muscled arms covered with black hair. He didn't know if the monster was his father or himself..

Repentance

"Well, I figured I'd try again," he told Steve on the phone. "I've only failed twice, right"? He wanted Steve to be enthusiastic.

Steve's voice is glad. But there's something else in it, something new. Weariness. Well, he's got a right to be sick of me. "You'll make it, young fellow," is all he says. That's all he ever says.

When he saw Steve at the next meeting, he knew something was wrong. There was a grayness about him, something besides the look of a man who had spent too many years drinking.

That's how I'm going to look. Maybe I already do. I'm only thirty.

The meeting room was filling.

Each time I come, there's new faces. And some have disappeared. This is a real game. A round-robin.

He recognized his arrogance and surprised himself by knowing it was bad, dangerous. He was an asshole. When would he ever change? Behind him, a couple of regulars were talking in hushed t ones.

I don't know why I'm listening. What do I care what they talk about?

But something held him. He heard the words six months and some kind of cancer. And he knew.

What I suddenly know sits silent in me, rips me like a knife, fills me with fear. I'm going to be alone again, alone with myself and the things I can't do, the things I'm too weak to do. I need you. I need you. Don't leave me.

*A*fter the meeting, when he and Steve sat in the diner with their coffee, he couldn't speak the thoughts that were screaming to be said.

I love you. I hate you. You're leaving me. I know how selfish I am. How hopeless. Can't you see I need something more than these rummies who are just as weak as me.

He began to choke on tears, the way he had after the night Steve got him back to his room and he woke up to see him sleeping next to him in that damn chair.

I'm an asshole. Want to be comforted, even now.

Steve was looking at him, saw his misery, Tadziu was sure, but didn't seem to think it was unusual. He just kept talking. "I've been sober now twelve years. It didn't feel natural at first. But it grew on me. One day at a time. It's time for you now. Other guys need you."

What the hell does he mean? I got to listen. No matter what he says. Does he think I'm gonna take his place or somethin'?

"Hey, not me," he started to say, but then shut up.

I can't believe what he's thinking.

The lights overhead blinded Tadziu, burned into the covering of the table, then settled into Steve's eyes like the flame of a candle. Tadziu stopped thinking, was caught up in a feeling he couldn't explain, a sensation that should be frightening, but wasn't. He was floating over the room, looking down at himself and Steve. Someone or something besides Steve and himself was in the room, something that held Steve and him together, like arms. The thing was stronger than the hatred he felt toward his father, made his hatred smaller and smaller, until it was almost erased.

Like sudden lightning or the explosion of thunder, he knew that Steve was no accident, but some kind of favor from somewhere, some kind of gift, he didn't know what, couldn't explain. He knew Steve felt something also. They looked at each other, but didn't speak.

I don't want this to pass. Steve doesn't want it to pass. I don't know what I am to him. I don't understand what he is to me. There's no word for it. No word for it. I don't want it to change. All things change. But some really don't. Not on the inside. No word for it. No word for it. Marysza. Jimmy. Steve.

Loss

Tadziu wasn't surprised to learn about Steve's cancer, but he didn't expect he would die that quickly. He and five other guys from the group were pallbearers. Spring was just beginning on the day they carried Steve's coffin to the burial site. The wind swept stray leaves and twigs that scurried along the path before them. The leaves turned back, scattered themselves, then moved on again. Sun poured itself onto the swollen earth, trying to coax it into life. But it was too soon. Beneath the sun's faint rays, the ground was still hard.

They listened to the clergyman's words. The sun moved behind a cloud and the wind took on a bone-chilling sharpness. Insipid drops started to fall, then grew larger. Tadziu shivered. Somewhere in the back of his head was an old fear—-his fear of the cold earth and the grave. He felt contempt for himself, tried to flip the thought away and think of Steve.

After today, I won't ever be the same. Won't be what I was.

The words kept repeating themselves.

Never the same.

After the service, he shook hands with other guys before they started shuffling away. Some patted him on the shoulder or back. Steve's son came to him and hugged him. Tadziu saw the tears in his eyes as they parted.

Never again the same.

He thought about the end. would be seeing it for a long time. Steve hadn't had much strength to talk.

We spoke no words, I must remember, no promises did I make. But there's still promises. Unspoken words. He said them so many times. I heard even though I wasn't listening, didn't want to listen. God-damn. He believed all that stuff. Now I got to believe it. Never the same.

The first thing has to be Jimmy. He told me over and over again. Always my son. No matter what. Always my son. My head hurts. I need a drink. Why do I have to listen to the words of a dead man? That's crazy. He's not just a dead man. He's Steve. That's crazy too. Steve's gone. Gone from my life.

A drizzle started to fall. He stopped beneath a tree. Another guy from the group approached, then more. They stood under the tree without talking, holding cigarettes in their mouths or backwards in their hands, embarrassed to look at each other, looking up at the gray sky as if something important was hidden there, something they would see if they just looked long enough. One man moved from one foot to the other, his shoulders hunched around his neck as protection against the dampness.

"You were sure important to him, kid," he said. The others nodded or said "yeah" in low voices, glad to have something to say, something to break the spell of the monotonous drizzle and the quiet.

Damn. Why'd the guy have to say that. Damn. Damn. Never again the same.

"Well, I gotta go now." one guy said, and threw his butt to the ground. "Gotta work today," he added apologetically. Someone answered him. "Okay. See ya." The rest of them were going to a restaurant to eat lunch. The chapter was paying for it, kind of a tribute. *Damn.* He didn't like leaving Steve behind. He pulled out from beneath the tree and started to run toward his car. He didn't want the others to see him cry.

New Memories

After Steve's death, his mind was always busy. He couldn't stop thinking of the things he didn't want to think about, of all the things Steve had said, words that seemed more powerful now that he was gone. Steve's death frightened him not because he was afraid to die, but because of something he never thought of, that someone could be taken from him. Never to return. When he thought of Marysza now, when Steve's death was like an open wound, he did not think of her in bed, but thought of them as children, of their games, of her grandmother. Thinking of them that way made death seem impossible, held any thoughts of death further away. He could never lose Marysza, anymore than he could lose parts of himself.

Steve was the only person he had ever seen die. He could still see himself in the hospital room with the other people. Friends of Steve's, all guys from AA. People who thought they should be there. Everything was quiet, nothing happening until Steve's son walked into the room. Tadziu knew it was Steve's son because he looked like Steve and because his face wore a different pain than the other faces in the room. As if Tadziu's mind were wearing dark glasses and he took them off, the scene became clear. Steve lying on the bed silent, his arm resting on the white sheets, a long tube extending from a needle stuck into a blue vein in the hollow where his arm folded, his hand turned upward, a white plastic hospital bracelet on the wrist.

Tadziu knew that Steve wanted nothing done to make him last longer, that he just wanted to die and get it over with. But things were never the way you wanted them to be. He was sorry to see all the tubes stretching from Steve like some kind of skinny octopus arms. Blood traveled through one of the tubes. He heard one of the guys whisper that the other tube pumped medicine for pain.

Steve was not conscious, lay still except for the slow rise and fall of his chest. Tadziu and the guys sat quiet, their heads bent low, their hands folded between their spread-out knees, barely moving except when someone left to go to the bathroom or have a cigarette. Now and then someone began tapping a foot against the floor but stopped, embarrassed when he became conscious of what he was doing, and everything became quiet again. Until Steve's son came into the room and more whispering and shuffling started. Everyone knew who he was. They were all silent because they didn't know the son or what to say until someone rose, introduced himself and shook the guy's hand.

Now the scene was blurred, as if a camera had lost its focus or Tadziu had moved back and was watching from a distance. He watched the men move slowly, their lips moving but no sound coming out.

Is this what death is? Just everyone quiet in a room, waiting. Wondering and hoping that the guy knows you're here. Knows you're with him. But you're not really with him. Because when the hours are over and they tell you to leave, you can go. The guy stays in bed with the aloneness. You say good-bye outside the room and ask who'll be coming back the next day. If there is a next day.

Tadziu thought all the guys who were there, standing and watching, probably felt as helpless and awkward as he did. He looked around. Some looked okay, even peaceful, as if they had been through this before, as if they knew something Tadziu didn't know, understood something about death he didn't.

Tadziu didn't know he would feel sorry for the son, the son Steve told him about, who said he didn't want anything to do with his old man. But the guy was here. He came. And Tadziu wondered if his father could possibly know he was here. Even though Steve's eyes were closed, Tadziu wanted to get up and go to the bed and look at Steve and tell him, "Look, Steve, he's here. Your boy's here. None of it really matters, you know. Your boy's here." He wanted so bad for Steve to know. But he just looked at the son, saw how miserable he looked, how he looked at his dying father with a frightened look.

I'm not scared. Because I loved Steve and Steve knew that. If he knows anything now, he still knows it. Something about that makes his dying not so bad.

It was a funny thing, the way an alcoholic old man could affect someone's life. He sat at a table with other guys at the luncheon. Waitresses scurried back and forth. It was a nice restaurant. Nothing like the diner where he and Steve drank coffee. It was a somber occasion but, except for new members, these guys talked easily with each other, shared something Tadziu had envied though he never admitted it.

Those who were new didn't talk except when they were up before everybody at a meeting and had to tell their stories. He was the same way. He didn't make light conversation easily. He thought about the first night he spoke.

I thought I was going to die. My tongue wouldn't move. I felt my hands shake. It wasn't just the regular booze shakes. Every single face looked at me, and I thought they were thinking how stupid I was.

Some of those guys had been pretty well-educated in their other lives.

"You gotta be kidding," Steve had said to him when he told him about his fear. "Did you ever hear Charlie talk. Or Mike. You sound like an astronaut next to them." So Tadziu listened to Charlie and Mike, and heard what he had never noticed before. "Besides," Steve said, "you could use a little humility." He laughed. "Guess you never noticed that, huh?" He became quiet. "Lots of us need help in seeing what we are."

After the next meeting, when the members had coffee and donuts, Charlie pointed at the box on the table. "Hey, pass dem donuts" he said. "Da shuga' too."

"Here dey are," Tadziu had answered and Charlie looked at him quizzically. Steve roared and winked at Tadziu. Charlie looked like he was hurt, but Steve patted him on the back.

"It's okay," he said, "just a joke. Nothing to do with you," he lied, his face becoming sober immediately. It would be a serious thing to hurt another member. Tadziu looked down.

Jeez, these guys really mean it when they say they care for each other.

After the next meeting, Tadziu held Charlie's hand when they said the "Our Father."

Ripples

Tadziu remembered other ways Steve had helped him, things he told him, things Tadziu hadn't paid much attention to at the time. He thought about the time he had taken the girl to his room. And told Steve about it later

Tadziu knew it wasn't fair. He needed a woman and he needed one bad. He didn't go to his usual bar but to a bar where he knew he could find one. He saw her perched on a barstool, a beer in one hand and a cigarette in the other. The heels on her shoes were like stilts and made her seem taller than she was. He didn't know if it was the sweater or bra that made her boobs look like small mountains formed into a V. but they were big. The skirt was a sweater too, made her stick out both front and rear. There were bands of flesh between her waist and her chest, bands that sat atop each other in a graduated series, large at the waist and becoming smaller as they moved up. He sat down next to her without speaking.

"How ya been," she said, pretending to know him, glancing back at her girlfriend triumphantly. He brought drinks for her and her girlfriend but he avoided looking at her face because he wanted to forget her as soon as the night was over. When he did look at her, he saw she was not much older than he was, maybe even younger than he'd thought.

What the hell's the difference?

His look would tell her what he wanted.

Most of the girl's boobs disappeared when she took off her bra. He knew she was nervous because she had trouble getting her underpants off, but she acted as if she knew everything there was to know about sex

. "Y'now what I mean," she kept saying, and winking at him after she made some remark she thought was dirty. And he was ashamed because he knew she'd do whatever he wanted. So he'd have to act impressed with everything she did when all he wanted was to get it over with.

I don't know if I can do this. She's just a kid who's probably too fat for her boyfriend.

Marysza's face kept coming from somewhere and attaching itself to the girl, moving in front of her like a mask on a long holder. But Marysza would not be sitting naked on some man's bed yakking about absolutely nothing.

They did what they were there to do and there was nothing sophisticated about it. Pretty basic stuff. All he needed. He came back to himself and heard more talking coming from her. He tried to pay attention but it required too much effort until he pieced together some of the words and realized she was talking about the two of them. Like he was her boyfriend or something.

"We could take a little cruise, just a little cruise on the weekend and be back for work on Monday."

"Whoa, whoa, I can't do that," he said and watched her face fall. He felt like slapping her the way you would slap a stupid kid. He controlled his voice and made himself turn away from his anger.

What am I doing here? Why am I down on this woman, girl, whatever she is, when I brought her here? Yeah, but she wouldn't be here if she was decent, would she? And I wouldn't be in this shit if it wasn't for Marysza. Aw, cut it out. I got what I deserved from Marysza. And this girl's just a kid. My sister Gina's age.

He felt his blood rise as he put Gina and this girl in the same thought. He realized the girl was talking about the Fourth of July weekend.

"I gotta go see my kid, my boy," he lied. "He's expecting me." Her eyes widened. She jumped off the bed.

"You been married, huh? I never been married. I like kids." She looked as if she was being punished, made to stand in the corner or stay after school.

Aw fuck, fuck.

He wanted to kick himself. Wanted to dress her and get her out of his room, out of his life.

"Maybe we could have a kid sometime." She put her arms around his neck. Then buried her face in his shoulder as if she couldn't look at him. This made it a little easier. Because he couldn't see her face. But she knew. Knew the whole thing, the story of him and her, the things he couldn't say. How women knew things he didn't know. But he wouldn't have to lie any more, wouldn't have to make excuses. She brushed against him with her naked behind. Deliberately. That was all she could do. To tempt him. Not much. But he was done.

"C'mon, c'mon," he said, pushing her toward her pile of clothes on the chair.

"You're a fuck, a shit," she said, whirling around, glaring at him with Marysza's face. Gina's face. Nobody's face. The face of anger, of hatred.

That's how it looks to be hurt. I deserve it. I wanted to use her. She knows that now. She's young and stupid enough that she thought it could be love or something.

He almost laughed.

But she knows now.

Without saying anything, he handed her twenty-five dollars. She pulled on her clothes and stuffed her stockings into her purse. Her hair stuck out in all directions. The waist of the skirt had two buttons but only one was buttoned which left the skirt off-center or something and its stiff fabric pointing in two directions at once. Like the two halves of a wooden panel. Her underwear showed. He wanted to tell her but he knew better. On her way through the door, she turned again.

"You're a real fuck".

"I know." He handed her more money.

Her face softened for a moment, then turned ugly again. Sounding like a horse walking on stilts, she clattered out the door. There was no way he could do anything about it. Maybe later, he could think of something that would make things better.

Be real. It's not possible.

He had thought she was a girl who knew the score. But there was something in her that was still innocent.

Damn. Damn. What Am I supposed to do?

Later, he told Steve about it.

"What the hell d'you do that for. You're divorced, for Crissake. You can go out with decent women. You don't have to look for whores."

Oh Jeez, oh jeez. That look's in Steve's eyes, the look that says "Now you have someone else to apologize to, to make amends to."

"Okay, okay," he said. "I know." And he was dumbfounded. He'd never thought of that, never thought a decent woman would want to go out with him. And he wasn't sure that girl could be called indecent. Stupid was more like it. He began to wonder about himself, about the things Steve had said, to wonder what he was, besides a rotten husband and father. Maybe he wasn't a rotten son. Maybe it was his father who was rotten. Steve had thought Tadziu was a pretty nice guy. But then why had he treated Marysza and Jimmy so bad? Maybe he could make up for that. He had to start making up for that, at least trying. It was one of the steps in the alcoholic program. "Atonement."

Tadziu didn't want to think about the program anymore. He had asked Steve more than once whether he was an alcoholic.

"Well, maybe not," Steve had answered. "but you're well on your way. Besides, none of this stuff is going to hurt you."

So Tadziu had started making the coffee at the meetings he attended. Steve said it was a way to get to know the other guys. And it was. Guys started talking to him, friendly-like. Tadziu knew they were all in the same boat with him when it came to booze. He began to feel as if he belonged, as if he had some friends, as if everything wasn't hopeless. And thought about his appearance again, kept his hair clean, washed his clothes more often and pressed his pants once in a while.

That wasn't easy. The laundromat was far away from his boarding house. He had to buy an iron and borrow the landlady's ironing board. He thought more and more about what he was. He had never been anyone, or anything. Besides a rhummy. But when he stopped being a rhummy, what was he? He didn't know the answer but because of Steve, he thought there was a possibility he might be something. That thought was frightening.

I can fail. Again. Big-time. I want a drink. I know I want a drink. To shut out the thoughts. Of Steve. Of my failures. But I don't want a drink. That'll be throwing things in Steve's face again. Like his jacket.

He closed his eyes against that memory.

If I just wait his one out, it'll pass. It'll pass. Never the same.

He heard those words in his head a lot. Said them a lot.

Whenever the need for a drink became strong.

Never the same. One day at a time, God-damn-it. Never the same again.

Chapter Seven

Beginning

Marysza walked on stairs covered with maroon carpeting, passing rows of seats that stretched before her like a sea...

If I sit *too far back, I might not hear. If I sit too close to the front, someone might think I'm too eager, too pushy.*

She chose a seat somewhere in the middle and, as if she had done this a hundred times, sat down and straightened her skirt with a slight movement of her hands. Groups of students wearing, jeans, T-shirts and old sneakers, came in talking and laughing, comfortable with themselves and their surroundings. A few older women wore skirts.

I'll never wear a skirt again.

A boy wearing no socks flopped along in sneakers that had no laces and were filled with holes. Marysza felt embarrassed, turned her eyes away and began to laugh. The boy turned and looked at her. His smile pulled air and sun from the open window and poured it on Marysza like a sudden shower.

Students sat all around, but no one sat next to her.

That's because there's so many seats. They'll never be full.

Seats began to fill fast, as if a warning bell had sounded, prompting a scramble in which someone sat down next to her, but Marysza couldn't turn to see because there was no time. The professor entered and began talking, saying words Marysza thought she had heard in a dream, the matter-of-fact beginnings of each of his statements building to an inevitable conclusion. Marysza was mesmerized by the ease with which the words tumbled from his mouth, the way they fell into the waiting silence as if they were planned to fall that way, by the way they sounded, as if they knew exactly how to sound, as if there were no other way to sound.

She regained herself and began to write the professor's words. From the corner of her eye, she saw that no one around her wrote as frantically as she did. She took a breath and tried to slow her hand but determined to capture every word, it had a will of its own.

This is impossible. I'm losing. I have to listen and write at the same time. How do they do it?

She could only write some of the words the professor spoke, the ones that stood out, that jumped at her like fish in a stream, and lifting her head, saw that now she looked like the students around her. They wrote at the same pace or slower than she wrote. Some didn't write anything.

Exploring

Marysza didn't know where to eat her lunch. The college was a big city and she was lost. She had a map, saw a building labeled "Lounge and cafeteria" but that didn't mean much because tables were scattered everywhere in the halls like random wildflowers and were filled with students eating and talking to each other, some tilted back precariously in their chairs, their feet resting on the backs of the chairs in front of them. She sat at one of the tables, took her sandwich from the paper bag in her purse and nibbled at it slowly, her eyes surveying, absorbing everything she saw. She was thirsty but didn't know where to get a drink. A girl wearing blue jeans and a jacket missing most of its buttons slid into the seat across from her.

"Hi," the girl said. Her long hair was fastened with rubber bands into sections as if it was being divided for a permanent wave but when Marysza looked more closely, she saw that the girl had braids that were coming apart. She twisted strands of hair between her fingers, drew them through her teeth and absent-mindedly chewed on the ends as she stared in consternation at the class schedule she held in her hand.

Marysza continued to watch, mesmerized as the girl began unpacking the canvas bag that contained books, notebooks, and anonymous articles of various shapes. A thermos bottle and sneakers jammed into a pocket on the back of the bag had broken its zipper. The bag, torn and unable to remember its original shape, sat before them like a deflated balloon. The empty and open pocket made Marysza think of a bedroom, of something private she shouldn't be seeing.

Between swallowing the contents of the thermos, the girl demonstrated her exasperation by pounding her forehead with her hand and raising the level of her voice by several decibles. Marysza stared in admiration at this unconstrained display of emotion.

"I'm not going to be able to get that class until next semester. I already know I'll have a full load."

Marysza thought the girl was going to cry, and not knowing whether the girl was speaking to her or to herself, listened intently and nodded her head in sympathy. After the girl had finished her last gulp, one that took so long Marysza thought she might be choking, she said "I'll see you," slapped the table in a final expression of frustration and walked away.

Marysza was filled with pleasure at the girl's matter-of-fact acceptance of her.

I'm happy to be fading, turning into a part of the scenery, like wallpaper or a lamp, an accessory in a room.

After the girl was gone, Marysza spotted a water fountain and quenched her thirst. She almost skipped to her next class.

As soon as I have the money, I have to get one of those bags. That'll make it a lot easier than carrying my books around in my arms. I don't want one of those leather schoolbags. Only older students and professors have them anyway.

Marysza stayed after her classes each day, exploring the college until it was time to get Jimmy. She found the library, the student aid center and the cafeteria and laughed at her pride in her accomplishment.

At first, she was afraid to talk in class, afraid that her answers to questions would be seen as stupid, so she seldom raised her hand. When she thought she might dare, she went over what she was going to say, wrote it down and practiced the words silently in her mind. The first time she was called upon, she hesitated.

I still see Mrs. Hoggenkamp looking at me and not seeing me. What makes me think I can be a part of this?

In the next instant, Marysza saw that thought was a false one, that she did belong here and that far from pitying herself, she should be grateful to Mrs. Hoggenkamp. The picture of the elderly woman who had been so kind to her in the hospital when Jimmy was born also flashed before her eyes.

She was so kind, so sweet. Mrs. Hoggenkamp was not sweet. But perhaps even more kind. I have found mothers in strangers.

The teacher is waiting. Faces are turning to look at me. I have to talk. I have to talk.

She said what she had been thinking to say, and no one laughed. The professor held his chin while he looked up at the ceiling thoughtfully. Students waved their hands in the air, wanting to agree or disagree. Marysza talked again. Defended her position when another student tried to knock a hole into her argument. She'd thought of his objection beforehand and worked it out in her mind before he raised it. The professor nodded his head at her before moving on. That was the closest to praise he ever got. Marysza kept her face in her book.

Does anyone see my heart beating? Does anyone hear it pound or see it fill with joy?

After that, she talked more.

Collaboration

The history professor had announced the first test.

Marysza gave Jimmy his bath and put him to bed before she sat down with her textbook and her notes. The phone rang. It was Martha. Martha, telling her about something that was on television that night and wanting to come and watch it with her.

"Oh Martha, I can't, I've got my first test tomorrow. I've got to study." Martha said "sure", but the sound of hurt was in her voice.

Martha, please understand. Please understand. Don't get goofy now

She thought of dialing her friend's number but she didn't. She was soon engrossed in her studies, going through her notes again and again until she was sure of everything. Jimmy called for a drink of water.

"Mama's coming," she said, but sat at the table too long. He called again.

Oh, jeez, Jimmy. I'm coming, I'm coming. Don't be so impatient.

She went to him, feeling guilty because she wanted to put herself into this thing she knew she could do, this thing that she felt was changing the person she was. Jimmy began to fuss.

"Jimmy, I can't stay here. I've got work to do. You've got to go to sleep."

"I can't sleep, mama. I had a bad dream. About a giant chasing me."

"It was just a dream. If you lie down and go to sleep again, you'll be fine."

"I won't, mama. I won't. You have to stay here with me."

For a moment, she glared at her child, wanting to leave the room and let him cry, hating him because he consumed so much of her, took so much away from the thing she wanted to do.

I'm every bit as smart as any of the other students. I can do as well as any of them. Why does Jimmy make it so hard for me?

In the next moment, she felt her face flushing and held her head in her hands.

What's wrong with me? He's a child. .

"Okay, okay, honey. Mama's sorry. Mama will stay right here until you fall asleep."

She went into the kitchen and brought her book into the bedroom, into the small circle of light that surrounded Jimmy's night lamp and studied there until he fell back to sleep. Then she crept back into the kitchen and studied until she felt sure she knew the answers to anything the professor could possibly ask. It was two o'clock when she finished. She had to have Jimmy at day care by eight.

Well, I might as well get used to it. This will be my life from now on.

She lay in bed, but couldn't asleep. Martha's face floated before her and she felt herself growing angry again.

Martha called again on Friday but Marysza had to study for another test. Impatience arrived wearing its ugly smile.

Can't she just understand how important this is? Cripes, how can I make her understand?

Before she set the alarm, she looked at her notebook one last time, at the dates of all her tests and exams. She wanted to be sure she was prepared for each of them. The weekend came and her course schedule told her she would be on a panel on Friday in Philosophy class. She had done all her library research but was nervous about presenting her material. There was a knock at the door and Jimmy ran to open it.

"Auntie Marthy, Auntie Marthy," he cried, reaching out his arms.

"Hi babe," she said, lifting him high and swinging him around. Marysza tried to make her greeting sound enthusiastic and then decided to be honest.

"Martha, it's not that I don't want to see you. I'm a nervous wreck," she confided. Martha was incredulous.

"That's ridiculous; you're probably the smartest one in there."

"Martha, It doesn't matter how smart I am. I have to convince everyone of what I'm saying. Win them over, you know." In desperation, the words left her. "I'll show you. Sit here and listen."

Martha obeyed and listened as Marysza submitted her arguments in several ways, lining up her points in a different order each time until she and Martha agreed on the way it should be done. Marysza felt the tension slide from her like old skin.

I'm confident now, confident because of her. Martha. Martha. She doesn't know how much she's helped me, has never believed how bright she is. I'm grateful it happened this way. I know she sees now what takes my time, what pulls me from everything else.

Jimmy was asleep on the floor. Martha lifted him carefully so he wouldn't wake and carried him to bed.

Helping me again. I can relax for the rest of the night.

Marysza's life became a routine. She studied diligently, tended to Jimmy's needs and always made time to be with Martha. Sometimes Martha read her papers and Marysza explained them to her. If Martha had trouble understanding, Marysza rewrote her explanations until the ideas became clear. She was surprised that the tests were not more difficult. At the end of the semester, she had an almost perfect average.

Changes

Marysza began to see the world through different eyes. Pictures emerged slowly, like the discovery of pieces in a puzzle she was trying to put together. Delight verging on joy filled her when a piece of the puzzle came into sight.

Sometimes it was a piece of history which unfolded itself, part of the story of the world and its people over large spans of time—the story of the privileged classes with their wealth, and the under classes, people like herself who were once peasants fighting to survive. Sometimes it was a piece of psychology which she grasped, with which she could understand elementary facts about the way people behaved. In science she learned about discoveries people made that helped them overcome the powerful enemy of their own ignorance about the universe and its workings.

She saw that what she most loved was her glimpses into people's personal experiences, their expressions of hope and despair, fear and joy, the record of which she could read in the world's literature.

She was overcome by a strange sensation, a kind of déjà vu, which told her she had lived through this encounter before, that the things she was learning were not new but had always existed within her, had only to be called forth and uncovered. She felt herself settling into a place of contentment, of happiness. Except for Jimmy and

Martha, her books and what they contained were becoming the most important things in her life.

She felt alive again.

I belong. I look like the other students in my worn-out clothes. But I know my professors see I'm alert and engaged. Some of the students look like they've just gotten out of bed and are still tired. Always tired. I thought it was because they were studying so hard. Now I know better. Their school life includes going to parties, staying out late and not getting enough sleep. When exam time comes, they stay up all night trying to learn what they should have learned all semester.

She laughed.

Oh, my god. I sound like an old crow.

At first, she envied the students, that they came from families who could afford to send them here, that they could be so sure of this gift of education that they were contemptuous of it. But after enough time listening to their complaints, her envy evaporated. She saw that many of them were children, not yet grown into adulthood. They didn't know what she knew, which comprised more than academic matters. Though they were the same age, she had arrived at a different place.

Progress

As the year came to an end, people at the social services office seemed more confused than Marysza. She didn't know what the next step would be, if and when her welfare grant would stop, but they knew even less. Marysza was told she had to bring her grades into the office, and with pride, she brought them.

As if Mrs.Hoggenkamp is my mother.

She smiled to herself as she listened to Mrs. Hoggenkamp talking on the phone.

"Yes Jerry, I know that, believe me," she said, sounding incensed at Jerry's stupidity, whoever he was. "At the end of the year, the program is over. But these people are supposed to be given help to apply for aid so they can continue. Who does this? Gives them this help? When do we stop their grants? How can we stop them if we haven't finished what the guidelines say we're supposed to do?"

Marysza had heard the words "apply for aid" enough times to know that her willingness to apply for aid was the condition she must meet in order to remain in the program.

I don't want this life to end. I've never been this happy.

She knew where the aid office was since she had passed it many times. She went there to fill out the application for summer school. By the time the Social Services department had decided how to implement the next steps of the program, Marysza had completed summer school and received twelve more academic credits toward a degree.

The summer classes were harder because more material was condensed into a shorter period of time. Marysza received her first bad mark, a C+ for chemistry, a course she had taken only because it was required.

An Ending

When Marysza saw Mrs. Hoggenkamp again, she couldn't control her excitement about the job she had landed at the college, a job which would pay at least as much as her welfare grant.

"The job's in the student aid office. I learned enough about that with all the applications I did for myself. I've juggled and managed so that I have a minimum amount of loans. I know I can help other students do the same thing."

She said all this in one breath, and went on to express her incredulity that school personnel had offered her the job. "Not only that, Mrs. Hoggenkamp. I was offered another job—one in the student day care center, but the student aid job pays more. Day care positions, you know, even at the college, don't pay much."

Mrs. Hoggenkamp did not speak for a few minutes. Lines formed at the corners of her eyes, first narrowed and then opened, travelling from her eyes and onto her skin like highways.

"Are you biting off more than you can chew, Marysza? Aren't you afraid a job will cut down on the time you need for your studies? For Jimmy?"

"No, no, I'm not. I can do it. I know I can. I'll be able to support Jimmy and myself. It won't be too much. And Jimmy can still be in the day care center while I work in the aid office or go to classes. The fee at the day care enter isn't much for students. It's set by what you can afford to pay. What do you call it? A sliding scale. It's all perfect. I know I can do it. Besides, I only need to carry twelve hours to be a full-time student and qualify for everything. Twelve hours is nothing. I've already carried over twenty." Marysza came to the end of her speech and stopped suddenly, as if a hand had reached out and silenced her. She took huge gulps of air.

Mrs. Hoggenkamp tried to hide her smile with her hand but it showed. It would be a heavy load but Mrs. Hoggenkamp's eyes revealed the faith she had in this girl who stood before her bubbling like a teakettle.

What she says is true. She won't mind the work, will rise from beneath her burdens like a newly-hatched bird shaking its wings.

Mrs. Hoggenkamp knew it was more than faith she was feeling. She was filled with envy, envied this girl's beginning, the expression of hope which sat on her face like a blush, covered her forehead and her cheeks, and traveled downward to her neck and the bit of her chest that peeked from the open collar.

Mrs. Hoggenkamp ran her fingers along the cord which held her glasses. A long time ago she had known that feeling, the feeling that nothing was big enough to stop her. She learned differently, had wrestled with the case overload, the bureaucracy of government, and most disillusioning of all, with the clients, until she reached the point where her faith in the motives of people disappeared. But with this girl, she could be proud of her judgment. The other two clients in the program could not compare to the progress this one had made. Despite what she had thought about this program in the beginning, Mrs. Hoggenkamp had helped someone.

That doesn't happen often. I should say almost never. Go on your way, young woman. Be what you can, what I wanted to be, what I started out to be. I have a part, hold a stake in you. Go on your way.

Marysza interrupted Mrs. Hoggenkamp's thought. "Who do I take my grades to?" Mrs. Hoggenkamp laughed.

"No one. You won't officially be a client any more. You'll still qualify for medical benefits and other benefits. But those are special programs, so you'll go to different offices. You won't come here anymore."

Marysza stopped her chatter. They were both silent. Mrs. Hoggenkamp moved the glasses on the chain from one side of her chest to the other. Marysza felt an unfamiliar lump growing in her throat.

I don't understand my feelings. I resented this woman. I know she helped me. I'll miss her. I'll miss her. What is this called? Nothing stays the way it starts out to be. Things change in ways you can't know, can't see. I want to touch her.

She moved to the desk, reached over and put her arms around Mrs. Hoggenkamp. "Thank you for everything." Mrs. Hoggenkamp stayed behind her glasses and cleared her throat.

Marysza's thoughts and emotions were in a hopeless tangle. She knew she had to hurry in order to get Jimmy on time but powerful feelings held her, held her in this office, to this routine that was so familiar.

Part of my life is over, will never be the same. I'll never be in this place again.

"Mrs. Hoggenkamp?"

"Yes, Marysza."

"You were right. You can call me "Mary".

Mrs. Hoggenkamp looked as if she had been entrusted with a great confidence.

"Okay, Mary. Thanks."

In all the times she'd come here, Marysza had never looked behind her as she left the office. Today, when she looked back for what was the last time, she noticed the glass on Mrs. Hoggenkamp's door, that it was streaked, smeared with the testimony of weeks, months and years of days.

I could clean that glass, really clean it, not just swipe at it like the cleaning people do.

She thought how silly she was, closed the door and walked to the elevator.

A New Question

At the end of the semester, the head of the Office of Student Aid told Marysza she could have the job again, could keep it for as long as she wished. She could tell he was pleased with her work. Marysza also was pleased. She felt good when she helped students find money to continue their studies, especially those who were as poor as she was. And there were many, she was surprised to find. But then, this was a state college. Students who were not accepted at or could not afford the university came here.

The tools of Marysza's job were thick reference books which listed all the colleges and universities in the country, their entrance requirements and any in-house aid they offered for undergraduate students. Another set of books compiled sources of outside aid, such as grants, scholarships, etc. A parallel set of books provided the same information for graduate students. Marysza began to know the books well. Students who were graduating and wished to work toward a higher degree became her favorite cases. She found herself poring through the books for these students as if her own interest was at stake and seeing that she could qualify for many of these graduate grants, began, in earnest, to hunt through them for herself.

She listened to the thoughts which came to her as easily as the words she spoke to student applicants and tried to ignore them.

I can't think of graduate school. I need to find a teaching job, a job with all the benefits Jimmy and I need. If I had a master's degree, I'd be permanently certified to teach. I can teach when I graduate but I'll have to earn my master's within five years. Why not work for it right away? Could I do it? Graduate school might be harder because I'd have to go to the university.

The word "university" was sufficiently ominous to halt her thoughts but they returned and began to run in circles.

I know I could get a teaching job when I graduate from here. It might be better to work toward a master's gradually. But if I put in two more years and start out with the master's, I'll be paid more at the start. The teaching shortage guarantees just about everyone a job. And if you teach in certain places, the government cancels all your debt.

Marysza hated the thought of leaving school. She heard the words she spoke each day in her office.

Go to graduate school right away. You're in the habit of studying now. It'll be harder to go back.

The tension surrounding the decision mounted and she saw that she was afraid.

Am I good enough, intelligent enough? It doesn't matter what I see on paper about me. The As and the Bs don't take away the fear, don't put assurance in its place.

Another Fear

She recognized the voice on the other end of the line and, with sadness and astonishment, knew it was the voice of her mother and that she, too, was afraid.

"I want very much to see you and Jimmy," her mother said, as if her breath were talking.

"It's not a good time for me," Marysza said. "I'm wrestling with applications for graduate school. If you could wait a while, it would be better".

"Of course," the voice breathed again and was silent, then, in a burst of emotion, exclaimed, "Oh Marysza, I'm so proud of you." It seemed she would say more but stopped herself. Marysza tried to forget the voice, told herself she was really too busy to give her mother any attention. But the voice was difficult to ignore, the way it rose hopefully and then fell, like a bird that had been shot down. She pushed away the sound of the voice and filled her head with the scratching of her pen on papers that rustled like dry leaves tumbling in the wind.

Love

Marysza didn't date. She told herself that her studies and her child absorbed her completely but she knew this was not the entire truth.

It's true that I'm too tired most of the time to think of dating, but that's only part of it. The real thing is that I can't be sure of my judgment with men.

She spent her free evenings with Martha which was not always easy because Martha had a boyfriend. David was a car mechanic, and a good one, Marysza knew, because he had a sizable following, people who asked for him in the garage where he worked. Martha told Marysza he was saving money to buy a garage of his own and open his own business.

When she met David, Marysza was struck by how well he and Martha looked together. She felt jealous of her friend, of the look of contentment in her eyes as she looked at the young man who had grease hidden under his nails and settled into the ridges of the skin on his hands and of the way David stood next to Martha proudly, somewhat possessively. Her jealousy made her ashamed.

I'm envious even of the scent of his after-shave.

She concentrated on looking interested as David told her about his business plans. He talked fast and furiously, about the equipment he was going to have and how much each piece would cost, laughing with Marysza as he heard the excitement in his own voice. She looked at his broad shoulders, his muscular build, the blonde hair and blue eyes that made him look Swedish and asked if he was. He roared.

"Pelosi? I don't think so." His smile was wide and spontaneous. His eyes revealed a confidence that was not overbearing, but nevertheless, secure.

"Cars today are more complicated than ever," he said, "so more tools and equipment are necessary in a garage. Expensive but necessary." Marysza nodded her head in agreement while David went into a long description of how engines were designed, and what parts were being replaced, but when he saw that Marysza understood little of what he was saying, he began drawing simple illustrations, and using analogies she could understand.

"Some things don't change much, though, thank God, so if a car overheats, or you see your engine leaking, it's probably that your water pump is shot, or your radiator has a hole in it, or got rusty or something. Even if the radiator design changes, it's still a part that does the heating and cooling, so it's got to have a thermostat and hoses to carry antifreeze and a pump to push the liquids through your engine, you know, like your heart pumps blood through all your veins and capillaries. You spring a leak anywhere in your body, you're in trouble too."

With large eyes and an open mouth, Jimmy looked up from the floor where he was playing with his toy cars and didn't take his eyes away from David's face. David looked so pleased by Marysza's interest that Marysza was afraid he would continue, but Martha saved her.

"David, leave her alone. Talk about something besides cars!" David reddened but Martha patted his arm reassuringly.

Jimmy came alive and closed his mouth.

"Martha, look at my new car!" he said excitedly, offering no objection when David took the car and turned it around in his hand, admiring it from every angle.

"Hey, little guy, do you know what this car is?" Jimmy shook his head no. "Well, it's a Buick," David said and sitting down on the floor, pointed to another. "And this one is a Chevrolet." He began to point out features on the small cars. "See the long body this one's got? And the big windshield here. This is a fancy car. But don't buy one because it breaks down a lot. Maybe you can work in my garage when you're big enough." Jimmy responded with a seriousness that made it seem he'd known David for a long time.

"O. K. I will!" Not wanting David to get up from the floor, he kept asking questions about the different cars. Marysza was relieved that Jimmy was now the recipient of David's technical knowledge but began to feel uneasy with Jimmy's endless questions.

"It's all right," David said. "I had six brothers and a sister." He tousled Jimmy's hair. "And this guy likes when I talk about cars, right partner?" Jimmy nodded emphatically and protested when Marysza said it was time for bed. Martha promised to bring David back again.

"He's really a nice guy," Marysza whispered to her friend. Martha beamed.

The door closed and as if she had been engaged in physical labor, Marysza was exhausted.

How happy she'll be with him. And I'm alone. Because I'm not as good as my friend at choosing men. She has a decent man. I'm glad. But alone.

"I thought we should just buy a house and use the garage for me at first, until we get on our feet," David had said. "And in the meantime I can finish school," Martha added. "You bet," David said. "It'll be nice having a smart wife."

The two of them making plans, giving each other secret looks.

It was quiet after they left. Marysza's books lay on the table, some of them open, one with its pages propped open with a plastic tumbler where she had stopped studying. The books looked out of place and superfluous, unreal things in a real world.

Why am I thinking of graduate school. I've been dreaming dreams I have no right to dream. I need a job right away. I need to be a real mother. It's selfish of me to think of anything else.

Marysza couldn't resume her studying and bent down to gather stray toys.

I know Martha will be happy.

One of the rubber wheels on Jimmy's green car was missing, the naked end of the axle sharp and dangerous. She put it up on a cabinet, out of reach.

But what will happen to our friendship. I'm more alone than ever.

Her thoughts continued their circling, making her feel they were drawing air from her lungs and she'd suffocate.

I know I'm smart. Other people think I'm smart so it must be true. But in another way, Martha is smarter. She knows how to get on in the world, how to find a partner who is decent. Like David. A good person, I can tell. Martha told me not to marry Tadziu. She sees things I can't see. I don't have her way of being smart, her way of seeing.

Marysza's head ached from thinking. She saw crumbs she had missed beneath the table. As if this would stave her inner turmoil, she reached for the broom again and swept them into the dustpan. The broomstick moved in circles.

Jimmy and I will face another strange world if I go to graduate school. We'll have to move closer to the university. Will he adjust? I'm afraid of newness. I know this flat, this building, this street. Can I hold these things I know? Things change from one moment to the next. But I don't want to change. I'm afraid.

The broom stopped and she plopped into a chair.

I lie to myself. Jimmy will be fine with the newness. I use him as my excuse.

Knowing she couldn't quiet the upheaval within her, Marysza closed her books and went to bed.

In the months that followed, Marysza didn't see Martha very much. She filled her life with her books, attempting to ignore thoughts that weren't new but always there, floating through the air like ghosts and coming to her with renewed vigor. She thought of her mother as she watched a young girl and her mother walking together on the street, their heads close together, the girl listening intently, and the mother solicitous, her arm around the girl's shoulder.

Am I like my mother? Be*cause her life was like mine? And my father? Why don't thoughts of him haunt me? Is it because he's dead? Or because he didn't leave me like she did? My mother grieved for the man she loved. Turned hurriedly to another man because of her loneliness, her despair. I can forgive that. I can't forgive her not loving me. Isn't that the first right, the right to a mother's love. I know. Because I'm a woman. And a mother. Maybe there's a psychology course I can take that will tell me if children follow their parents' patterns. If I go to graduate school.*

Chapter Eight

An Invitation

Marysza had asked about his family. He thought about his sister, of her last letter. Helcza, now Helen, the second oldest, next to him down the line.

Sometimes in dreams he saw her, felt her two thin arms encircling him, holding him close when everyone else cried, and holding him so that when it was over and everything was quiet, he could close his eyes and travel to other places. Helcza, who had somehow managed to get away from it all, to escape. And become a nurse. His beautiful sister. Who knew about recovering. Making recovering her business. Her life. The same open arms his mother once had. But not afraid. And so she could walk away. My beautiful sister. My beautiful Helen. He carried her letters in his wallet. They were grimy, and smudged where the folds were. He took out the last one and read it again.

Dear Tadziu,

I think about you all the time. Sometimes I wish I did not live so far away but California is so beautiful. When I moved here it was like starting a new life. The only thing I miss is never seeing you and the twins and Gina. I hear from them every now and then. The only one who never sends a letter is you. I know your little boy must be getting big. I've never seen him. I've never met his mother. That hurts me. Please think about coming sometime. Maybe at Christmas or something. We have plenty of room and the children could have a lot of fun. We could take them to Disneyland. Imagine Tadziu. Disneyland. I never thought I would see such things. I am sending you a picture of Jerry and me with our children. I told you I had another baby. Mary is almost a year old now and crawling backwards to get where she wants to go.

Please don't think Jerry wouldn't want you to come. He's such good man Tadziu. You would like him, I know you would. He is so good with the kids when I have to work. I've been doing the second shift so I don't get home until late and they're already sleep-

ing. He even gets Mary off to sleep okay. I got a promotion at work. Now I supervise other nurses.

I wrote to ma and told her she could come here and live. I didn't get an answer for about six months but when I did, it was no. She didn't say much else. Just that her place is with pa. I knew she'd never leave him. I wish I could say the same thing to Pa but I just can't. Tadziu, do you ever see them? You're still there. Ma's handwriting was so shaky. I know she never writes letters but still I worry. Could you just let me know how things are with them? It would relieve my mind so much.

Gina is doing fine. I talked to her on the phone the other night. Her classes are good and I think she loves the guy she's been going with. He seems very nice. I don't know what to do. If they get married, I'd like to have it here. Would ma and pa come? And if they did, would seeing pa spoil things for Gina? Or Tommy and Johnny if they came? Tommy's still in that garage fixing cars. Johnny's taken an exam to be a corrections officer but he won't know the results for a while. He's had all kinds of jobs. The two of them live together and they're kind of funny. The first time I went to see them, the place was a mess but this summer we stopped when we were on vacation. I guess they finally figured that someone had to clean up the place. It looked pretty good. They told us they divided the chores evenly. We laughed. They always make us laugh.

They ask about you all the time. So does Gina. I tell them you're okay but I don't really know that. The only letter of mine you ever answered was when you got divorced. I never even met your wife.

Tadziu, maybe you think I'm a pest and wish I would quit bothering you. I can't. My life is so good I want it to be good for all of us. You were the one who had things worst at home We all know that. I remember how you brought things home for us. You were such a good brother. I know why you had to get away, to disappear for a while and not see any of us. But it's been years now, Tadziu, and maybe you've figured things out.

Please let me know if you would come here for Gina's wedding. I know that if Tommy and John knew you were coming, they'd come too. I don't know about Ma and Pa but I'll worry about that later. Please answer my letter. Love. Helen

Jesus, what am I supposed to do now? Do I want to see them? His sisters and brothers were lumped together in his mind with everything else. Twin boys walking around on fat little feet. His mother nursed them for a long time. So they stayed babies. Played with anything that was around because they never had any toys. Dragging the few pots and pans his mother had from the cupboards. Sitting on a kitchen floor slopped with whatever they had in their mouths. Sleeping in the same clothes they wore all day. But laughing. Always laughing. Until their father was around. Then suddenly quiet. Expectant. As if they sucked the quiet from the air. Janina. Now Gina. Not a helluva lot older than the twins. Quiet in a different way. Didn't laugh much. Even when the old man wasn't around. As if she was always scared. She was. With teeth that grew in crooked. Turned in all directions. Still pretty. Always skinny. And once they started school, she could read better than he could. And so he was jealous. But he still loved her.

And Helen. Always. Running to him when she knew their father was after him. Trying to shield him. Once standing in front of him. Because the old man wanted only him. The first one to stop crying. And helping the others to stop. Including their mother. Who seemed to age ten tears for every year he remembered. Who was an old lady when he left. At thirty five maybe. Or forty. Helen was wrong if she thought he'd figured things out. He'd never have them figured out.

He had a funny thought. Another old lady. Marysza's grandmother. She would have knocked the shit out of the old man. Hit him with a frying pan if she had to. He laughed out loud at the picture of Marysza's grandmother hitting his father with a frying pan. The old lady was always good to him. And not afraid of much. Swore sometimes too. He always liked her.

And now Helen wanted him to come. To where they'd all be. And now she was married. Would she understand he couldn't come? How the hell she got to California he didn't know. Something in her got her places. Like Marysza. Even when she was afraid. Something else in her was stronger than being afraid.

And I'm nothing. I don't want them to see I'm nothing.

Pain rose in him like bad food he'd eaten and had to get rid of. He saw all of them. All at once. Like a portrait. Each of their faces. And knew he wanted to see them. Even though they'd see he was nothing. Would see he was a reformed alky who couldn't drink. He wanted a drink now. His throat and his tongue were parched. His veins about to burst. There was a booze store up the street. Just this once. He had nothing good about himself to tell his brothers and sisters. Just this once. He started out the door. Trying not to think of Steve. Or Marysza. Or Jimmy. Or his brothers and sisters. Just this once.

The store was empty, lit up with red and green. Christmas must be close. He stared at all the bottles on display. Stacked in rows. On shelves. Little silver bells lining the window. Marysza was gone. Joe was gone. He was alone. Was always alone. Why the hell would they want to see him? But her letter said it. Maybe Tomasz and Janek would come, Tommy and John, she called them.

I wonder if they remember their new names yet?

If he came. Something depended on him. He didn't know what. Gina was the one he remembered least because she always seemed to be hiding, like a little mouse. She didn't need him to get married. Or Tommy and John either. Maybe they'd come, Helen said. If he came. If he came.

He wished Steve was here. Steve would know what he should do. Steve would talk to him. He felt tired. He couldn't think anymore. He leaned his head against the window of the liquor store. Closed his eyes to shut out the sight of all the bottles. Some guy passing by looked at him.

"Hey buddy. You okay"?

"Yeah. Yeah."

He straightened up. Started to walk away. So the man couldn't know he was an alky. A failure. Where was he walking to? Marysza was gone. Steve was gone. He didn't want to call any of the other guys from AA. He knew what they'd say. He could say it himself. Or Jerry or Hank, the guys who were still his friends. He didn't want to talk to them. It was too personal or something. He wanted a drink.

If I come. If I come.

He kept putting one foot in front of the other.

If I come.

*I*t would probably cost a lot. To fly to California.

If I come

Mother

He didn't like to think of his mother or the way she looked the last time he saw her. He could still remember when he was a boy and he saw in her eyes that he was important and she was proud of him. That was when their house was clean and she cooked for all of them. She loved Helcza and Janina too. The three of them fought over who would be first to sit on her lap, the first to reach her when they came in from playing outside.

Tomasz and Janek were babies then so their mother shushed all of them if they made too much noise when the babies were sleeping. She let them watch the babies drink milk from her breast. It made Tadziu happy to see the baby look at him with big eyes, his head almost upside down in his mother's arm, his mouth never releasing his hold on the nipple. He didn't let go even if Tadziu tickled his fat feet. It made his mother happy too. Sometime when they were done nursing, she gave each of them a baby to hold. They sat on the couch next to each other while she sat next to them, smiling and saying quiet words in Polish. Some of the words he still remembered like *piekny*[40] and *niewinny*[41]. Even Janina got a turn but he was the biggest so his mother let him have the longest turn. He remembered those times. Sometimes his mother even sang when she did her work.

He couldn't remember exactly when it was that his mother changed, when things began to change in all of them. His father starting to hit him, hitting him more when his mother tried to protect him. Everyone screaming and crying, Helcza hitting their father until he pushed her aside like a dog in his way. But his father never hit Helcza. Only him.

His mother stopped cooking, stopped doing much of anything. She cried a lot, sometimes into one of the babies all wrapped in blankets. Tadziu remembered thinking she had gone blind because she didn't seem to see any of them anymore, didn't remember to do things for them.

Tadziu and Helcza did whatever they could to help their mother remember to make food for them. They played with the babies so they didn't cry and washed the dishes in the sink. When they had no more clothes to wear they pulled out the big machine so their mother knew it was time to wash. Then they put the clothes to dry on the big wooden racks in the kitchen. When things were quiet, Tadziu played pretend games with his sisters, mostly Helcza. Gina didn't always want to play so he and Helcza teased her until she started laughing. Then she would play and made up better games than he and Helcza did.

Then he met Joe and had to start going to school. His sisters went later but they were behind him. He liked what he learned in school but he worried all the time about what would happen to him at home. From the fuckin'old man.

He wasn't sure why he did it except that it made it easier so he told himself that his mother died. That didn't work for long and he started thinking of her again. She was an old woman who wasn't really an old woman. A shadow. With a look of shame in her eyes all the time. He didn't know why she looked ashamed but he couldn't stand looking at her that way. It made him angry with her and angry with himself.

He thought again of his sisters, that he'd only thought of them a few times in the last years and mostly of Helcza. But now he saw Janina too. The three of them running in the cold mornings in their flat to sit before the gas heater and dress. Janina wore her slippers because she always put them in a safe place. Sometimes Helcza wore hers but he could never find his when he needed them. He was so cold he wanted to cry but he didn't because he knew that would frighten his sisters.

He invented a new game. His sisters and he dared each other to see who would be first to take off their night clothes. He tried to trick them but after a while they didn't trust him and wouldn't be first. Tadziu remembered thinking that his mother didn't feel the cold, that she didn't feel anything.

He could still see her coming to tell them to hurry. She was a silent ghost, her bare feet sticking out at the bottom of her long white nightgown, her hair in a braid down her back. Then they would all count to three, throw their night clothes off together and hurry to see who could be the first one dressed.

Their mother would turn up the gas heat of the stove where they sat and pad into the kitchen to start the fire in the kitchen stove, a stove divided into two parts, one part for heating and the other part for cooking. She used something that looked like a can opener with a silver handle to lift the black circle on top of the stove, then put paper and wood down the hole to make a fire. The yellow glow of the flames made a roar when the fire started and popped and crackled when the cover was replaced.

The sound of that crackling made Tadziu think he was warm but the house would not really be warm until they came home after school. Sometimes not even then if his mother forgot to put more wood in the kitchen stove because the gas heater wasn't enough to keep the whole place warm. One day, Tadziu got brave and did what he had seen his mother do. He lifted the cover, put wood into the fire and turned the handle that looked like a coil half way up the stove pipe. When he played with the coil, the fire got bigger or smaller.

He wasn't afraid anymore and built up the fire in the stove in the morning and after school. He felt his sisters thinking he was a hero. Another day, they watched him with big eyes and held their breath when he turned up the knob on the gas heater. But nothing bad happened. The orange and blue fire behind the glass got bigger and when they were warm enough he turned the knob down. After that, his sisters depended on him to keep the house warm. He did. He wasn't sure his mother noticed except one day she put her arms around him for no reason and held him close for a long time. His sisters watched silently. He could still feel the warm skin of her face and the powdery softness of her graying hair.

The babies were out of their cribs then and played with toys on the small colored rug near the stove. They didn't cry as much so Tadziu knew they were warmer too. His mother had made the rug and many of their other things from rags. She cut the rags into long strips and used the strips to crochet rugs and blankets and warm slippers for their feet.

But then his mother didn't get out of bed in the morning anymore. After he did the fires in the morning, he'd find whatever food he could find for himself and Helcza and Janina before they went to school. Sometimes they were still hungry and they never had any lunch. Sister gave them some things, even to take home, that looked to Tadziu like leftovers from someone's supper.

Then his mother seemed to remember they needed lunches. They came home one day to a smell Tadziu had almost forgotten, the smell of baking bread. All week they had lunches of huge slices of bread and the jelly his mother had made during the summer. For a while she even baked placek, [42]the crumb cakes he could remember having at Christmas and Easter, a long time ago. They could smell the bread or the placek before they reached the door and knew their mother was well that day.

But that ended and she would stay in bed again, sometimes all day until their father came home. Tadziu thought his mother was sick. He didn't know what to do when she cried so he just tried to pretend it wasn't happening. But Helcza put her arms around their mother and kept telling her how she loved her. When she did that Janina would follow her and do the same thing. Finally she only got out of bed when the babies cried and when it was time to cook for their father.

If the babies cried a lot when the old man came home, it made him mad. He'd yell at their mother and shake his fist until she cried. And that made Tadziu and Helcza and Janina hate him more. When his father hit Tadziu, Janina—-he kept forgetting, her name was Gina now, before that, he thought she was Jeannette—would cry and run away, but Helen stayed and screamed at the old man. Then she came into the bedroom and put her arms around Tadziu. Sometimes he cried. But that was only in the beginning

"Poor Tadziu, I love you," she would murmur into his ear until he could stop crying. When they were older, she talked with him about how they could run away.

Now she was asking him to come to her house. In California.

It's impossible, Helen. I have no money. I just got a decent job. I'd have to work overtime from now until then to get the train fare. Then I'd have to take two weeks off from my job.

It's impossible. Impossible. Don't you see? Why do I give a shit if Tomasz and Janek don't come to Gina's wedding? Why should I give a shit about Tomasz and Janek at all, or you or Gina either?

He wanted their faces to go away, to leave him in peace. In peace.

He wanted a drink. How could he go to this wedding and let them see that he couldn't drink. His sisters. His brothers. All in better shape than he was. He was a failure. Just like his old man said. They would see that he was a failure. Why had she bothered him?

Helen, you make me want a drink. My life's a mess. You ask what's impossible. Just like all women. My mother with her eyes, you with your arms around me, Marysza with my need for her

I want a drink. I can't drink. But just one or two.

He walked to the corner bar. There was no Steve to call. A woman sidled up to him but he turned away. She was pissed. Too bad. All women were trouble. All your life. Trouble.

He had a drink. God, it tasted good. He ordered another. That tasted better. He was no good anyway. Why shouldn't he drink? No one cared about him. No one cared. He heard the voice in his head. He knew what the voice said wasn't true. He also knew he didn't want to admit it was untrue and that something about that was wrong.

"You fucker, you", he said aloud. The guy next to him turned his head and stared.

You want this excuse. You want this. I can't turn liquor away. They say so. Once I start, I'm sunk. You fucker. You want to prove they're right. You want to fail again just like you failed with Marysza and Jimmy. Then with Steve and Joe. Joe, you don't belong with Steve. I never knew if you loved me. Maybe you did a little. I always wanted to ask.

He got up from the barstool. He could walk away. Could prove they were wrong. That he wasn't an alky. That he could have two beers. He wanted to turn back to the bar and have some more to drink. He knew something was at stake here. His legs felt like lead as they moved through the door and into the street. He was being pulled to return. He was being pulled not to return. His mother's face and Marysza's and Helen's and Gina's were all pushed aside by Steve's.

"Don't leave, don't leave," he whispered, as if Steve were beside him again.

I need you, Steve. Let the damn Higher Power send you back to help me. Please help me.

He opened the door and stepped outside.

Don't let me return. Don't let me return.

He felt more uncertain each minute.

Just put one foot in front of the other. One step at a time. One step at a time.

He felt he was walking in a trance, kept putting one foot in front of the other. With each step he was unsure of whether he would continue forward or go backward. His muscles strained, pulled at invisible ropes, ropes that tied, tried to halt him.

I can't do this. I can't do this.

Now he heard Steve's voice.

"One step at a time."

He began to count his steps, concentrating hard on the counting. Turned around to look at the bar. Almost couldn't see it.

“One step at a time.”

Then he began to believe it, saw that he was walking away. He had drunk two beers and he was walking away. He began to hurry. Now he couldn’t see the bar. He felt like more than himself, like every person who battled an enemy. The odds weren’t in his favor. He had to give it his best shot. He reached his car, for a moment looked back into the darkness and then began driving home. He drove pretending there was no difficulty, that he was just another normal person.

The battle continued. He wanted to stop at each bar he passed, drove past each one, counted them all, kept driving.

I’m closer now, just a couple streets away.

Still wanting to turn around and go back, he turned off the ignition. Then he was running up the stairs. He didn’t know to what. Slammed the door behind him. As if he was escaping, hiding from an enemy that chased him. Like a robot, he kept putting one foot in front of the other all the way to his bed. He fell asleep immediately.

The next morning he realized he’d forgotten about his car. He’d parked it on a side street and walked home without even thinking. He thought that was funny. Because he wasn’t even drunk. When he walked to the street, his car was still there, waiting for him, but in a different way than all the other things that waited for him.

He loved his car. He kept it together and it paid him back, always dependable, always there, like now, when he turned the key and it started immediately, the motor so quiet and smooth you almost couldn’t hear it.

Looking In

There was no way out of it. Helen had asked him to look in on his parents.

His old man leaned against the door. It was amazing how his eyes held nothing when they looked at him. Only the thing Tadziu remembered. The old menace. A tired menace. But still there. Making itself big. Glaring at him. Trying to make him afraid. The old man was about half the size he’d been. Shrunk. Thin. It would be easy to hit him now. He was nothing but a little old man. With eyes trying to get back their threat, trying to recapture the only thing he’d been. With thin strands of hair covering the growing nakedness on top of his head. And his slippers. The same slippers he’d worn each night of his life after he returned from work. He was stuck in a world where nothing changed, a world where everything remained the same.

A half-smile crossed the old man’s face. The only greeting there would be. No words. The pitiful challenge of his eyes was the only thing left.

He’s made of holes, big, gaping holes.

And his mother. The only one his father ruled anymore. Walking on the sides of feet that were twisted and gnarled, like roots gone crazy in their growing, the ankles like knobs that were collapsing, trying to touch the floor. Pulling the rest of herself so she could stand. Looking at him with the same plea in her eyes. “Please understand. I’m helpless,” they said, and his silence telling her she was forgiven. That he could take her from this. From his father. But memories lay on the ground between them like corpses. And he knew she wouldn't go. Wouldn't leave his father. He could have told his sister that too, saved her the trouble of trying.

A Trip

He decided not to go by train because it would take too long. He had never flown anywhere. Helen wanted to send the airplane ticket but he said no. Actually, his new job made it easier to get the money together than he had thought. He tried to control the pounding in his chest when he stepped up to the window to buy the ticket, handed over all the money casually, as if it were not important to him.

The airplane rolled along the runway, building up speed like a car driven by someone with unrestrained confidence. He thought of the way he used to be with his cars. A little too sure of himself. A little too fast.

I hope the guy's not showing off the way I used to.

The plane began to ascend. Tadziu felt his stomach flip. The ground was a checkerboard with no color, a grid of squares that began to shrink until they disappeared. His body tensed when the plane began to jerk from side to side. He heard the pilot's voice came on some kind of radio. He said it was mild turbulence and would soon pass. God damn thing. Moved through the air just like a bird, bouncing when it hit some bad spots, turning so that you thought it would be on its side, then righting itself and passing through whatever it was that made them bounce.

And he was in it. Right in the middle of it, surrounded by clouds, wondering how safe it was, thinking of what he would do if it suddenly shot down like a deflated balloon, then forgetting to be frightened, filled with astonishment again as he saw that he was still surrounded by clouds. Some of the passengers actually slept, their heads leaning back in their seats, moving from side to side on the padded leather.and looking like they were cut off from their bodies.

He never closed his eyes once. His stomach felt queasy when the plane began to descend. As if hit by a brick, a sudden jolt told him the wheels had touched the ground. The plane ran crazily down the runway as if it could not stop. The whoosh of screeching brakes attacked his ears. Finally, like a car coming up against a wall, the plane stopped. He stood up and looked around in triumph at the other passengers, wanting to say, "There, we made it. That wasn't so bad, was it?" No one noticed.

Bumping and banging, he moved down the aisle with them, then into the airport, carrying his brand-new bag, excitement in his stomach as if he were a little kid. He moved as quickly as the others, an ocean of people all flowing in one direction, all heading toward a gate. A crowd of faces on the other side stared.

Jesus, I don't know who to look for. I don't know what she looks like now.

Then he knew. There she was. A young woman. Blonde, with a man and a boy at her side.

His nephew. His nephew.

But what about Jimmy? My son. My son.

Awkward, not knowing what to do until she hugged him and he hugged her back. Hesitant. Then sure. Her head moved in the hug and over her shoulder, he saw her husband smiling and the boy's eyes timid and searching.

The guy is stretching out his hand to me. My sister has water in her eyes. Women always do that. What kind of people are these? Dressed well. Who is she now?

They rode in a nice car and moved into the driveway of a nice house. Palm trees and flowers in the yard, swings and slides for children. He felt a vise in his chest, squeezing, tightening until his breath was almost cut off.

And Jimmy My son. What does my son have?

They took him into their house, gave him a bedroom. He felt them opening what they had.

They're a family. A family.

"You're part of this family," his sister's eyes said. But he didn't know it. Didn't feel it. Unsure of who he was. Her brows were a pencil-thin curve above her brown eyes. The hair that hung to her shoulders covered her eyes as she moved her head or looked down, keeping him from looking into her. She was also afraid.

Her husband broke the thing that sat in the air, the thing that kept them from talking to each other past the hellos and the kisses. The guy talked without stopping and Tadziu had to answer all his questions.

"Yes, the flight was good. Yes, the plane was full. The weather back home was cold. What the hell you want? It's winter." The husband laughed and Tadziu could feel some of the tension in his shoulders begin to give way. He thought then how hot it was here and felt his skin prickling inside his long-sleeved shirt. Helen's husband was still talking and then the boy too. Calling him uncle.

Uncle.

"Here the climate's pretty stable all year," the husband said. Cool at night. Good for sleeping." The boy asked him about snow. And for a moment, he forgot to answer.

"Mama says we can take you to see the ocean, Uncle Tadziu."

A little girl appeared from somewhere. She had the face he remembered, Helen's face. Then the husband was offering him a beer. He hesitated, then thought of how he walked away from the bar after two, and that maybe he was a normal man. He took the beer. Swigged it down. Too fast. The husband brought him another. Tadziu's words stumbled. He couldn't remember the husband's name. Then he heard Helen call the guy "Jerry".

"Thanks Jerry," he said, trying to sound natural. He was careful to drink slow this time. No more was offered. When more was offered, he declined.

Good.

He could barely keep up with the talk. "Yes he wanted to see the ocean. The dinner is delicious."

Some strange things I've never had. But good.

The little girl was shy. Didn't want to finish her supper, left the table, came back bringing some paper dolls to show him.

"She likes you," his sister said. "She doesn't let everyone see her paper dolls." His sister's skin was tan, the color of wet sand, her arms rounded curves. Tadziu tried to hold the paper dolls. The boy got jealous and brought some trucks and cars to show him. Tadziu laughed. His first laugh. They all laughed. He admired the cars and trucks. The boy was pleased.

What does my son play with? My son. Jimmy. Sleeping on his back in the crib, his fingers closed into a fist, his eyelids brushed with a faint blue color. My son. My son.

And then the first day was over and he was exhausted, lying on his bed.

She hasn't spoken to me really. She's afraid. I'm afraid. What do I say? Remember when we were always hungry? Remember when pa used to beat me up? When ma cried all the time?

A Family Reunion

Helen wasn't there the next morning when he came into the kitchen, shaved, wearing his only good shirt.

You stupid fucker. You could have more shirts. You could have a lot more of everything. You're not in the factory any more. You get paid enough.

Everyone was excited, anxious, running around for things connected to the wedding. So he was lost in the movement, didn't have to say much. Then Gina was there. Looking like his other sister. But somebody had fixed her teeth. They were white and straight and shiny, He thought he'd never really seen how beautiful she was. Big blue eyes. Long lashes. A figure like a movie star. The kind of girl other guys would call a dish and roll their eyes. Until he whacked them. She gave him a kind of hug, her arms floating next to him, barely touching, like a quiet whisper he couldn't hear, couldn't feel. They were strangers, walking around a house, trying not to collide, apologizing for everything.

I don't know her anymore. Why did I come? Quit being a wimp, you asshole. Helen asked me. Helen wants me.

Then Tomasz and Janek were there, both loud, thank God. Both tall. Good. The old man was short. That meant something else was in them besides him.

There was more shaking of hands, more words getting lost, not said, held behind a gate straining to open. But Tomasz and Janek rallied

It looked like something had been mixed up. Janek, with dirt under his fingernails, the old man's big arms, big shoulders and bulging muscles, but something Tadziu could see in his eyes, making him look too soft to be a corrections officer, and Janek knowing the two of them should be polite, punching Tomasz in the arm with his bulging muscles when he thought no one was looking and his brother was saying something stupid, then trying to hide his hands with the car grease under his fingernails until Jerry said, " hey, relax, that's honorable grease, and Janek, grinning, said "yeah, I think so too, but," pointing at Tomasz with a ""ha-ha" smile "my brother here don't think so',' and Tomasz beginning to answer," yeah, but for a wedding…"until his voice was drowned out by the overwhelming laughter that enveloped them all and Tomasz, free of any ill feeling, turned to Tadziu and said, "hey Tadz, guess what?"

Tadz?

"What?"

"I was an altar-boy just like you."

"Oh yeah? I'll bet you were especially picked."

Janek broke into laughter again. "Yeah, he was. Not me. I wasn't picked." This time Tomasz punched him in the arm.

"Well,"—-Tadziu was surprised at the sound of his own voice. Like an authority. Or a teacher—-"it don't matter how you were picked. It's still an honor." The laughter stopped abruptly, like camouflage that was no longer needed. For a moment, there was no movement except for Jerry stroking his chin.

Tomasz and Janek. Two babies. Carried in blankets while Ma cried. So they cried too, into the air, at nothing, until they discovered each other, learned to play. Screamed only when everyone else screamed.

"Who're you guys?" Tadziu asked, "Tomasz and Janek or Tommy and Johnny, or Tom and John?" The laughter returned as Tomasz waved his hand in dismissal.

"Who knows," he said. "Hey Tadz, Helen says you saw ma and pa."

"Yeah," Tadziu answered, but he knew it was a polite question, that Tomasz didn't care how they were doing, and for some reason he didn't understand, Tadziu resented this.

At least his mother. He should care about his mother, their mother.

And as if he could read thoughts, Janek said, "How's ma?" without mentioning the old man, as if he were dead, as if he never existed

"Not good," Tadziu said, knowing they knew without him telling them. Everyone was quiet but his answer broke some rope that tied them all, and they all began talking at once, except for Jerry and the children, who listened with wide eyes until Helen told them to go and play. Tomasz spoke first, his face no longer smiling.

"What's wrong with her?" he asked, and Tadziu answered, "She's all bent up. Has trouble walking. Rheumatism, I guess." Tomasz looked sad, then angry.

"She won't leave. We've tried to get her to leave." He looked at his sisters and Janek. "All of us wanted to chip in. To get her out of there. But she won't come."

"Not without him!" Tomasz said. "And I'm not going to worry about him!" Janek nodded. "The way he treated us," Janek continued, then stopped, and looking at Tadziu, his voice became the voice of a small boy again. "especially you, Tadziu. Nobody can forget how he was to you." The big corrections officer was close to tears, swallowed hard.

"So no one wants him. No one wants our father," Tadziu said, in a kind of summation, as if a trial had occurred.

"Nope, not after the way he treated you," Tomasz repeated, and glared at everyone. Helen looked away. Gina looked sad.

They remember? They know? What it was like. Because of me, they won't take our father. Because of me?

He couldn't find words to say. There were no words, could never be words. Tomasz's voice rose, picking up where Janek had left off. "I don't care if he rots in hell!"

Helen put a hand on Tomasz's shoulder but he didn't seem to notice.

"I know he hasn't changed one bit. I don't know why the hell she stays with him!" He lifted his arms to heaven, and spat on the floor, gestures meant to indicate his exasperation. Gina's lip began to tremble the way it did when she was a little girl.

"I know why," Tadziu said, almost whispering, because he was part of Gina, of Tomasz, of them all, of those he thought he'd lost but could never lose. "Because he's the only thing she knows. And she's afraid of anything else." Helen nodded her head. "And hey," he said, pointing to Tomasz, this ain't a bar. That's your sister's floor you're spitting on." They looked at him then as if he was some kind of leader.

"Oh yeah, Jeez," Tomasz said. His face reddened and he fell to his knees, hunted unsuccessfully in his pocket for a handkerchief, and so Tadziu handed him his own, and Tomasz began cleaning up the small round of frothy spittle on the floor, rubbed, then went to the sink, wet the handkerchief, and went back to his cleaning, rubbing until Tadziu wanted to laugh and told him to stop.

"You'll take the finish off the floor."

"Oh yeah, yeah," Tomasz said, his face a mixture of guilt and embarrassment as he stared at the wet handkerchief in his hand. Helen took it from him and hung it on the sink.

Son of a bitch. I'll die before I drink too much in front of them.

Tadziu's voice was quiet. "She won't abandon the old man," Tadziu said. "He's her husband. Our father." Voices started to rise again but Tadziu raised his hand like a traffic cop.

I see now. Helen was right. I matter. I have to be here. They need me. They need me.

And he was taken back to being a boy, to the times when his insides felt broken because there was nothing he could do to fix their lives.

"Hey Tadz," said Tomasz, with a beer in his hand, and offering Tadziu one. And he declined. Because he'd already had two. The name brushed across him like a breeze on a hot summer night. Tadz. Tadz. "Women leave men all the time," Tomasz announced, like some kind of swami." For dumb-ass reasons." Tadziu was the only one who said anything.

"She's Polish. It's not that way for her. Her kind of women stay until they die." And then, he didn't know where it came from but he was still talking, saying what he'd never said to anyone.

"My wife left me. Took our little boy. Threw me out. I was drinking too much. Getting nasty. She was right. My wife had balls. Ma can't help it. She's got no balls."

The words sat like rocks on the ground before them. He felt them moving back, looking at him with something in their eyes he remembered. They were children again and he was bringing home a bag of food from Joe's store. One of his brothers brought them back to where they should be.

"Hey, you married Marysza, right? That girl you hung around with." Someone offered him a beer. He shook his head. "Boy she was a dish," the voice said, filled with sympathy.

"I gotta watch what I drink now," Tadziu continued, "so it doesn't happen again." The beer was like a statue Janek held in his hand. Tadziu kept talking as Janek drank his beer. "Gotta make it up to my son." _

There, it was over. He'd said it. Got it out of the way. And felt good, as if he'd been to confession and been absolved.

Then Gina spoke from somewhere in her sad eyes.

"You will Tadziu. He loves you. You never hurt him."

Tadziu looked at her. They spoke to each other as if the others had disappeared.

"No. I never hurt him," he said, his voice becoming thick, "not like pa". Gina's voice became a bird flying over water, swooping down, touching the waves lightly, then flying away.

"I still love pa," she said. "I know he hurt us. Mostly you." She touched Tadziu's arm. "But I love him." She shrugged her shoulders, as if she knew Tomasz and Janek disapproved but there was nothing she could do.

As if a bell rang, a new round started. Tomasz sputtered.

"You crazy? You must be nuts." Janek was disgusted, shook his head.

"He's an old man now," Gina said, loud, as if she didn't expect to be heard. "And it's all over. Over."

Tadziu tried to say the word to himself.

Tomasz almost spat on the floor again, but caught himself and only said, "the old cocksucker!" Janek covered his brother's mouth.

"Shaddup already. I know what she means."

"Yeah right," Tomasz said. "You know what she means. My ass. You talk about him worse'n me." And Tadziu saw that his brothers were kids. Just kids. And competing to impress him.

To impress me. I'm the oldest. They're treating me like a father. Janek's had too many beers. He's starting to blubber.

"I'll never forget you comin' home with those brown paper bags, Tadz. Bringin' us food. Ma was too out of it to know whether we ate or not. But you brought us food. Brought us food." Tears streamed down Janek's face. One hung from his nose and sparkled in the sunlight like a diamond. He hugged Tadziu with one big arm. His other hand held a beer. Tadziu hugged his brother back and took the beer from his hand.

"You've had enough," he said. And so it went. All afternoon. The girls left. They could see it would be endless. And Gina had things to do for the wedding. He stayed with his brothers.

His brothers. His brothers.

Making sure they didn't get too drunk.

The Wedding

The day of his arrival had gone fine, but on the day of the wedding, fear was the first thing he felt. It sat on the edge of the bed waiting for him to awake. He went into the kitchen, drank coffee with Jerry, Tommy and Johnny and tried to keep out of the way but even the kitchen filled with commotion. Gina was off somewhere getting her hair done. Then she was back. Helen sent Jerry on some errand. Tommy and Johnny went outside. He heard Gina's voice, tearful, upset. "She left the veil," Helen told him. "At the hairdresser's. She took it to make sure her hair looked okay with it. And forgot it." This appeared to be a tragedy of major proportions.

"I'll get it," he said.

Where the hell's the hairdresser? Can I find it?

Helen was handing him the car keys, drawing a map. He had about an hour to get the veil back and get himself ready. The sun blinded his eyes and he had no sunglasses so he missed the first turn and had to pull to the side of the road to read the map again.

Women. What the hell kind of map is this?

Tadziu stopped to ask directions from an old guy in overalls and work boots, telling him why he had to hurry. After explaining the directions three times and quizzing Tadziu each time with "dyou gettit?" the old man, with something like sadness for a personal failure, gave up, seeing, as he said, that Tadziu was a "ferenner", and jumping into the car, ordered him to "drive" pointing out each turn with a five-second notice until they came to an ear-shattering halt at the front door of "Joanne's Beauty Shop". Tadziu wanted to drive the old guy back to where he'd been but he refused.

"Naw, I kin get back meself. I know these parts better'n you. You gotta hurry." He grinned. "Jus' kiss the bride fer me." He waved. "Kiss the bride." Thirty-five minutes later, Tadziu rushed back into the house, the white veil trailing behind him like a kite. Gina embraced him as if he were a soldier arriving home safe from war.

Then suddenly they were in another scene and Gina was all in white and so beautiful he almost staggered. Smiling at him. At him.

Took his arm, an arm that shook like the vibrations of a violin string. And he was walking down the aisle of a church somewhere in California, slowly following two little kids who marched down the aisle smiling at everyone, the boy pulling the girl's hand whenever she slowed down. Shaking hands, giving her to the boy, stepping back into his place. Everyone's eyes on him. But on him in a good way. A very good way. He heard the two shy voices saying words he'd never listened to before, not even at his own wedding. Heard the words of the minister, or priest, whoever he was, talking about what love was supposed to be. Pretty good stuff. People dabbed at their eyes, blew their noses. Tommy and Johnny's eyes were shining. They looked as if they just had their hair cut. As if their tuxedos were made out of cardboard and they couldn't move.

Then he was standing in a line at the back of the church with everyone shaking his hand and saying how glad they were to meet him. And Gina danced with him later under the tent, looking like a princess with him supposed to be her father but really her big brother, people applauding while they danced and when the dance was over, she kissed him on the cheek and he could feel the wet of her tears on his face.

I didn't fail them. I didn't fail them. And they don't think I ever failed them.

There were more tears when Helen kissed him goodbye at the airport. Tears, tears, tears. Women were like that. He was embarrassed. Because he was not used to anyone thinking he was that good. And because her husband was watching and he didn't know what she had told him about their life as kids. But what the hell Jerry was a nice guy.

And I didn't fail them. Not even at the party. Watched my drinks. Knowing I would rather kill himself than get drunk and spoil anything for Gina. People watching me and smiling. More people than smiled at me my whole life. And me watching Tommy and Johnny. Keeping them in line. And them listening to me To me. As if I mattered. As if they respected me. I fucked up lots of things but not this time. No, not this time.

The memories would stay with him. How for that one weekend, he'd felt good. Almost proud of himself. Because they needed something from him.

And he gave it.

Whatever it was. Whatever it was. For once, I didn't fail.

Chapter Nine

A Giant Step

As graduation approached, Mary saw changes in her appearance. Her inner voice told her she remained the old Mary, dreaming things that would never come true. She turned it off as if she were changing a radio station. An invisible curtain was removed and allowed the entry of light. Her eyes shone, she smiled more often and her face became luminous.

I'm a college graduate. I'm entering a new world. I've done what I thought was impossible and it was only hard work. I'll never be afraid of anything again.

The stage was a huge platform beginning to sag in the middle. Mary stepped off the wooden steps and walked holding the cap on her head, the folds of her black gown fluttering like wings. With each step, she felt her grandmother's presence becoming stronger but when thoughts of her mother tried to gain entry, to become part of this moment, she shut them out.

She saw the perspiration shining on the dean's face and heard his weary voice. Aunt Irene and Uncle Ben, her cousins, Barbara and Jimmy; Martha and David, and of course, her son Jimmy, were in the audience. David snapped a picture of her shaking the dean's damp and lifeless hand. She saw her son and her cousin standing and cheering as she walked back and took her place on the portable bleachers, Aunt Irene whispering to them, trying to be stern, and the boys sitting down.

The bright lights blinded her and became a wall that separated her from the audience. She imagined her grandmother taking a seat in the front row, her face wearing a look that said she didn't approve of Mary's refusal to think of her mother, but this disapproval was tempered, as it had been when Mary was a child, by her grandmother's pride, a pride that spread through Mary as surely as the heat of the sun had spread over the earth that morning. There would be a time when the issue of her mother was resolved, although Mary didn't know how. She could hear what her grandmother would be saying now.

"You and Jimmy come first at this time. But soon, you must think of your mama, must forgive her."

Maybe, grandma. Maybe. I'll try.

Mary couldn't wipe away the water that filled her eyes because she didn't want to knock off her hat.

It's okay. They'll think I'm crying with happiness.

It grew hotter each moment. The microphone muffled the words of the speeches. The only sound one heard was the crying of babies.

Family

After the ceremony, people stood outside, the men smoking, the ladies fanning themselves with folded programs. Mary's uncle wore a white shirt and tie and carried his sport coat on his arm, her aunt a sheer summer dress that was feminine but, Mary knew, out-of-style, and sandals with worn heels and open toes that displayed her neatly-polished toenails.

The older Jimmy began chasing his cousin but Barbara stood quiet, her self-consciousness evident, until Mary, remembering how awkward things had been between them when Mary first arrived, how they had later become friends, the times she had baby-sat Jimmy, and the sympathy her face had always worn when Tadziu's name was mentioned, went to her cousin and hugged her.

"How you doing with the fellows?" Mary whispered and Barbara answered, "could be worse," to which Mary bellowed an "a-ha"! that made her cousin Jimmy, who wore an embarrassed look, halt abruptly in his tracks. The younger Jimmy, Mary's son, having no one to chase him, looked confused and stopped running. Mary stared at her cousin Jimmy with amazement as if he should not have grown, should have remained the small Jimmy who followed her around in her uncle's house.

He looks embarrassed. I'll bet he thinks we're whispering about his few stray pimples. How did he get to be an adolescent?

"We're not talking about you, silly," she said. Her cousin was quiet until he saw the younger Jimmy jumping from one foot to the other and groaning, "I gotta pee, ma."

"Go behind a tree, why doncha," the older Jimmy blurted as his younger cousin continued to jump and squirm. Mary laughed.

Well, almost an adolescent. Whatever it is that lies between childhood and adolescence.

"Jimmy," Uncle Ben said sternly to his son, "take him over there to the men's room."

"Sure, Dad. C'mon you little weasel, you."

"You're a weasel. A big fat one!" came the retort. The older boy laughed patronizingly and Barbara looked up to heaven.

"This will never end," she said to no one in particular. Mary couldn't explain the joy that filled her, a joy that couldn't exist apart from those she loved, those who surrounded her now. In that moment—instinct made her aware that such moments were uncommon—-she was freed from the boundaries of the self and its narrow concerns and linked to other lives that made her whole, lives from which she couldn't become separated without loss to her own self.

"Oh Mary, we're so proud of you!" her aunt gushed. Her son jabbed his mother lightly in the side, shook his head with what he thought was a sign of sophistication and gave voice to an embarrassed "ma!" as if Aunt Irene had taken her clothes off.

"Jimmy, you be careful with that baby," his mother commanded.

"Ma, he's not a baby," Barbara said, sighing and looking around at everyone else. "He's five years old." Aunt Irene ignored both of them.

"Jimmy, listen to your mother," Uncle Ben said, looking reprovingly at Barbara. Things became quiet until her aunt broke the silence.

"Mary, pretty soon we'll have someone else to be proud of," she said in a confidential tone, a remark that confused Mary. She knew Barbara was still in junior college.

The cheeks beneath her aunt's eyes were red with excitement. She looked at Uncle Ben as if he weren't her husband, but someone she didn't know,

Mary remembered.

Uncle Ben must be finishing engineering school. I'd forgotten. He waves his hand dismissing what Aunt Irene says but his face looks excited and proud. Life will be better for them now.

"Roosevelt's G. I. Bill is a good thing," Uncle Ben said in a subdued voice.

"He's already got two appointments for job interviews," her Aunt whispered as Uncle Ben looked away, pretending he didn't hear.

Mary's cousin Jimmy continued to chase her son Jimmy as they walked back from the lavatories through groups of people that covered the lawn like dandelions. Holding the center of attention in each group was a young person wearing a flowing black robe and carrying a blue satin book beneath his arm. Laughter floated through the humid air, pride radiated from parents' faces and impatient children hung from their parents' arms until they escaped and ran away to play games.

One small boy's white shirt was covered with dirt. His mother dragged him by his arm away from the other children and pointed to a spot near her where he was ordered to stand. The boy looked defeated and rubbed his fingers through his hair, his mouth turned downward in protest at the injustice, perspiration and dirt tracing a path down his face, shirttails and suspenders hanging from his pants.

Mary did not immediately recognize the woman who came and hugged her. Mrs. Hoggenkamp! She wore a suit with a jacket and blouse, its bow tied at the neck like a scarf, perspiration like half-moons growing under the arms. Her eyes were wearier, her face more lined than Mary remembered.

I never knew her, never saw the kindness in her eyes.

"How did you know?" Mary asked...

"I do read the newspaper, you know," Mrs. Hoggenkamp answered, thrusting a card and a small package into Mary's hand and playing with the ends of her scarf the way Mary remembered her playing with the long chain on her glasses. They were silent for a moment, the air between them heavy with unspoken words until Mary remembered to say "thank you" and murmured something about how thoughtful Mrs. Hoggenkamp was.

Martha and David tried to hold Jimmy's hand and Aunt Irene held her son's arm as the two boys laughed and swung their captors around as if they were on maypoles, while they swiped at each other with their free arms. In the midst of the excitement and confusion, Mary introduced Mrs.Hoggenkamp.

"How d'you do," David said and held out his hand. Mary's Aunt and Uncle and Martha and Barbara joined him. Mary knew they suspected but weren't sure of Mary's connection to the woman who was smiling and nodding her head. Mrs. Hoggenkamp took some tissues from her purse and wiped beads of sweat from her face.

"My god, it was hot in there," she said. Mary's Uncle agreed. They stood silent and awkward until David spoke to Jimmy.

"Your mama is finished with school now. She graduated." Jimmy replied with an indignant "I know," a response for which David swatted him playfully. "That means she's real smart," David continued. He turned the pages of the program and bent down to Jimmy.

"That's your mom's name. Look at the star she has."

"She was a good girl in school, huh?" Jimmy said, with an impish look on his face and they all laughed, the laughter breaking the tension that stood in the air like an uninvited guest. David turned to Mrs. Hoggenkamp, whose name Mary knew he could neither remember nor pronounce.

"C'mon with us. Have a drink. We'll find a cool place."

"Oh no," Mrs. Hoggenkamp replied, in the old voice that Mary remembered, the voice that said her mind would not be changed. "Congratulations again. I knew you would do well." Her voice rose with emphasis. "I <u>mean,</u> graduating "magna cum laude". She turned to Mary's aunt and uncle. "You should be so proud." Her uncle nodded solemnly.

"You're not kidding," Martha chimed in. Mrs. Hoggenkamp put her hands on Mary's shoulders and looked into her eyes.

"Don't stop here. You can do much more."

"I've applied to the masters program at the university," Mary said with excitement, as in the old days when she had reported her grades to Mrs. Hoggenkamp.

"Good. Don't stop there either. Go all the way, Mary," she said matter-of-factly, leaving Mary momentarily breathless. Mrs. Hoggenkamp had put into words what she herself had never dared to think. The heat and noise disappeared. Serenity settled on Mary like fresh air.

I can do more. I can do more.

But a vague disquiet entered, one that promised to grow. At what price? Women who have careers don't marry. Mrs. Hoggenkamp never did. Had she been happy without the other things? Is it that she was never chosen by anyone? Did others think she'd never been chosen, never picked?

Mary realized she had to think hard to remember a time when Mrs. Hoggenkamp had looked happy.

"You have a good time now," the older woman said to Mary, and turned to her family. "It was nice to meet you. You too, fellas". She made a mock bow toward the two Jimmys who'd been making a ruckus as she arrived.

"Likewise," David replied, and as if she'd never been there, Mrs. Hoggenkamp disappeared into the crowd. Martha guessed who she was. Mary told the others.

"My welfare caseworker."

"She's a nice woman," Aunt Irene said gaily, and everyone agreed. Mary smiled, thinking they couldn't know the depth of her feeling for Mrs. Hogenkamp. But silence settled on the group, an instinctive respect for the woman who'd just left, a silence finally broken by Uncle Ben.

"Boy, that was five hundred hands that guy had to shake." David nodded. A page was turned. David's voice, insisting they go to a restaurant for dinner and drinks made everything normal again.

"Our treat," he announced, putting his arm around Martha and kissing her cheek. Above Uncle Ben's "no sir," Aunt Irene's, "we want to pay" and the boys' laughter as they held their stomachs and said "no sir" to each other, they all walked toward the car.

Another Step

The aroma of coffee filled the air. As she sat at the kitchen table filling out the application for graduate school, the feeling of déjà vu overtook Mary.

Many decisions had been made at this table, many journeys begun. The furniture is still worn, the painting Tadziu and I did is chipped again.

Jimmy was asleep. His school supplies lay on the other side of the table—a black and white composition book, a clear plastic pencil case and a book with a cover made of brown paper cut and folded from grocery bags. Jimmy never asked for help with his homework anymore and was insulted if Mary offered it.

"Ma, I can do it myself," he'd protest, and she saw again that his face, as he worked, was Tadziu's face, strong and determined, and, she worried, also like his father's in the speed with which it could show anger in the face of frustration. She was jolted from her thoughts by the ringing of the phone. Martha wanted to know if she was filling out her application.

She's a mother hen. Sometimes mother hens can be irritating. It's difficult to tell her I'm frightened. She thinks I'm smart and shouldn't be afraid of anything.

Mary's voice hesitated as she answered her friend, telling her how nervous she was.

"You'll get used to things," Martha told her. "It's not like you're moving to another country."

"I'll miss you guys a lot."

I mean that but there's something else, something lurking like vapor in my head. Do I want it to reveal itself? Martha, Martha. Do I want to leave my old life behind? Do I want to leave you behind?

"We can visit you. It'll be fun."

Mary didn't answer.

She thinks it's because I'm anxious. I am but it's more than that. More than that. I'm sad. And ashamed. I've already left you. Martha. The life you want for yourself is different than the one I want. You and David will marry, settle in a nice Polish neighborhood, have a family and do the same things your parents did. You'll be happier and more satisfied than I'll be, I'm sure, but I can't live that life. I don't know what life I should live but it's not the life of housekeeping and babies and more babies.

A rope tightened around Mary's shoulders. She wanted to run until she reached a place free from the guilt of her thoughts about Martha. She loved Martha and envied the ease Martha had concerning all the basic matters of life, the matters at which she herself failed.

But I'm not Martha. I know I'm not Martha. I don't know what I am. Do I really want to be a teacher? Being a teacher or maybe a nurse are the only ways I know to be something other than a housewife. So I guess I do.

She moved away from her thoughts and answered her friend.

"I know you will. But you can't come often. Depending on who accepts me, it might be expensive to come. And you can't expect David to take off from work."

"I can come alone. I'm a big girl."

"I know that. It still might be expensive."

"Mary, unless you go to school in Australia or something, I can drive. That's about as cheap as you can get. We're not that poor, for cripe's sake."

I'm not saying the things I want to say Martha. I don't know what I want to say. I love you, Martha, I love you. But I can see us floating away from each other like leaves in a stream.

Jimmy woke and with his "grown-up" voice of inquiry, a voice he tried to make deep and masculine, asked who Mary was talking to.

"To Auntie Martha," Mary called, thinking again of how much Jimmy loved Martha, remembering him confiding, when he was about three, as if it were an important secret, that after Mary, Auntie Martha was the one he loved best in all the world. The friends finished their conversation

"Good-bye, Martha."

It will be good-bye soon enough, my love.

Mary hung up and sat at the table biting the end of her pencil.

I'm ridiculous. Nothing will change. My new life will still include Martha and David.

The ticking of the clock became the thunder of rocks tumbling down a staircase. As if she had been asleep, she awoke and returned to the application.

She knew the questions were only formalities, that the thing which mattered most would be the recommendations. Her professors had led her to believe they would be supportive but nothing was ever certain. There were other reasons she could be refused. State college was not the most prestigious institution to be coming from, and there were students who'd done better than she had, even if there were none who loved more what they were doing. She stopped writing and ran her pencil through her hair.

Why am I doing this at all? Why am I trying? I should look for a job and make things better for Jimmy and me.

She paused.

I've gone over this before. I'm not going to do it again.

The ticking of the clock became louder. Mary felt a wish beginning to take shape, a wish imbued with her grandmother's spirit. She knew why. She wanted her grandmother to lift this latest burden from her shoulders, to make the decision she was finding so difficult to make. Her heart beat loudly. Everything else was silence.

She's refusing to come, refusing to do for me what I can do for myself. She handled her own obstacles, had something inside that kept her from complaining about the difficulties of her life, a strength that was acceptance without being resignation. I don't have that. Protest lives inside me, comes to the surface at times, shows the face of anger, rage at the facts of my life, a life which seems less and less my own responsibility. Things happened to me. People betrayed me, including my own mother.

The strong odor of coffee percolating on the counter changed the direction of her thoughts. If her grandmother were here, she would frown and tell Mary that such excuses were nonsense. Mary wouldn't feel the comfort that flowed from her grandmother, a comfort that would settle on her like the sun's rays on a cold winter day. There would only be a look that told her to get up and get on with it. She'd have to make this decision alone. She rose from the table and began walking the short path between the table and Jimmy's bedroom.

"I won't think anymore," she said aloud. The sound of her voice made her realize how tired she was. She went to bed and slept soundly. The next morning, she finished the application and mailed it. "Thank you, Grandma", she whispered, "for the good sleep. It makes everything clearer."

The coming of summer made Mary uneasy. Her rational mind told her she had overcome many obstacles, yet each time a new one stood in her path, her apprehension resurrected. She reminded herself that summer was not long and though nothing was certain, if she heard from the university, she would receive money in the fall.

She'd find a job. It would be waitressing, because the tips made it a more lucrative job than others and because it offered the most flexibility in schedule, a flexibility she could maximize by trading work hours with other waitresses.

And so it was. She found a job and enrolled Jimmy in a pre-school summer program that offered numerous activities and found that, on most days, she managed to arrive home before he did.

On a hot July day, she started out for work early in order to stop at the day care center. She knew the kids walked to the swimming pool at about this time each day and though bewildered by the uncertainty of exactly what she wanted to see, she hoped to see Jimmy without him seeing her.

As the building came into view, she saw a line of ten or twelve children walking through the double doors and marching down the sidewalk like miniature soldiers. With outstretched arm, each child held the shoulder of the child before him, bumping into his predecessor whenever the teacher, her hand held high like a policeman, blew her whistle to halt the line, at which point some soldiers, including Jimmy, fell, exaggerating the force of their fall, the entire exercise resulting in repressed giggles that turned into open laughter.

Watching from behind a tree, Mary saw Jimmy frolic with the other children, saw him acting silly with the boy in front of him until the teacher blew her whistle and reprimanded them, the girls in the line looking reproachfully at the two offenders.

Parents had been instructed not to come to the outings because it was disruptive to the children. Mary covered her face and silently crept away.

I'm a spy, watching from behind a tree to make sure my child is properly taken care of.

She left knowing that Jimmy was having fun as well as learning, that he was with other children, having experiences richer than she alone could provide.

Summer was almost ended when she received the letter accepting her into the master's program in the English Department at the Sate University. The aid package was generous enough that she only needed a few more school loans in order for her and Jimmy to survive. What relieved her more was that Jimmy and she qualified for an apartment on campus in the married couple's dormitory. The school gave her 10 days to reply. Mary mailed her acceptance immediately.

Martha

"I know things will be good for you. You were always so smart." Mary listened to Martha's usual song and dance and felt her irritation turning into anger.

The look in her eyes is envy. I don't want her to envy me. We've been through this so many times. I've tried to convince her to apply to State next year. But she has her own fears, the very thing she thinks I should be immune to. Because I'm smart! Yeah. Sure.

Thinking of her own fears, of how, at the last, there had never been any way to be rid of them except by plowing straight through, made Mary want to deafen her ears to Martha's spiel. Then she thought of the many situations in which her friend had helped her and felt her face redden with shame. Digging her fingers into the palm of her hand, she took a deep breath and began her own familiar speech.

Martha was silent. The look on her face alternated between doubt and hope. Mary knew Martha thought she wasn't "smart" enough to think of any kind of college. The very word probably caused her to tremble.

"Listen Martha, I went to State with kids who were not as smart as you are, and they all finished. If you're not sure about State, you can start by taking a course at the Junior College. You'll know whether you want to continue and if you do, most of the courses are transferable to State. If you don't like it, you can quit. You won't lose much."

Martha protested that she wouldn't know what to take, that she didn't even know what she wanted to study.

"But it has to be something with children," she said vehemently. Mary smiled.

"There's all kinds of things you can do working with children. There's teaching, there's child care, there's social work, like adopting or foster care, even working with delinquent kids. You'd be terrific working with kids who needed a helping hand. Do you like being a waitress so much that you want to be one forever"?

"Are you kidding, Mary?" The question was a plea. Mary took her friend by the shoulders and looked into her eyes, whether from impatience or affection, or both, she couldn't tell and it didn't matter.

"Martha, would I kid you? C'mon. That would be like setting you up to fail. Do you think I could do that? I'm telling you the truth. I know you can do it." This last statement was spoken with such emphasis that Martha's expression changed and though she said nothing, Mary saw the flicker of a smile on her face..

At the end of the week, Mary helped Martha her fill out the application forms for the local junior college. She was accepted.

Martha's brother was the pride of the family because he had won a scholarship to college and was doing well. Mary had listened to her friend brag about him relentlessly. Now she heard her friend laugh gleefully when he was home.

"You're not the only "big shit" in the family," Martha taunted. "I'm going to college in the fall." Martha's parents said nothing when they looked at Mary with gratitude in their eyes.

Graduate School

Mary's campus apartment, located in a remodeled old home, smelled of soap and pine disinfectant. There was tile throughout, tile which resembled wood and gleamed as if its protective coating had not yet worn off. The small refrigerator and stove in the kitchen also smelled new and, as if freshly removed from factory boxes had unmarred surfaces.

Mary liked the bathroom best. At home, the bathtub resembled an ancient white boat with huge claw-feet, its porcelain floor scored by black lines that looked like games of tic-tac-toe. Mary had made a shower for Jimmy and herself with a rubber hose that had a sprayer head attached to the end, a spray Jimmy could use to show his bravery when he was a baby, putting it on his head and letting the water stream down his face.

This bathroom had a real shower, a yellow tile stall into which you stepped and drew a plastic curtain across the entrance. Mary opened the small medicine cabinet and placed her items inside, relishing the feel of the new plastic containers of shampoo, toothpaste and deodorant, entranced by the way they fit exactly into their spaces like pegs on a pegboard. On the bottom shelf she placed her lipstick, her slender gold tube of mascara and a bottle of hand lotion. The last item was a jar of fluffy white cream she'd asked Martha to buy her for Christmas.

"I'm not kidding, Martha, it's what I want. I'm telling you, you have to start at our age if you want to prevent wrinkles and sagging." Through her laughter, Martha sputtered, "then we'd better put it on our rear ends too," but Mary received the cream. All these toiletries sat in the small chrome and glass chest, taking up not even a quarter of its space.

After she finished unpacking, filling all the drawers, inhaling the smell of their new wood, then standing back and surveying the apartment, she opened and closed all the drapes, imbibing the views of the campus, feeling that its grass and trees, its weathered buildings, were a gift and belonged to her in the way that her grandma's home had belonged to her. She'd found a new home, a home in which she could feel she happiness in the walls, a home in which everything was clean and bright without her having had to scrub it.

A small minority of the students disturbed Mary. They walked through the hallways holding their heads in a certain way, a mannerism which said, "I'm here. I've arrived," while they looked around pretending not to care whether others noticed them. The majority of students looked as glad as Mary to be there, as grateful as she was for the chance to further their education, to make their lives better.

The ratio of men to women in the class was about three to one. Mary sensed that when a professor called upon a woman student, the air held a pause, a silence which said that allowances would be made. The men's silence was one that expected the woman to say something ridiculous, the women's silence one which held its breath, hoping the woman would do well. That state of affairs lasted even when it became clear that the women were as bright as the men. But though the question of gender was never forgotten, both the men and women were too intelligent not to understand the truth, to know that it was irrelevant. They understood what was most relevant, that they were all hungry for success, that they were surrounded by bright minds and that these minds all represented competition.

Mary wrote letters to Martha until classes and studying began to consume all her time. The message in her letters was always a variation of, "I'm so happy. I can't believe I'm here."

And Martha sent the same message to her friend:

Dear Mary,

I've started with a composition course, like you said. You were right. All those times I tried to help you helped me. I'm afraid I might be punished if I say it's a breeze, but so far it is. I really love it, Mary. I feel like I'm a different person.

Love to you and Jimmy

The day care at the university had many supervised activities for students' children—picnics, parties, and educational outings. The time Jimmy spent with other children allowed Mary to socialize with the students without feeling guilty. Young mothers, the wives of students or students themselves, were always willing to exchange baby-sitting services.

On the night a dinner party was being held, Mary stood before the mirror scrutinizing her outfit. Thoughts flowed through her brain like a clear stream..

Soon, I'll be drinking cocktails, laughing and talking with people who love what I love. It seems only yesterday that Jimmy was a baby and I sat in despair, looking through the kitchen window at the few birds who pecked at the hard black dirt. The only place I could take Jimmy was for a ride on the street in the wagon Martha bought him for Christmas. Tonight he won't even miss me. Day-care at the college was good, but here it's excellent. My child is luckier than most. I work hard. But others work hard and are not as lucky, don't find themselves in the happy situation I'm in. Thank you, God.

The tone of her thoughts and feelings intoxicated Mary. This was what people meant when they called themselves "happy". Jimmy's words— "you smell pretty, mama,"—as he walked around her, admiring her evening dress and smelling her perfume, were like expensive champagne. The dress, shining with the luster of satin, made her feel she was a part of the world it represented until she heard the inner voice that told her she didn't belong, that the dress would scream its sale-rack origin.

She cut the tag that hung from the sleeve and did what had become increasingly easy to do. She turned her back to the voice.

It's an expensive dress. It was marked down several times at the end-of-the-season. I'm good with money, good at spotting quality things. No one will know.

She twirled around for Jimmy.

"Mama, I'm your boyfriend. I want to dance with you." He bowed deeply, in imitation of a minuet he had seen somewhere, held one hand at his waist and stretched out the other while trying to hold his feet at right angles, a maneuver that resulted in much wobbling, until finally, with legs hopelessly twisted and peals of great hilarity, he fell. Unflustered, he rose again. "And kiss you too! Yeah, kiss you too"! He laughed in appreciation of himself.

"I don't have a boyfriend. I'm just going to a school party." She tried to sound matter-of-fact but his playful manner infected her and she laughed with him.

"Oh yes, you do mama. Your boyfriend's name is Mickey Mouse and he's going to fall down when you're dancing. Just like me!"

Mary knew Jimmy's capacity for fun. This could go on forever.

My intelligent child is also a clown.

"Make sure you're good for Jeannette," she said, trying to sound firm as they walked from the apartment, Jimmy continuing his merriment until they arrived at Jeanette's, the night's designated baby-sitter, where he saw the other children and became quiet, Mary knew, because he didn't want to look like a baby.

The party-goers greeted each other, instructed their children, and left their directions with Jeannette, a small, slender girl with wispy blonde hair, large eyes and long, tapered fingers, who was the wife of one of Mary's classmates. Mary was struck by her beauty and her name.

She looks like she stepped from a Botticelli painting. And her name in Polish would be "Janina", the name of one of Tadziu's sisters.

Holding a tearful infant in her arms, Jeannette waved good-bye, her delicate voice telling Mary to have a good time and not to worry.

She's not resentful, knows her turn will come. Everyone here is happy.

Mary saw Jimmy move shyly toward the other children. "He won't be quiet for long," she told Jeannette, knowing, as the words left her, how normal Jimmy was, how well he was developing, and how that knowing increased her happiness.

"You can collect him whenever," Jeannette said, and shifting the baby to her other arm in order to see Mary better, her voice filled with admiration.

"You look terrific. I love your dress."

Michael

Mary was aware of Michael in the way one was aware of the sky, or the earth, as someone who was always there but never called attention to himself. He was six feet tall with large shoulders he held back and straight as if he thought a man should walk that way. His lips widened into an easy smile. His eyes, which looked directly at you, were etched with laugh lines that seemed permanent until one saw them move like lightning when his mood changed. A few stray freckles were scattered across his cheeks, like something left over from being a teen-ager and gave the impression of an easygoing and somewhat ingenuous nature.

After Mary knew him, she saw he was incapable of cynicism, but sophisticated when his self-interest was involved, a self-interest that included the welfare of those he loved. Not a complicated man. As if she had been waiting, his entry into Mary's life did not surprise her.

"Well, what do you think? Can we manage it? I think this is the weeding-out class." He was referring to research methods, a class notorious for its difficulty.

Mary moved toward the window, turned pages and studied the notes in her hand, knowing that the sunlight breaking through the glass and falling across her face would be flattering.

"It is tough but everything else depends on it. If you can't do basic research, you won't make it."

"Would you like to take part in our study group?" he asked. "Jill Winer and Paul Machowski are in. You'd make four, just the right number for a group." Her yes was spontaneous. She began attending sessions in which they quizzed each other, argued and discussed, each session demonstrating further to Mary the distance she had travelled since she left the State College. Although she was often nervous and unsure, her uncertainty was different from the one she had felt then, an uncertainty that had questioned her own value, her right to be one of those privileged to attend school. Now she began listening to the sound of her voice as she spoke and liked what she heard.

During one of the first meetings of the study group, Paul challenged a position she had taken on literary criticism and she defended herself.

"What Pound says is true, that it's invalid to base an ethic on a belief about men without examining that belief. The problem lies in whether one's perceptions concerning men are true or untrue. It's difficult to accept Pound's ideas about bad art, art which lies about the nature of man, without dealing with this issue." Mary's earnestness did not make her unaware of the smile Michael made no attempt to conceal.

"What're you laughing at, Michael?" Paul demanded. "You haven't read the chapter on Ezra Pound either. Who the heck reads ahead in the text anyway"?

"Mary does," Michael said, and their laughter acknowledged the truth of his statement. Mary blushed and pulled at the wire binding of her notebook. The pleasure Michael took in her intellectual ability wasn't lost on her. Her feelings of uncertainty stood more and more in the shadows and though she knew they could reappear, she also knew that Michael helped to weaken their strength.

Michael didn't pursue her. They drifted toward one another, as if driven by an invisible current, a movement that made Mary uneasy, resembling as it did, the way in which shed' been drawn to Tadziu, the way in which she had closed her eyes, believing herself to be helpless, ignoring the inner voice that exposed her lie, that screamed she was an accomplice in her own pain. Her face became hot as she thought of the last days with Tadziu and the self-doubt they had strengthened, the doubt of her ability to "take the measure" of any man, to believe what she thought she was seeing.

Michael, Michael, you don't understand why I don't want you to love me. I can't let anything interfere with this prize I've won, this chance to change my life and Jimmy's.

So that when he asked if they could get together and she didn't respond, he laughed and said, "Over coffee, I mean. Nothing serious. Nothing we can't take back anyway." They both laughed.

"O.K. Michael. We can have coffee. A drink even." His easy manner, his sincerity, was difficult to resist. And she was lonely.

Coffee became a weekly affair. Students grew accustomed to seeing them together and began greeting them as a couple. At first, this made Mary uncomfortable, but she told herself this reaction was foolish, since Michael seemed to sense her fear of becoming romantically involved and followed her lead in referring to the two of them as "friends". Without noticing, she began to rely on him for favors that made her life easier—helping with Jimmy or fetching items from the store because he had a car and she didn't. When she saw how much help he had become, she told herself he needed her in the same way she needed him, that she helped him also.

But that's not true. He wants something different.

They had returned from a school affair and were drinking coffee in his apartment, when he kissed her, lightly but positively, holding her face in his hands, as if she were fragile and valuable. The air of youth and romance turned to embarrassment when he asked why she had never married, and she had to answer, "I did."

"It's okay," she said, reassuring him that he wasn't intruding. "I'm okay. I don't talk about it much. We were young and starry-eyed, married three years before we knew we weren't meant for each other. We parted amicably." She played with the chain of her necklace.

That's a lie. I wish we had. But in a way we did. Tadziu was ill. And I never hated him, never stopped..........

The thought became suspended, taunted her and she faced the truth she had always known. She'd never stopped loving Tadziu.

Michael's voice became thoughtful.

"That must be nice. I wasn't so lucky. We didn't part amicably." She didn't ask what he meant but he told her about his marriage at eighteen, about his young wife who was not ready, as he expressed it, to settle down, and began seeing other men, no one in particular, just men who made her think she was still the prettiest and most popular girl, which she was, "but high school was finished. We couldn't work it out." He laughed ruefully, a laugh that aroused her sorrow and distracted her from thoughts of her own past. "Nothing was amicable," he ended.

Because he didn't ask, it was easier for her to say, "My husband, Jimmy's father, was disturbed. He drank a lot. I married him, I think, to have a place of my own, some-one of my own. My parents were gone and I was living with my aunt and uncle. They were good to me. I should have stayed with them. But I didn't." His hand stroked the back of her shoulder. He looked up at the sky pondering what she'd said, giving atten-tion and thought to her words.

"Don't you know we all have those things, things we should've done but didn't, or never should've done, but did."

She wanted to put her head on his shoulder, wanted him to hold her.

"I guess I don't. I've always felt guilty about my mistakes."

"How can such a smart woman be so innocent?"

"Don't you mean naïve?"

"No, I mean innocent. About life. I like that. It's what makes you different. It wouldn't occur to me to feel guilty over my mistakes." His eyes looked puzzled, as if he had realized something. "You know, the strange thing is I never think about her. Like it never happened."

He's trying to make me feel better

She put her hand on the door and hesitated. "I have to go now, Michael."

"Okay, just don't disappear on me. I love you."

And Mary heard the words of her inner debate, the debate she'd tried to ignore but nevertheless heard conducting itself, quietly, persistently, secretly, like something shameful that must be hidden. She wasn't sure when the debate had begun. Was it only now, with Michael, because he was the first serious threat to whatever it was that was at stake?

I love you, Michael. I don't love you. I love my life and the life I can have.

She heard Mrs. Hoggenkamp's words..."Don't stop, Mary. You can do much more"—-words that echoed like a children's rhyme, much more, much more, more….. She imagined Michael holding her, as Tadziu had held her, imagined him burying his head on her chest and her mind drifted away, wouldn't be found, because she didn't want it to be found, because she was conscious only of the pulse that beat within her and could almost hear the pulse beating within him.

She saw pictures of him holding her by the elbow, directing her as they crossed a busy street, opening his wallet to pay her way to school functions before she could offer, driving her to places she couldn't reach without a car. Men did those things for women. She thought of the times he defended her from the unkind remarks of other male students and said the words she wanted to say but couldn't, of the times he calmed her when she was upset over assignments she failed to do as perfectly as she thought she should have, of the times he brought or returned her books to the school library.

He stood close by but never made her uncomfortable. She was made whole by his protection, by his shielding her even from her own mistakes, although for some reason she didn't understand, that caused resentment in her. She saw the number of times he had been kind to Jimmy, helped him with what she couldn't—-carving a piece of wood into a respectable representation of a car for the cub scout requirement, attending father-son events, teasing him out of an unhappy mood, telling silly jokes that made him laugh.

Then she imagined herself struggling to carry heavy packages, trying to fix something that was broken, taking her car to the garage for repairs knowing her bill would be excessive because she was a woman. She saw herself trying to raise Jimmy without the help of a man. It was easy when he was a baby, or even now, but teen-agers and young men were different than babies or children.

Can I do it? Am I enough for Jimmy, for myself?

She felt the certain stigma she would know as a divorced woman, a woman alone.

People judge divorced women, consider them as fair game. I'll be the object of dirty jokes, bawdy remarks people think I can't hear. Even getting a job might be more difficult. I could lie, could say I was a widow. Someone would find out. That would make it worse.

Her thoughts were a welter of confusion.

Cherishing this growing sense of independence is real but the picture of myself alone cuts into me, drains me like a medieval blood-letting. Knowing I'll go to bed alone, sleep alone, awake alone. Knowing I'll live without the touch that can't be explained, the touch that brings life. Won't know that someone seeks me, won't have the irreplaceable knowing that I'm the one without his telling me.

Another Mary stepped onto the stage, a Mary who had become what her grandmother saw, whose accomplishments were many, who spoke before a class the way the college professors at State had spoken. A Mary who knew many things, whom others admired and sought to emulate.

I would help other girls, help them see that life has more possibilities than marriage and children. Or teach. Or nurse. I don't know where I might land. I don't know why I have ability if I'm not to use it. Things won't be this way for women forever.

And there entered thoughts she didn't want to recognize, thoughts she didn't know she was capable of having

It's not a question of loving someone, but of being with someone. There are times that Michael irritates me. Not anything he does or anything he says. It's simply because he's there, and in my way. When I don't want to be bothered with anything except the work I must do, the work I want to do. She heard the word "must", was aware of the emphasis she placed upon it, an almost clandestine emphasis, as if her thoughts feared their own content. I'm irrational. Michael would understand and leave if I said I needed to work.

But he wouldn't leave forever, couldn't understand if I wanted to be alone for long periods of time, alone with myself, my thoughts and the products of those thoughts, if I wanted to worry about no one or anything except myself. Just rise in the morning, begin my work and sleep at night with the taste of that work still on my tongue, have the work sleep with me, stay with me in my dreams, giving birth to images and sounds that feed the work, enlarge it, and I able to see creation happening, the thing coming to be because of me, moving through me so that I am forever and indelibly stamped on its face.

If I wanted to live for nothing but the work. Bound by no one, not a lover, not a friend, child or pet, not even a plant. Nothing that needed my care or thought.

I'm irrational. Michael doesn't need my care. Yes, Michael needs my care. In the most basic, most consuming way. Demands, because of his need, all that lies within me—-my emotions, my thoughts, my concern. Like a bird that sits on my finger and won't be ignored because it knows I won' ignore it, stares at me with pleading eyes, speaks from deep inside its throat what I alone can hear. "Love me. Give me food, water to drink, all of yourself, your awareness of my needs, your attention, your care, your life. So that I thrive, can be what I must be. My throat trilling splendid music, my eyes aglow, my feathers large and fluffed. Because of you. Because you are here. For me to feed upon, to absorb."

I'm irrational, irrational. I vacillate, move from pole to pole, can never decide what it is I want. And what the work is that I am to do, that pulls at me like the tide desiring to return to the sea. I don't know what it is but I know it waits for me.

In the week that followed, Mary wouldn't allow herself to think about Michael.

I have work to do. Thinking about love makes me inefficient.

When Martha met Michael, she gave him unconditional approval. "Mary, this is a wonderful guy. You better grab him quick." Mary was quiet.

I have nothing to worry about. He's mine. I'm in control. The way it was with Tadziu. Michael wants me, always waits.

She thought about the differences between Tadziu, coming from poverty, so unsure of himself and Michael, who came from a comfortable family, was educated but did not flaunt it, slipped easily into any world, wore his suit and tie as if he was born in them and drank at the corner bar the same as a working man, his eyes wide with concentration as he listened to someone's story. When Mary was in a bar with him, it became more than just a bar.

I like the looks of the other patrons looking at me, knowing how it is between us. I like that he sees them looking at me. I absorb their looks. Like nourishment. I'm a lady. They all know I'm a lady. A lady coming into the bar with a nice man. Michael is a nice man.

She'd loved Tadziu but he was never a nice man.

She'd told Michael he was causing her to be inefficient, and when he looked puzzled, said that she spent valuable time thinking about him. When he looked pleased she felt guilty.

I'm encouraging him. My feelings are not the same as his. I don't know what they are.

"There can never be anything between us," she told him one night, after a department dinner dance.

"Okay," he said, but she knew he was hurt. He danced with other women students and didn't look at her.

Now I'm jealous. At the way he holds her. Wouldn't it be wrong if I weren't truthful? Why do my arms ache, feel tired, exhausted? My body hurts because I've hurt Michael.

Completion

"It's been great, hasn't it?" Jeannette asked, standing in Mary's kitchen on a night when Mary was the baby-sitter and Jeannette had come to retrieve her little girl.

"It sure has."

Today, Jeannette's blonde hair was drawn into a kind of soft sweep and held by a clip at the back of her head so that her small features and the dimples at the corners of her mouth were accentuated. She looked like a little girl playing dress-up.

"Oh Mary," she blurted, enclosing her friend in her miniature version of a bear's hug, "I'm going to miss you. Promise you'll stay in touch."

Mary knew the promises she and Jeannette made to each other would be broken, that they'd forgot their temporary lives when their real lives resumed.

"I will," she answered and even as she heard her words, felt the old fear beginning to rear its head, her fear of the new and unknown. She and Jimmy had been happy here. Now they would face change again. She extricated herself from Jeannette's hug and moved away, like someone not wishing to become more attached than she already was.

Leaving

"I don't think Chris and I can ever forget the friends we made here," Jeannette continued. "You know, Chris has accepted the offer from that high school in New York City.. It's a good move, I think. It will be exciting to live in the city and lots of his loans will be forgiven for teaching in a targeted area. Have you decided anything yet? You should consider it Mary. Your loans would be forgiven after five years."

Mary shook her head. Jeanette barely noticed. "Oh, you'll be good no matter where you teach. Everybody knows that. Chris says so." With those words, the matter was settled, as if Chris were the Pope and what he said was infallible..

A child ran from the bedroom carrying a blanket and rubbing her large and frightened eyes. "Mommy, mommy", she cried in a relieved voice, and hid her face in her mother's skirt. "Jimmy played house with me and Mary. He was the father."

"Oh that's nice, honey."

The child looked at Mary from within her mother's skirt. Mary noticed how small she was next to Jimmy, and feeling a sudden wistfulness, lifted her. The girl stared quietly at Mary, but didn't protest.

Jimmy's not a baby. I have no baby any more. He seems so grown up next to the toddlers.

She handed Susan to her mother, as the child struggled to separate her thumb from her blanket. Finally succeeding, she thrust her thumb into her mouth and her eyes began to close. The door was shut and everything became quiet until other parents began to arrive. Children were collected. Greetings filed the air. Gossip was exchanged.

"Hey Mary."

"How was he?"

"Great time."

"You should have seen the dean. He actually had a new suit." This remark because it was a universal joke among the students that the dean of studies wore the same suit to every function.

When everyone was gone, Mary leaned against the wall.

Jimmy sleeps soundly, doesn't worry about our next adventure. He trusts his mother implicitly.

She moved from the wall to the couch, sat without moving as if her stillness could keep the evening, the two years from ending and looked out the living room window at the round yellow globes on tall stems which lit the walkways of the apartment complex. She couldn't put into words all that she'd learned here, but knew it involved lessons more important than the subject matter of her courses.

I saw how foolish and self-absorbed I'd been to think that I alone came from an under-priviledged background. If anything, I had more than some others. A family—Uncle Ben and Aunt Irene—who would help me whenever they could. I just never asked. Stupid, stubborn pride. And humiliation at the mistakes I'd made.

She thought of Ronald Everett, a classmate who was rumored to have had a police record of some kind. He seemed harmless enough to Mary, a nice guy. People on the admissions committee must have been impressed with him. They hadn't been wrong. He was graduating at the top of the class and had already been offered at least five excellent positions she knew of. Or Jane Knox, who came from a family of nine kids on a dairy farm and dressed, as Mary's grandmother would say, "jak prostytutka". [43] Mary smiled. Jane was away from home for the first time and no doubt acting out her new freedom in the clothes she wore. Like Ron, she was bright.

Maybe I could tactfully speak to her about her outfit before she goes for a job interview.

There were more stories, other class members who had overcome difficult odds to reach graduate school. How had they found such courage?

How arrogant, how egocentric of me to think I was the only one.

Mary continued to watch the glow of the lamps outside. Their light became mist, falling and covering the ground with the shimmer of dew. She watched the lamps intently in order to fix the scene in her memory, to etch it on her consciousness amd recall it when she was gone from this place.

Chapter Ten

Beginning Again

The good feeling stayed with him for a while after he was home but then it began to wear off. Maybe it would be better if he lived closer to his sisters and brothers. But then he'd be further away from Mary. Everyone else called her Mary so he began to call her that, though she'd always be Marysza to him. And the boy. The kid he didn't know yet. He knew what was right. If he started to wonder, Steve's face was there to remind him. He could hear his voice.

"Just because you're divorced from your wife, you're not divorced from your kid."

Yeah, yeah, yeah. Okay Steve, okay. Boy am I crazy or what? Talking to a dead man.

Anyway, I can't move anywhere. The apprentice program lasts at least two more years. I have to go to school besides the training on the job.

Steve was right. His friends were still his friends. They didn't seem to drink so much anymore. Jerry already had three kids. Dave had given his girl an engagement ring. She pretty much called the shots and didn't want him going out with the guys. Tadziu couldn't resist saying. "Got your own ball and chain now, huh?" Dave answered by punching him in the arm.

It had been six months since Steve's death. Before he died, Steve and some other guys at the AA got Tadziu into a tool maker apprentice program. Tadziu worked at the job during the day and went to school two nights a week and Saturdays. He had passed some kind of aptitude test they had given him to get in the program but he still had to get a GED.

So he went. Went to classes in an old high school in the city. Between those classes and the apprentice classes he spent half his life in school.

Keeps me out of trouble. I'm too tired to drink.

He liked everything about tool making. Because he was good at it. The stuff he was supposed to learn fell into him easy, like things he had always known without knowing he knew them. He offered to work overtime whenever they needed someone. What else would he be doing anyway? Besides trying not to drink.

It was the GED classes he didn't like. History and geography stuff. Even spelling, his worst thing, and writing. He'd rather measure things than try to spell them. He was scared shitless of the exam. If he flunked it, everything would be messed up. And before he started the classes, he was scared shitless of the other students because they would think he was stupid. Like his father did. He almost turned around before going into the classroom. Until he thought of his job and the apprentice program and how much he loved it. If he wanted to keep that, he had to do this.

Shit. Nothin' in life was free.

He remembered Steve saying most of the things you were afraid of weren't so bad once you faced them. Steve was right about this one. Most of the people in the class were older than he was. Some of them couldn't speak good English. They all looked tired and worried. No one bothered to look at him. He went to all the classes, even tried to help some old guy who was having trouble with his writing. In one class, the man turned to Tadziu, looked at him with some kind of desperation in his eyes and waved his arms like he was crying for help. Acted as if Tadziu could help him.

"How yoo sey excooz, excooz too ah lay-dee? When she in da way? A mahn too. In da way, yoo nauw?"

The man's face grew red and his hands shook.

Oh- boy, this guy thinks I can help him. That's a good one. I don't know what he means. "When she in da way?" What the hell's that?

The man stood up and walked in front of Tadziu and stood there, blocking his view.

"Layk dis! Layk dis"! He waved his arms and his body like he was sending an SOS. When Tadziu tried to look around him, the man moved and blocked his view. Tadziu was puzzled and on the verge of anger. The guy wouldn't let him see, kept moving whenever he moved. "Ay sey sahmthin," the man insisted. "Ay sey sahmthin' too yoo nauw!"

A light went off in Tadziu's head. "Pardon me!" he roared, and the guy dropped into his seat like a rock, hit his head with a closed fist and rolled his eyes to say "at last!"

"Yah, yah. Nauw yoo rite it," he said, handing Tadziu his paper and pencil as if it was natural that Tadziu should do this for him.

So Tadziu became a teacher and printed the words "pardon me please" in large letters the man could see and use them in whatever he was writing. Tadziu watched him labor over the paper. It seemed forever until the man finished what he was writing and handed his paper back.

"Yoo reed, pleez," he said, "and tell mee watt."

. So Tadziu read the man's story about a woman and a man eating dinner and the man dropping his fork and then his plate and cup and saying "pardon me please", to the woman each time. The damn story went on and on and the man in the story said "pardon me please" in every second line for one thing or another. Tadziu tried, with the help of his small dictionary, to make sure all the words were spelled right.

When he handed the paper back, Taziu thought the man was going to jump up and kiss him but he just looked at Tadziu with wonder and said, "Yoo nayss boy." After that, Tadziu didn't mind the classes so much but he was still afraid of the test. He hoped the old man passed it. He was probably taking it for some reason that was necessary like Tadziu was.

The letter came in the mail. He was afraid to open it so he threw it on the table and let it sit there while he looked at it.

Shit, this is stupid. One way or the other, I gotta know, gotta face it.

His hands trembled like a little kid's opening a present. The letter didn't waste any words.

Thaddeus Wreblewski———. 79 Pulaski St,———. GED exam site Fillmore Junior College. Congratulations. Score 83. Passing grade 65. Test copies available in room 217 until 5/27.

Tadziu's legs were too weak to hold him. He sat down.

The math part was pretty easy. The sisters made sure all of us knew how to add and subtract, multiply and divide. Even numbskulls like me had to go to the blackboard and prove it or we got a whack with the ruler.

He laughed, thinking how he couldn't count the number of times he got whacked. He thought about how they had to memorize the times tables. Each kid had to stand up and recite them, all the way from two to twelve. Even if you were unconscious, you knew them after hearing them so many times.

Two times two is four, two times three is six…three times two is six, three times three is nine…four times two is eight, four times three is twelve….all the way to twelve times twelve is one hundred forty-four.

He remembered when it was his turn to stand up, Martha always turned around in her seat and looked back at him.

Hoping I'd mess up and get zapped.

He laughed out loud. Funny, how he never got mad at Martha, how things between them were some kind of contest or something. Sometimes he'd win and sometimes she'd win.

He never thought he'd be grateful to those sisters and their rulers but he was. Knowing arithmetic and the little algebra he did helped him get into that apprentice program. And now he could stay in the tool and die program. And out of that goddamned factory.

Searching

He tried to put the letter away and forget about it but he couldn't. He took it from the drawer and read it again five or six times.

I want to show this to Mary and Jimmy. If I can find them. Maybe she won't be interested. Hell, I'll show her anyway.

He didn't know how to send money for Jimmy because Mary didn't answer the phone when he called.

Well, I tried. No, I didn't. Who'm I trying to kid.

This was going to be harder than taking those classes. Jimmy wasn't a baby anymore.

He won't even know who I am. He'll never know who I am if I don't do something. But what? I don't know where the hell she is. Maybe her aunt and uncle would know where she is.

I can't go there. Her uncle never liked me. Didn't think she should marry me. Well, he was right.

Then he heard a voice, a damn god-damned voice that sounded exactly like Steve's.

"I guess you don't want to see your kid bad enough, huh?"

So he went. Another Jimmy answered the door. It was Mary's cousin, looking shy, like he was thinking you were staring at him.God, the kid had grown. Tall and skinny. Like his body had grown too fast and wasn't ripe yet. Like he might trip just opening the door. He was probably in high school now. The kid remembered him and said "hi Tadziu" as easily as if the years hadn't passed at all. That was the neat thing about kids. Mary's aunt came to see who was at the door. Her eyes opened wide in surprise. But she didn't let the surprise show in her voice.

So he sat there. On the couch across from Mary's Aunt Irene. The old man wasn't home from work yet.

Boy, he'll be glad to see me sitting here when he walks in the door.

Mary's aunt knew he was nervous. He remembered how she always knew things like that. She offered him a beer.

"No thanks," he said.

He didn't know if she offered him the beer because Mary never told her about him or because she forgot. With Aunt Irene, you were never sure of the reason.

She told him that Mary was doing her practice teaching at one of the schools outside the city so she was gone for long hours. She hadn't moved from her old apartment yet and the drive was a long one so she left early in the morning. Jimmy was in an after-school program. Tadziu could probably reach Mary by calling early in the morning.

He looked at Aunt Irene's face. He'd always liked her. For a moment he thought of showing her his letter, letting her know he'd passed that damn test.

Nah. That's stupid.

She said that when Mary was done with this practice thing, she'd be looking for a real job. It could be anywhere, even in another city. Unless she went to graduate school. Then Lord knows where she'd land.

Then Aunt Irene's face was lit by something inside and she told Tadziu that Uncle Ben was studying to become an engineer and was in some kind of on-the-job training until he finished school. Tonight he was in class.

The whole damn family's studying somethin'. Good for the old man. Maybe he's not so bad if Aunt Irene thinks he's so great. She's not dumb about things like that. Anyway I don't have to see him.

He thanked her and the boy and rose to leave. She held his hand at the door.

"Now Tadziu, you come visit us whenever you want."

"Thanks" He moved to hug her but felt awkward and stopped. She saw the gesture and completed it, holding him close, like a mother bear embracing one of her cubs.

"Okay, I will, I will."

"Ma, you're gonna suffocate him1" Jimmy cried.

Pretending to gasp for air, Tadziu laughed with Jimmy and waved good-bye.

At least he knew where Mary was. Still in the old flat. Right here. For now. She wouldn't stay here, wouldn't come back after she was a big shit. Maybe for Christmas sometime to see her aunt and uncle but that'd be it. If he wanted to see his son, he'd have to go wherever she was.

Mary will take my son away. Is that fair? Take him away and not give a shit about me at all.

The words rolled around in his head and flung themselves against his skull like heavy balls.

We were the same. We grew up and went through a lot together. And she left me. Took our son and went off to some fancy school. And now maybe another one. He knew her. There'd be another one. What the hell. How's she think I can follow her all over the damn place?

He thought about the days when he called Mary teacher's pet, when she was skinny and scared-looking, just like he was. But she was pretty and she wore clean clothes. Like a princess. Her house was two streets away from where he lived but it could have been another world. It was like a castle. Always smelled like soap. And had a table where she did her homework. An old one that wobbled. But still, it was hers and belonged to her alone.

Christ, she even liked to read, used to show him her books and tried to get him interested. Sometimes she read out loud and he had to listen. He said the books were dumb but he remembered how the words sounded when she said them, like something you had to stop and listen to, and that he liked them. But he wouldn't tell her that.

Her grandmother worked at her sewing or crocheting while they read. Like someone watching over them. Keeping them safe. Yeah, that old lady would shoot anybody who tried to hurt them. He just knew it. He always knew it. He was included in her protection because he was Mary's friend but mostly she loved Mary.

Mary always had so much more than I did. Now she's going to take my son.

Words crashed into each other inside his head again. He knew something about the words was a lie but he wasn't sure what. It was too hard to sort out.

It wasn't hard to picture Mary as a teacher. He tried to give her face a bad look. Told himself she was sleeping with other men and neglecting Jimmy. But it didn't work. He knew that was a lie and that she was a good mother.

He couldn't think about her sleeping with other men. He still had the crazy feeling that she belonged to him, that they belonged together. Maybe he could fix things if he had a chance. God-damn, how could he have a chance if she went away?

Like dice turning to a new number, Mary's face was replaced by Jimmy's.

Okay, Steve, okay.

He had to see his son, had to become a part of his life or the kid would forget him. He wasn't sure how to do that. He'd have to write to Mary. He could probably write a half-way decent letter now. Thanks to the teachers at the GED place.

Once he started the letter, it got easy, easier than talking to her. The words were hard to hold back, as if they knew he had waited a long time to say them. And he liked the way they looked on the paper, as if they were different, better than spoken words. But in some ways writing a letter was harder than talking. It wasn't just for practice like in those classes. He had to choose his words. And choosing meant a lot of thinking.

After what seemed like a long time working on the words, he picked up his paper and read the letter out loud so he could make sure everything sounded okay:

Dear Mary,

I miss seeing Jimmy. I miss seeing you too. I know you have a new life now and it does not include me but it should include me in the welfare of my boy, our boy.

That was a good sentence. He was proud of it.

I would like to come and see him, to have him stay with me sometime so we could get to know each other. Don't worry, I haven't been drinking bad for about three years now. Believe it or not, I can take it or leave it. Anyway, I would never drink around him because I know it would worry you. I don't know how you feel about this. I wish we could talk. I don't want to come and upset you. If you could answer this letter, maybe we could work something out. Sincerely, Tadziu.

The "sincerely" part was something the teachers called "the closing" and had to be included. He wanted to write "love" but he didn't. Why should he write "love"? What good had his love for Mary ever brought him? Except unhappiness. And a drinking problem.

Aw cut it out. She didn't cause me to drink.

There were things about himself he'd never understand, things that made him feel helpless, like a man on the edge of a roof, about to fall, like now when he admitted he was telling a lie, yet still, in some ways, couldn't admit it.

Mary, Mary. I'm alone. So alone. I wish you felt alone. I wish you needed me.

Thoughts became pictures that floated past his eyes like a movie in slow motion. He saw the two of them sitting at their desks in school, saw himself laughing out loud when his spitball hit the back of her head. She kept doing what she was doing, never turned around to look because she knew if she did Sister would know, but Martha turned around when Sister's back was turned and shook her fist at him.

He saw Mary and himself playing cards at the kitchen table in her grandmother's house. He felt the need to win, as if he was carrying a bag that was too heavy, and losing would make the bag heavier until the muscles in his legs burst open.

He saw the hospital room when he went to visit Mary after Jimmy was born, how she looked helpless and he wanted to protect her, until the nurse brought the baby and then he watched Mary enter some private world, a world where he didn't belong, where only she and the baby could go. Even though she invited him in. The baby was more hers than his. He could only sit and try to smile.

It was different now. Jimmy was older and didn't need his mother twenty-four hours a day. He could do some things with his old man.

He slammed his hand on the kitchen table. Hell, his life had other things besides Mary and the kid.

Who'm I kidding? I'll never stop thinking of her.

Why did he feel so edgy? Probably from writing the letter. Wondering if she'd answer. She'd better answer. Or he'd go there anyway. He had a right to see his son.

Aw hell, this is shit. Just words, words, words. Even my words sound like threats. God dammit. Just like my old man. And my head hurts.

He thought of calling one of the guys to go for a beer, but they couldn't go so easy any more. They were all attached. Only he was single.

Aw hell, I don't need anyone to go with me. I'm all grown up. I can go alone.

He got drunk. He hadn't been drunk since he could remember. It wasn't worth it. It made him feel worse. The next morning, as if someone wanted him to know, he woke up thinking that he hadn't put his address on the letter. How could she answer him? So he put his name and address at the bottom of the page, sealed and stamped the envelope and went to the mailbox.

When he received an answer to his letter, she told him to come anytime. She was probably just trying to be nice. He felt as excited as a kid who'd caught his first fish.

First Visit

He and Mary sat facing each other across the table but Tadziu didn't know what to talk about. She asked him where he was staying. He told her the name of a nearby motel. There was a pause so he talked about how nice the motel was and that it wasn't expensive, that he could only stay one day because he had to get back to work and he had an eight-hour drive home. He thought he must sound like an asshole, a motor-mouth, but he was afraid of the silence there would be if he stopped talking. But she started.

She's telling me about practice teaching, acting as if I know what she's talking about, how she might be going for a master's degree in the fall. I'm paying attention, pretending I understand all of it, but I'm really looking at her face and at how happy she looks. Her hair has sun and shade in it, looks just the way my mother's used to look.

Her legs could wrap around me like ribbon. She's older, looks as if she knows more than she did. before. Could wrap around me while I hold her until she's ready for me.

A boy ran into the room. His boy. Tadziu looked at him closely. It was like seeing his son for the first time. Jimmy stopped when he saw him.

"Hi," he said. His eyes were unafraid, held a hint of mischief, like he was waiting for a chance to show his cleverness. A shock of blonde hair stood up on the back of his head, sort of like a feather.

How can I tell him about me? Who I am? She said she'd told him nothing important. What did that mean? That she told him what a bum his father was. Be real, you jerk. She wouldn't do that. You know she wouldn't do that.

There was that half-lying thing in him again.

The boy had been running, was breathing hard, fell backwards into a chair exhausted, then popped up again, as if he had sat long enough and had to be about some business. He had a dimple in his chin. Looked like any cute kid he ever saw

Her eyes. Behind the mischief. Yeah, her eyes. I wonder what part of him looks like me.

I don't know how to play with him. Maybe I could learn. How? If she's taking him away. And herself. What's wrong with me? I've been away from her for four years. Lost years. I lost them. She's not going to run her life for my convenience. Just because I decided to make an appearance.

Okay this was more like the truth. He was truthful. It didn't help much. He still felt lost. And sad. And alone

Tadziu watched Mary's movements as she heated food on the stove in a dented pot he remembered. Her hands shook when she held the heavy pot and offered some to him but he felt awkward and told her he'd already eaten, which was a lie. She offered him coffee and he said "Sure," and sat there drinking it and watching Jimmy eat.

This is my family. My son. And the woman who was my wife.

Now the boy is shy, sits across from me looking at his mother. Maybe he's shy because she told him I'm his father. He doesn't know what to do with a father.

A carrot rolls from the boy's s plate onto the tabletop.

He stabs at it but misses, looks from beneath blonde lashes to see if I've seen. I pretend I don't. A black and white striped cat jumps onto the table, starts rubbing itself against the boy's cheek. The kid giggles, then stops, thinking I'll think he's a baby. I can tell that look. That's how boys think.

"Harry, get down," Mary said.

Tadziu laughed out loud. "Harry! Who named him Harry?"

"I did," the boy said proudly as he lifted Harry from the table and placed him on the floor in a firm, grown-up manner.

"That's a good name for a cat."

The boy looked pleased. Mary didn't say anything.

She doesn't want to interfere. How long will it take for me to know my boy? Is she reading my thoughts? Why does she turn away?

He talked more to the boy, saw how easy it was to make him laugh.

The dark sheet falling slowly across the window told Tadziu it was getting late. Her face filled him, held him like the falling light held the world.

Mary told Jimmy it was time for bed but he didn't want to go.

Tadziu wanted him to stay up talking about school, about his friends, about anything. He asked if he had any girlfriends.

Jimmy let out an indignant "no," the loudest noise he had made all evening. .

"Well someday you'll like them," Tadziu said. "Someday you'll love one." He didn't say, "The way I love your mother." Warmth fell across his shoulders like the last rays of light, grew and spread itself through him.

The way I love your mother.

"It's okay to tell," he teased. "All boys like girls."

Jimmy screamed louder, held his stomach as if he was in pain, and began telling Tadziu the many ways that girls were stupid. Mary flushed, as if she was hot and returned to washing dishes.

The boy was silent and looked at them. Tadziu sensed the boy understood that feelings of love existed between his father and mother and that Tadziu would always be present in their lives.

As if he were answering a formal invitation, Jimmy said yes, Tadziu could come to see him again. With a hidden smile, Mary said yes and the boy shook Tadziu's hand. Tadziu reached out and held him close for a minute. Jimmy grew stiff and turned away.

I should have known better. It's too soon.

Mary wiped her hands and took the boy to his bedroom.

Does it mean anything that she avoids my eyes? Her letter said I could come as often as I like.

When she returned, Mary looked at Tadziu as if she'd never seen him before, and was remembering who he was.

"Jimmy likes you." It was quiet until she asked, "do you want more coffee?" He nodded and forgot what he'd told her earlier.

"Sure, it'll keep me awake on the long ride home."

"I thought you were staying at a motel"?

He admitted he lied when she asked him where he was staying.

"You'll have to drive all night." There was concern in her voice.

"Yeah." He waited, not wanting her voice to stop so he'd have to get up and leave.

"It would be better for you to start out in the morning."

"Yeah." He waited again. As he'd always waited when he was a boy. To see if he could go into her grandmother's house.

Will she let me in? I must go in. I must stay. I must stay. She knows.

"Do you want to sleep on the couch?" She looked sorry the minute she asked.

She's uncertain. Could it be she's afraid she might love me again?

Tadziu felt happy.

Could it be? And afraid I might go back to what I was?

Tadziu didn't want to answer too quickly, to let her know his longing. She'd thrown him out. She'd left and taken their son. He resented that. He heard Steve telling him that was nonsense. He didn't need Steve to tell him that. He knew.

What the hell did I expect her to do? Live with someone who threatened her?

He tried to convince himself that Mary had done the right thing but he felt the anger that lay brooding in him. Anger because she'd left. Part of him thought she should've been loyal. That was what his father thought about his mother, that she would stay no matter what. And she did. Because she couldn't do anything else. Yet he resented Mary because she was strong enough to do something. And he still felt the blood pulse in his veins when he saw her. Still wanted her. And resented that too.

He watched her put blankets and a pillow on her couch and they both laughed nervously when she said she didn't think it was a comfortable couch. And that touched him somewhere deeper inside himself than the anger and washed it away

She was right. The couch wasn't comfortable. But still better than riding in his car for eight hours.

Who'm I kidding? It has nothing to do with the drive. I'm here because I want to lay here, thinking about her in the room next to me, wondering if she's awake or sleeping and the low breathing I hear means her lips are parted the way they were when we slept together.

Tadziu remembered how sex exhausted her, how he would lie awake after she fell asleep, wondering how a girl like her could love a creep like him. From the time they were kids, he was afraid. Each time he was with her. That it would be the last time. And now, lying on her couch, miles away from the place of their childhood, or the place of their short married life, he was wide awake. And he heard something beneath all his thoughts, something loud and clear, as if someone was talking to him, a voice that told him fear was a terrible thing. Not physical fear, like being afraid of another guy, but mind fear, the kind that lived in your brain and told you what a shit you were. He thought of how afraid he'd been to take the GED class. He thought of Gina's wedding, of his fears of spoiling it, and how those fears had almost kept him from going. Fear could keep you from doing things. Could keep you from living your life. He wasn't sure what knowing that meant except that somehow he'd have to smarten up, stop being afraid of what life was going to do next, of what was going to happen to him.

Mary's silence was like a light blanket covering the night noises in the apartment—-the refrigerator motor humming, a clock ticking somewhere, the complaints of the couch each time he turned. He knew she was awake.

"I'm just going to use the bathroom, okay?" he whispered, as he walked past her door. He remembered that door. It never closed properly and he'd meant to fix it.

"Sure," she answered and he went on his way. Walking back, he thought he heard her mattress creak, as if she was tossing and turning. He lay back beneath the covers on his couch and again thought he heard Mary's bed creak. The lumps in the couch cushions hurt his head. They hurt his shoulders. He turned some more, got up to go to the john. Again. She coughed. He stared at the ceiling. A feeling in his gut told him this was one of those moments that were important. He couldn't explain why. He just knew. He got up again.

"You having trouble sleeping?" he asked at her door. "I am." She was quiet. "Mary, I know it's late but can we talk?" There was no answer.

She's pretending she doesn't hear me. Pretending she's asleep. But she came out, wrapped in a robe that covered her from her neck to the floor, only her toes sticking out and her hands playing with the collar on the robe.

She's nervous. Is she afraid? Of me?

He was silent, filled with sadness and anger. The light from the street lamps moved through the blinds on the kitchen window, fell in stripes against the wall and settled in pools on the floor. He looked into her face, then turned his eyes away.

As if I'm some man she doesn't know, some man who wasn't her husband.

His hands felt heavy at his sides. The ticking of the clock became louder.

"I'm sorry," he said, "sorry for everything."

"I know."

"I want to be Jimmy's father."

"You can. I won't ever keep you from seeing him...as long...as long as..."

He finished her words. "As long as I'm not drinking."

"Yes."

He didn't know what else to say.

I want to lie down on the bed next to her and she doesn't want to hear that. Does she? I can't fail. I'm failing.

When he reached for her, she settled into his arms with the sureness of an old habit.

I don't know how this is happening, how I'm holding her and she lets me, isn't moving away. I can't tell her I love her. She doesn't want to hear it.

He was a drowning man watching his lifeboat move away. With each tick of the clock he felt more desperate. He couldn't stop the movement of the hands, couldn't stop the night. He'd have to move away from her. Would have to go. Mary pulled herself from his arms.

She's sorry for that moment.

"I really don't drink anymore," he repeated, and knew it was stupid the minute he heard himself say it.

"I'm glad. You're a good man."

"You must be kidding." He laughed. Then he thought about Gina's wedding. He was getting better in the goodness department. "I'm trying," he said, and then the words he knew he shouldn't say, rushing from him like water in a flood, "I want us to be together again." She turned away.

Mary. Mary. You loved me. I know you did.

He had the terrible feeling he was one of those men who was going to love only one woman in his life. He put the few things he had brought into his bag and left. She didn't try to stop him.

A Second Visit

He sent money to Mary twice before he went to see them again. He remembered the frightened look she had on his first visit when they talked in the middle of the night. He couldn't say, "I don't know how it is for you but for me, it doesn't matter how long we've been apart. I want to come as close to you as I can, to reach out and touch your hair, your mouth and your neck." And he held back. Always held back.

I'm afraid of you, Mary. I was always afraid of you. You had something I wanted, something more than your body alone could give. I don't understand any of it. Except the part that needs no thinking. I'm drowning in you. Again. Drowning

"I wanted to tell you the money will keep coming. This time for real." He looked around the apartment and laughed. She looked at him. "The red linoleum," he explained. "It's he first thing that hits your eyes. Kind of like a beacon. Or a light-house." Toys were stacked neatly in a bookcase made of some kind of imitation wood.

Cheap. Everything cheap. But clean. No change there.

He sat down in a kitchen chair. She sat across from him. He felt himself quiver because of her white arms on the table, their curves covered by almost invisible golden hair, so that he had the picture of her naked and exposed.

"It's cold in here. You should be wearing a sweater."

"I know." Her laugh was embarrassed. "I was getting ready to go to school. You know how the gas bills are. I try to keep the thermostat down when Jimmy's not here." She was talking fast. He took her hand and quivered like he was getting a cold.

"He's in kindergarten" she said and took back her hand. .

"Oh. Yeah," He felt stupid. For not knowing his kid was in school. Yeah, he remembered what kindergarten was. That fact let them talk about how Jimmy was doing. She got up and came back with a sweater. Blue. Like a piece of sky against her skin. Her face told him that something new came between them, so that their words were no longer natural, free and flowing like a stream, but clouded, covering their meaning. They talked for a while about things he wasn't interested in and he could tell she wasn't either.

She asked, probably out of politeness, about his parents, and he answered no, that he didn't see them, and was forced, by her question, to face what he had avoided.

Jesus, it'd be too hard. I'm not ready for that.

He wanted to talk about himself and her and Jimmy. Instead he handed her a check. She started to say it was too much, more than the divorce papers ordered, but he stopped her.

"I want to. I can afford it. I'll send that each week." There was nothing more to say. A rock fell inside his stomach. He'd have to get up and leave

"But I'll be going to graduate school and the address will be different, and…." She stopped, the rest of the words disappearing as she turned her face away and played with the button on her sweater

He paused and breathed hard. Tried to sound natural.

"Well, you can give me your new address. The post office is still in business."

Her face flushed, the way it did when she was embarrassed. And he understood. She needed the money to come regular while she was at school and didn't know how to say it. And she worried whether she could depend on him.

Again he reached to touch her hand, one of her fingers where she played with the button on the front of her sweater.

"I won't miss sending the check".

Their words came back to the way they'd been. They were together again, hiding nothing. He felt himself fly, like a bird newly free.

"Do you want some coffee?" she asked, like she had just thought of it. He felt the rock lifting. She didn't want him to leave.

"Sure."

It doesn't matter what she means or doesn't mean. Jimmy is my excuse to come back. The money is our tie.

Words repeated themselves.

I'll see her again. I'll see her again.

He walked down the stairs of a hallway that seemed different, not as dark as the last time. She wouldn't be here much longer but he'd worry about that later.

But the worrying started right away,

Jesus, how the hell much could you study? She said having more degrees meant she could make more money. But she'd be taking Jimmy. He didn't know the kid yet and she'd be taking him. And God knows where they'd land when she finished and got a job. She might go so far he'd never be able to see his son. Or her.

She's a good mother, ain't she? The kid looks happy. She said she'd always send an address so I'd know where to send the money. Why should I send money? She's probably going to make more than me. Jesus. What's wrong with me? I'm sliding back. Because he's my son, that's why. Fathers support their sons. Yeah but fathers should be able to know their sons. Cut it out. No shittin' around anymore. The problem is that I want to see her. Mary. Mary. Like yesterday.

She still stirred him up. Could another woman ever do that the way she did?

He reached the bottom of the stairs. He had to go back to his room. Alone. But he'd been alone. Some crazy thing had made him hope. Hope what. He didn't know.

It's going to be tough tonight. I haven't had a drink in 18 months.

He knew because he counted the months.

Routine

He went to see Jimmy each week. He wanted to see him as much as he could before they left. His visits were usually on Sunday because he went to tool making classes on Fridays and Saturdays. That meant he had to drive most of Sunday night and work on Monday without much sleep. But he didn't care. On his last visit, Jimmy had called him daddy.

"Daddy, will you bring me a present next week?" he asked with that "please" look in his eyes that kids got.

"Sure," Tadziu answered. "What d'you want?"

Jimmy answered without hesitating, "a horse."

"A horse! You want me to bring a horse?" With great exaggeration, Jimmy fell to the floor and held his stomach with laughter. Tadziu kept his face serious.

"I suppose I'll have to ride him all the way."

In the toy store he looked at stuff for boys, but there was so much it was confusing. He tried to think back but that was useless. He never had any store-bought toys. He asked the store clerk what a boy Jimmy's age would like. She helped him choose some cars and trucks and an erector building set he thought looked like fun. And they found a small toy horse. Looked real too. A nice brown color with a mane and tail that felt silky but tough

He looked at the building set in the bag when he got home. Three times. Then he took it out and tried it. It was an hour before he put it away.

Mary thought it was funny when Jimmy was faster at building than Tadziu was. Tadziu pretended to be puzzled.

"How d'you do that? I practiced at home for a long time, you little shit, you." He covered his mouth as if he'd been caught using bad language, but Jimmy seemed thrilled to be called a "little shit" and overjoyed that he was faster at building than his father.

"I guess I'll have to find some easier things," Tadziu said, sounding sad and watching Mary cover her mouth to hide her amusement.

"Mom, it's Dad," Jimmy would yell each time he saw him.

Sometimes Tadziu felt doubtful.

How can he like me already?

Then he remembered Joe, how he hadn't warmed up to him at first but it wasn't long before he loved him.

Each time his visits at Mary's were over, he tried to linger until Jimmy went to bed. When he said good-bye, he looked at Mary carefully so he'd remember how she looked that day. All week long he thought about going back. At work, it was not as hard because he had to concentrate and couldn't let his mind wander. Being a toolmaker was not the same as being a factory worker. Your work was more important. A lot of other things in the plant depended on it. But it was impossible not to think of her on the long rides back and forth.

It would have been his sixth trip. She called to tell him that she and Jimmy would be taking some things to school and she'd be having an orientation. He could come to the apartment and take it as it was because she'd be packing. So he went. And found out they'd be back the following week to pick up the last things before school started. Just like that. He wouldn't see Jimmy unless he went to the school.

But it wasn't as bad as he thought. Just over the state line in Pennsylvania. A long drive but nothing impossible. He couldn't do it weekly but he could do it sometime. Monthly maybe He was always careful keeping his car in top shape and it never gave him trouble.

"Everything's going to stay the same in the flat so we can come home for vacations and holidays and have some time when I finish. I'll need to find a job and a better place. Her eyes were lit with excitement and she spoke fast. Like when he got the letter about the GED exam and couldn't believe it was true. "Uncle Ben says the landlord will hold the place and keep our stuff for us because we were good tenants." That sounded funny to Tadziu because he remembered what a hard ass the guy was but he didn't say anything.

She said Uncle Ben would be driving them. He reached out to shake Tadziu's hand.

"How you doing Tadziu?"

Jeez, didn't seem like any hard feelings there.

And when it came time to leave, Jimmy cried and clung to him.

"Will you come see us, daddy, and bring me some stuff?"

"Yeah," you little shitburger. We'll find some things to do in Pennsylvania. Don't worry. They got the same things there we have here. Jimmy was goofy with excitement or something. He fell on the floor, laughing hysterically.

"Ma. Ma, Daddy called me a "shitburger", a "shitburger!"

"Okay, Jimmy, okay, quiet down." Uncle Ben laughed but Mary looked at Tadziu with reproof. He shrugged

"Well, you are a shitburger," he whispered to Jimmy behind his hand, which started his giggles again.

Okay, she's nervous and tryin' to pack and stuff. I better get going

He wanted to kiss her good-bye, hold her and feel her against his chest but of course he couldn't. Instead, he handed her a check and said, "I'll be waiting for that address. More than an address. A map of the school and where you are. Jimmy, you help your ma to make a map for me. I don't think she's good at that and I'll never find you." Jimmy stopped laughing and turned serious.

"Okay dad. I will, don't worry."

That sounded nice. A kid and his father kidding about the woman they loved.

He swooped Jimmy up and hugged him hard. Even kissed him, though Jimmy wiped the kiss away and hollered, "Yuk, boys don't kiss." Then he started to cry. Tadziu didn't expect his own eyes to mist over. It was getting easier and easier to love this kid.

"Once in a while when it's important, it's okay, for boys to kiss. And cry too." Jimmy was serious again.

"Okay, dad."

And Tadziu was gone.

Schooldays

Tadziu found the school without any trouble. He wasn't surprised by anything when he got there. It was the kind of place he always knew Mary would be in. It felt important and even the chilly fall air told you everyone here was important.

If he wasn't meant to be here his son probably was so he might as well get used to it right now.

There ain't any "no trespassing" signs, right?

He laughed at himself and began to enjoy what he knew was beautiful.

The buildings looked like they were from another time, something you might see on the front of a greeting card, constructed of something he'd never seen, long, thick bricks of gray stone that made you think of a church or some kind of fortress. Some had ivy climbing the stone and he thought of how he knew that wasn't good for the mortar but these babies could probably hold up under anything, probably already had. One building had a tower with a clock. The hour was just changing and he listened as the chimes boomed their message and traveled through the fallen leaves. The walking paths looked worn smooth by a million feet, and you could see the footprints, as if they were inviting you to try them yourself. He passed students who hurried and carried books, Some looked like they were thinking about something and looked past him, but most were friendly and smiled or said "hi". When he asked a guy his age how to find the library, he even offered to take him there.

It's nice here

"Naw, I'll find it."

"I'm going in that direction. C'mon."

So he walked with the guy and talked about where they were from.

"I was in Buffalo once. Nice city. Nice people. Went to see Niagara Falls. We looked at it from both countries. The U.S. and Canada. It's amazing. And went on that boat that goes right under the Falls."

"Yeah, that's fun." Tadziu had never done that.

That'll be a good thing to do with Jimmy.

The guy waved good-bye and Tadziu walked up the steps like he was going inside. He looked through the glass doors. Looked like thousands of books on miles of shelves. Then he went and sat on the steps—because Mary said they'd always meet at the library—-with guys who looked just like he did. Girls too. They were laughing and fooling around but without any big deal they included him. One girl was smoking. Her hair was in her eyes.

"She thinks she's Greta Garbo," one of the guys said to Tadziu.

"She looks okay to me," Tadziu said and the girl gave him a big smile. He was glad he was wearing his good clothes.

Then he saw Jimmy running up the path with Mary behind.

"Dad, dad, what're we gonna do?" Tadziu lifted him and pretended to try tossing him into the air.

"Holy smokes. Guess you're getting kind of big for that. Well, I thought we could go to the show or something. Whatever you want." Mary hugged him, actually hugged him. Maybe she was homesick or something.

"Thanks for coming. He's been so excited." She stepped back, held his hands and examined him closely.

"You look good."

"Thanks. You too."

"You look like a student." Handsomer than most, too." She started to say something else but stopped herself.

Then they were waving to her and Jimmy was talking non-stop about what they should do. There'd be no problem because Tadziu had picked up all the pamphlets at the visitors' station. He tried to pay attention to Jimmy but he couldn't stop thinking that Mary looked at him the way she did a long time ago when she loved him. He knocked himself in the head.

I don't care why. I'll take it. Just don't get carried away, buddy.

But he couldn't help it.

The way she looked when she loved me

It was still warm so they went to the zoo. The next time he came Jimmy was wearing a heavy jacket and gloves so they went to the movies. He kept looking at Mary for that look again but was never sure it was there. Jimmy paid pretty close attention during Singing in the Rain but he and Tadziu laughed out loud at the Mickey Mouse cartoons

And then it was Christmas vacation and she was home for almost a month.

When he went to the apartment, Jimmy ran to him, circled Tadziu's legs with his small arms, and began butting them with his head.

"Hey, you a goat or something?" Tadziu asked, which sent Jimmy into one of his laughing fits.

When they were on the floor playing with the miniature train Jimmy got for Christmas, Jimmy told Tadziu they were at Michael's house on the weekend.

"Michael is mama's friend. He's nice." Tadziu felt a sinking feeling in his stomach, but he didn't flinch, never looked up at Mary. He was proud of himself. She'd never know how something began chewing him up inside.

He got drunk when he got home. It had been so long since he had done any real drinking that it didn't take long. He walked home from the neighborhood tavern and went to sleep immediately. The next day, the pain was worse, both in his head and in his thoughts. He knew the drinking wasn't worth it. But there were times you just couldn't do anything else.

All that week, he tried not to think of her but he couldn't help himself. Then he stopped trying. A part of him was angry with himself, an anger it seemed okay to have.

I'm letting her make me drink. I'm letting her take everything away, not just herself, but myself and whatever the hell it is I've worked for. I shouldn't give myself up so easy, like a boxer just letting himself be hit. I'm a better fighter than that.

He didn't want to do it, talked to himself all week so that he wouldn't do it, but when he got there, he started questioning her.

"This guy you're carrying on with," he began, surprised at the sharpness in his voice.

Am I crazy? We're divorced. She can do what she wants.

Mary stared at him as if his voice were coming from some far-away place she didn't recognize. She turned away from him, then turned back.

"It can't be us anymore, Tadziu. You're a good man, but it can't be us."

"Good man, good man, what's this shit? I don't want to be a good man. You know damn well what I want." And then, in a voice that ran away from him, a voice that was no longer under his control. "Mary, what're you doing this for?"

Jimmy came to Tadziu and put his arms around him. Tadziu didn't know what to do with any of it. Not only her but the boy too. Mary didn't seem to notice.

"Mama," Jimmy wailed, in a voice that, Tadziu noticed, always got his mother's attention. "Tadziu's my daddy. You said so."

Damn, damn. Even the kid's sticking up for me.

"I know, Jimmy," Mary answered. Her calm voice made Tadziu want to hit her. "Your daddy can come to see you as many times as he wants. Even take you on vacations." Jimmy looked at Tadziu hopefully.

Fuck, fuck. This is no surprise. I expected it, knew she'd find someone else. I'm no good. Why should she want me?

He wanted to leave but he couldn't when he looked at Jimmy's face again, when he saw that his son knew he was hurting.

How could kids be like this? How did they know things? As if they had some kind of radio inside, wires coming out of their heads that caught everything, didn't let anything escape.

He remembered thinking, after Jimmy was born, that Mary had that kind of radar too. He remembered his own childhood. As a kid, he'd always known when his mother was hurting. Even though she never said anything.

His anger with Mary grew. The muscles in his back tightened. He saw the lines in her forehead deepen. Joey looked at the two of them, his face moving back and forth, like the little rubber ball attached to a paddle with a long rubber band. She tried to change the subject and asked him and Jimmy if they wanted a snack.

He wasn't going to help her. His voice was more abrupt than he intended it to be.

"No thanks!" Tension filled the room like water in a rising flood. He saw Jimmy's lower lip tremble and heard his voice.

"Carl says his mother and father are divorced and they fight all the time."

Jesus. I don't want to hurt my kid. Do I? My kid.

"Jimmy, your mama and me won't fight anymore. Right Mary?"

"Right." This with gratitude in her eyes.

Pis. I have to face it. I already got drunk. I'm not going to let her make me get drunk again. The bitch. Who knows what she's sleeping with. Aw, cut it out. I'm a big asshole.

He told Mary he was hungry, real hungry. He sat there with Jimmy and ate crackers with peanut butter. It stuck to the roof of his mouth. He pretended he couldn't talk, that his jaw was glued together, that he tried to pry it open but couldn't. Jimmy tried to help him open his mouth.

I'm going to be alone. Bullshit. There's other women. Bullshit. I'll always be alone.

The emptiness in him couldn't be filled, would never be filled. At the door, he wanted to tell her he'd be around if she changed her mind, but he wouldn't say it.

She knows. The bitch. I want to kiss her with an open mouth, feel her tongue. Take off her sweater and her clothes, suck her all over until she gives in, cries for me and comes, is over, finished before me, then falls back and I have to move her legs apart and feel the tightness that holds me when I go in. So that I can't stand it long and I come too. And we lay together, our hips and our legs touching. And I smoke a cigarette, watch the smoke climb while she talks to me about anything, nothing. It won't be that way with anyone else.

O Christ, Steve, what do I do now? C'mon Steve, you told me how much you loved your woman. And you lost her too. Help me.

Jimmy climbed onto his lap.

"Okay, you bum," he said to his boy, heard himself laugh, wondered how he could do it. "Whatcha want me to bring you next time I come?"

Next time. Jesus.

Peals of laughter. "An elephant!"

"Now an elephant. Horses aren't big enough, huh?" He pretended to drop Jimmy in surprise. "How am I supposed to get him here once I find him?" He couldn't stop thinking about her sweater, the way the skin of her breasts was softer when you moved toward the nipple. Jimmy would not give up.

"Just bring him, Daddy. Then we can ride him together."

She turned, filled his throat like a stone that was lodged there and couldn't come loose. He wanted to get away, tried to move to the door. Jimmy held on to his leg. He pretended not to notice and opened the door as if he would drag Joey right through. Mary stopped the game.

"Let go of your daddy," she said sternly. Jimmy let go, then put his arms around Tadziu's waist, and hid his face in Tadziu's stomach.

"Okay, fella, I gotta go." Tadziu took him by the shoulders and looked into his eyes. "See you next week."

"Okay, daddy. Hurry, okay?" The pit in Tadziu's throat went deeper, hurt more. Could he come back? Did he want to do this anymore? Did he want to see her? Could he stand not seeing her? What about his kid? Who wanted him to bring horses and elephants. Who laughed the way he never laughed when he was a kid. Who, for some reason he couldn't understand, loved him.

He loves me. He loves me.

He told Jimmy he didn't know when he'd be back, that things were getting busy now at work. He watched the kid's face fall, saw him trying to act like a big man who didn't cry.

A Big Step

During the week, like crazed horses, Tadziu's thoughts ran in all directions.

Mary doesn't want any part of me. Okay. I get the message. I'm not going to get on my hands and knees for any woman. Not even her. Jimmy loves me. I used to cry the kind of tears Jimmy was crying when I was a kid.. The kind that don't show. I was a big man.

His anger at Mary made him want to hit someone. Because she wouldn't take him back. But he couldn't hurt her. Except by hurting Jimmy. Because she loved Jimmy too. He knew that was crazy. Hurting the kid to get at the mother. He didn't care. He thought of his old man, got ticked off at himself for being just like him.

There's nothing I can do about it. Like father, like son.

Then his thoughts changed, became something else, like black and white turning into color, trying to let something in that pounded at him more and more lately. He knew he wasn't his father. Would never be his father. Something about him was the same. But something about him was different. Very different than his father.

What am I, some kind of woman, that I can't think straight?

He heard Steve's words. "You don't divorce your kids when you divorce your wife. You have to separate them."

Separate them? I think of them together now. Mary and Jimmy. Mary and Jimmy.

He was some kind of woman. His thoughts continued to zigzag back and forth like a flash of lightning you saw drawn in comic books. If he went to see Jimmy, he'd see her. It was too hard to see her. He'd always get angry, just thinking they'd never be together, that he'd always be alone. It would be better if he got lost, went somewhere far away. He'd still send the money.

But then the kid would grow up and wonder what it meant for his father to say he loved him. Nothing. The same story. His anger grew until it filled him. His anger at

Mary because she deserted him. His anger at his life. Why should he worry about his son when no one ever worried about him? The thought stuck in his head like glue.

No one ever worried about me. Jimmy. Born into bad luck, just like me. But my luck was worse than Jimmy's, worse than anyone's. No one ever had a father like mine.

He went out and bought a bottle of whiskey and put it on the kitchen table. Just so he could use it if he felt like it.

He lay on the bed in his room staring at the ceiling. He saw Jimmy's eyes looking at him, searching for a sign. From him, from his father. Approval. Recognition. Whatever it was. Something Tadziu couldn't give. Didn't want to give.

His eyes are hers. Have the same color. The same look. If I let them in, they'll fill me.

He wanted to sleep. Closed his eyes, turned out the light. Turned it on again. Walked around his room. Smoked. Put on the television he'd bought himself.

Late-night talk shows were on. He hated them. Too many wise-asses who thought they were hot shit. He switched channels. Jack Paar was okay. He got tired of him too. Switched from channel to channel. All the movies were old. Had old stars in them, with names like Carol Lombard or Clara Bow. Their clothes looked old and their cars looked old, although that did interest him, seeing what cars used to look like when he was a kid or before. They looked as big and as heavy as tanks. He found a war movie. He liked those too, seeing the kinds of guns that were used, watching soldiers run from cover to cover while bullets flew all around them. One guy got hit in the leg and fell face down into the mud. He lay there groaning until another soldier, his buddy, dodging all kinds of bullets, reached him and dragged him to safety.

Yeah, sure, as if anyone is stupid enough to believe that—one soldier sacrificing himself to save another one.

He lost interest in the movie, switched channels some more, watched some commercials before he decided to turn the television off.

Damn, Steve. You know how hard it is to separate the two of them. The wife from the kid. You couldn't do it. I can't do it either.

He heard Steve's voice.

"Can't. Don't give me can't. Just do it." He almost looked around to see where Steve was hiding. His head was playing games with him. It didn't matter if Steve wasn't there because that's what he'd say anyway. He fell into a half-sleep, thought of the whiskey bottle on the table. That thought turned into the ringing of his alarm clock and it was time to get up for work. He passed the bottle, still on the table. Full. Unopened. It made him glad.

For some reason he didn't understand, walking past the whiskey acted like some sort of signal. He looked at himself in the bathroom mirror. Held up his hands.

Okay, I give up. I don't know how I'm going to do it, but I'll try to separate Jimmy and Mary.

A huge chain snapped. A weight fell from his shoulders. The muscles in his neck and back relaxed. Jimmy's face floated before him like a picture missing its frame.

"Hey kid," he said aloud. "I'm not gonna leave you. I don't know what's gonna happen between your mom and me."

Yes, I do. She'll never take me back.

"….but no matter what happens, I'm gonna stick around for you."

Some magic took effect from saying the words out loud, made him feel as if he meant what he was saying. He walked out the door to head for work, his voice becoming louder with each step.

"I'll see ya next week, kid!" He laughed. After a while, he started to whistle.

His week in work was strange. He was always busy but the job was becoming more automatic, sometime giving his mind the chance to wander. He didn't allow himself to think about Mary, told himself he had to stop thinking about her and when he succeeded, felt pleased with himself. Whenever he felt thoughts of her threatening to take over, he filled his mind with thoughts of Jimmy. Jimmy and himself at the zoo, Jimmy being faster than he was with the erector set, Jimmy not wanting him to leave, holding on to his leg until Mary yelled at him.

He thought of that night he had sneaked into Jimmy's bedroom when he was a baby. How he had been amazed at his perfection, a perfection he had never seen because he didn't look at him when Mary was around. Because he was jealous. And how he was amazed when he saw that Jimmy looked like him. So he belonged to him. As well as to Mary. You never could tell. The kid might like him when he grew up. He felt a smile covering his face. Jimmy liked him already. He could tell. Then something stood still inside him. He didn't know what it was or what to call it but it filled him with fear. Like the fear he felt before going to Gina's wedding, the fear that he would disappoint her.

Now the stillness inside him told him how much he loved Jimmy, how he didn't want to disappoint him. Even if he didn't get Mary back, he didn't want to lose him. The new thought battered his brain.

Maybe I'm not like my old man. You can't decide to love someone and decide to keep loving them if you don't already love them. Right? I'm a hell of a lot different than my old man.

He felt sadness rising to the surface, like dead fish floating to the top of the water, the sadness that was always there, hidden and submerged, but always there.

My old man didn't love me. Never felt the way I feel about Jimmy.

All those thoughts should have been confusing but they weren't, were as clear as all the other things he ever understood for certain. They stood in his head like kids in school waving their hands, wanting to be called. So one-by-one, he called them. One-by one they stood up and were recognized. He knew he had to do something his own father never did. He had to stand by his son. He had to be a father. He was slapped in the face with the thing Steve had told him, a thing you couldn't just be told but had to be smacked with hard. Loving his son was separate from anything that happened between him and Mary. And he had to stop being afraid, the way he was afraid of the GED classes or of going to his sister's wedding. Because like the poison from a snakebite, fear would paralyze you, would keep you from doing anything.

A few weeks later, when they were eating ice cream at an amusement park, Jimmy told him they didn't see Michael that week. Something in Tadziu jumped. Maybe Mary and the guy had a fight. He couldn't stop himself from asking why. Jimmy didn't know. That was really being an asshole. Asking his kid, like some spy, why his mother didn't see her boyfriend anymore. Mary would shield the kid from those kinds of things. He and Jimmy went through the park at least twice.

Parenting

When he drove to Mary's place the following week, his car moved through slush, parting it like a boat parting water. And flew into the air to land with loud splatters on whatever was in its way. The sky was as gray as the cover of dirty snow melting on the ground. Winter was easing and spring lurking somewhere. Mary and Jimmy were home from school for a break so his trip was easier. That didn't cheer him. His thoughts were like a heavy load he carried on his back. He wished he could be sure of himself but he didn't know what the sight of Mary would do to the decisions he'd made. Yesterday's thoughts had lost their strength, seemed old and useless, like the snow.

When he saw Jimmy, he felt strong again until a new and unexpected feeling overtook him. His feeling of strength began to seep away as Jimmy made him more and more impatient. He didn't know what the hell had happened to the kid. He was more full of pranks than usual. Stupid pranks. Nasty pranks. When Mary scolded him, he stuck out his tongue and continued whatever he was doing. It embarrassed her, and Tadziu wasn't sure what he should do, so he kept quiet. Jimmy was jumping up and down on the couch, something his mother asked him not to do. Tadziu thought that if he wasn't there, Mary would punish Jimmy. But he wasn't sure. He felt her nervousness crackle in the air between them. Jimmy continued to jump. A lamp tipped over on the table at the end of the couch.

This is stupid. The kid is doing whatever he wants to do.

Before he knew it, he reached out, grabbed Jimmy by the arm and sat him down on the couch, hard.

"That's enough of that." Jimmy began to cry. Tadziu didn't know if Mary was angry with him. He thought he saw relief on her face, a relief that for a moment short-circuited the tension between them.

"You heard your father, Jimmy. Stop crying," she said sternly, but Jimmy continued to whine, sobs that sounded fake to Tadziu, and were accompanied by profuse tears running down his face, causing him, like a drowning man hunting for air, to take mighty breaths, breaths as loud, if not louder, than his cries. Mary took Jimmy in her arms and began comforting him.

Like a limp balloon being filled with air, Tadziu's anger grew.

Now what the hell good is that going to do?

"There, there," she whispered, rocking Jimmy in her arms. "Just don't do that anymore." Her unsaid words—so that your father doesn't get angry— were clear. Tadziu glared at her, wanting to say things he couldn't say. It was worse because he knew she knew it.

Jimmy stopped crying and looked at him with something in his eyes Tadziu didn't want to see, something that said, "I don't have to listen to you."

When Jimmy went to bed, Tadziu stood silent and awkward.

I'm just a third wheel here. She runs things. What I think doesn't matter. Maybe I shouldn't come back.

He drove home through deeper slush than before. His mind wouldn't shut down.

How dumb am I? I can't be a real father to the kid. I've been away too much. She's bringing him up. She's a good mother. It's better if I just leave them alone.

He told himself that all he way home. But a voice in the back of his head didn't agree.

"Jimmy could turn into a brat," the voice said.

Yeah, but what can I do?

The next week, he asked Mary if they could talk after Jimmy was in bed and watched her pick her nails as she answered "sure" in an uncertain voice.

Jesus. Why does she look nervous? Do I still make her afraid?

"It's not right," he began, then realized that was a bad beginning and started again. "You can't say something different to him when I say something."

That's bad too. She raised the kid by herself for years. Now I come in telling her what to do.

"He's a nice kid, Mary. You've done a good job."

"Thanks" Coldly. Okay, he could understand her resentment. But he continued anyway.

"It's not good if I tell him one thing and you show him something else." Silence. Continued coldness. "Look, if you want me to get lost, say so. I will." Now he was angry. "But I'm not going to be quiet when he acts up."

"Oh no Tadziu," she said, with something like alarm. "Jimmy needs you. He needs a man."

"Any man? What about your boyfriend?" She ignored that.

"You're his father."

"Then let me be his father."

"I let you see him whenever you want."

"That's not what I mean."

"What do you mean?" Both of their voices were raised now.

"I mean you can't spoil the shit out of him. If you let him do whatever he wants, he'll grow up wrong!"

"I don't let him do whatever he wants."

"Yeah you do. You don't stick to what you say. And you gotta back me up!" Her face changed. Her voice became bitter.

"Who the hell do you think you are, coming here now and telling me how to raise him!" It went on and on. Jimmy started to cry.

Aw shit. This ain't worth it.

He slammed the door behind him. The next week he didn't go back

A letter came in the mail. Addressed with large letters written in blue crayon. It said:

Dear Daddy.

I miss you. Please come. We can go to the zoo. I'll buy you ice cream. From your son Jimmy

The little shit. Maybe he really did miss me. She must have helped him with the letter.

The longing he had shut within himself escaped and headed for the sky.

Yeah, Jimmy, I'll come.

There were other times Jimmy acted like a piss pot. He was a kid. Tadziu tried to lighten up when he told him to cut it out. And she didn't butt in, didn't interfere with what he said.

After his visits and the long trip home, he always lay in bed thinking, trying to quiet himself.

It's not easy for me. I can see it's not easy for her. I guess we're meeting half-way or something. Jimmy's in the middle. Things get confused. The line separating the kid from the adults, I mean. I must be dumb. I'm the adult. Sometimes I feel like a kid again. I'm supposed to be the one giving direction to Jimmy. That scares me. Even Steve failed, lost his son. When he was a boozer. I'm not a boozer anymore.

He got out of bed, stood at the window and looked down at the street. Thinking. Things came to him this way, were clearer at night when everything was quiet, when the radio in his head was turned off. Light from the street lamps and windows made the black pavement shine like an oily sea. In houses where children sat down to supper with their families. He had always thought of other lives as different from his own, filled with all the happiness he never had. Maybe it wasn't true. He knew nothing about other people's lives. Maybe all the other bastards were in the same soup, or some kind of soup. Maybe what he thought they had, what he envied in them was his own dreams, dreams of a good father, a mother and kids who were happy. The pool of light beneath the window expanded into a screen.

He saw Stan, another kid in school who had a tough old man.

Stan coming to our house because his father is looking for him and he needs a place to hide. His eyes are wild and his face is streaked with dirty tears. Begging ma to hide him. A miracle happens. She's scared but she does it. Does for him what she could never do for me. We hide Stan under Helcza's bed. I hear mama's voice shaking, say-

ing over and over again, "O Jezu, Jezu!. [44] *I see her almost falling to the ground with fright when she hears my father's footsteps on the stairs. I'm quiet and my sisters are quiet all through supper, dumb with fear of what my father would do if he knew.*

I start to be glad we're hiding Stan because it makes me think we're fooling the old man, that we're smarter than he is. Until the old man gets up from the table and heads for his bedroom. Stan's socks and shoes are on the floor in the hallway where he left them in his hurry to crawl under the bed. My sisters and my mother look at one another in terror. And I'm scared again. It doesn't change. I've never been brave. Another miracle happens. My father doesn't notice the shoes. As soon as he closes his bedroom door, we pull Stan from underneath the bed.

Stan has no place to go and I want him to stay there all night but my mother won't do it. She's already done more than I thought she could. I picture my father walking into the dark bedroom. I think bad things.

"Turn off the lights and hide, old man, ugly old man with your little eyes and your red eyelids."

My mother goes in there and closes the door. She hides with you, ugly old man. To protect us. The next day Stan wants me to run away with him but I know I can't leave my mother and my sister and brothers. Later when I know all about the stuff men and women do together to make babies, I don't know why my mother does it. Stan's family moves away and I never see him again.

None of it was ever going to change. It didn't matter how many times he thought about it, tried to figure it out. Maybe he shouldn't think about what he remembered anymore. Close the screen forever. Impossible. That's what he was, what he was made of. His father, his mother, all his brothers and sisters, himself. All that shit The way they lived and grew up. That's what he was. But it was gone, over. Would never come back. Or change.

Help me, Steve. What do I do with it? With all of it?

The stars disappeared. Light rose gradually from inside the darkness. He knew what Steve would say.

"Never look back. Only ahead. One day at a time. One day at a time." He thought he felt a hand on his shoulder.

I'm nuts. No, I'm not nuts. Steve is somewhere. He knows. Okay Steve. I'll close the screen.

He climbed back into bed. Slept soundly until the alarm clock rang.

Chapter Eleven

A Visit

When Mary arrived home from the university and opened the door to the old apartment, she caught her breath. She didn't wish to remember what she'd left behind, the grief that had almost disappeared at the university when she was another person.

She and Jimmy had been home only two weeks. Michael stood in the doorway like a child expecting a reprimand, the uncertainty on his face and in his voice breaking into a wide grin that revealed his happiness when she invited him in.

"I know you didn't expect me. I was in the neighborhood and couldn't resist stopping in."

She thought of the words she had spoken to him at school. He couldn't have forgotten them. He didn't believe she meant them. It didn't matter. She didn't know whether she meant them either. She thought of the condition in which the flat still remained—the linoleum, the window sashes, and the lumpy furniture—and knew that with him it was unnecessary to make apologies, that she did so only from habit. He walked into the kitchen, his eyes resting on her, unaware of the surroundings.

"I don't have much to drink," she said. "My supply is limited. But I have coffee."

"Jeez, I was afraid it might happen. After I come all this way, you don't have any spirits." Their laughter came easy. Before hanging his jacket on the back of the chair, Michael snapped at her behind, and falling into their familiar playfulness, she shook away the memory of the words she had spoken to him like drops of water after a rain.

Michael, my beautiful Michael, is here now.

They drank coffee, his face now the way she remembered it, relaxed and transparent, and hers, she knew, blushing each time she looked into his eyes.

"Mary, I heard about this job." He said this with the tone that again told her she was valuable to him, and this knowing was accompanied by a truth she didn't wish to recognize, that she took his feeling for granted. "I think you might be interested. The school's in a suburb not far from your place here, but more important than that, it has some really good programs, even one for gifted kids." She listened without telling him she had three other interviews lined up. "It's a good job for anyone but you'll have a better chance because you're a woman." Pretending to be angry, he teased her about the unfair advantage women had in the teaching profession.

"Oh sure," she retorted, as if warming up for the heated debates they had engaged in as students, "which doesn't say anything about the fact that we have barely any chance at all in the other professions." He opened his mouth to speak, then, as if thinking the better of it, loudly closed it again, and hung his head, which renewed their laughter. He consulted a notebook which he took from his pocket, one that was divided into the days of the year, the kind she also used but could never keep as carefully as he did.

"Jeannette and Chris and a few others are coming to Buffalo this weekend. We're getting together at Cole's, yeah Cole's, on Elmwood Avenue." He faltered for a moment, attempting to recall the address." I told them you'd be there."

"I know where it is," she said, and with a dry "oh, really, he pretended to raise his eyebrows.

"Does anyone need a place to stay?" She hated the sound of hesitation in her voice. "This isn't much but we could manage. There's the couch and Chris and Jeannette could have my bed"

"No, they've made arrangements. Kind of like a second honeymoon for Chris and Jeannette, I think." He didn't say, "but I could use a place", and she said nothing. "I guess Buffalo has some impressive architecture by Frank Lloyd Wright and a few other things they've lined up, like Niagara Falls, of course. They're looking forward to it. David's coming too. He's signed on for a job in New York city and wants to celebrate. We decided that Buffalo would be a good half-way place to meet." Then peremptorily, "so be there"!

The Interview

She tried to be confident at the job interview but had the nervous feeling that all her hours of practice were wasted. Mr. Lawson listened but mostly watched her and read snatches of the university file he held in his lap. His eyes were youthful at the same time they were aged, held what appeared to be an ingenuous quality as well as one of wisdom, so that despite his shiny bald head she couldn't tell his real age. He scratched the top of his head and looked away periodically, as if aware that his look could be intimidating.

I'm in the presence of a gentleman. He makes me think of Michael.

After a few questions, he seemed satisfied.

"You don't have to answer," he said, "but are you married? Single?"

He's thinking I'll only work until I become pregnant.

She found herself telling him about Jimmy, about being divorced, somehow knowing that with him it was all right. His eyes opened with interest and for a moment she regretted what she had revealed.

"I have a daughter raising a little girl alone," he said. "It's not easy." He didn't say whether his daughter was divorced. "How did you manage to go to school? Your father help?"

"No, I did it myself," she said, not wanting to elaborate, then felt sorry she might have sounded terse, and panicked when, as if a signal had sounded that her time was up, he rose and held out his hand.

I've failed, messed it up.

"We'll see you in the fall," he said, as if it were a thing she should have taken for granted. She learned later that he had been one of the principals in the district and was now a superintendent. From time to time, he did personnel duty, because he liked to interview people. No one objected. He was too important. She was filled with pride when she told Jimmy she got the job.

"That's great, Mom!" he said, beginning to run out the door, then stopping and turning, with concern in his eyes.

"Will I have to leave Danny and Carl?" Mary was truthful.

"We'll have to move because I want to live closer to the school. You can see each other but probably not as often. I'll drive you when I can. And they can sleep over on weekends." Her voice softened. "You'll be making lots of new friends, honey." Jimmy thought about that for a minute.

"Okay," he said, and ran outside.

I must be doing something right. I worry about his life and he's content.

Friends

Mary stood at the mirror and rolled mascara onto her eyelashes, then stepped back and examined herself. She wanted to have a sophisticated look. Her eyes were now shaded by long lashes and her new dress flattered her figure.

I can afford it. I've landed a job with a salary that seems like a fortune.

Her friends were well into the celebrating when she arrived. She and David had landed jobs and were the purported reason for the celebration.

"I'm glad you guys have me and Dave here to give you a reason to drink," she announced above the noise and the laughter. As the evening wore on, laughter grew louder. Dave stood on a chair, and with great effort, tried to make a speech, but finding that his tongue wouldn't cooperate and his audience wouldn't pay attention, shrugged his shoulders, gave up and tried to hop down, an effort that would have ended in disaster if two of the guys hadn't moved fast enough to catch him.

"Whoa guy, whoa," they hollered, as if they were in better shape than he was. And the laughter rose again.

Dave slapped Mary on the back in the way he had when they were in school.

"I know you'll knock the crap out of those kids Mary," he said. "They might even like you." She pretended to be insulted but beneath the mischief, his words were packed with a tenderness that filled her not only with the pain of parting but also an anxiety aroused by the words' unintended challenge.

How many of my high school teachers did I like? I'm going to be so good. They'll remember Miss Jargosz, the teacher who made a difference in their lives.

She was here with people who wanted the same thing. To make a difference in kids' lives. The room was bright with the faces of these people she had come to love, all travelling with her, all skaters on a smooth pond, moving together in the same direction, in a world that held them close, would keep them safe. She remembered this sense of well-being, remembered knowing it with her grandmother when she was a child, when it seemed that everything good was hers and she was held in invisible, solicitous hands. Her friends sat with her now in the semi-darkness of the club, laughing, drinking, reminiscing, while, like a skater, she moved in and out and between them, her joy like a golden chain that held her, suspended her in time as she touched those friends and felt them touch her.

Their questions about the job interview were eager and excited.

"What did he ask?" Not much," she answered truthfully. "He just seemed to like me," and her reply was greeted with a cacophony of "oh-ho", "ah-ha", and "sure-sure." Then she remembered and before she could catch herself, told them he had asked if she was married, which she had thought was a logical question on his part, and this was greeted with an even louder chorus of humorous remarks.

"Did he say anything about yearly increments? How are they granted?" And she was forced to confess, "forgot to ask," as she tried to appear casual, to wear a look of unconcern, and felt the presence of Michael, who sat slightly apart from the others, quiet, not yet drunk, one leg crossed high over the other, his hand supporting his chin, his eyes seeing only her, watching her with pride, while she heard her inner voice, loud and clear, saying, "he loves me," and thought she didn't know what to do with her knowing but didn't want to be without it. Today, he wore a sweater over his white shirt, its collar unbuttoned, and knowing that his casual pose was an attempt to mask his love, the ache of her longing was aroused.

How long, how long, have we been together? For as long as I can see, as long as I can remember, as long as I have dreamed. You will wash him from me, will wash Tadziu away. He'll be like the class-notes we remember today but will no longer recall next year.

When they'd left her apartment, she'd taken his arm, watching Jimmy and the sitter wave goodbye from the window.

So easy. So natural. To take his arm. The kind of man who is conscientious in the things he feels are important—-his job, his family, the woman he loves. No deception lurks in his eyes. It would be easy for a woman to take advantage of him.

Her friends were still teasing about her casual attitude.

"Hope you asked when to show up, and the address of the school." Mary downed another drink.

"Nope. Forgot that too." But I get excellent medical coverage," she said, and felt Michael hearing this, felt him knowing this was the thing most important to her. Because of Jimmy. And again felt his pride, like heat sinking into her bones, warming her core. Someone remembered she hated beer, ordered her mixed drinks, one after another. Her thoughts traveled through haze to reach her.

If I know more about who I am, if I value myself more, am less afraid, it's because of school, because of these friends.

The evening passed like a page she turned, a single page in a new book. She didn't know who paid the bill.

The Oldest Friend

She was tired, but too excited to sleep. Alcohol always did that, filled her with restlessness, with thoughts that raced through her head like wild horses. It was senseless to lie there; she would write a letter to Martha. Even if she saw her before the letter reached her, she'd give it to her. She just wanted to write. The words came slowly at first, more quickly as the alcohol wore off.

Dear Martha,

I've found a great job teaching at West Bend, a suburban high school not far from here, about fifteen minutes by car. It's not in this district but maybe that's better. I don't know if it would be good or bad for Jimmy if the kids knew his mother taught in his school. And it won't be too many years before he's in middle school. Hard to believe, isn't it? I went to the interview on Friday. I was so nervous that I thought my tongue would stick in my mouth. But it went well.

Do you remember how you helped me prepare for my first panel discussion at State? Well, the day before the interview I wrote down every question I could possibly be asked. Then I wrote out the answers, lengthy answers that covered more than I could possibly need. I practiced them, practiced speaking and articulating, even looked up the meanings of any words I wasn't sure of. I must have been at it for a long time because Jimmy came into the kitchen and asked who I was talking to. I don't know if I was imagining that he looked a little alarmed. He is so grown up, such a little man, and so worried about me. I told him his mother had not lost her mind, that I was only practicing a speech I had to give. But he was too smart for that, asked me who I was making the speech to. I had to tell him the truth, that I was going for a job interview. He very seriously told me that I was doing the right thing, that practicing something is "always smart", and walked away with his hands in his pockets, looking satisfied with himself for telling me what I needed to know.

When I walked into the school, I felt the stares of the other teachers in the hall. I smiled at everyone and most of them smiled back. I don't know how it's possible to be happy and afraid at the same time. I know what you're thinking. I know that if you were here, you would tell me what I've always told you, that I don't believe in myself. Then you'd tell me that this comes from thinking I was deserted by my mother because I deserved it. I guess you have your own psychology book now. And in my defense, I'd say another thing I've always said, that you'll never know how lucky you were to have the family you had, that you were born with an arsenal—your mother, your father and your siblings, especially your brother. Scrapping with him made you strong, because it was really love. You're thinking I should stop feeling sorry for myself and asking yourself who's using psychology 101 now. It always jolted me a little, you know, when you told me I was feeling sorry for myself. Well, you know what your brother always says, that you've always been sharp-tongued (he uses different words) but I love you anyway. I know that right about now, you'd laugh and punch my arm. I miss you. I've made new friends. But no one can ever take your place.

I'm glad, but not surprised, that you're doing so well in school. All my love. Mary.

She addressed the envelope, climbed into bed, and as she did when she was a little girl in her grandmother's house, pulled the covers over her head, and fell asleep immediately. Her last thought was how stupid she had been to think she could ever forget Martha. The next day, as she emerged from the covers, she reasoned that a drunken state causes one to revert to childhood.

She'd even forgotten what was important. She'd meant to tell Martha that she'd been doing something for herself in whatever time there was left from the things she had to do. She'd been writing some poetry, some short stories, the things she'd always loved reading. One of her poems had been published in an obscure literary magazine and she was waiting for word on the short story.

She thought about how she loved the writing, how she loved the struggle of making the words fall into the right pattern, the right form. But perhaps it was better she hadn't told Martha. She'd never told Michael or Tadziu. The fear of failing at some distant goal, some dream had kept her from telling anyone. Except grandma, when she thought of her before she fell asleep at night.

Decisions

Mary didn't expect it to be easy to leave the old flat, to find her elation at beginning a new life free from a sense of loss, the loss of what was embedded in the walls, the windows and the floors, those moments of profound unhappiness she and Tadziu had suffered as well as those piercing moments of love and passion they had shared. She looked at apartments, and found one she liked on the third floor of a new building with a view from its living room window that made her think of scenes in a movie. The panorama of the city— lights, apartment buildings and houses—scattered, isolated, clustered—seemed like a pattern arranged by a giant hand. The hundreds of lights became one, a living body that, from its silence, spoke to Mary, spread its light and its excitement through her until she became a part of that life, felt her heart throb in unison with its own. She stood at the window, overcome by the scene before her, her mind a welter of thought.

The city schools are good and the city holds advantages for me. I would gladly forget who I am in all that it would make me become. I would pursue its people and its places, its glories and its shames, as it wrapped itself around me, engulfed me in its embrace. I would absorb its offerings like a sponge, immersed in what I have always dreamed would claim me, in what I have always believed was my birthright.

But I'm not alone. I have Jimmy and though he also needs culture, he needs other things. Tenants in the apartments are primarily couples beginning their lives or those at the other end of the spectrum who are retiring. There are not many children.

In the end, she decided it would be better for Jimmy to grow up in a house, in a neighborhood with families and other children. She continued her hunt.

A New Home

She bought the house during the summer so they would be settled before school started. She was glad there was so much work to do when they moved in. She washed woodwork and floors, hung curtains, arranged and rearranged the few pieces of furniture they had. There was no time to think. She went to bed exhausted each night. And slept soundly.

The neighborhood was not a new subdivision but one of older homes. Many of the people had lived in their homes for many years and seemed to keep to themselves most of the time. There were some younger families with children and before a week had passed, Jimmy found kids on the street to play with. Each day, she recognized his excited voice, the steps that rushed through the door and moved, in a manner already certain, across the room, heard the voices of the other boys he was bringing with him and heard the thud of their paraphernalia as it hit the floor. She thought with reluctance of him becoming a teen-ager, of the innocent child who would be gone and the new challenges there would be in raising him. Even now, being a mother absorbed more of her each day. Michael would have made that easier. But Jimmy never questioned her about Michael.

"I know mom, I know," he had said, patting her arm like a father. "You have to do what you have to do."

He understands. I don't know what or how but the little pot understands.

She admired the elaborate gardens in the yard next door and saw her new neighbor, an elderly woman who tended them. On a Saturday, the woman was outside on her knees, cleaning leaves and debris from what looked like it might be a rose garden. Mary introduced herself.

"Oh Lord, There's such a lot of work," the woman said, conversing with Mary as if they had known each other forever, telling her how nice her boy was, saying, "my, my," when she learned that Mary was a teacher, and listening to her classroom stories with admiration. When she stood up, Mary saw she was a small woman. The distance between her head and her waist was too short, and she walked with a limp, her body leaning to one side. The red cotton pants she wore reached to her knees, did not cover the thin and spindly calves that were covered with what looked like bruises. Her hair was short and too black for a woman her age. She laughed easily but it was a laugh that seemed to be an apology. A slow-moving cocker spaniel followed behind, adjusting his pace to hers, so they both moved very slowly, although the dog did not seem old.

On the weekend, Mary met Eddie, the woman's husband, a white-haired man with a loud laugh who sat inside the open doors of the garage, out of the sun, watching his wife at her gardening. When she finished, they both sat in the yard in folding chairs and drank beer.

"C'mon over. An' have one," Eddie boomed, and she did once or twice, talking to them about things in the newspaper or on television, finding that he worked for the railroad and she kept house, and that they had never had any children. Each time Eddie told a joke or said something his wife thought was silly, she looked at Mary as if to say "Isn't that just like a man, but her eyes followed her husband just as the cocker spaniel followed her. They had a long name—Schottenhamp— and had been married forty years. They talked to Mary about the people who owned the house before she did, and told her about the other people in the neighborhood.

"That one over there," Eddie said, cocking his head toward the house across the street, is always working on his place. Never stops. He thinks he owns the neighborhood and can tell every one else what to do just because he knows a few people in Town Hall. Big deal!"

"Now Eddie," his wife chided, patting his hand.

"It's true, it's true!" Eddie boomed. Mary glanced at the house Mr. Schottenhamp indicated. It was very well kept, had awnings and a patio and a huge lawn without a single dandelion. The Shottenhamp's lawn and gardens were far from perfect.

"Don' let him bother you," Eddie continued. Once he sees you outside an' starts talkin', he'll never leave you alone." Jimmy liked Eddie immediately and talked about him as if he'd known him a long time.

"Ma, you know what Mr. Schottenhamp said. The guys who work on the trains have to pee out the window when the train slows down." Mrs. Schottenhamp told him "go on," like she always does, but he says it's the truth." Before the summer was over, Mary asked Mrs. Schottenhamp if Jimmy could come to their house after school until she arrived home. Mrs. Schottenhamp seemed flattered. Her face turned red and she had trouble finding words.

"Of course, of course," she said, over and over, looking past Mary, as if she were embarrassed. "We'll love it. We'll love it." She lowered her voice and looked around, as if someone might overhear her words. "You know, we had a boy once. But he died." Mary stammered something about not realizing that it might be difficult for them to watch Jimmy.

"Oh no, dear, no," Mrs. Schottenhamp said, raising her hand, palm out, in denial. "That's been over for a long time."

Mr. Schottenhamp made a project of teaching Jimmy to cut the grass and Jimmy performed the chore without prompting. Mary tried planting flowers, starting with geraniums because she did not know if anything would grow and she did not want Mrs. Schottenhamp to see her fail.

The geraniums took well. Mary found herself admiring their ordinary beauty—the green centered foliage edged with cream, the flowers in varying shades of pink, some almost red, all extraordinary because they marked the house that each day became more and more hers and Jimmy's home. She thought of buying a tree for an empty space in the back yard.

The back yard could use a tree. I don't know much about planting trees but I'll learn.

She thought of the tree she had planted with her grandmother the summer before her grandmother died. It grew. When spring came, she remembered touching the hard buds, still black, swelling at intervals along the naked branches, and the rough green that, almost overnight, broke through the softening crusts. One had fallen off and she held its head between her fingers, crushed it to feel the outline of its life, the slippery fibers that clung together tenaciously beneath the skin.

I remember. I **am** *good at growing things.*

It was Saturday and Jimmy was home. "Mom, mom," he cried, bounding through the room like a gazelle. Joey and Kyle are gonna stay for super, okay? Kyle's mom doesn't care. She's working and won't be home until tonight. Joey's doesn't either." Mary learned that Kyle was the son of the woman across the street who had waved to her once or twice. Jimmy threw his jacket over the chair. She could see excitement flow through him like an electric current, lighting his eyes, making them seem larger and happier. His happiness spread to her. This was the first time he had asked his friends to eat with him.

"Sure," she said, trying to sound casual, but feeling pride in him, in herself, in the house. "Do you like spaghetti," she asked the two boys. Their "yeah" was filled with gusto.

We have spaghetti a lot," Kyle offered. "My dad likes it." A part of her joy broke off and plummeted.

How does Jimmy feel when other kids talk about their fathers?

Jimmy was absorbed in the Monopoly game they were setting up on the floor.

"My dad likes it too," Jimmy said absent-mindedly. A note of bravado began to creep into his voice. "He takes me out a lot when he comes. My mom and dad are divorced." The boys didn't look up. Joey spoke in a mature voice.

"Yeah, I know about that," he said. "My mom's divorced, but my father never comes. He ran away with another lady." None of them seemed interested in the subject anymore. Their heads were bent low, absorbed in the game.

"Last time, I had Boardwalk and Park Place before my Dad had anything," Jimmy boasted. Kyle whistled between his teeth in admiration. Mary felt the moving seas within her begin to calm. That evening Jimmy announced he was going to ask his father if Kyle and Joey could come with them the next time he came. He told Mary their mothers already said it was okay.

Teaching

Mary wondered if she should smile at the two people who stood in the back of the room. Her palms were sticky. There was a lump in her throat as if a piece of food had failed to go down and was stuck. She had been told they would be there, that she would be observed and evaluated by two senior teachers. It was routine. She was a new teacher, after all. They had to check and make sure she was doing whatever it was they judged to be a good job.

One of the observers was a short, stocky man with a red face and thick glasses who kept grimacing and putting his finger between his shirt collar and his neck. Perspiration like grease coated his face. She wasn't sure whether he didn't like her or whether his collar was too tight.

Maybe that grimace is really a smile.

The second man was tall and thin. His face looked white and dry. He had a smile that never changed, a line across his face that looked like it was pasted there. She thought of the nursery rhymes she read Jimmy when he was small.

Jack Sprat could eat no fat. His wife could eat no lean. That doesn't make me feel better.

Her lesson plans had been approved and she'd been told what the evaluators would look for. She straightened her skirt and patted her hair where it wouldn't stay in place that morning.

Will they make allowances if my voice cracks or if I forget something and have to consult my notes? C'mon now, what's the matter with me? They're not monsters. They have to do this. They know how nervous new teachers are and that they make it worse. How can anyone enjoy such a job? My brain and my mouth worked pretty well when I was a student. Why should they quit now just because I'm on the other end?

The kids were aware of the two people in the back. They fidgeted in their seats and turned around surreptitiously. Except for one boy whose eyes looked absolutely filled with glee.

Because I'm nervous. The little creep knows I'm nervous and he's happy.

She looked at her seating chart.

Oh my God. Are they serious? Charles Darwin. The kid's name is Charles Darwin.

She certainly couldn't forget him.

She took attendance, reading the names in her role book aloud. Joy Adams, John Abramowitz, Jeannine Borzawski (nice Polish name), Joseph Bernard. They each replied "here" except for Charles Darwin who silently raised his hand and stared at her, his eyes a bold challenge.

"Please say "here" so that I can hear you," she said, knowing she should say it, that they would all notice if she didn't.

"Sure," said Charles Darwin, "here," louder than anyone else, his compliance as much a challenge as his silence. She made an effort to keep her voice calm and looked him squarely in the eyes.

"Charles, please use a normal tone."

"Okay," he squeaked, imitating a mouse and the rest of the class tittered. She wasn't sure what to do next. She couldn't back down or she'd be sunk. She knew that from her Methods class but words in a textbook were so sensible, so believable, so unlike reality.

"Charles," she said quietly, fighting not to raise her voice, not to walk over and strike this kid who was threatening her, ruining her first day, "that's not normal either. We're wasting valuable time because of you. Let's try again." She was afraid of what he might do next but he only sneered and answered in a tone as normal, she knew, as he was going to get. She finished the roll call.

Now, she'd have to teach. She had planned a unit on poetry and everyone knew that was tough to teach. The lump was back. Her hands shook as she instructed the class to open their textbooks and asked a student to begin reading a selection from a poem by Walt Whitman, *There was a child Went Firth*, one she had chosen because it was springtime, and the poem spoke of lilacs blooming and apple trees covered with blossoms and because she loved it, loved the description of the earth awakening from winter, loved Whitman's descriptions of the people whom the child in the poem sees.

They were bright, these kids, students who were headed for college, and Mary knew she had been assigned this group because they thought she could handle it, that her school records showed she was interested in gifted students and her grades indicated to them that she herself was bright.

I've judged correctly. The lines of the selection don't intimidate them, but they're sufficiently challenging for such a group. I can't be sure, though, if their attention is because of the two observers in the back of the class.

She heard her voice, the not-yet-familiar sound of her own words.

"Whitman tells us about the many things that become a part of who we are."

Had she said that? Where had the words come from? What secret part of herself had kept them hidden? Would they reveal themselves again? I remember how I felt the first time I heard a professor in college speak. I sound like that…no, I don't sound like that. I'm getting carried away. I deserve that look of admiration in their eyes No, I don't deserve that look.

The spell was broken by a taunting, sneering voice.

"This sounds silly. This kid is being stuffed like a turkey with all these things he sees. C'mon. Who you trying to kid? If this happened to every kid, there wouldn't be any kids left. We'd all be turkeys." Charles looked around the class, hunted for smiles, for laughter. There were a few uncertain giggles. His voice grew more indignant.

"This Whitman guy's lying, just lying." He was protesting something she knew how to answer but because of her surprise at this challenge, her mouth wouldn't open. She saw one of the teachers in the back of the room look slightly alarmed.

I can't do this. I can't do this. Charles Darwin is calling my bluff. Now I'll look like a fool to all of them.

From somewhere, she again heard the voice that was hers, the voice that continued to appear like a beloved friend, and surprise her.

"Charles, we're not going to look for literal truth here. We're going to look for something poets use all the time, something called symbolism. She turned to the blackboard and wrote the word "symbolism", then turned back to the class and asked, "Who can tell me what a symbol is?" The two faces in the back of the class relaxed, looked pleased again. A girl raised her hand. There was no way she could remember their names yet. She just smiled and nodded at the girl, who, like an angel, smiled back and said, "a sign".

"Of course, and what is a sign?" Another girl raised her hand.

"Something that points to something else." And it went on from there. They began talking about the meaning of symbolism and she smiled to think she was taking advantage of the opportunity opened up by Charles Darwin and that inward smile grew because she knew the two in the back of the room would appreciate her skill and because it was so easy, so natural to proceed from one thing to another. She asked them for examples of symbolism in the text and they all gave excellent answers, one student bravely offering that the child himself was a symbol for all children, and the springtime a symbol of childhood.

"Being born is kind of messy, isn't it?" she said shyly, and Mary was not sure what that meant but the girl explained that it had to do with going from "the spread of purity" to "salt marsh and shore mud." Mary thought hard and saw what the girl was trying to say, how sophisticated the observation was and told the girl how well she had interpreted the lines. Then she had to explain the girl's example to the class and time was moving quickly, the bell would ring and the evaluators would be gone.

"And after we're born, we get more beautiful each day!" one boy burst out enthusiastically and the entire class laughed, except for Charles who looked angry at the entire proceeding.

"We certainly do," Mary agreed. And she told the class to read through the poem again at home and write at least a page about the symbolism they saw. That assignment would reveal their writing skills to her.

When the bell rang, the line pasted on the thin teacher's face spread open like an icy river that cracked and was flooding. He came up to her, rubbing his hands as if he had done something well and was pleased with himself.

"That was excellent, Miss Jargons, just excellent." She breathed hard, as if she'd just finished running a race, but her smile remained steady.

"Thank you." Her voice was quiet. Her face felt damp.

"Yes, the other man agreed. The look in his eyes said, "A born teacher" and Mary thought her voice might return. "The way you handled Charles was excellent, just excellent, the first teacher said. It appeared that "excellent" was his favorite word. "The lesson was excellent and your choice of material was excellent." The second man told her that Charles was difficult for other teachers as well. She listened to the words of the two men only half-hearing them. The deepest part of herself knew she had been good, and because she knew that, it didn't really matter what they said. She could teach! She could make it! She thanked them again.

That night, she read students' writing at home, was amazed at their observations and the creativity of their ideas. The next day class went well. But she didn't trust that it would continue, knew that her encounter with Charles wasn't finished. His eyes were sullen but watchful. He sat on the edge of his chair and looked, she hated to think, like s snake, looking out from piercing eyes as if waiting, holding his breath and preparing to strike. In Wednesday's class, she returned the papers with their grades. She asked if there were any volunteers to read their papers. There were many students who raised their hands. She used the examples the students themselves had chosen to illustrate the meaning of symbolism as the material for her lesson. Charles snickered at each of the papers.

She ignored his antics the first time but knew she had to do something. She asked him to leave and go to the principal's office. He leered at her as he passed and she knew that going to the principal's office meant nothing to him. He had been there so many times.

In one way or another, Charles continued to disrupt her classes, whether it was insolent behavior or asking senseless questions. She knew what a defeat it would be to ask the principal to take him out of her class. He would think that after all she couldn't handle things as well as he had thought. Yet she would lose the respect of the class if she allowed the situation to continue. A large unnamed feeling began to move in and out of her. Charles' face filled the classroom and the walls of her bedroom at night.

I hate him. After all I've done, some smart-ass kid is going to defeat me.

Resentment welled inside her like a festering sore. She recognized its poison but didn't try to fight it.

I have the right to hate him.

He didn't come from the best of homes, observer number one had said on her first day.

So what? A lot of kids come from messed-up homes. Does that give him the right to ruin things for other people, for me?

She continued reading the students' papers at night, always haunted with thoughts of Charles. She thought about the ways she could penalize him. Extra homework. The threat of failure. No one would blame her. Certainly not the principal. They knew about him. But she couldn't determine the feeling of the other students. Somehow she knew that was important.

And something made her uneasy. There was a look in Charles' eyes, a look she had seen before, somewhere, sometime. She pushed the thought aside and turned back to the paper she was reading, one written by a second-generation German immigrant.

"No one appreciates what it's like to be German in this country." The student went on to explain that the crimes of Hitler should not be blamed on the German people. The tone of the girl's writing was so sincere and confidential that Mary knew she was being entrusted with private feelings. The paper filled her with happiness because she was a teacher. She saw not only the practical results of her efforts—the students' critical thinking as expressed in her writing —but also the fact that she could help students with their feelings. Literature did that, brought out things that were difficult to articulate, even to recognize, let alone share with others. In this case, a poem they had read about war had acted as a catalyst. She would ask the student if she wanted to read the paper to the class.

Mary bit on her pencil and stared at the wall. She gave the paper a good grade and wrote an encouraging comment. "The hurts brought on by the war are still very fresh in the minds of many families who lost loved ones, but not everyone blames the German people." She bit her pencil more, stared at the wall, and thought about the books she had read by authors who did blame the German people and wouldn't accept the claims that they didn't know. Sympathy filled her as she thought about this young girl who certainly wasn't responsible and read her own comments again. She was satisfied.

A feeling intruded so suddenly that it seemed like a person had entered the room and struck her in the face. She tried to recognize it.

What am I doing? What is happening here?

She turned and saw light from the window filling the room. In the moment of seeing that light, she felt her grandmother's presence. Understanding moved over her like a gift she had been given and unwrapped.

I've let this thing turn into a personal battle between Charles and me. And he feels it. He's too smart not to feel it, not to know he's already won, that he's in charge.

For the rest of the evening, she didn't think about Charles but concentrated on reading her papers as if he didn't exist, as if the problem had already been solved.

Next day's class arrived. She listened to Charles' mutterings, and the constant comments he made beneath his breath.

This won't be easy. It'll last the entire year.

She stopped her lesson and turned her gaze on him.

I mustn't waver, not for a moment.

"Mr. Darwin," she said, in as calm and assured a voice as she could manage, "it's obvious that you don't wish to learn but there are students here who do. You are disturbing them and me. You may take out your homework from your other classes and work on it. Just don't disturb us."

"I don't have any other homework," he said with contempt, always contempt.

"All right then, tomorrow, you may bring your own reading material to class. Any book or magazine you're interested in. But I must warn you. I'll still hold you responsible for the work we're doing."

He glared at her. The next day, he brought in a pile of comic books and flipped the pages noisily while she taught the class, but Mary saw he was listening to what she was saying.

Charles did well on the first test but continued to read his comic books. Mary never called on him or asked him to read and so she was surprised when he raised his hand to answer a question she posed, giving a good answer and a penetrating analysis of the assigned reading: Walt Whitman's *Captain,! My Captain!*

"Yes the ship is a good symbol of our country," he said, emphasizing the word symbol as if he had a microphone so that Mary couldn't help but laugh with the rest of the class, "because the civil war was tearing our country apart and the ship is taking so many hits it's almost sinking. And Lincoln is a symbol," the word again loudly emphasized, "because he was the leader of our country, just like the ship's captain fighting to save it, when some asshole shot him. Walt Whitman is crying over the death of a great leader."

You stinker, you're very bright.

She used his comments to pose additional questions to the class and a lively discussion ensued.

This is good but I can't get carried away. I have to put an end to this comic book thing before I lose credibility with the rest of the kids.

After class she told Charles she could see that he had rejoined them and should leave his comic books at home.

"Yeah sure," he answered, with a look in his eyes that said, "You think you're smart. I can teach this stuff as good as you can." She stopped the resentment that tried to take hold of her, kept herself calm and didn't allow herself to think she was failing.

I'm handling this. I'm coping.

At the beginning of the next week, Charles was absent. Mary was glad. He was also absent the second and third day. She turned in her roll call reports and thought of him vaguely, behind all her other concerns. On Friday, at the faculty meeting, Joe Clancy, his eyes downcast, said to her, "What d'you think about Charles Darwin, poor kid." Mary dropped her pen, and forgot the stupid notes she was writing. The week had been so peaceful and now, knowing that something was wrong, she felt guilty for having enjoyed it. The principal was talking about the usual things and Mary lost the words as fast as he spoke them. Fear settled in the pit of her stomach.

"No, I haven't heard," she said. Joe pointed a silent finger at Mr. Clark, the principal, just as he said the words "Charles Darwin."

"It's not easy for teachers to recognize the signs of such distress. Charles Darwin was angry. We don't see it as part of our job to try and help kids with their emotions. But it is. All I ever heard about Charles was complaints. No one saw that the kid was in trouble. We've failed, just failed." Mary was mesmerized, afraid to hear the next words. Joe was shaking his head, a frown on his face.

"Yeah, well, what're you supposed to do with a kid like that?" he blustered under his breath. Mary twisted her hands.

"Joe, what happened to Charles?"

"He's in the hospital," he said, from the corner of his mouth. "Tried to kill himself. They're not sure he'll make it."

Charles's story came to her in bits and pieces. He had two alcoholic parents. Social workers had gone to the house and their report was harsh. The mother and father weren't even sober for the visit. Younger kids in the family had been taken away but Charles was old enough to decide for himself and he'd chosen to stay.

Charles, Charles, how could I have been so stupid. Hating you like all the rest.

Joe's mouth held a sneer but another woman teacher looked distressed. After the meeting, Mary approached her. She was older, more experienced.

"I just let him do what he wanted. I tried but there was nothing I could do. The boy needed help. Mr. Clark knew that. Everyone told him about Charles. He has no right to accuse us. If you want to use the word failed, he failed." Her voice was bitter but softened when she turned to Mary.

"I'm sorry. I'm Mrs. Coatwright and I shouldn't be complaining to you. Mr. Clark isn't being fair, that's all. Some of us did try."

"I know," Mary mumbled. "I know."

That night, Mary listened to Jimmy's ceaseless chatter as he told her about school, watched him at his homework, saw the happiness on his face. She prayed to the God she hadn't approached in a long time.

Please don't let Charles die. Don't let him die. Thank you for helping me with Jimmy. Thank you. Thank you. Thank you. Help me know what to do about Charles. I don't even know how to tell the other students in my homeroom. Or what to tell them. I don't have to say anything. They'll know anyway. No, that's not right. I'm their homeroom teacher. Charles. Charles. You were so bright. You did well despite what you went home to.

She remembered the way Tadziu's face had looked when he was drunk, of the hatred that emanated from him and the helplessness she felt. Charles had two people he couldn't escape, people he loved and couldn't help, people who made him walk a tightrope and turned their faces as they saw him falling. Because they were also helpless, had chosen their initial step, and each step after, had become more locked in their own hell. She knew that was a judgment she didn't wholly accept.

A face appeared before her, a face from some reservoir inside herself, a reservoir that held memories she no longer knew she had. She was carried back to her grandmother's house.

She remembered the little girl Michelle, who lived in the flat next to her and grandma, a child who had been neglected by her young parents, parents who—could it be—had neglected her without knowing, because of their youth and their ignorance? No, it couldn't be, because at some point everyone knew the consequences of what they did, the pain they continued to inflict, even if, desiring blindness, they closed their eyes, so they couldn't see. That was the contrasting judgment.

Mary hung her head in her hands, She shouldn't ask these questions because they couldn't be answered. She smiled as she remembered grandma who wasted no time on such questions but went to the parents' flat, banged on the door and told them, in no uncertain terms, to shape up or she would report them to the police. The parents were afraid of grandma and watched their behavior after her visit. They even paid Mary to baby-sit when they went out. Michelle wasn't left alone again.

She saw Charles' face again, his eyes ringed by darkness, probably from lack of sleep, the corners of his moth trembling slightly, even when he was at his smart-alecky best.

The atmosphere at school was sober for the rest of the week. Charles was forgotten by the teachers because their work was demanding, but her students were quiet when Mary told them. Some came to her after class and said they wanted to do something. Mary promised them she would tell them whatever she learned and they could decide on a plan. Mary talked with Mrs. Coatwright. The answer was always the same. Charles was in critical condition. Critical condition for two weeks.

He's hanging on by the skin of his teeth.

Again she told her students. They began writing to Charles and sending him cards. Some hidden string tied them to him.

"He'll just go right back home when he's well," Mrs. Coatwright said, with sorrow and frustration in her voice. "I don't know what needs to happen for them to do something. Sixteen. Sixteen years old and they can't remove him." Later Mary heard that if Charles recovered, he would be placed into foster care.

Mary remembered Tadziu running away from home when he was fifteen, and of his reluctance to tell her why. She thought of his bravado, of his talk about pushing his way through whatever stood in his way. She'd known his boasting was a mask, a disguise that kept others from seeing what he wanted to keep hidden. She was right to leave him, right to keep him from hurting Jimmy and herself. Tadziu had to exorcize his own demons, find a way through the thicket of his emotions. Charles would have to do the same. If he could.

Her thoughts fell from her like useless garments. There was only Charles' face. And his voice that day in class when he talked about Whitman's eulogy to Lincoln. He said that Lincoln was a hero not because he was more special than us, but because he tried harder to be more special. Something like that. And ordinary men could be our heroes, our captains, if they tried that hard. She heard his confident, slightly wavering voice, the silence of the class listening to something they sensed was momentous though they didn't know why.

A week later she found herself in the hospital room, speaking standard words because she didn't know what else to say, seeing the long thin body and pale face, the bright eyes staring at her from blackened hollows that surrounded them like frames. Mrs. Coatwright had visited Charles and told Mary not to expect much, that his attitude hadn't changed. She was right.

"Charles," Mary said. "I'm sorry for what's happened. If I can help you in any way, please let me know."

"Yeah, sure," he snapped, in the old defiant voice. She felt her heart cracking, falling inside her like heavy pieces of metal.

Nothing has changed for him. Nothing will change.

Her eyes traveled around the room, tying to find a place to settle, seeing Tadziu's face before her, Tadziu with the false face and swaggering gait, his tears after he had been out drinking and was contrite.

At least he had me for a while. At least I loved him for a while. I wish somebody loved Charles. But how can they? He'll make it as difficult as Tadziu did for me.

She sat there for a while talking about inane things, to which, rightly, she thought, Charles didn't respond. He only stared at the ceiling as if she were disturbing him. After forty-five minutes or so, she rose and approached the bed, and half afraid he might hit her, kissed the top of his head. He said nothing, she knew, because he didn't want her to say anything. At the door, she heard his raspy voice, a voice exonerating her, forgiving her for what she couldn't do.

"You were nice," he said. That was all. She turned but his face was already toward the wall.

She couldn't help him. There had been other times in her life when she couldn't do anything. But helplessness was always a fresh wound.

Michael visits again

The next time Michael came, he carried a package which, because of its shape, Mary thought, might be flowers but when she removed the wrapping, an exquisite Tiffany lamp appeared, the green, blue and red squares of its globe marked by silver boundaries and perched atop a slender gold body.

"Fooled you, didn't I?" His voice had a smile, his face betrayed his pleasure at her pleasure. "Your first house-warming present. Even before you're in the house."

I want to kiss him, to put my arms around him and feel his closeness, to smell the skin of his neck and his hair.

"I don't deserve you," she said.

"But you do. No one else will have me." Mary said nothing, thought about the ridiculousness of his statement, about the girls who gazed at him admiringly when she was with him and then turned to look at her with envy, sometimes anger in their eyes.

He knows I love beautiful things. The lamp is in excellent taste. I'll never find anyone this good, anyone who understands me, knows me so well. His face displayed strong feelings.

"I want to be with you," his eyes said. "We can have life together."

It would be happiness to be in his arms each night, to feel safe and cherished.

Why am I hesitant, filled with doubt?

"C'mon," he said, "let's get Jimmy and go find something to eat." "Hiya chief," he called and Jimmy's eyes lit up.

"Hiya chief," he answered and pretended he was preparing to jump into Michael's arms. Michael groaned and held his head.

"Have mercy," he cried in mock terror.

Michael stayed that night, and so again, Mary remembered the way it was to lie in a lover's arms, to be touched with hesitation until hesitation ceased to exist and they were pulled into a current that swept them away, cast them like fallen branches into a river. The next day, without speaking, Mary knew the matter had been settled. Michael would return. On weekends, he drove from the school where he was teaching. For two days, she had a husband and Jimmy had a father. She knew Michael wanted this to lead to marriage.

The next weekend, as soon as Jimmy yelled to her that Michael had arrived, she saw him pulling on his jacket and watched him as he headed out the door.

"C'mon mom, c'mon. We're going. You want to come? What's the matter with you? Hurry up!"

I can't answer, can't give my son an answer. I don't know what's wrong, what holds me back.

She watched the first evening shadows move along the walls.

It's always evening, lovely evening when he's here. He'll always be here for me. I'm standing in the middle of my happiness. It can't be better. Why don't I feel closed, finished? Why don't I see the story's happy ending?

She listened to the clatter of Jimmy's shoes running out the door. Of Michael running with him, laughing, playing games with her child, her son. A threesome. Nothing more could be asked.

But what if she didn't want to be a threesome? Is that how her mother had felt? Wanting to run away. To leave behind the things that claimed her, to escape from having to worry about someone else. No. Her mother had run from her pain. She knew the story. But what if part of that running had been towards her freedom, toward herself?

I can't know. I can't know. Even about myself. I'm a good teacher. People respect me. Is that enough? What is enough? Perhaps if one could run away for a while, could find out what there was to run toward. Like escaping from the gray of winter in the month of January, when all the lights and ornaments are packed away and the stores are empty. Why had her mother run? Am I like her? Selfish. My mother's child.

"A penny for your thoughts," Michael said. He touched her hair and she sensed the certainty in his fingers. Michael would never have such thoughts as hers, was always sure of his feelings, was grounded, had structure.

Do I live anywhere except my grandmother's house? With her, whom I know I loved, or with Tadziu? Am I arrested in that time? Never able to leave? Or have I become like grasses blown by the wind, unable to settle, to find my place?

I am steadfast, have always been steadfast. A good friend to Martha. A good mother to Jimmy. A good teacher, model to my students. But a good wife? To no one. Because here is a good man who loves me. And I can't be his wife.

"Ma—ma—c'mon!" Jimmy ran up the stairs, grabbed her hand, and, in his eagerness, pulled her. "Michael's taking us for ice cream. Hurry up, Ma!" He jumped up and down, as if he were on a pogo stick.

C'mon. How uncomplicated. The concerns of a child. Never so simple again.

She thought of Martha's parents, of her father's heavy eyebrows, now turned gray. But the look on his face was always the same, held the trace of a smile, even when he was serious. And Martha's mother's eyes, so solicitous when she looked at her husband, eyes that said what she couldn't speak, that he wouldn't live, that they couldn't live forever. Was it her imagination that Martha's mother looked more concerned for her husband than for herself, concerned that he not be left alone, believing that she was stronger and could survive alone longer. In those eyes, Mary read the words, "For better or worse. Till death do us part." Through children. Through anger. Through forgiveness.

But it was easier for them. They had no careers. They had no goals. Except their children's lives, their children's welfare. And each other.

I can't measure up to that simplicity. That strength. I'm not like Martha's mother. I don't love enough.

"I'm coming, Jimmy," she called and Michael reached out to help her down the stairs. A gentleman, like Martha's father, who, she remembered, always extended his arm to Mary, took Jimmy from her when Jimmy was a baby and she carried him. She walked down the stairs with Michael. Jimmy ran ahead, kept turning around to look, stopping to wait, then running ahead again.

Confession

Before the weekend ended, Michael told her again that they should marry. He was uncomfortable in the situation not only for himself, but because of Jimmy.

His honor demands that he act as a husband and father, that he do the right thing.

She heard herself telling Michael she loved him but couldn't marry him, and he answering that this was ridiculous, contradictory. Somewhere within her, words struggled to take form, to emerge from the prison of feeling and be set free. As they freed themselves, they chanted.

I'm afraid. Afraid, afraid, afraid. I'm afraid.

Other words arose, tried to cover them but they wouldn't be denied.

I'm afraid.

The hurt beneath Michael's words would not be denied, was transformed into anger.

"What do you want?" he demanded. "What the hell do you want?"

"I don't know," was all she could answer. The silent voice inside her asked him to stay, not to leave her alone, not to take away his strength, to make her safe. Then a face emerged from within that plea, the face of her self, the self she had always known, the self she had kept through all the foolish roads, the wise roads, the uncertain roads, and, that now, placed itself against her fear. After his rage, his leaving, that self would survive. "I don't know yet." she said again, having no doubt of her words' truth, knowing her uncertainty must be faced, by herself as well as by Michael, knowing she must claim that right for herself, must usurp the time.

Her arm felt warm. Sunlight beat its way through the wall of green that swayed outside the window and settled in islands that floated on the walls and floor of the room. The faint smell of his after shave invited her to touch his face, to claim him. She saw his hands shake, knew he wouldn't betray himself, wouldn't relinquish his pride and so she loved him more. The ticking of the clock broke the silence into measured pieces that dragged themselves through the room. He spoke with effort, the words leaving him slowly.

"I guess you've made your decision then." Mary knew, even as her words left her, how feeble they were.

"I wish you wouldn't leave," she said, "I mean, not permanently. Life can't be the same if you leave for good."

"Mary, I don't understand you. You want me to hang around, just hang around in the background, on the sidelines or something, right? What do you think I am?"

She had no answer, didn't look at him. Her life was sweet, so sweet. She couldn't lose it. But neither could she think of never being in his arms, of never again knowing he wanted her..

She thought of the young wife she had been, of having to leave Tadziu because of her fear for Jimmy, a hungry fear which tried to devour her. She thought of the time when she lived alone with Jimmy, her fear existing then as a soft-spoken, persistent friend, a constant companion. She tasted fear in her mouth even now because she understood only that she didn't want to lose herself. No one knew her feelings. She couldn't say them. She had told Michael about her life, but he couldn't know the elation which came with each day, each day that told her she could take care of Jimmy and herself, that told her, even though she was alone, she need never be afraid again.

She couldn't give up this life, this freedom from fear she had earned. And the luxury that freedom gave her—the chance to find herself and what she could do.

The anger in Michael's eyes turned back into a wound. She knew he wouldn't say anything more.

The closing of the door sounded like a gunshot. She didn't run after him. She would survive. Survival would be hard, the slow passage of hours, of days from which the color, the life, had been taken.

She didn't hear from him and tried not to think of him. Her dreams were filled with images that fought for recognition, arrived slowly and vaguely, like people walking toward her in a snowstorm. She saw childhood days with her grandmother, when happiness was a gift, when tomorrow was only a continuation of the joy that belonged to her, was her right. She saw herself and Tadziu as children, saw them in the heat of summer, running together through the spray of cool water in the city pool, through drops that sparkled like rain falling through sun. She saw them lying in the grass at the pool's edge, looking up though the leaves of tall, ancient trees that waved back and forth slowly, like huge lumbering giants, then disappeared somewhere in the blue sky. She saw herself in her grandmother's house, a child staring out the window at winter's endless night, thinking she could hear the sound of veins cracking in the black trees and thinking of Tadziu, wanting him to be safe, as she was safe, from the winter and the cold.

She saw Tadziu later, in the days of their marriage, saw him controlled by his drinking, as surely as he had once been controlled by his father, saw herself unable to help set him free. Fear had ruled her then like a tyrant. In her dreams, she recognized that first, most merciless fear, as a black figure with a naked white face. She saw Mrs.

Hoggenkamp refusing to give Jimmy food, watched her as she pushed Jimmy and herself through the doors of her office. She felt the pain that was absorbed into the fabric of those days.

Now they returned, invading her sleep. In one dream, she saw herself sitting alone in an amphitheater of empty seats, saw smartly dressed young women pass by the classroom door, jeering at her, pointing at her hair and her clothes. She woke exhausted, seeing truths about her life and remembering, with renewed surprise, the symbolism of the last dream, that the lack of women's things—clothes, haircuts, beauty—had been important to her. She was like her mother, the woman her grandma described as thinking she was "real pretty".

The dreams continued. Night after night, a battle was being fought and she was, balanced on a precipice, unable to fall, unable to climb. She dreamed of her grandmother, saw her face as clearly as if she were in the room, but could not understand the expression on her grandmother's face. She felt cheated. Her grandmother had always helped her find answers.

She wrote to Michael and tried to explain.

Dear Michael,

I know it is difficult to understand why I don't want to marry. I'm afraid, my dearest. I don't trust my own judgement. You love me. I 'm not sure that will continue. I think one must work very hard to maintain love. I don't want to fail.

I can't lie. There's something else I don't want to give up and that is my life. I have dreams, though I can't define them, don't yet know what they are. I don't know how much you would require of me, how much of my dreams I would have to leave behind. In favor of yours. I don't think you can know either. These doubts, these fears live inside me, grow monstrous when the subject of marriage enters. Forgive me for the hurt I've caused. I know I love you. That's all I know.

Absence

His shoes were in the closet, large shoes, the rich brown of their leather making her think of masculinity, of stretching out on the bed and wedging herself in the crook of his arm. Michael, Michael. With his strong shoulders, his easy laughter, his ability to pull her into his laughter. To make her feel protected. Safe.

Aloneness settled on her like a shroud. Frightened her. She wanted to push it from herself. To run to him.

I can't run to him. I've lost him. He's right. I can't have it both ways. He won't stay without the restraint of marriage. He says it's because he cares for me, because marriage is a protection. I know he believes this. He is honorable. It will be better when Jimmy and I leave this apartment, leave behind all the memories.

Mary looked in the mirror. Light that fell into the room from the window became shadow, turned the gold in the earrings she wore into gray, accentuated the curves of darkness that lay beneath her eyes.

I look like this because I don't sleep peacefully. She saw herself as unnatural, a grotesque person, a kind of androgyne, part of her accepting Michael's love, another part loving herself more. How dare she do this? Who did she think she was? What was the face in the mirror anyway. Just a face. Alone.

She saw that she was turning, running in circles, would come to no end, unless she made one, unless she stopped thinking. "You think too much," Michael had said to her. Because from the place where he stood, some things didn't need to be thought about, should be taken for granted. Like love. Two people who loved each other being together, marrying. But he didn't stand where she stood.

Alone

Mary walked up the street, rather, was yanked up the street by the dog.

I'm not a good dog trainer. He's supposed to slow down at my command. And halt when I tell him to halt. Why did I take in this creature? Just because Jimmy begged? No, let's be fair. Because the dog was freezing and starving in the street and because I couldn't resist the strange combination of breeds which created him. Big feet like a Labrador even though he's no taller than two feet, long ears like some sort of spaniel, black fur with white spots, a kind of reverse Dalmatian. And the biggest saddest brown eyes I'd ever seen. And now the eyes are happy. Especially around me.

It was almost twilight. A low sun hung in the sky, a golden apple heavy with its own weight, red and orange streaks in the backdrop like paint spilled on a canvas. The picture filled Mary with peace. The dog's heavy breathing as he strained against his leash moved Mary's attention from the beauty overhead to the earth and the laughable picture of her charge. She leaned down to soothe him and he covered her with wet kisses. But trying to teach him not to yank on his collar was hopeless. She began to run because she couldn't stand the sound of his choking.

Tomorrow is a holiday and I don't have to work. Jimmy's going on an outing with his friends. A bus will pick them up and bring them back. I'll have the entire day to myself. Just me and my pal here.

When she walked in the door, she looked at the empty boxes stacked in the corner. Everything was unpacked and in place.

Each day she loved her job more. She was beginning to think ahead, to imagine further possibilities for herself. She and Jimmy were embarked on a new stage of their life. They had neighbors and friends, even a dog.

A Visit

Uncle Ben still acted as the go-between

"My sister said she'd come on Saturday, Mary," he murmured, turning his face and looking away. Mary thought of how much she loved her uncle. She thought of the words he had just used, "my sister", and how that must cause him to suffer.

She told Jimmy they would be "having company."

"Who, ma, who?" His questions lately began to sound like demands.

"Just someone from the family you don't know."

"Who, ma, who?" She didn't answer. Jimmy gave up.

Before the doorbell rang on Saturday, Mary looked through the window and saw a summer day like a woman adorned and changing her jewelry, the sky turning from gold to crimson to blue, the grass and trees heavy with their green, moving in the breeze and reaching toward the burning light of the sun.

Some moments are always remembered. This time, this evening is one of them.

The woman stood in the open door, outlined by the light as if belonging to its brightness, an extension of its beauty. She was middle-aged, her hair full and thick, her mouth sensuous. The blue eyes were startling, luminous against the gold of the skin and showing the faint beginning of wrinkles at the corners, in the same place as grandma. The expression was furtive, as if she wished to hide. She wore a light summer dress with a small blue pattern that accentuated her eyes and her skin. Mary's resentment was aroused. This was a woman who spent time in the sun, sitting in a chair and rubbing suntan lotion on her arms.

"Mary."

"Yes," Mary answered, glad at the woman's discomfort when she stepped forward and attempted to place her arms around Mary and Mary didn't move to meet her. Mary felt her skin growing red, thought of Jimmy standing stiffly behind her like a soldier, wished she hadn't asked him to be there, then glad he was, because, if only for a moment, her thoughts were free of the woman, her eyes and her unspoken demands..

"Jimmy, your mama is so proud you. Your Aunt Irene and Uncle Ben too." Jimmy beamed, as always, revealing his feelings.

He likes her. Does he recognize something I don't?

She felt the woman's eyes searching, felt the effort she made to look at Mary directly and her inability to do so. So Mary did it, felt the coldness in herself like a winter chill, looked at her mother's face without seeing it, looked past it, but not entirely past, her eyes catching the top of her mother's head and its brown hair, hair she remembered from somewhere, the upper layers leaving the thickness below, floating above her mother's head like a mist and settling on her shoulders like a cloud. Without thinking, Mary reached out and touched it, touched her mother's hair. The woman's eyes lifted and, for a moment, were filled with joy.

The word "mother" sticks in my throat, won't leave. She must call herself "Elizabeth." She was "Elzbieta" to grandma.

"This is Elizabeth," she told Jimmy and he was satisfied.

"Would you care to sit down?"she asked and her mother headed for the couch, as if it were a boat that would save her from drowning. Mary felt the radiation of her mother's despair, the heat leaving her body like breath, like life. Jimmy sensed the woman's emotions and plopped down next to her, as if, like one of his friends, she were shy and needed reassurance.

"Are you related to my mother?" he asked, and Mary held her breath, felt again the longing of her girlhood, wished to embrace the woman and say, "Yes, Jimmy. She's my mother." But she didn't. Elizabeth said nothing.

"She's part of our family," Mary said and again, Jimmy was satisfied.

"You look like our family," he added enthusiastically. "Where do you live?" Elizabeth looked grateful for Jimmy's lightheartedness and for having to stop and think.

"In Chicago," she answered and Jimmy said, "Wow! That's far away. How long are you staying with us?"

"I can't stay," she answered, her eyes like those of someone being pursued, her slight movements in the corner of the couch awkward and stiff.

She wants to fade, to disappear.

"Maybe…maybe I can stay another time," Elizabeth mumbled from somewhere in her throat. Mary gave no reply. She felt her own cruelty but didn't know how to end it.

She looked at the woman again, tried to hide her looking as she took pride in the woman's beauty.

I must be as attractive as she is. She's my mother.

In the next instant the resentment returned.

She left me. She left me. How could she be so different from grandma? How can I ever forget?

Shame settled inside her like the growing darkness of the sky. She didn't want to be a part of this woman. She looked at her mother again, saw the rigid manner in which she sat, watched her tearing at the handkerchief in her hand. Pity began to enter Mary's shame. Confusion covered her like a blanket. She wanted to be a child again. Since grandma died, her emptiness never wholly left, appeared like the regularity of winter, was never filled, even by Tadziu.

She began to relive it all—how alone she had felt, how she had married Tadziu despite the part of her that knew it was not good, how she had not wanted to be a burden to Aunt Irene and Uncle Ben.

How could I forget, even for a minute, what my mother caused?

Jimmy whispered that she was a "pretty lady" and chattered on as if he would never tire, then announced he had to go to his friend's house. As he turned to leave, a shadow appeared behind him, a shadow that hung loosely, like a breath of air taking shape. Mary knew. She turned her face. Her mother's voice trembled but continued.

"You've done a beautiful job with him, Mary. He's a wonderful boy." Mary said nothing. Her inner self heard her grandmother's reproving voice.

"Your mama didn' do right but she didn' control your life. We make our own decisions, Mary. You know that." Her mother's voice became stronger.

"Mary, I didn't know Ma died. I would have tried…tried to come sooner." Her grandmother's form began to fade but her words continued.

"It's true, Mary. She didn' know." Mary straightened her skirt.

"I think it would be better if you didn't come back," she said, suddenly conscious of the thin gold chain she wore, rolling it between her fingers, wishing that all the talking would stop and she could return to yesterday when she wasn't the person she was now. "Not for a while."

Mary's mother looked helpless. Resignation came down and covered her face like a curtain and, as if years had instantly passed, changed her into an old woman. After the door closed, Mary twisted her necklace until it broke and fell to the floor. She thought of what she'd done, wanted to call her mother back and erase everything she'd said. But she couldn't. The word "forgiveness" tried to enter her thoughts but she pushed it away..

She was imprisoned, a figure frozen in a picture. She looked around the room. At the rose-colored drapes at the windows, the rose-patterned rug in the center of the room, the lamp with the white-patterned shade.

I've earned my home, worked hard for everything. Her way was different. She didn't care enough about me to take me with her. She didn't even know grandma died. Why should I care? She's not part of my life.

Desolation descended, landed on her shoulders like an ugly bird, a desolation she recognized, remembered from other times—when her grandmother died, when she had made Tadziu leave. It was she who was alone, abandoned.

She walked to the window and watched the departing figure. Her breath came in shallow spurts. Salty tears stung her eyes and, like needles, carved canyons down her face.

I'm sorry, grandma. I'm sorry. I'll bring her back. I'll fix it, Grandma. I'll fix it.

But she knew it would never, could never be fixed. No one could ever return, ever retrieve what had been lost.

Chapter Twelve

An Approach

"Here I come"! Jimmy yelled, announcing his intention to jump into Tadziu's arms. His attempt was a conglomeration of movements that included climbing his father's torso and swinging from his neck. Tadziu staggered.

"Hey, you're bigger now, you know. You almost knocked me over." Jimmy looked delighted, then, as he remembered something, the expression on his face changed and he became quiet.

"I'm sorry, Daddy." Tadziu's mouth fell open. He whistled and threw his hands into the air.

"Is this the same kid we were fighting about?" he asked the sky. Mary looked at him with vindication. A point had been proven.

"He's really a good kid."

Oh Jeez, I never said he wasn't. Women are crazy. She's got that hurt look on her face.

"You do a great job with him, Mary."

"You've been helping a lot, Tadziu."

"G'wan, I only see him once a week."

"I mean it. He loves you. He needs his father."

Silence. Awkward silence.

Now what? What do I say? We've passed the compliments around. Might as well go for it.

"You're his mother, Mary. A kid needs both." He was swinging by his bare hands from the edge of a cliff.

"I know."

"Can he have both? Can we get back together, I know I'm not much, not like you but I'll work hard. I won't mess up." He didn't know what the look on her face meant. Her "no" sounded like it was coming from someplace deep inside.

She didn't even hesitate. That no's been sitting in her a long time. All ready and waiting.

"No? Just no? Is there someone else?" He knew this Michael guy from school had been hanging around.

"No, there's no one else." He had trouble hearing her voice. He saw this was hard for her.

"Then why? You hate me that much?"

"I never hated you, Tadziu. I love you. As much as I love Michael. I know it doesn't make sense."

"No, it sure as hell doesn't. You love two guys? Me and this Michael."

"Yes." She paused and wonder filled her eyes, as if she knew something she hadn't known before.

Mary, you're nuttier than a fruitcake. That's okay. I always knew that. Brainy. But nutty.

"You gotta make up your mind." He stretched out his arm and touched her shoulder. Some piece of knowing was rising to meet him. It wasn't a contest between him and this Michael. He didn't know what it was, but it wasn't that. He scratched his head.

"I don't want to be with anyone, Tadziu." She turned her face away so he couldn't see her. I don't want to marry again."

"That's crazy. What, you queer or something?" She laughed. "I don't think so. I just want to be alone right now."

"Right now? What does that mean?"

Without looking, she brushed stray crumbs from the table. "I don't know."

"What d'you mean you don't know? How long before you know. What d'you expect a guy to do?" He knew his voice was rising but he didn't care.

Mary saw the way his mouth set itself into a line, turned away from seeing the hurt in his eyes, from seeing his hands hanging at his sides, forming a fist, relaxing, then forming a fist again

He's fighting so hard. Fighting for control over himself, all the things he is. He's changed. It would be so easy to fall, to pick up the habit of loving him from where it has lain since I left him. His reaction so similar to Michael's. Wanting to possess, to own. Then I'm caught in that circle, the circle of someone else's life. With only segments, pieces left over for myself.

She was quiet, didn't answer, and didn't try to explain.

Tadziu forgot his pride. "I need you a lot."

Mary felt herself hardening, closing, then opening, like a door. "No you don't Tadziu. You'll manage fine. You've got your drinking under control."

He's not an alcoholic. Just a man who drinks when he can't cope. He's so tall. Can hold me, brush all the places on my body, his hands settling, exploring.

"I don't get it. I don't get it," Tadziu said, opening his fingers, running them through his hair, like a comb. Her answer sounded like a speech she'd rehearsed.

"I loved you. It didn't work for us. I've gone in a different direction now. I want the chance to find out what I want. I can't do that with you." Then she added, "Or Michael."

"What the hell are you talkin' about? I won't interfere with anything you want to do."

"You would Tadziu. You wouldn't mean to but you would."

"Boy, you're goofy, I mean, tough to understand." She was quiet

"Is there a chance for me?"

Why does he ask me these questions, pin me down. Why doesn't he leave it alone. Why does he need such certainty .

"I don't know." Silence.

She's not lying. She doesn't know. Sometimes she scares me. She always scared me in a way I never understood..

He forgot that he wanted her at this moment, forgot her body, the body he'd thought about with every woman he saw. They all became her. Through the window, he watched the sun fold in half, its light slowly disappearing. Her fingers were long and thin, the upper arm curved as if someone had carefully shaped it. He wanted to press his lips to her fingers, her arm. He knew he couldn't, that he never could again. The knowledge settled in almost like a relief. What he had feared and expected was now real, had been said out loud. Anger swelled, threatened to come from that place where it always hid inside him. It didn't matter if he told himself she didn't deserve his anger. He was angry at her for having been in his life, for having loved him, for his having loved her.

A Meeting

He went straight to a bar. He saw a woman, a girl really, with large blue eyes that looked like a picture of what was going on in her head. The picture in them changed so fast he couldn't stop looking at her. When he sat down and mumbled a surly hello, the eyes looked nervous, confused, like she didn't know if she should say something back. She turned away and kept talking to the guy next to her, putting her nose in the air, nervously smoking and ignoring Tadziu. He knew she was nervous because he saw the fingers that held the cigarette shaking like a leaf in the wind. He knew she was trying to be sophisticated. He would have laughed out loud except that she looked something like his sister Gina and if he laughed, he could just see the beaten look, the sadness, in her eyes.

For Christ's sake, she might even start crying.

He was here to drink so why the hell should he care anyway?

She looks so young. The guy talking to her looks pretty crummy. What does she see in that asshole? She could get into real trouble with an asshole like that.

The guy pointed his hand in Tadziu's direction, his face filled with contempt.

I can see the word on his mouth. He's asking her who the jerk is. That means me. *I'm the jerk. Oh well, what the fuck.*

Before he got off the bar stool, Tadziu saw her eyes, wide with water moving in them like it was trembling, understood then that she was talking to the asshole because she was afraid not to. That pissed him off more. He looked the guy square in the face, daring him.

"Who you calling a jerk, mister?" The guy had his thumbs hooked casually in the waist of his pants. His knuckles curled into a fist.

"Who d'ya think, buddy?" He rocked back on his fake leather cowboy boots.

Again, Tadziu felt like laughing, but this time a different kind of laughter.

Maybe that's supposed to scare me. He looks like a kid in fifth grade except he's taller, bigger around. Who gives a shit.

He glanced at the girl on the bar stool, saw her hold her hands on her ears as if they hurt, her eyes so wide she looked like someone riding a real bad roller coaster. From the corner of his eye, he saw the bartender summoning the bouncer. The guy before him reached out, and tried to grab Tadziu's chin

Something inside Tadziu went off like a firecracker on the Fourth of July. Filled him with an energy that grew larger and turned into steel so his voice came out loud and steady.

"You son of a bitch. Think you're hot shit, huh?" Tadziu saw the bouncer hurrying from across the room and swung at the guy before the bouncer reached them. Caught the guy square. The guy swung back but Tadziu moved quick and the shot just grazed his shoulder. Tadziu couldn't be sure of what he did next because the dim lights made everything blurry and his rage blinded him more but his next shot knocked the guy to the ground. Tadziu knew it was good. Something that had been beating at him to get out was released. The guy got up from the floor, ready to lunge at Tadziu again but the bouncer, a guy who looked like an ape, pinned back his arms, held them and began dragging him outside.

"You too mister," the bartender said, pointing at Tadziu.

A guy at the bar said, "It wasn' him, Chuck. The other one started. He's always lookin' for trouble." Another guy agreed. They were older men, "regulars." Tadziu had always seen when he went into the place.

A third man piped in, also older and a regular, insisting that Tadziu was not the one who made the trouble. "He did ya a favor," he chortled to the bartender. "Maybe Benny won't come back."

"Okay, buddy. Jus' watch yourself." the bouncer said and Tadziu sat back down. He looked at the girl. She stared at him with eyes as round as saucers, formed her hands into a steeple and held them to her mouth, like an old lady praying.

"Oh Gee, why d'you do that? she said, in a voice as quiet as a whisper.

Tadziu was breathing hard but he felt like he was waking up after a good sleep. The poison was gone. He smiled at the girl.

She's probably going to think I did it for her. Girls are like that. But she's too much of a kid to get involved with a shithead like that. I wanted to hit something anyway. That asshole deserved it. Oh, what the hell.

He asked her what she wanted to drink.

"Nothing," she said, still looking scared, like she thought he was going to hit her too, and added the word "thanks" quickly, like something she had forgotten. Then she just sat there, staring at him with those saucer eyes, stiff, as if she was made out of wood, a statue that couldn't bend, couldn't talk. Tadziu told her his name, kept asking questions, trying to show her he was not another jerk. Finally she talked. But not much. Her name was Amanda. She was not as young as she looked, only a couple years younger than he was.

He saw her the next weekend before starting out to see Jimmy. She was perched on the barstool holding a glass of beer, her cigarette dangling from her fingers. She wore a tight black skirt and an orange turtleneck sweater. She made Tadziu think of Halloween but he couldn't say that. The sweater showed off her small boobs. Her dark eyelids were coated with something black that looked sticky like it might glue her eyes shut. He bought her a drink and she must have started to trust him because she started telling him about her life, as if she was eager, as if she knew he would listen. She told him she didn't know anything about her parents, that she'd been brought up in foster homes.

"What d'you mean you don't know anything about them. Where d'you come from?" He felt bad the minute the words left him, could see they struck her like gun-shot. Her eyes showed the pain of it, then turned away, like a deer falling. He was quiet. And sorry. He'd have to be careful.

"From Father Baker's. My mother left me there. I was a baby. The sisters said she knew they'd take care of me. She loved me." Sounding as if she had said this a thousand times.

Oh Jesus.

She kept talking, her words like rope holding him, making him listen, not letting him get up and leave. She told him the people in the foster homes had been good to her, had treated her like one of their own children.

"They're always asking me to come down. They have reunions, you know," she said, as a kind of afterthought, her eyes brightening, then, suddenly looking down, losing their brightness, as if she was aware that her one great pride might not be what she'd always thought it to be. He felt himself being pulled into wanting to be with her, wanting to keep her out of bars, but he stopped himself.

The thought of starting this thing, of asking her out confused him. He didn't want to surrender, to give up his hope of being with Mary again. She was his childhood and his manhood.

But I know I'm defeated. It won't happen. So what am I giving up? I don't know but I'm giving up something. It's all a joke, a thing that laughs at you. Gives you a taste of what you long for, what can't be yours.

Mary came to him in dreams, sometimes a child, sometimes a woman. Sometimes he was a boy. Sometimes a man. They played games, mostly cards. They walked together through snow, huddled together to keep warm. They made love. She brought him into her wet darkness, resting her head on his chest afterward, bringing him pain at the sight of her body.

When he awoke, he didn't understand any of it, only the thing that never changed, that he'd always love her. Sometimes he was tired of his love, but that didn't make it go away.

At other times he dreamed of the old flat, the place he and Mary lived in when they were first married. He saw the room where Jimmy slept, remembered going in that night to look at him. He saw the shiny linoleum in the kitchen, the worn-out brown couch he sat on after supper, the television in the corner that he watched when he drank his beer. Before he got too drunk to see.

Oh God, did I ever get drunk. Nights I didn't even remember. Would've kept on that way if she didn't leave me.

He'd said all these things at AA meetings but now he really heard them, really listened to his thoughts.

I was jealous of Jimmy because he took Mary away from me. Now, sometimes I'm jealous because I know he loves Mary more than me. Boy, am I crazy or what?

Amanda

The next time he saw the girl in the bar, looking around expectantly, probably for another asshole guy, he lost it. She didn't know he was there until the stool next to her opened up.

"Amanda, why d'you do the things you do? Coming in here. Taking a chance on getting involved with scum. You're better than that, honey. Better than that." She got that frightened look, as if he was her father scolding her. Tonight she had on a sweater like a blouse that dipped low in front so that it looked like she had bigger boobs than she did. The heels on her shoes were so high he wanted to laugh. She might kill herself climbing off the barstool. But he was angry.

"And why d'you dress like that?" She brushed back her blonde hair. Even in this light you could see the dark roots. But her face was pretty. Under all the make-up, she was real pretty. "C'mon" he said. "I'm taking you home."

"But I was only waiting for you," she whimpered, like a little kid. That made him angrier.

"Well, I'm here," he said, the words coming out like a growl.

"It took me an hour to get dressed, Tadziu."

"Yeah, I'll bet." He was immediately sorry. The trembling came into her saucer eyes again, as if he'd hit her or something. She was just like his sister, Gina. Except Gina never hung around in bars. He tried to form a picture of Gina in a tight skirt and a low-cut sweater. But he couldn't. He just couldn't. With heels a half-foot high on her shoes. And long earrings, something that was probably supposed to look like gold because they shone like hell.

"Oh honey, you don't have to look like this. Don't look like this," he said as they walked to the car. "Like a streetwalker," he wanted to say, tried to remember the Polish word his father always used when he talked about cheap-looking women. It had begun to snow, small, fluffy flakes that were starting to stick to the ground. He realized she could not keep up with him in her high-heeled shoes so he slowed down and took smaller steps.

"Why not Tadziu? What's wrong with the way I dress?" Now it was she who was angry. Her voice rose. "How am I supposed to dress?"

He couldn't say "so you look like my ex-wife." The picture of Mary pasted itself against the darkness like a mirage. She always looked so—he had trouble naming it—so high class.

"I don't know but not like that." In the car, he felt her trying to calm her anger, looking at him, concentrating.

"I could dress any way you wanted me to, Tadziu. If you were my guy."

Oh boy. I shouldn't be doing this. It isn't fair.

"Look Amanda, you're a nice girl. I just think you should dress like a nice girl."

"I am dressing like a nice girl."

"No, you're not. You're dressing like a girl trying to attract a guy."

She sounded exasperated, as if he was the stupid one.

"All girls try to attract guys."

"Yeah I know, but you should be trying to attract the right kind of guys."

She gave up, started to cry. Through snow that continued to fall slow and lazy, he drove her to the apartment house where she said she lived.

Oh, for god's sake, just leave her alone. Let her go ahead and dress any way she wants.

But he couldn't shut up.

"In a nice dress, Amanda. A nice dress. Loose, so it doesn't show your boobs. Or your other stuff, either." That was all he could think of. Then he almost said something dumb.

Dress so that I can take you to see my kid.

Black stuff from her eyes ran down her face as she cried.

"Don't wear so much makeup," he added.

Oh Christ, what am I doing to this poor girl.

He saw the curve of her small breasts, thought of the small curve of her behind.

Her boobs can't even fill a sweater decently. She's small all over. She'd fit nicely in my arms. Maybe my sister could teach her something about dressing and stuff. What the hell's wrong with me?

He opened the door, wondering if she'd go back to the bar after he was gone.

I can't do anything about it if she does.

"Good-night," he said. But if she heard, she didn't answer, just slammed the car door, went up the stairs of the house and disappeared into the blackness inside.

Well, I deserve it. I guess she's had enough of me.

Women

Tadziu looked up at the window of Mary's s apartment. He was here for Jimmy. He wondered how long it would be before he stopped thinking he was here to see her, before the feeling that he belonged here would go away, before he stopped hoping she would take him back. She smiled when she opened the door. It meant nothing. She always smiled. Jimmy was behind her.

"Daddy! What took you so long?"

"So long? Hey look chum, I've been driving for four hours. There's things like traffic jams and I have to stop sometimes to take a leak, you know." Jimmy laughed at Tadziu calling him chum, and at his saying he had to take a leak.

He's a great kid. He laughs at everything I say.

Jimmy ran to get the equipment he had piled in a corner. Like a squirrel scampering after his supply of winter nuts, he began picking up and dropping things. "I'll get my stuff." Tadziu laughed.

"Let me help ya here, kiddo." They were going camping. There was no getting out of it because it was Jimmy's birthday and Tadziu had told him he could pick whatever he wanted to do. When he said camping, Tadziu groaned. He had to borrow a tent and all kinds of gear from his friend, Jerry. That was okay. The kid wanted to go camping. He said all his friends went camping, that next year, he could go camping with the Boy Scouts and he needed to practice.

Okay, by God, they'd go camping.

Mary wore an amused expression as Tadziu explained to Jimmy the things he needed to know.

"What d'you mean we have to walk to the bathroom?" Jimmy asked. "Can't ya just go behind a tree?"

"Sure," Tadziu told him, "as long as no one's looking. You can crap behind a tree too, but I myself think I'd prefer an outhouse."

"Jeez. He's so happy, because he thinks I don't know what the hell I'm doing and he does. And he's right. Is this real? I have to listen to my pal Jerry, the father of three kids, telling me what to do when I take my kid camping. I can't believe I'm doing this. Why not? I'm a father, ain't I? Yeah but I really don't know what I'm doing. Shit, how hard can it be?

They loaded Jimmy's supplies into the car—-a backpack, a water canteen to take when they went hiking. And assorted gadgets rolling around in the bottom of a huge duffel bag. Jimmy lifted it carefully. Tadziu couldn't imagine how he could lift it if it were full. He said nothing, nodded when Jimmy, in a solemn voice, told him, "Mom bought me that."

Tadziu had purchased sleeping bags and they stopped at Jerry's to pick up a tent. He told Jerry he didn't need the heater. He couldn't believe it would get cold enough for that.

"It's July, for Chrissake." Jerry made him take it.

"Yeah, you'll be surprised at how cold it can get at night," he warned in a know-it-all voice. "Especially next to water. You're camping at the lake. Ain't you?"

"Yeah," Tadziu mumbled.

"You need to take cooking stuff. You can't take Jimmy out for a hamburger in the woods, ya know."

"Just keep it up, Jer. I'm gonna hit ya," Tadziu threatened but Jerry couldn't control his teasing.

Jerry's wife Joan, a woman half Jerry's size, balanced their third boy on her hip, a six-month-old whose face was a miniature version of Jerry's, and who seemed slated to be just as big. Trying to hide her amusement, Joan giggled and told Jerry to leave Tadziu alone. The baby laughed out loud at nothing.

"See," Jerry guffawed, chucking his son underneath his chin, "even the kid knows you're a am-a-chur and headin' fer trouble," as if he were putting the word "amateur" into bold print.

"You weren't so smart the first time we took the kids either," Joan said.

Jerry looked offended. "Whad'ya mean. I been campin' all my life."

Joan shifted the weight of the baby from one hip to another. "Yes, but the first time you forgot the boys' fishing poles. And the second time, your hiking boots, remember?" It was Tadziu's turn to laugh as Jerry grumbled under his breath. As if he were on automatic pilot, Jerry reached out and scooped the baby from Joan's arms as easily as a stuffed toy.

"Yeah, and who was doin' the packin'? See what you're doin', Tadz? A fam'ly argument. Startin' fam'ly arguments."

By this time, Jerry's two older boys were there, their eyes traveling from one parent to another, enjoying an obviously familiar scene—-their mother and father kidding with each other. They liked it. But it was clear who was in command. Joan, whose frame and bones made Tadziu think of a bird, looked like a teen-ager but her eyes gave you the clear message that she was the boss in the outfit. The two boys looked at their mother as if she were an admiral and they were getting ready to salute. Jimmy stared at them good-naturedly and they stared back.

"Don't worry, kiddo," Jerry said, ruffling Jimmy's hair. "If your dad gets you lost, Uncle Jerry will cum an' save you. Just as long as you don't pick up any bears!" Jimmy was captured by the fun, lost his shyness, and surrendered to convulsions of laughter. The other two boys joined in and all three became "bears" chasing each other.

Something heavy settled inside Tadziu.

This could be Mary and me. She's a lot smarter than me. She could boss me around.

He became impatient with himself and left the thought behind like a light he was turning off.

When Jimmy and he left, on a sudden impulse, he drove to Amanda's apartment. It was the weekend. Maybe she'd be home. She was. "She's my girlfriend," he told Jimmy. "Maybe she'd like to go with us."

Jimmy's face fell. "Aw dad, I thought it was just going to be me 'n you."

"C'mon, Jimmy. You'll like her. She's a lot of fun?"

What the hell's the matter with me? How do I know if she's fun. Why am I trying to convince my kid? And disappointing him?

"Hey Jimmy, she likes camping. She knows a lot about it."

Maybe he won't know who's dumb and who isn't.

He laughed. He knew better.

"Just pretend you're in the army," Jerry had laughed as they left.

He told Jimmy to wait in the car. She answered the door in her bathrobe, her eyes full of sleep. With a clean face and no makeup, she looked even more like a kid.

"Hi," he said.

"Hi." She rolled the tie on her bathrobe between her fingers.

"What'r you doing this weekend?" he asked.

She stared at him. There was no answer.

"You wanna go campin'? I got my kid in the car."

"You mean with you?"

"Yeah, with me and my son."

"Your son?" She said the word with a kind of reverence in her voice. "You want to take me with your son? Camping?"

Tadziu was beginning to think she was hard of hearing.

"Yeah. We need a female presence." She looked puzzled. "We need a girl!"

She looked past Tadziu at Jimmy sitting in the car, then back at Tadziu again.

Oh Jeez, I don't have to worry. By the time she decides, the weekend will be gone.

"You wanna go or not?"

"Yeah, yeah, sure." Holding the tie on her robe so tightly that her knuckles turned white, she looked at Jimmy as if he were a prince and she had somehow been dropped into a medieval court. "I'm very happy to meet you," she said, and Tadziu found himself hoping she wouldn't bow.

Jimmy looked at her dubiously, and then, with the kind of radar kids have, knew about her, about the kind of person she was.

"Me too," he said, and broke into a wide grin. Then began telling her all the things they were going to do. Like hike in the woods. And find snakes. And sleep in a tent. And fish.

"You'll like it," Tadziu told her, because he didn't want her to be nervous about something she'd never done before.

My kid's a nice kid.

"Yeah," she said, "I camped a lot with the girl scouts. And earned a badge." Hearing the excitement in her voice, she paused, then said, more quietly, "I like snakes."

Jimmy looked ecstatic. "You do?"

"Yeah, I have a book about all kinds of snakes."

Tadziu was startled.

"Biology was my best subject in high school," she said, again quietly, as if she didn't want to brag, but couldn't hide her enthusiasm. "I know what kind of snakes we have in this country. They're not as big as the ones in Asia or India. Like pythons, or cobras, but..." She stopped suddenly and looked at Tadziu, like someone who has been caught doing something bad.

Oh brother. I don't believe this.

He smiled at her. He'd never smiled at her. Jimmy wanted to hear more. She started to tell him about her biology project, how she had cut out pictures of snakes from *National Geographic* magazines and pasted them on poster board. She told him she had to draw the ones she couldn't find. From library books. She listed all the snakes that had impressed her. Talked too fast. Like Tadziu was listening to her, waiting for her to make a mistake.

People go through life worrying about what someone else is thinking. Always apologizing. For what they are. Amanda is worried because some guy, some asshole like me, won't like that she likes snakes. She knows she's safe with Jimmy. What an asshole I am. They're forgetting all about me, going from snakes to elephants. Then lions and tigers. Holy shit. She knows a lot about animals.

He found his voice and tried to be part of them. "What happens if we run into one of these big snakes in the woods, Jimmy?"

Jimmy lifted his eyes to heaven and shook his head. "Oh daddy, that's silly," he said, as if their roles were reversed and Tadziu was the child. "Cobras don't live in this country, right Amanda?"

"Right Jimmy. Only in Asia or India," then added, "well, Africa too, some even found as far as parts of Australia and New Guinea."

"Thank God," Tadziu said, in mock-relief and Amanda looked at him again.

She thinks I'm making fun of her.

He looked back at her and smiled again, putting the smile into his eyes. Even though Jimmy sat between them, he could feel her body relax, and like a balloon losing air, some of the tightness leave her. The ride to the campground was good. He started singing a camping we will go, to the tune of the only kid's song he knew, *The farmer in the Dell*. "C'mon Jimmy, c'mon," he urged, and Jimmy sang. Finally Amanda broke in. Tadziu was overtaken by a feeling he didn't recognize, one that stayed with him throughout the weekend.

When it was over and Tadziu brought him home, Jimmy ran into the living room like something shot from a cannon.

"Mom, mom, mom, we had this great time. Amanda caught a trout fish. She even cooked it. She took off all the scales and stuff. Daddy didn't know how. Then we had a campfire with some people and one man sang songs and played his guitar. Raccoons came at night and wanted food. They knocked our garbage cans over. And made lots of noise. Me and Daddy looked outside. One looked right at me. Can I go again, ma? Please."

Tadziu watched Mary's face, and for a moment, was confused. But then he understood.

She's trying to smile and look happy. But she's pissed. Looking past me, over my head, wanting to see Amanda.

He looked at Mary and without talking, put words into the air that fell between them.

The hell with this. What's your problem now? I'm doing what I'm supposed to be doing. It's tough shit if you don't like that I took a girl with us.

"Of course you can go again," Mary said, with ice in her voice, as if they had interrupted her in something important. Jimmy's eyes moved back and forth desperately, feeling the new thing, not understanding it, wanting it to be gone. Tadziu couldn't take it. He turned to leave.

"Wait daddy, wait," Jimmy pleaded, reaching out his arms, wanting Tadziu to pick him up.

"Can we go again, daddy, please?"

"You bet kiddo." Tadziu said, lifting Jimmy in his arms, hoping that Mary saw how Jimmy loved him and what a good time they had together.

What the hell is this? We're fighting now. Quietly fighting. Over what? Women are nuts.

Tadziu jumped into the car and slammed the door. Amanda's eyes became small with uncertainty. Tadziu knew his feeling was turning into poison and would spread to her but he was powerless to stop it. At her door, he said a short good-bye. He knew he was being lousy and that it wasn't her fault, but he needed to get a beer. He felt the old frustration sweeping over him, the frustration he always tried to fix with a beer. Sometimes it worked.

He downed two beers quickly and felt his anger growing. He ordered a third and threw it down his throat. His head ached, and was starting to spin.

Goddamn. Why am I doing this. Letting her make me drink. I don't even want to drink in this mood. When it was such a great weekend. I think something important happened but I don't know what it is. I can't keep track.

He got up from the barstool and went to the phone. He knew Amanda was on the other end but no words came from the ear piece.

She won't talk because she knows it's me.

"C'mon Amanda, I know you're there," he said, sorry that his voice sounded the way it did.

She sounded scared. "What did I do?"

For Chrissake, I hear her crying.

"What's wrong with you?" he yelled into the phone.

"Nothing."

"Then why do you act so scared all the time. As if everything in the world is your fault. It's not, you know. That's something you gotta learn." She stopped crying and was silent. "I mean you didn't do anything to anybody, Amanda. Ever." He made his voice sound calm. "This was a great weekend. You were wonderful. And you don't believe it. Just because some asshole like me is pissy to you."

"You're not an asshole, Tadziu."

His voice was getting louder.

"Yes I am."

"No, you're not."

"Amanda, I am, I am." He was close to losing control.

"Okay you are," she said. "I love you anyway."

Oh Christ. Christ. What the hell is wrong with me? A nice girl. She said she loves me.

"Amanda, wait there okay?"

"Okay."

When she opened the door, he put his arms around her. Held her a long time without talking, then said, "Thanks for being so nice to Jimmy. He likes you a lot." A smile fought to break out on her face, came and stayed there all the while he held her. When they slept in her bed, he felt how clean it was, how like a woman it smelled. He gave her as much pleasure as he could. But he didn't tell her he loved her. He couldn't say that. He just couldn't say that.

Afterward, she didn't talk, just looked at him with the rest of that smile in her eyes, a smile she held back until he chucked her beneath the chin and turned it into laughter. She leaned against him with her small breasts pressed against his chest, didn't ask anything, just drank him in as if he was water and she was parched with thirst. When she rose from the bed, she wrapped her robe around herself tightly.

"Do me a favor," he said as he left, "Don't go to that bar anymore."

"Okay," she said.

I shouldn't have asked that. It could make her think things. What? Things I don't want her to think, things I'm not ready to have her think, might never be ready to have her think.

Still, as he closed the door, he thought of taking her sometime to meet his sisters and his brothers. She belonged with nice people. His sisters were nice people.

Changes

Amanda began to change. She dressed in big, baggy pants and T-shirts, never bothered with make-up, and walked with her head and shoulders held high as if whatever had been on her back had fallen off. She began to sound proud of herself. And Tadziu began to change. Without thinking about it, without noticing how natural it had become, he spent more and more time with her.

On a weekend, he took Amanda and Jimmy to a circus, a three-ring affair that made Tadziu tired about half-way through. All the acts began to look the same but Jimmy was so excited he couldn't sit still.

"Look dad, look," he yelled, pulling at Tadziu, and then at Amanda on the other side. Amanda also acted excited and Tadziu could tell it wasn't just to please him. She liked the circus. And she liked watching it with Jimmy. If he pointed at something, she pointed at something else. In a between-the-acts diversion, clowns ran in and did all sorts of clown things. One was hopping on one foot.

"Look Amanda look, his shoe's on fire!" Jimmy yelled. Amanda's eyes grew wide with amazement. She looked intently and in the next second, placing her hand under Jimmy's chin, turned his head in the other direction and shouted, "The firemen are coming, Jimmy. Look." The clown firemen took out big hoses and squirted the fire but only small spurts of water came out. The crowd roared with laughter as the clown's foot continued to smoke and he hopped from one foot to the other. The clown walked over to the firemen, silently complained and pointed at his burning foot. The firemen listened and aimed the hose at the clown again. This time, a large stream of water knocked the clown over.

Jimmy was hysterical with laughter, but Tadziu became fidgety and wished the acts would move faster.

"Look Dad look," Jimmy cried, pointing at another clown but Tadziu didn't answer. He could feel Amanda's eyes. With her arm on Jimmy's shoulder, they turned together toward the ring just beginning its act.

Why does he have to jump up and down like that? She's picking up my feelings. She knows how impatient I am, knows I know it too and that I know it's wrong to be like this with my kid.

Jimmy put his arm around Amanda's waist and they watched the string of horses prancing around the ring, their backs covered with colorful blankets and ballerinas balancing on their toes. Jimmy was speechless. "Wow!" was the only word he said, over and over again until Tadziu thought he was going to scream. Jimmy moved closer to Amanda.

Shit. Does the kid know? That his old man's got no patience?

Amanda watched every movement with Jimmy.

Jesus, how does she do it?

The smell of animals and peanuts filled the tent, seemed enough to make it topple over, like a paper kite in a high wind. A man came down the aisle yelling. "Kot tun. Kan dee. Get your kottun kandee here." Surrounded by the sugary smell, Tadziu felt his stomach doing flips. It was almost as bad as a hangover.

"Oh dad, can we get some, please, please?" and Tadziu groaned.

"Sure Jimmy." As if he had ears all over his head, the guy appeared in the row before them and seemed on top of them.

"Come around here please," Amanda said to the man, and he moved to the end of the row of seats and stood in the aisle. She ordered two and Tadziu passed her the money, a ridiculous sum, he thought, for garbage. Amanda gave one to Jimmy and began eating the second one. With a puzzled face, Jimmy looked at his father who didn't have one, but then turned back to the excitement of the ring. Amanda ate all of hers and Jimmy kept eating, but slowly, so that the blue and red sugar began to dissolve and run in a stream down his chin.

"I don't want anymore, Amanda," Jimmy said, handing her the no longer recognizable concoction. She told him that was okay, took the gooey mess and folded it into a tiny package that she threw beneath the seat. Then she reached into her purse and produced some magical wet thing, a cloth wrapped in an old plastic bread wrapper. She used the cloth to wash Jimmy's hands and face. He bent over to let her do this without taking his eyes from the horses and their riders. Tadziu asked her where she got the idea for that.

"I always carry one with me," she answered. "It comes in handy."

"I'll say," Tadziu said, with appreciation in his voice, and she looked away from him the way she did lately when she was proud of herself.

As they walked to the car, Jimmy slept on Tadziu's shoulder. Inside the car, Tadziu handed him to Amanda and she held him until they reached Mary's place.

A little too much circus I guess," he said to Mary and with no acknowledgement to Amanda, she asked him to carry Jmmy into his room.

She might be silent because Jimmy's asleep and she doesn't want to wake him. Nah, who the hell do I think I'm kidding?

"Good-bye dad," Jimmy murmured in a voice rapidly fading. "See you next week." Then he was out like a light.

As he and Amanda walked back to the car, Tadziu didn't know how to break the awkward silence, didn't know what to say about the way Mary acted. He couldn't figure it out. Mary was usually so polite. Amanda spoke first.

"It's okay, Tadz," she said. "I understand. You can't do anything about it." Tadziu was so grateful he could have jumped into the air. Amanda was thoughtful, then said, "She loves you."

Tadziu was puzzled. Bad. "No. she doesn't," he said, louder than he meant to..

"Yes, she does."

"Look Amanda," Tadziu began, "she's told me at least a hundred times that she doesn't, that it's over, done, kaput." He was prepared to argue but Amanda changed the subject.

"He's the best kid," she said and with a relieved sigh, Tadziu just said, "Yeah." He wasn't up to the subject of Mary. Not after the circus and clowns and cotton candy. He wondered what was so funny that Amanda started to smile to herself, like a little kid with a secret. "Men!" she uttered mysteriusly, and Tadziu kept quiet, didn't ask what she meant.

Tadziu slept at Amanda's place because he was tired and driving home would take too much effort. And it was nicer than his place. He watched as she undressed, saw how changed she was from the girl he had met in the bar. Her hair was cut short like a boy's so you could see more of her face, a face in which you were forced to look at the eyes. They no longer made her look as if she was about to cry. Now they held laughter, laughter that poured forth from someplace deep within where it had been hiding, waiting to break free, and change her look from sadness to happiness.

She came from the bathroom wearing a large white towel. Looking at her made him feel dirty so he also cleaned up, relaxed as he lay back in the tub, thinking of how he wanted to kiss her all over when he got into the bed. But she was sleeping.

"I love you," she murmured. Just like Jimmy. And just like Jimmy, she went out big time.

"Okay kiddo," he said, kissing her shoulder. "catch you in the morning." He thought she smiled and he lay there watching her. She looked so young. He thought about her stories of the foster homes, of never knowing her own family.

She needs someone. She's lonely, not strong like Mary. Hell, I have to live. I'll never hurt her. I could take care of her. The way I should've taken care of Mary.

A Coward

The thought that he should be more responsible toward Amanda kept returning to him all week. It began to frighten him. The next weekend he didn't take her with him when he went for Jimmy. Made some excuse when she looked at him. Tried not to see the hurt in her eyes.

At Mary's, he sat at the kitchen table and waited while she said good-night to Jimmy. He looked around the kitchen as he had done so many times since he'd started coming and saw how neat it was, how it had only the basics, nothing extra.

She's still making the best of things, working and trying to furnish her house, doesn't see that she could have it easier with me. I've got a decent job. I could pay for her house. She wouldn't even have to work. I'm a real creep. I'd be with her in a minute if she'd have me. And leave Amanda behind. I don't like being a creep. I want to stop thinking about Mary. No, I don't. That's a lie. Her blouse pulled tight across her boobs that way is enough to get me going. It's not the same with Amanda. I've never left Mary. She's always there. In my head. I'm a real creep.

"Mary," he began, not knowing how to say it again. She knew. "Okay, it's no secret. I want to come back to you and Jimmy. Will it ever happen?"

She turned her face, as if she could not look at him. "I don't want to hurt you, Tadziu." The way she said it made him believe her. She wasn't the one dragging him through all of it again. He was. He knew what she'd say next, but her "no" was quiet, almost a whisper. She didn't turn, stood there as if frozen.

I'm the one frozen, Mary. My beautiful Mary, my Marysza. Frozen in time. The time with you. It'll never change.

He closed the door behind him. That night, Tadziu told Amanda about his childhood, about his father. About how his father hated him. About how he hated his father. She listened and concentrated hard, then wrapped her arms around his neck. "I hate him too," she said.

Another Change

He didn't notice, wasn't aware of how it happened, and when he did notice, didn't understand it. Happiness crept in from somewhere and settled in a corner of his consciousness. He never believed in happiness. Things just happened the way they happened. Some things were good and some things were bad. That was all.

But the entry of Amanda into his life didn't n seem like an accident. It was like something that had been planned. That was crazy. That would mean the day he walked into the bar and sat next to her was meant to happen. That was crazy. Wasn't it? He'd be thinking like a woman if he believed that. He shook his head. He didn't know anything anymore.

A Visit

"Ma," he tried to tell her, "you don't have to stay with him anymore. Helen and Jerry want you to come and live with them. In California. They have a nice house and you'd have your own room." She listened to him but he knew it was useless.

He saw himself filling his mother's eyes. They took him in, the way a sponge absorbed water. Her eyes no longer had that frightened look. They were that blue he never could describe, not the blue of sky or water, but blue that made him think of peace, of safety, like knowing the moon would come out each night and the sun would come up each day. It was the color of his thoughts when he thought about Jimmy or Amanda or Steve or Joe.

He thought about Amanda a lot lately but never stopped thinking about Mary. He remembered what she had said about loving two guys. But still, there had to be one who was the most important. He felt like a little kid taunting another kid, trying to outdo him, saying, "I'm better than you are" or "she loves me best." He wished he loved Amanda best. He wished Amanda wasn't smart. She never said it but he knew she understood about Mary. Since she had come into his life, his love for Mary had moved to a different place, still part of him, something that was always there but, like breathing, something he didn't concentrate on. He thought again how it was necessary that she always be there, that he wouldn't exist, would disappear if his mother or Mary didn't exist. He had to know they were somewhere, even though he wasn't with them.

His mother's hair was now streaked with gray, although the blonde was so light he almost didn't notice. She still wore it wound into a bun behind her head. Her waist was gone. She no longer tied her housedresses at the back but let the ties hang loose at her sides. She walked in a way Tadziu didn't remember, shuffled along as if she could not pick up her feet. Her ankles looked swollen. Small knobs of flesh sat on the knuckles of the fingers that Tadziu remembered as long and graceful.

Oh ma, ma, where are you? Am I so dumb to think you would never change, would never grow old?

She wouldn't listen to his talk about California. "And what about your father?" she asked, and Tadziu couldn't answer.

You know none of them will take him, ma.

She held Tadziu's face in her hands and looked into his eyes, wanting, he knew, to change the subject.

"And you, *moj*[45] Tadziu, is there a wife yet for you?" She told Tadziu things he had never heard before. That his father and she had been about this age when they married and came from the old country. Life there was so hard. Never enough to eat. No money no matter how hard you worked because landowners took it all in taxes. Life was so good in America. They thought there would be nothing but happiness here. When Tadziu asked what happened, if his father was always the way he was, she only said that his father was the oldest of five sons and worked on his father's farm. Her face fell. "Jego ojczym byl niedobry,"[46] she said, and would say no more.

Ojczem. Stepfather. Okay. So what? His stepfather was mean to him. It's no use to push for any more. Why am I asking these questions? Thinking of these things makes her tired, unhappy.

She made Tadziu sit in a chair so she could bring him food. He became impatient, couldn't remember what he'd told himself, couldn't stop his mouth, said more than he wanted to say, knowing even as his words left him that he was sorry for them.

"Ma, I don't want you to wait on me. I want to know why you stayed with him."

Why am I hurting you, making you face what I suffered, what I can't forget.

She looked at him as if she didn't understand the question. She didn't.

I know your thoughts, ma. How could a woman leave her husband? How could these words be coming from your son?

She looked past him, her voice patient, falling into the Polish she used whenever she was nervous.

"Your father worked hard. Babies came. The country was poor. Everyone was poor. It was hard to pay bills, to buy food. Many men couldn't work. Your father had a job. The boss kept him because he worked so hard."

"He wasn't good to you ma. He wasn't good to us. To me." She turned away, looked at the wall, pretended she didn't hear. He knew she was finished, wouldn't talk anymore. She brought meat and potatoes from the refrigerator, and began to heat them. "Ma, I don't want to eat. I'm not hungry." She wouldn't listen, stirred the food vigorously, placed a plate of pork chops and boiled potatoes, all covered with onions, before him, sitting on the other side of the table, watching, waiting for him to start eating. Tadziu couldn't taste anything, but he sat and ate while she watched him, her face telling him that she thought everything would be all right, that the food would make it all right, would take away all his questions.

You don't know, ma, that things are changing. You couldn't know. You never went anywhere, never talked to anyone except the old man. Women leave their husbands now. Women like Mary don't stay with a man like my father. You're not like Mary.

His thoughts tired him. His feelings confused him. He was giving Mary credit for her guts. Still, he had to be fair. Not many women were like her. Most women, at least poor Polish women born into the old-world ways, never thought of leaving their husbands, no matter how bad they were. They just shut up and took everything. Like his mother. And they always, always served food to whoever came to their home. It was a good sign she was serving food again. Not fading into darkness like she was when he was a kid.

When he had downed every last morsel of food, his mother took his hand and pulled him into the bedroom. It was so dark he couldn't see. They never wasted electricity because his old man yelled about that. His mother knew exactly where to find what she wanted. She took a picture from her drawer, a picture that was old and brown. Tadziu took the picture to the window. He could make out the two of them, his father, young and looking uncomfortable, wearing a suit that was too tight, looking into the camera, probably not seeing very much because he wasn't wearing glasses. His mother stood beside him, smiling a shy smile, holding his arm. Now she stared at the picture as if she had stared at it a thousand times before, placed it flat on the table and pressed it with her hand to straighten the creases.

She knows I've never seen this. Am I supposed to tell her something?

"You see," her eyes said as they studied his face, "you see the answer to what you ask, how handsome he was, how good he was. You see the man I married." Tadziu saw what he knew, what he didn't want to know.

She loved the bastard.

He asked no more questions. It was too complicated for him to understand. He'd never understand.

A Phone Call

It was a month later that the phone rang, took him from his sleep and filled him with dread. Phone calls didn't come in the middle of the night unless they were bad. Unless it was some drunken bastard dialing a wrong number. He knew it wasn't. It was Helen. Crying.

"Tadziu, it's ma She's sick." He sucked in his breath, hard, saw the clock on the table next to his bed, crooked because one of its metal legs was broken, his dirty socks on the floor where he'd left them. He had the desperate hope that seeing all the ordinary things would make everything normal, would make the phone call and his sister's crying go away. He always knew it would be like this, somewhere inside himself had always been waiting.

I'm not ready. I'll never be ready.

It didn't matter that he never saw his mother much. She was always there in the back of his head. That was the thing that tied him to everything else.

Now I'm going to float free, get thrown around with no mooring, no anchor. Mama. mama. Wait for me. I'm coming, mama. I'm coming.

He drove for three hours, was the first one to get to the hospital. The others were on their way. As far as he could figure, his father had called the landlord when his mother collapsed and the landlord called an ambulance.

His mother was a long thin body under white sheets. How could she be so thin? The veins on her hands stood out like roads. The lids of her eyes were closed like shades. When she opened her eyes and saw him, she tried to put her arms around him the way she used to do when he was small and his father had been at him. Now she needed protection. From what was coming. From what they all knew was coming.

He couldn't let her see he was scared. She thought he was strong. Since Gina's wedding, they all thought he was strong.

"They said that radiation and chemotherapy would give her a little more time Tadziu, but it would cost her so much in pain. It's not worth it," Helen said, searching his face for agreement. He nodded.

The next few hours were loud in the way that whispers could be loud when everyone was arriving. Gina with her new husband, Michael, her eyes red and swollen from crying, Tommy and Albert, their eyes also red, Helen's husband, Jerry, in the background, quiet, shaking his hand again.

"Where's the old man?" Tadziu asked Helen.

"At home," she said. "He wouldn't come. Jerry and I tried to bring him but he wanted no part of it."

"Nie. Nie,"[47] he kept saying, as if he was begging us not to drag him here." Tadziu could just see him, his eyes, whatever they felt, impossible to read, so small and black, sunk into his head like the eyes on the side of a lizard's head. "He's scared," Helen said.

"Who cares," Tadziu said to himself, louder than he thought. He sat by the bed next to his mother, with Helen on the other side. Helen bent down and kissed her. His mother kept her eyes on Tadziu, kept repeating, "Moj synek, moj synek," [48] and reaching toward him with her thin arms, over and over again, as if she'd forgotten she'd already embraced him. He went to her each time. But she couldn't hold him for long. Her arms shook, trembled like small tree branches in a storm, loose skin hanging from them like white sheets on a line. Knobs protruded from her elbows, like they protruded from her ankles the last time he saw her. He let himself be held, let her wrap her arms around his face, became a boy, once again felt his desperate helplessness. His mother brushed the hair back from his forehead and kissed him. Last kisses, fervent kisses.

"Mama, mama," was all he could say, all he could think. Her name, her face filled him.

His brothers and sisters let him be first, stood behind him and waited. "She loved you most," said Janek, in a voice free from resentment. No one else spoke. Their agreement was silent.

She loved me best. Her first son. I know it, always knew it. Whenever I taste a woman's body, whenever there's Mary, or Amanda, I'm there with them because of her, because of mama. All other loves come from that first love, her love for me. Now she talks only in Polish. I don't understand all the words. I've forgotten so much. But I understand her saying she's sorry. She says it many times. She can't say what she's sorry for. I don't think she knows how.

Then, in a look as swift as lightning, her eyes told him that she knew, and he saw that the sorrow for it had always been there, a huge stone inside her, its sharp edges cutting her into pieces. Now, like the rest of her, the pain and sorrow were fading. The darkness outside the hospital window began to threaten them all. His mother spoke but so quietly he could barely hear her. She said he must forgive. Forgive? He'd forgiven her a long time ago. And then some words in Polish about not letting him die alone.

The old man. She was talking about the old man.

He pushed it away.

"Mama. Mama," he cried, tried to tell her in Polish, whatever Polish words he could remember, that he knew everything, that he did forgive her. He said nothing about the old man. He couldn't. He couldn't. Helen came and touched his arm

All right, all right, goddammit.

He bent down and in the best Polish he could remember, told his mother he forgave the old man too. Her eyes looked at him as if she were kissing him for the last time.

Mama. Mama. Don't go. Don't go.

He lay his head on her chest, held the hands that were cold, their skin like paper, and wept, felt the front of her white hospital gown turning wet from his tears—his mama, who could never help him, but wanted to, because she loved him—told her again and again that he forgave her. And his father too.

Mama, mama.

"Moj synek," she whispered again, her face relaxing at his words, because of his words, as if she had waited for them, and holding his hands in her own, she kissed them. Kissed his hands, and closed her eyes.

Mama. Mama.

Her hands fell. Everyone behind him was crying, touching him on the shoulder, holding him, as if he'd fall. Helen cried quietly. Gina sobbed uncontrollably. He turned around and held her. His brothers came closer. They all stood together. They all held each other.

Another Visit

It was six months' after his mother's funeral when Tadziu remembered his mother's words about the old man. He hadn't made any promises but he didn't know if his mother had understood that, didn't know what she'd understood. He tried to forget the old man but he couldn't. On the weekend, he went to the old flat where he'd grown up, where his parents had remained. Helen had asked him if he wanted her to come but he told her he could handle it.

He stood there, looked at the decaying building, at he bricks loosened from their mortar, so that some hung at various angles in the wall, and some looked as if they might fall at any minute. There were four or five flats in the building but from the outside it was impossible to tell in which part of the building they were located. All the windows were the same—- long, double-hung, some cracked. A small portable screen, the kind that fit into the bottom of a window, had become caught by a loose piece of metal at its corner after the window was closed. It swung back and forth in the wind like a rusty wing that would never fly. Paint the color of mud peeled from the window frames and the doors. Tadziu didn't remember it looking this bad. Taking a deep breath, he went inside, steeling himself against the hatred he expected to feel. He felt only an old, familiar fear, told himself he was crazy, that there was no reason anymore to be afraid. The fear had become a habit, was carved into him somewhere, like a scar from an old wound.

The same brown paint that peeled on the outside of the house peeled from all the wood inside. He knocked on his father's door but there was no answer. He tried the doorknob. It opened. That was not like the old man. He kept everything locked up tight. The empty kitchen smelled the way it once did, before his mother was sick, like potatoes and cabbage boiling on the stove, transforming themselves into steam that traveled into every corner.

Where's the old man? He must be in the bedroom.

Tadziu opened the door to the bedroom and looked in.

His father lay on the bed with his eyes closed, his legs stretched out, one arm thrown over his face. The covers lay crumpled at the foot of the bed, as if it were too much effort for him to reach for them. There was no snoring, the kind Tadziu heard coming from the bedroom when he was a kid. In those days, his father worked every day, long days. He was gone before Tadziu got up for school. On the days Tadziu loved best, his father came home late, after they had eaten supper and gone to bed. Now his father lay in an old man's sleep, not the sleep that followed the fatigue of a day's work but a restless sleep that waited for something late in coming.

Tadziu closed the bedroom door and looked around the kitchen. He saw little mounds of unknown dirt piled into the corners. Spills that were now dry and sticky, who knows how old, formed a glaze covering the pieces of linoleum that were slapped onto the painted wood in the pantry and served as countertops. A utensil that looked like a fork was stuck in some oil that had congealed in a pan on the stove. He remembered when his mother was sick and she lost interest in the place. At its worst, it never looked like this.

Tadziu heard a noise behind him and turned to see his father. Neither of them spoke. Tadziu stared. The old man had shrunk or something, was stooped over like he was carrying something on his back. His black greasy hair was now white and didn't look greasy anymore. Kind of powdery and thin, as if, like the rest of him, it had begun to disappear. He wore the same slippers Tadziu remembered him putting on when he came home from work. All those years. Everyday. The same slippers. But they had once been blue and red corduroy with some kind of pattern, flowers or something. Tadziu had always known they were women's slippers, that his mother had bought them in the five and dime, without knowing. And his father wore then because she gave them to him. Tadziu wanted to say, "Hey stupid old man, do you know you've been wearing women's slippers all these years." But he didn't say it. Bitterness rose in his throat like something that tasted bad. Pity wrestled with the bitterness, and, for one moment, made him angry with himself.

His father's small eyes were rimmed with red, as if he'd been crying. Tadziu knew he didn't cry. Not ever. The eyes watched him, pierced his back as he walked to the table and deposited the bag of groceries he had stopped on the way to buy, just in case. "Nie nie," his father said but the voice was small. Tadziu ignored him. He half-expected the old man to knock the bag of groceries to the floor. He walked to the door, glad that his job was over, turned around once more and looked at the old man, wanting to say something, but he couldn't.

You bastard, I heard the same words from your mouth all those years. Always at ma. Or me. That she was stupid. That I was no good. Ma and me. The others sometimes. But not as bad. You never hit ma but you blamed her for everything in your life including us kids. You hit me plenty.

The bitterness came again and filled Tadziu's eyes so he couldn't see, could see only the picture of himself trying to shield himself from the old man's fists. Trying to run. Trying to hide. Which he did most of the time, but sometimes couldn't.

Helen hit you once, pounded you with her small fists, screamed for you to leave me alone. And you grabbed her, raised your hand. But you didn't hit her. That one moment was enough time for me to run away. And for your anger to run out. Helen found me and cried with me. Under our breath, we called you all the swear words we knew. Only yesterday. Helen and me sitting on the floor together in the bedroom. What a little tough she was. Survived it all. We all survived. You old bastard, we all survived. Even me. It was close. But even me. I lost Mary. But I got Jimmy back. And now there's Amanda. Who have you got, old man? Who cares whether you live or die?

He wanted to scream these words at his father. Wanted to see pain in his face. He looked around once more at the ugly place his father lived in, the place where they'd all once lived.

We don't live here anymore old man. You live here all alone, all by your fuckin' self.

He closed the door and left.

"Tadziu," Helen said to him over the phone, "he's there all alone."

"Yeah, so?" He didn't know what she wanted from him.

"He never leaves the house. I know he never leaves the house. Mama told me. She used to get all the groceries and tried to keep the place clean. Even though she was sick. The house was bad then, ma said. And she's gone now. He's going to die there, all alone." She was quiet, waiting for him to say something.

"Yeah, so?" Her voice began to sound tired.

"He's our father. Ma told me. She told you. We promised something."

"What? What did we promise, Helen?"

"I don't know, but you know what she meant. She didn't want him to die there alone."

"Jesus, you don't want much do you?"

"It's not me. She wanted it. And I don't know, maybe I do too." Tadziu snickered. Helen sounded as if she was going to cry.

"It's a lot to put on you. But I'm not there. Gina's not there. Tommy and Albert said they'd take turns with you. Looking in on him. Once a week. Just do it. I'll come in when I can. Gina will come in when she can. About once a month. Her husband says they can manage. We promised her, Tadziu." Tadziu didn't remember any promise, but he knew Helen wouldn't bring things out of nowhere.

Fuck.

In the deepest part of himself, he knew they'd have to do something about the old man.

Why me? Because ma loved me best? So she put this on me. She knew I'd do it. Mama. Mama. I hate him. Why'd you do this to me? This is hard. I love you, ma, but I want to be free. Free of him. Of him. What did I promise you? I don't know. I only know how much I hate him.

Tadziu went to the house again two weeks later. He could tell that Tommy and Albert had been there and tried to clean up some things. The floor looked as if it had been mopped. There were no dirty dishes in the sink. The old man didn't want to take the groceries again but he objected less than the first time. Tadziu plopped the bags on the table and left. But the picture of the old man stayed in his head like something burned into his brain. He seemed even smaller, thinner than before.

Every day another piece of him disappears. Everyday he becomes more of a shadow.

Helen came into town and stayed with the old man for a week. Tadziu went everyday because she was there.

Tadziu looked around more than he had when he came alone and only wanted to get out fast. The house seemed dead, the life that once sat inside things, even old things—the upholstered chairs with their worn seats and arms, the lace curtains with their holes, the lamp with its crooked shade—all were gone. The old crib still sat in his parent's bedroom, untouched, a knitted yellow blanket folded and hanging over the rail, as if some baby were going to return and occupy it again. The room Tadziu shared with his brothers was the same as he remembered it, the only piece of furniture a big iron bed rammed against the wall, the wooden hooks they had hung their clothes on protruding from the opposite wall.

"Do you know what he's doing," Helen asked and ignored Tadziu's answer that he didn't know and he didn't care. "He's saving his social security checks. They're all in a drawer, uncashed. The landlord says he hasn't paid the rent in about a year, long before mama died, but he felt sorry for him so he let him stay."

The guy probably couldn't have budged him anyway," Tadziu laughed. Helen didn't laugh, never laughed at his comments anymore, just continued what she was saying.

"I tried telling him the checks were for rent and food and things he needed but he wouldn't listen. The only food he eats is what we bring him, Tadziu. He's going to have to go into a home. He can't make it alone."

Okay, she's starting to irritate me. What do I care if the old man eats or not? Or if he piles up checks in a drawer. He's loony.

On his next visit, the flat was dark, as if morning had never come. A sour smell filled the air. Tadziu didn't want to go in.

The old man was lying on his bed in the same clothes he'd been wearing the last time Tadziu was there. He looked at Tadziu with indifferent eyes.

That's fine, old man. You don't care about me and I don't care about you. I'll do what they want me to do. Report on what I see.

When Gina called him, he told her the old man was a mess. Dirty. Not even walking around. Albert called and talked to Tadziu like Tadziu was some kind of manager, as if he was in charge.

"Hey, what d'ya think, Tadz? He sure ain't good. What d'ya think?"

Tadziu wanted to say, "What d'you mean what do I think? I think I'm sick of this and I don't want to see him anymore." But he said. "I think that's the way he's gonna be. He belongs in a home. He can't make it by himself."

So Helen dealt with the county and did all the official stuff. Thank God she knew about things like that. He sure as hell didn't. And came back so they could take him to the home together.

They went to the flat on a Saturday but Helen said they couldn't take him the way he was. So Taziu had to carry the old man to the bathtub, carry him in his arms like a baby and strip him of his clothes. Thank God, his sister was a nurse. She could wash him. He didn't want to look at the white skin, at the ribs sticking out like stairs that some bird could walk on. The nails on the old man's hands and feet were long and yellow but the skin was even whiter than the rest of him, as if the blood had been drained.

He must be cold. Goose bumps cover him all over. But he won't complain. He won't say anything. He knows it's me. He won't look at me. He knows it's me.

The old man let them immerse him in the water. Tadziu and Helen both washed him, Helen with a kind of professional detachment, Tadziu squeamishly at first because he had to touch him. When he got into it, he scrubbed hard, maybe too hard because the old man winced and Helen looked at Tadziu with one of her silent looks, a look that told him she was not pleased.

Tadziu smiled to himself.

She's a supervisor. She probably looks at the nurses that way when they do something wrong.

He wrapped the old man in a towel and then a blanket. Helped his sister to pull on the new underwear and socks she had brought with her. The old bastard still had his own teeth. Helen thought they should clean them but they couldn't figure out how to do it. When they gave him the supplies, the old man knew what they wanted and he brushed his teeth, slowly, methodically, and spit into a pan.

Tadziu carried him to his chair in the living room, next to the gas heater where they all used to run on cold winter mornings to get dressed. He turned the gas up high so the old man could get warm. But the heater did not look the same either, the orange and yellow flame not as bright. When Tadziu covered him with another blanket, the old man looked him squarely in the eye and said "Dziekuje."[49] Helen heard it. She said nothing, knew that Tadziu didn't want her to say anything. Tadziu looked down, tried to straighten the old man's legs in the chair, tried not to think of the words he'd never heard from his father, of all the times he had wished for anything from him that would tell Tadziu he was glad Tadziu was his son. He looked up now to see his father's face covered with wordless confusion, his hands waving excitedly in the air.

"What the hell's his problem?" Tadziu said to Helen and then understood. It was the sign of the cross. The old man was making the sign of the cross in the air, blessing Tadziu.

Jesus. As if nothing's ever happened. As if he doesn't remember how much he hated me. As if God could make everything okay, could make things different from what they were.

Later, his sister told him he should start thinking of forgiving his father. "That's bullshit," said Tadziu, feeling betrayed.

The old man sat wrapped in his blanket by the gas heater, with his tiny bird-like eyes staring at everything Tadziu and Helen were doing, watching them sort his clothes, moving forward slightly each time they threw something into the garbage box, as if he wanted to drag it back. He fell asleep, holding onto the blanket, looking like a baby wrapped tightly in winter, his head covered, his eyes closed.

He would almost fit into the crib. A baby in the crib again.

They cleaned everything and paid the landlord.

"All those checks in the drawer. It's a shame he didn't cash them," Helen said. Tadziu thought they would get sent back, or the home would take them. He didn't care. He wanted nothing that belonged to the old man. Not even money.

"You should cash them and split the money," he told his sister. There's got to be a way to do it. Gina could use it. Tommy and Albert could use it. The old man owes them that." His sister's silence told him she agreed with him. Before they left for the home, she managed to get his father to sign all the checks and somehow cashed them. They paid the landlord everything their father owed.

"He must be a good man, Tadziu. He looked surprised, like he didn't expect to get anything." Tadziu nodded.

When it was all over, the old man in the nursing home, and Helen and he back to their lives, Tadziu smiled every time he thought of Gina, Tommy and Albert getting their unexpected windfall.

Chapter Thirteen)

1967

The Longest Days

Waiting

It had started with Uncle Ben. A simple phone call asking if he could come over for a while.

"Of course, Uncle Ben. You don't need to ask."

Something told her the visit concerned her mother. Poor Uncle Ben. Always the messenger. Overcome by anxiety and uncertainty, she tried to prepare herself. Uncle Ben sat at the table and reached to hold her hands.

I love you, Uncle Ben. Close to my mother, bringing her close to me. The blood knows, carries its memories through the body, my body, memories stored before remembering, memories of you, my mother, you whom I loved without knowing, you whom I wish to punish, to hurt, and so hurt myself as I hurt you, I who share your blood, I who know you, who have always known you.

"Mary, for whatever it's worth, I was around when your mother left. I know how she loved your father and how crazy she got when he died."

"Yes but…"

He stopped her by raising his hand. "I know, I know, that doesn't excuse the fact that she left you." He ground his teeth silently. "Never will. But I didn't come here for that."

"Is something wrong, Uncle Ben? With Aunt Irene or the kids?" She heard the word kids as it left her. Barbara was as old as she was, for God's sake, certainly not a kid. She'd done well, received her degree from State College and was teaching second grade. Martha would have been launched on a similar career path if she hadn't become pregnant but she and David were happy with that. Martha gushed each time she saw Mary and never tired of telling her how happy her parents were. Jimmy, Uncle Ben's son, the other "kid," had been accepted to an out-of-state college that specialized in chemistry, always his favorite subject. Mary teased him constantly. "Jimmy, how can you like that stuff? That was the worst grade I ever got." And he'd parry with, "Yeah well, Aunt Mary (he called her "aunt") how can you like that stuff you like, poetry and yuk things like that?"

"No, no, everyone's fine. I came to tell you something I thought you might want to know, even though your mother asked me not to tell you."

Mary sighed but covered her mouth so Uncle Ben wouldn't hear.

How many secrets can she have?

"Mary, when you went away to school, that night we were packing everything, that landlord wouldn't in a million years hold that flat until you returned. In fact, he wanted more money to hold it at all. I discussed it with your mother. She insisted on paying the rent for the time you were gone."

Mary became perplexed, then angry. Why would her mother do that? What did she expect to gain by it?

"You tell her I'll pay back every penny."

Uncle Ben put his fingers gently on her mouth. "No I won't do that. She wanted things to be kept for you the way you left them so it would be easier when you came back. If you want to tell her that, you'll have to do it yourself." His voice was the closest to a reproach May had ever received from him.

The blood knows. She's his blood He can't forget.

She sat there after he was gone. She knew grandma wouldn't approve of the way she had treated her mother. But Uncle Ben too?

He and Aunt Irene would never leave their child. They wouldn't even leave me. I can't tell my mother I'll pay back all the money. I can't throw back her gesture in this bitter way. A child throwing mud. Trying to humiliate her and so dishonoring Uncle Ben. I'm trapped in resentment and never thought of him. He loves her. I'll be left alone with my anger. What do I do about her? My mother?

She placed her head into her hands and tried to pray. She knew God couldn't shut his eyes to her plea and if He tried, Grandma wouldn't let Him.

She tossed and turned that night, seeing the look on her mother's face when Mary told her not to come back, and hearing grandma'a voice. "An' don' be too hard in thinkin' on your mama. Cause she'll be hurtin', real hurtin' in the end." Grandma forgave Elizabeth just as Mary would forgive Jimmy. Because they were mothers. But a child? How much could a child forgive a parent? Parents should act in ways that needed no forgiveness. In that half-sleep, half-awake state in which she was held, she saw the rueful smile that crossed her face and felt the tears that filled her eyes. Such a world didn't exist. Would never exist.

She fell into a sound sleep, her mother's face moving through her dreams as clear as the flow of crystal water. Mary heard words she didn't speak. A wordless knowing settled in her as naturally as the air she breathed

Forgiveness is the essence of blood, a distillation of the life-force. Without it we are paralyzed, kept from the dance. Dead. Life is forgiveness. To live is to forgive. Forever. Without end.

The next morning was unusually cold, even for western New York winters. The radio announced that Mary's school was closed because a boiler had given out. She sat at the kitchen table until she could think no more and the knowing that had come was set within her, no longer uncertain. She went to the telephone.

"Elizabeth, this is Mary." She couldn't use the word mother. Just couldn't. Not yet. "I thought we should meet again."

The house was quiet. Jimmy had gone to school. She went back and sunk into the warmth of her bed. She would work on her papers later.

Two days at home because it's cold and a boiler in school needs fixing

*Time dropped into the days I know, days when I guard and shield myself, when I fill, overfill my mind with what is waiting, always waiting, needing to be done, and my thoughts are kept from breaking free, until they gain strength to emerge and I'm forced to see what I tell myself I can't see, to know what I tell myself I don't know. These will be days when the memories of mind will not rule, will drop into sleep, when the body's memories will prevail, will step forward with their unerring logic, a logic that uncovers what the veil of thinking s*eeks to hide.

Throughout the day, Mary felt memory rolling over her like waves grown too large, and threatening, to immerse her in depths from which she couldn't arise. It was more than the thought of her mother.

Drowning, drowning. I am drowning in memories. The body's memories. The body's memories. A feeling. A touch. A look. Tadziu. Michael. Their faces melding, flowing into each other. Then there is only Tadziu. I've never left him behind.

She wished she could abandon Tadziu like clothing she had outgrown and no longer needed.

Because I know my weakness. The sharp edge of my need. That it can blind and divert me from what I can be for me. I must shut him away.

She held the gloves he had forgotten once when he came to the flat for Jimmy, the gloves which she had packed and brought with all the other things, held them now to her face like dead flowers in which some lingering scent might remain.

She remembered his last visit in the old flat, before Jimmy and she moved to the house, how he looked at her with that look of resignation, and said, "I wish we could get together again," and how she shook her head without saying anything. His next visit with Jimmy was at the new house where he told her he'd be leaving for a trip. Her confusion must have shown because he laughed and said it wasn't that kind of trip.

"I've signed on for Vietnam. They were kind of amazed an old man like me was volunteering. I think they thought I was running away from something but changed their minds. Gave me some tests and said I must be good with machines. I said that I could fix any machine or engine there was, that I got machines in my blood." He said this with pride, then became quiet and stood holding his arms with his elbows crossed.

"Machines and guns must be kind of alike or somethin'. D' you suppose?" She didn't answer, couldn't answer. "They gave me enough shots to last the rest of my life. Made me sick as a dog for a week." She knew he was waiting for her to say something but she couldn't. Anger filled her.

How can he think that his senseless action, his volunteering for the marines will influence me, will make me accept him into my life again?

There was also guilt. She knew she was a part of the decision he had made. She wanted not to care what he did.

"Anyway, I guess they can use guys like me. I don't know how long I'll be in training because after boot camp I go into training for airplane mechanics, helicopter mechanics, I guess. I want to tell Jimmy," he said, in a tone that wasn't uncertain, that told her she should not interfere.

"Yes, of course." she replied.

That was eleven months ago. She looked at the calendar on the wall. He would be leaving soon. Surely he wouldn't leave without seeing Jimmy again, without saying good-bye.

Eleven months ago. Eleven months.

She sat, not knowing what she could do, afraid of her thoughts, her feelings, herself. Her hands trembled and she tossed the gloves to the floor. Dark shadows surrounded her, their heaviness bearing down, compressing the air in the room, making it difficult to breathe and making her afraid, though not of anything she could name. With a sense that had never failed, she felt that something was being set into motion, something determined long ago and now coming to maturity. She looked out the window, half-expecting to see storm clouds descending or a swarm of locusts moving over the house.

She had turned her mother away. She had turned him away many times. Tears filled her eyes, one or two sliding down her face. With a flick of her hand, she brushed them away like pesky flies or mosquitoes. Her initial anger with him had disappeared. Filled with dread, she looked out the window.

Something is going to happen. I know. I just know. Where's Jimmy?

She had long ago recognized that when she felt stressed, when she had troubled thoughts or difficult decisions to make, Jimmy's presence grounded her, made the most painful realities shrink to manageable size.

Where is he? Why is it taking him so long to come home? He's probably with his friends.

She thought again of how she was not one of the normal mothers, how she could not be here after school as she was today. Her child was alone. In the next moment, she saw that thought was nonsense. Jimmy did fine when she worked, was probably better because of it. The Schottenhamps loved him as if he were their own, spoiled him, she knew, but nevertheless provided another influence besides her own overly-maternal one. His school reports were excellent.

He has strength, his own strength. I've seen it.

Yesterday Mary watched him from the window when he didn't know she was watching, watched him banter with the girls and exchange confidences with the boys. She heard him laugh, saw how at ease, how right he was with his friends, how comfortably he fit into his life. She had done something right. Now she waited to hear his voice.

She was frightened at the foreboding which held her in its grip and tried to believe she had the power to disperse it. Like a wheel stopped by an object in its path, she felt her body pause. She looked in the mirror, and with an automatic gesture, pushed the hair back from her forehead. And for some reason she didn't understand, her anxiety began to fade, transforming itself into curiosity, almost anticipation.

What's coming? What am I waiting for?

She saw her eyes no longer looked frightened. They were sharp and clear, searching for the invisible thing she couldn't name but knew was there. Her hands stopped trembling. She placed one into the other and felt pleasure at contemplating her long fingers and the sheen on her nails. She felt lighter, as if discarding a weight that had been tied to her shoulders. She breathed deeply, concentrating as the air entered, filling her with its sharp, clean life, then departed, leaving its energy behind.

Why does peace fill me now?

Then she knew. Of course she knew. He stood in the doorway, his presence filling the room, absorbing her.

I haven't seen *the changes in him.*

His face in the semi-darkness was the face she remembered, held the same tenderness it always had, a tenderness that was almost reverence. But it also held a new confidence, a confidence not arrogant but one that simply stated his certainty in who he was. His arm brushed her and his hand came to rest over hers. He held it there and looked at her intently. She didn't move it away.

She settled into the sight of him like a bird finding a familiar path after it has circled endlessly, depleting its strength, then discovering the route it has always travelled. His eyes drew her into himself, told her what she knew, what she had always known. She was tired of resisting, of trying to forget her beginning. He reached for her and she forgot thinking, settled into him with silent relief. She felt the thick, curly hair on his arms, touched the prickly black hairs growing on the back of his neck. The taste of his mouth was a taste she'd never forgotten.

Because they were in the living room with its cushion of carpet, he drew her to the floor, and for a moment, she was hesitant and shy, until that passed as the years had passed, disappeared into the ribbon of pain that trailed behind those years. Her arm caught in the shoulder of her blouse and he helped her remove it, touching her carefully, slowly, as if she might be hurt. She shivered at the sudden cold against her skin. He saw and said in a low, husky voice, "You're cold," while he rubbed her arms and her legs with his hands and enclosed her in himself.

"Are you warmer?"

She told him she was and drew herself tighter against him. She saw his hair had a few strands of gray, and that the exposed muscles on his arms were as firm as they had been when he worked in the factory.

He remembered how to please her. Years of days and nights, of denying her the right to think of him were concentrated into this one night.

"I love you," he said and she did not answer at first because from force of habit, she was afraid of what it might mean. But she knew she would always love him, and the words broke from her like a flood, a release of pressure, a dam cracking wide at its center.

"I love you, Tadziu. I love you." Her words were covered, lost in the insistence of his mouth, his tongue. They moved to the bed. And so the night was spent.

That was the last time she'd seen him. Now she sat at the table correcting student compositions, trying to direct her thoughts, to pull them away from thoughts of that last time, that night they had spent together. When he was a different man. Yet the same.

The last time. The last time. The words interjected themselves between the words of her students' sentences, repeated themselves like a line of long-forgotten poetry. The last time. The last time. She closed her eyes, willing the lines of his profile, the strength of his arms to become present. She saw his face when he held her that night, saw it speak silently of the strength in his knowledge and wished she had that same knowledge, that assurance she had always known he possessed, that lay beneath his doubts and carried him through his worst days. She had only an imitation, a half-knowledge she was ashamed to admit.

His eyes had been clear, accepting, telling her he knew their making love did not mean finality, did not mean the question separating them had been answered, but no longer concerned him, that he loved her through all her feelings, whatever they were or would become.

"I'll always love you," he had whispered. That night. That last time. She wanted to live that night again, wanted him to be here, for them to come together again, easily, naturally, as if they'd never been apart, as if the years had not happened, and they could return to their first knowing of each other.

She looked out the window and thought how sad it looked, an early evening at winter's end. Unsure, the remaining rays of light hit the tops of the trees and fell searching to the ground. The door slammed and broke her thoughts. Jimmy ran into the room, his face lit with excitement, an excitement that had been there ever since Tadziu had told him he was leaving for Vietnam. She didn't want to believe what she was again hearing, this time in her son's voice. Again she became angry.

It's the kind of thing he'd do after I turned him away. Leave to fight in Vietnam, leave and try to lose himself in something larger, something more important than he is. Or me.

She twisted a sheet of paper in her hands. Jimmy's voice sounded far away.

"The last time he was here, Mom, Dad said someone had to fight the Communists and it was always Americans who did the fighting." She saw and heard the pride in Jimmy's eyes and voice. "I told that to the other kids. I'm going to tell Miss Borowski, so the class can all write letters to Dad. There's already a homeroom that's writing letters to soldiers." Mary knew he watched for her reaction.

He always watches for my reactions in anything that has to do with his father.

"You should be proud of your father," she said, hearing her words and knowing she meant them. Jimmy's face broke into a wide grin.

"I know," he said, throwing his books on the table, and running from the room. "I'll be at Kyle's." The door slammed behind him.

"Be home by five," she yelled and heard a faint "okay" in reply. She returned to the compositions, remembering the nights years ago, when she had lain in bed, listening to the sounds of beer bottles opening and wishing that Tadziu loved his son. She looked at the wrinkled paper in her hands and wondered what she'd been doing with it. For a moment, she felt the old fear well within her.

How do I know his old anger won't return? Can I ever be sure, really sure of him?

Now she became angry at herself.

She remembered, felt his hand on her back, felt the rise and fall of love that moved between their bodies, and in the same instant, saw him as a boy, sliding on the ice outside her grandmother's window. She saw him after their divorce, walking into the door of the flat when he came to see Jimmy, the way he had of grinning, laughing through the secret pain that only she could see. She saw him in his muddy clothes after Jimmy and he returned from a fishing trip, remembered thinking that the mud didn't seem to bother him the way the dirt from the factory always had.

She knew he'd never fished in his life, remembered him taking Jimmy to buy a pole, tackle and bait, trying to sound as if he knew what he was doing, not wanting to appear stupid, then surrendering to his ignorance and saying to his son, "Hell, it can't be that hard, can it? We're bigger than they are, right?" She remembered the laughter at the end of that day, as she looked in disbelief at their meager catch, how their laughter —Jimmy and she and Tadziu— sounded so natural and free, and she knew that the size of the catch didn't matter, that being together was what the fishing was all about. She was happy.

The picture shifted and she saw herself years before, sitting alone in their flat before Tadziu returned from work, saw herself holding Jimmy as an infant, waiting for the door to open, waiting to hear the tone in his voice, the tone that would dictate the atmosphere in which they lived that night, the tone by which she'd know if the hours would be even and measured, or frightening and unpredictable.

She stared again at the twisted paper in her hand, tried to remember the composition she had just read, told herself that the emotions claiming her—the fear and sorrow and regret—would pass. Jimmy returned, ran into the room like a runaway train, halted abruptly, and stood before her, demanding her attention.

"Hey ma, are you going to write to Dad?" he asked, his tone exasperated, impatient with her, as if he knew she was lost in her own thoughts and it was his responsibility to bring her back to what was important.

"I don't think so," she told him and his eyes opened in disbelief. She corrected her mistake. "I mean, not tonight. Tomorrow. I have too much to do tonight." Jimmy's face remained taut.

"What're you going to say?" Mary felt a smile beginning to form.

There's no way to have privacy when you have a kid like this.

"I'm not sure yet," she said, and watched as the wheels in his head turned, saw him preparing to tell her what to say.

"Tell him you're proud, Ma. Let him think you still love him. Even if you're not sure." She was astounded.

How does he know these things?

Sadness filled her, for her son and the reversal of roles that was taking place, because her child was now the protective parent. She touched his forehead but he moved away.

"Okay, okay," he said, then, in an authoritative voice.

"He's fighting for our country, Mom, just like Ike did." Jimmy belonged to a political events club in school." They'd recently held a debate on the question of which president had performed the most meaningful duties for his country. Jimmy had chosen Eisenhower and had become a veritable expert on the man. His father was receiving a great honor by being placed in the company of "Ike".

"And he's in the Marines, Mom, the toughest guys."

"Okay, okay," she said, imitating her son. "I'll remember. I'll remember."

Again he ran out the door. "Hurry up with your work and write the letter," he called out.

Mary stared at her schoolbag.

There's no way around it. Teachers always have work to bring home. I've never minded it. Why should it be different today?

She opened the bag three times. And closed it three times.

How long will he be gone? How long before I see that look on his face that tells me he still belongs to me?

She took out papers. And tried. Tried to read them. Her mind wouldn't absorb the meaning of the words. She saw Tadziu's hands fumbling nervously with the buttons of her blouse. The schoolbag fell to the floor and scattered its contents. She bent down and slowly, methodically, began gathering them, barely taking note of what her hands were doing.

My work is important. I love being a teacher, feeling that I'm making a difference for kids. I make good money. No one in my family ever had this much money. I never thought I would. This is the way it is, the way of being a woman. I can't have the other things if I want this. If I want me. If I want me.

She saw herself in the early days of her marriage to Tadziu, saw them scrubbing and painting the flat together and knew that nothing she could buy now would please her as much as the cheap curtains and the flowers she'd bought then.

Some of the papers had fallen beneath the table. She looked at them, saw they were white, lifeless things, and did not go after them.

I can't disappoint Jimmy. But what will I say? I must write. Business paper won't do. I must have plain white paper somewhere.

She rose and walked to the desk in the corner. The schoolbag fell to the floor again.

I'm doing this because Jimmy wants me to. Because Jimmy wants me to.

She sat in the chair and held her head in her hands. Sadness engulfed her, reached into her bones, made her shiver with cold.

I know he has someone else. Why wouldn't he? Jimmy's told me about Amanda and how good she is. What can I say? I'm not good. Smart and strong. But not good. Why am I thinking nonsense? I'm different than Amanda. But also good.

She began to write: *Dear Tadziu,* stared at the words, and felt Jimmy behind her, reading over her shoulder, then giggling.

"Great start, Mom. Miss Borowski would be proud of you." Miss Borowski was his English teacher. Mary swatted him playfully on the head.

"I teach English too, you know. To bigger kids than you. Get out of here, you little pot." He ran, turned before he left the room and said, "Hey, all your papers are on the floor." Then he was back, running again, always running, and dropping to his knees, gathered the papers into a patchwork pile and placed them before her on the table.

"Here Mom," he said, his voice subdued, and walked quietly from the room.

She was alone with the letter again. She turned on the teakettle, put a teabag into a cup and waited for the kettle to whistle. The blank paper stared at her. She would write anything, just to get started, and began with:

Jimmy and I are very proud of you, She looked at the words and crossed them out.

I don't know how to sound. I've never had trouble writing before.

She turned as the cat came into the kitchen. Her elbow knocked over the teacup and she watched the tea spill onto the floor and the few stray papers Jimmy had missed. She moved quickly and saved most of them but it took some time to clean up the mess. She'd have to let those papers dry out before correcting them. When she gave them back, she'd explain to the students what happened. They were good kids. They would laugh. She began to write furiously:

I don't know what to say to you. Jimmy is very proud of you and so am I. I pray God keeps you safe. I know how terrible it must be. Some newspapers say we are making great gains but others say this is a war impossible to win and that we shouldn't be there. Everyday there are more protests, more marches. It's hard to know what to believe.

I try to assure Jimmy you're fighting Communists. He's too young to be aware of all the differences people at home are having over this war. The other day he came home with the story of one of his friend's brothers who was drafted but refused to go. The boy's father is a World War II veteran and I think the family is in turmoil. I tried to talk to Jimmy about medical exemptions and conscientious objectors. He seemed to understand everything I was trying to explain. I barely do myself. But I know he thinks the boy's brother is a coward. All he really cares about is his pride in you, your courage in doing what, as a young boy, he thinks is right.

Mary chewed on the edge of her pencil and stared into space.

The night we spent together before you left grows more important to me each day. It brought back the happiness of the early days of our marriage. I loved you very much then. I don't know what my feelings are now. Nor do I know why things happen the way they do. I know Amanda loves you, that you'll marry again and be happy. I want you to be happy. I want you to forget me.

She paused and stared at those last words.

We've become different people. I was honest when I told you I'm not sure I want to be married again. To anyone. I thought my life was satisfying to me. Now I'm confused. Perhaps I no longer believe in happiness, believe only that we must do what we can in order to make the best of things. I hope we can talk when you come home. Mary.

She read the letter over, biting her lip. She read it a second time. Then tore it up.

The next version was little more than a note:

Dear Tadziu:

When I think of us as children, I wish it could be that way forever. I know it can't. Time passes. People change. That makes me afraid. I've never loved anyone as I loved you. I think I always will. I don't know if the love we knew together is enough to overcome the differences that exist now. I simply don't know. I pray God keeps you safe. Mary.

She read that over, tore it up and began again.

A gate that was locked opened and she was set free. Conflicts that had seemed so important melted like ice in the sun. Simple words flowed from her pen like rain, reviving, bestowing new life, life she could feel and for those moments, the world was a simple and beautiful place. She wrote several sentences and read them several times, feeling satisfied as she felt the words drawing him closer.

The letter was short. It ended with the words:

I love you. I always have and always will. I long to be in your arms again. Please return to me, my beloved. Mary.

She sealed and stamped the envelope.

But she wasn't finished. She needed to write another letter. And so she wrote to Michael, told him the truth, that it was Tadziu who claimed her love, Tadziu whom she would rejoin when the war was over. She said all the usual things such letters said, that she would always remember him and hoped they could remain friends.

Jimmy could ride his bike to the mailbox and mail both letters.

She sat at the desk with her eyes closed, her energy drained but the tiredness, a friendly thing, was good, the fatigue one was left with after an important undertaking was completed.

There was no need to mention Amanda. He knows I know about her. He'll know what to do.

She cradled her head in her arms on the table.

Without you, there is nothing, my love, my love, my love.

Chapter Fourteen

1968

Vietnam

Tadziu was anxious and surprised. Why had the Lieutenant Colonel called for him? He was a mechanic, spent his life on the helio pad fixing up his Hueys with as much care as the docs in the field hospitals gave to the guys brought to them, guys bleeding, missing parts, sometimes screaming, wanting to lie down in the dirt and die. Sometimes the Hueys almost seemed alive, coming back to him battered up, their parts screeching, not sounding smooth and easy the way they had when he sent them out. But he worked on them, nursed them until they were good as new again, which was more than he could say for the guys brought in on stretchers.

After emergency treatment in one of the field hospitals, about as lucky as one of them could get was to be sent to a navy hospital ship. Unlucky again was being sent to Japan for R&R so you could be sent back here. When you were knocked up real bad, you went back to the states and a hospital near home.

I guess it depends on your definition of lucky.

Tadziu had seen guys who wouldn't have to fight anymore, who would get a medal because they were missing an arm or leg. He left his thoughts and turned his attention back to Lieutenant Colonel Whiting.

"Those two planes were medevacs sent to pick up guys from the Alpha platoon, some wounded pretty bad. The Huey took a couple .50 caliber rounds. Didn't hurt the pilot but the bird started having trouble. The pilot radioed he was experiencing control problems and had to set the bird down. The Huey's in as good a place as he could manage. Must be a tight spot because the VC haven't found it yet and the pilot's just sitting there waiting for orders. The co-pilot and two gunners are holed up with him, one with a possible shoulder dislocation from the hard landing that I bet doesn't feel good but won't put him out of commission. The other Huey made it back okay. Even brought in some wounded. But I don't know how many are left, whether they're wounded or dead, nothing. We have to make another try, send the Huey back and hope it can secure a landing zone. If the chopper can spot the downed plane, our guys will be nearby."

Then the lieutenant colonel said Tadziu should go with them in case there was any chance the downed chopper could make it home.

He knew I could save any bird with anything left of it—- part of an engine, broken blades, even a door that wouldn't close. He was right. Tadziu smiled, remembering his words to the captain.

"I'm a non-combatant," he said, kidding him, "a corporal who's a mechanic, ya know." He looked at me, kidded me right back.

"You forget how to use your M-14?" he asked.

I see the pain in his face. Because there aren't enough of us. Just a couple kids on the helio pad workin' with me. Not until headquarters sends more men. And by that time, any guys left out there could be killed, or even worse, captured. The old man has no choice. Either send back a plane he might also lose or forget the grunts out there.

"Yeah", Tadziu told him, "I remember how to use an M-14. Just make sure those stupid grease monkeys put enough oil on the propellers so we can all get back." He saw a slight smile trying to happen on the old man's face.

Tadziu remembered the trip. All the guys from Mike Company. The day was dark. Solemn. Like a warning. He could still see everyone climbing aboard. Funny, how your mind could be so clear when you were scared shitless. There were ten of us. Two corpsmen with their equipment and their stretchers, three grunts, two gunners, the pilots and me with my metal toolbox and my m-14 just in case.

The pilot revved up, a grim look on his face. He knew our chances. They all knew. We had one shot. No one talked much. The gunners were tense, the muscles in their arms bulging as they clutched the weapons that made the whole goddamn plane shake when they were fired so you thought your brains were being scrambled. But everyone knew we had to go after our guys, had to try. Then I said to Frosch, one of the grunts who looked about eighteen or nineteen, "how come you're in first class," because he was in one of the seats that faced straight ahead and I was sitting behind the pilot, facing backwards. Frosch laughed nervously and a couple of other guys too.

Tadziu could still hear the steady drone of the Huey and feel it lift into the air like a big wind-up toy someone had aimed right. He remembered looking up, like he always did. Because no matter how many times he flew in one of those birds, he could never believe the feeling. An army in the air. The workhorses of the war.

And I'm part of it. My company a part of the cavalry. Kind of thrilling, really. If you're nuts, I guess. Not that anyone can be comfortable, scrunched up like a sardine in a can, but because for a minute you feel like you're seeing the whole world from up high and heading straight into a cloud. Problem was, the only way you could see anything was by looking up at the sky. Looking down and trying to spot that knocked-down Huey would be like trying to find fly shit in pepper.

The goddamn jungle was a thick green carpet already with the rainy season starting so that whatever was brown and dry six months' ago was popping up again. After long months of rain, they'd be back to brown and dry, heat that grew until it was like the inside of an oven no matter where you were or what you were doing. Easy to forget the rains that would sometime reach into your bones and make you shudder like you were cold.

There was enough wind to rock the plane at times. That wouldn't make it any easier down there. You knew there were things moving underneath the green carpet but you couldn't see them. Just outside the green of the jungle were neat rectangles of brown earth outlined with canals of water. Rice paddies that were quiet until you got too close. Then a boat you missed seeing in a deep enough channel could start riddling you with machine gun fire. They passed over the open land and were looking down at jungle again.

Nobody knew how many were wounded and waiting. As far as the old man had been able to tell, including the downed plane, ten or eleven guys from the company were still missing. Maybe they were all dead. "Nah, not everyone," Tadziu remembered telling himself. "Couldn't be, could it? They'd find some." He remembered holding his M-14 closer. And feeling for the bolt of the rifle. Even after they dropped guys, someone had to cover while others were lifting stretchers.

He remembered it all. They saw the downed plane and colored smoke and knew their guys were down there. That they could hear the chopper coming. But the mortar shells were coming fast and furious so they hovered in the air for a while like a giant hummingbird. The pilot made a quick turn as if he was going back. But he didn't, was just trying to fake out the yellow bastards and made a nose dive that felt as easy to Tadziu as if the guy was shooting a dart. Tadziu and five other men jumped out and disappeared into the green growth like caterpillars and the helio flew away, a mama bird that had just dropped her babies and they had to manage alone.

Tadziu ran to the fallen bird. It looked peaceful and undisturbed in the tall grass where the pilot had landed, as if it were just waiting for someone to come and take it home. They had plenty of cover. Like parents watching their kids, helicopter gun ships seemed to be using all their ammo as they fired around the downed helio. Tadziu saw the pilot hidden in the brush behind the plane and hoped he didn't move while all this strafing was going on.

He ran to the waiting Huey, climbed inside, grabbed the controls and tried to get her going. All he got was the sound of gears straining, unable to engage. Someone, he couldn't see who, but something told him it was Frosch, lay on the ground behind him, firing away, keeping him covered. He saw their guys appearing from two directions but nobody wasted time talking because they were either carrying poor bastards or helping others who could still walk and everyone knew this was a chance in hell.

He jumped back out, his heart pounding louder than a hammer hitting iron, yanked open the door of the motor housing and plunged his hands inside, touching parts all the way down the line to see if they felt right. Isolated bullets flew and bounced off the copter's metal as if it were a big toy in a shooting range. He turned around for a second, his hands still exploring, and saw Frosch on the ground, his rifle aimed straight past him and the downed Huey, an eighteen year-old sounding like he was firing as much ammo as a whole goddamn platoon.

Then he found it. A hydraulic connection he'd checked on a hundred planes back at camp. Probably hit by a round from a .50 caliber. A piece of cake. He had the connection in his small toolbox. Lucky the pilot had suspected hydraulic problems. Not lucky, really. That's the way it was. You got to know the feel of your plane when you flew it or worked on it enough, could tell things about it someone else would never know. He unscrewed the old connection, tossed it to the ground where it became lost in the empty shells, pieces of shrapnel and debris that littered the area around the plane and clamped in the new connection. From the corner of his eye, he saw guys dragging stretchers and supporting hobbling men to what was the landing zone for the other "copter," the one that had dropped them and disappeared. Jesus, the zone was filling fast.

Mortar shells whistled past, some exploding so close they tore up the ground near him. He didn't bother looking, just kept his head down as he worked. He wanted to run but he couldn't. They needed this machine. And more.

"Don't worry," Frosch called, "I ain't goin' anywhere." With bullets still pinging off that metal bird and VC rising out of the grass and falling with what always seemed to Tadziu their inhuman screams, the place was a regular beehive of activity. He had to disconnect the hose once, but when he re-ran it, it fell into place nice and tight. He got that motor turning, screeching as if protesting, but turning. The firestorm let up and the bullets stopped as if they weren't interested anymore.

And then, Tadziu didn't know how but that god-damn helio appeared again like an angel from heaven and the guys on that LZ worked like fuckers to get those men onto stretchers and into slings while the gunners in the copter fired at anything around them whether it was moving or not. And that sweet bird rose up into the air again loaded with its cargo, the gunners still working away like crazy until it disappeared, gone and on its way back to camp and the field hospitals. Tadziu watched that chopper growing smaller and felt like crying. Because it was such a beautiful machine. And mostly because of what they'd done. But neither he nor anyone else had time to breathe.

It was his turn. He counted fast and saw there were five guys left on a landing zone that was nothing more than a stretch of beaten-down grass—two men on the ground, one in a stretcher, a single corpsman still working on them and a single grunt who could load. That meant with him and the pilots with their two gunners and Frosch who was still spread out behind him, there were eleven who had to get into that battered-up bird and fly home. Could she make it?

The bullets started again, directed at him and Frosch, angry, he was sure, because of the helio that had tricked them and escaped. Jesus. How was he going to handle this? He motioned to Frosch to keep low and inch along on his belly toward the Huey and he did, shooting all the way. A couple grenades exploded where Frosch was and there was a momentary silence.

Jesus, not the kid. Please, not the kid.

The firing from Frosch resumed and Tadziu breathed again. He didn't know how many VC were in their trench but he knew there were more than two.

Don't those geeks know they can overrun us now?

The pilot didn't have to be called. He heard that motor revving up and like a lover finding his lost girl, came out of hiding, his head ducked low, reached the plane, and jumped into the pilot's seat, Frosch covering him all the way. The co-pilot held his shoulder and walked slower. The two gunners who had been hiding with them also reached the Huey and plopped into their places like missing puzzle pieces. Each of them took a magazine from his pack, thrust it into their gun's belly and resumed firing, as if they'd never stopped, covering Frosch until he was inside.

They saw the line of VC, screaming with fury, shaking their fists at the first helio that grew smaller and smaller in the sky, and running toward them while their rifles hammered away, but the gunners cut them down until there was a respite. Then it didn't matter anymore who was supposed to be doing what because they all knew they had only a few minutes. Tadziu and Frosch jumped out to help load those guys. When they slammed the doors, no one talked. They were too crowded, pressed against each other's sweat and blood and too scared they were going no place. Tadziu was afraid the overloaded plane wouldn't fly but the pilot gave it all he could, floored it repeatedly and it rose into the air like a fallen angel, slow but resurrected, moving, flying.

The gunners kept shooting while Tadziu, Frosch and the corpsman did what they could do for those who were moaning. Tadziu prayed to his mother to help them as he watched the pilot keeping his foot to the floor. In a few more minutes the plane seemed to gain life from somewhere and rose directly up and past the reach of any fire. Still no one talked. All the way back to base they were silent, as if they were afraid their luck would change if they made a sound and the helio would fall out of the sky back into enemy territory. It wasn't until they were back at the base that Frosh and Tadziu shook hands and said "good job" to each other.

Back at camp everything was normal. Tadziu laughed as he thought there should be some kind of celebration for what they'd done. Like the parades they held in Times Square at New Year's. It was the morning of January 31 and water fell from the sky like waves of gunfire, stopping only so it could start again. There was no place dry to sit, no place dry to lie down but the Lieutenant Colonel wouldn't allow them to build plywood hootches that would keep them off the ground and enclosed. "I've seen that backfire a few times," he had said tersely, so they had a kind of "half-hootch", a hole that had plywood reinforcement and an overhang of corrugated iron. They kept widening the trenches at the perimeter as they filled up with water. They took turns going into the officers' quarters to smoke and dry off for a while but had to come back to their wet bunkers and take their turns at guard duty sleeping in the rain.

As much as he respected the Lieutenant Colonel, Tadziu thought that was hard-assed. They said it wasn't cold, that it was only the end of January. But even though you wore your poncho liner, the constant rain seeped right into your skin, making you shiver even though the temperature said you shouldn't. When you were tired enough on watch you could fall asleep standing up in a poncho dripping water. Tadziu was in the bunker at the section of the perimeter nearest to the helio pad fighting to stay awake and keep watch while two of his buddies got some shuteye

The night was funny but he didn't know why. Except for the dull sound of rain landing on earth soaked to capacity and the plump of larger drops falling into the stream at the bottom of the trench, the camp was quiet, abnormally quiet. As if it was Christmas or something. Tadziu leaned against the mud wall, rivulets of water collecting on the edge of his helmet and falling like a sheet just past his nose. Thinking that he didn't trust the quiet.

That's the worst thing. You never trust anything, never relax.

About half an hour ago, there had been a mail call and the marine had handed him a letter which he stuffed into the pocket inside his poncho. Probably from Helen. Or Amanda. They wrote all the time. Thinking of Helen made him think of Gena and how she had hugged him, her eyes filling with tears when she said good-bye. That made him think of his brothers, how glad he was that their tour of duty was over and they were in Okinawa waiting to be shipped home. They had been zapped, caught just like that, right age, good health, everything. He had no one but himself to blame. He followed right after them and signed up for this rat's ass duty. Still, he couldn't complain. The marine friends he'd made were the best buddies he'd ever had. And his job as helicopter mechanic sure as hell couldn't hurt him when he finished his stint here.

Now he took out the envelope and looked at the large handwriting. It's Jimmy. It has to be Jimmy. That's a kid's writing. He held the envelope inside his arm, trying to keep it dry but drops fell on it no matter which way he turned. His eyes moved across the paper. There was some light left and he had the tiny flashlight under the red lens on his key chain. He moved it under his hand along the paper and read one word at a time. He felt he was swallowing them.

My kid's writing to me. My kid's writing to me.

Dear Dad,

I am telling all the kids in school about how you are in the Marines. They all think you are great. For fighting the communists. Everyone hates the communists. Everyday we say the Pledge of Allegiance and prayers for all the soldiers. I am proud of you. The teacher is letting other kids in my class write to you. You will get lots of letters. Yesterday was my birthday. I had a party. Mom let me invite six kids. But no girls. I do not want any girls. Our new house is nice. There is a lot of grass. I help Mom with the yard each week. Please be brave and tell me all about how you are being brave. If you have time to write me a letter. I can't wait until we see you again. Mom and me pray for you. I love you. Your son, Jimmy.

My kid's having a birthday. How old is he. Ten, I think. Not one spelling mistake. That's pretty good. Smart, like his mother.

There was another letter inside Jimmy's letter. He unfolded it and recognized Mary's handwriting.

Dear Tadziu:

I can't stop thinking of our night together. I feel you near me, your hands, your arms, and your tenderness as you enter me and we own each other. We've always owned each other. Your love is part of me, part of everything I have done, everything I have lived. I know you've helped me, have made me strong. For so long, I wasn't able to place the difficult memories of our marriage behind me, wouldn't allow myself to see the different person you've become. You told me I wouldn't lose myself if we were together but I didn't believe you. I believe you now, but that doesn't matter. Whatever difficulties lie ahead, I can't be without you. I love you. I always have and always will. I long to be in your arms again Please return to me, my beloved. Mary

Tadziu sat down.

If I wasn't stuck in shit up to my neck, I might faint. Mary. Mary.

Just saying her name took him to her, carried him back through years of loving her as if none of those years had passed.

Mary, Mary. We're playing cards at your grandmother's kitchen table. Your grandmother watches while she crochets. Mary. Mary. Why so long? I asked you once how come you don't crochet. You say your grandma tried to teach you but all you could ever make was chains. And you'd rather read a book. My Mary. Brainy, smart.

A sigh moved through him, stopped in his chest and sat there for a while before it left him.

I'm here. In this hell. But I'm home. Because Mary loves me.

He saw Amanda's face, thought of how her face and her eyes had become different since they had been together, how he didn't want to take that away. He remembered the crazy thing Mary told him once, about loving two men. Maybe he was feeling something like that now. Not really. It made him tired to think about it. Mary was first, always first.

I won't think of that now. Won't think of anything. Nothing that happens to me here matters. Mary wants me to come home. Jimmy wants me to come home.

He put the letters into his wallet with the other letters he carried—-Helen's letters. Amanda's letters. And slept. Against the mud wall at his back, he slept. At first he dreamed of gunfire and the sound of shells but he knew he was dreaming. With the same will you have when awake, he pushed those pictures away and forced them to stay at the edge of his dreams, like strangers pounding at the door. He wouldn't let them in, slept through the pounding, slept and slept. And continued to dream. Confused dreams. At first they were colored with gold. Like the sun. Like warmth. He was wrapped in warmth, held in its kindness like a blanket.

In another dream he saw the place he was in, and allowed himself to dream the truth, saw that now it was always wet, the ground flat and brown where it had not turned into mud. There were no trees anywhere. In his dream that made him sad, made him think of trees that were here before the bombing blasted them away, before the fighting wiped the land clean. He saw waves of wet heat leaving the ground, floating upward, then falling, settling on everything. Until the waves turned into coolness. Like ocean breezes. And he was happy.

He saw himself sliding on the ice in his shoes, blowing on his hands to keep them warm. But he didn't have to do that. Because it wasn't cold. Mary waved to him from the window of her grandmother's house. He wanted to go to her, to hold her. She knew, reached for him, invited him inside. He saw himself moving into the house, settling into Mary like a shadow, his body disappearing into hers. Without sex. Just disappearing into her. Like he needed her to be himself, to be complete. Amanda stood away from them, balanced herself on the edge of his dream. Without sadness. She knew he belonged to Mary. She'd always known.

He understood then, even while he slept, that dreams pulled the truth of things from everyday life and placed them before you with no pussy-footing around, none of the clutter that filled your mind during the day. He held Mary and ran his fingers through her hair. It was right. Amanda saw it was right.

He awoke with a start. Gonzalez was shaking him.

"Tadz. Tadz. Wake up. Something's happening." Tadziu remembered his feeling earlier and knew his instincts had been right. Something was happening and it was big. The trail of rockets lit the sky like fireworks on the Fourth of July. Flares illuminated the camp as if they were streetlights. The noise was deadening. A million piercing screams landed like grenades, one after another. Howitzer shells exploded and opened craters around them. At first, it seemed to be a dream, one of those crazy nightmares you have when you're small and you think you're being attacked by something. But they were being attacked! The screams connected themselves to men, hordes of enemy soldiers running through the camp, crossing the perimeter like it was a stream they needed to jump over to get into their fort. A game. It was just like a game. And their base camp was being invaded.

Tadziu was fully awake now. This was no game but an attack. From every direction. They were taking fire from up high somewhere, as if those geeks were sitting in the trees with machine guns. Confused, guys were running in all directions and being picked off one by one. "Stay down," Tadziu screamed to his two mechanics and grabbed his rifle. Seeing him, they grabbed theirs also and the three of them fell into the trench and fired at the forces streaming by.

Our rifles ain't enough. I've never seen so many of them.

Tadziu felt his lips grow dry as the officers' quarters became the target of heavy fire and parts of it started to burn.

Oh God, I hope the colonel isn't in there.

"Holy shit," Gonzalez screamed, "what the fuck's happening?" Joseph, the smart Jewish kid, looked perplexed at first, then said, "I think we've been set up. It's a raid. A big one."

"Yeah," Tadziu answered and they kept shooting, until Gonzalez screamed and fell, blood trickling from a neat hole in his forehead. There was no hope of a corpsman anywhere. Tadziu felt Gonzalez' pulse and saw he didn't need one. He felt numbness trying to push through him, to block out this time, this day, this hour. Gonzalez had been one of the best mechanics he'd had, but more than that, one of the best guys in the outfit. Always trying to make peace where there was resentment.

What's the sense of this?

Joseph looked at Tadziu solemnly, his bright eyes saying, "We're next anyway." And Tadziu marveled again at the courage of these kids, because that's what they were, kids, taken from the safety of home and turned instantly into men.

Artillery and mortar fire kept coming from every direction. Tadziu knew this mortar fire was from those 60mm bozos that looked like cannon. He'd seen our guys firing them once, then turn away to hold their ears. It seemed the yellow bastards had AK-47s with ammunition that never ran out. Tadziu kept low, afraid to lift his head to see. He had the nightmare picture of an entire battalion of men running in circles and crashing into each other before they fell into their own blood and brains. He could see the line of Ontos exploding, then going up in flames, even the Amtraks left from some operation.

It was not the silent, the dead who bothered him. It was those who were mortally wounded but not dead, lying in their anguish, writhing, screaming. There was nothing he or Joseph could do. The fire was too heavy. There were too many sappers, enemy soldiers running through their camp armed with explosives intended to hit every bunker and hard target they could see. Tadziu did something he thought he'd never do. He shut his eyes and turned away. He didn't know how much time passed. Then he saw his helio pad and his hootch "garage" being consumed, could almost hear its corrugated roof sizzling with flame, and saw the Hueys, hurt and falling to the ground, as if melting into a pool like the "wicked witch" from long ago, when he and Mary had watched the "Oz" movie. He watched the wounding of the beautiful cobras and the heroic medevacs, helicopters like the one he'd flown in to rescue the guys who were downed.

The explosions seemed to lessen but the ak-47s kept up their ack-ack-ack. Tadziu turned his rifle onto someone who jumped into their trench and almost pulled the trigger until he saw that it was Frosch, Frosch finding him in all this confusion! Another guy jumped in and Tadziu saw he was also one of theirs. They recognized each other without talking.

Now there was some answering fire from the trenches of their perimeter across the way. Tadziu remembered what the old man had said about not trusting hooches, and prayed silently to his mother that the old man had not been caught in the incinerated officers' quarters.

Joseph and Gonzalez and I complained about having to dig the trenches.

The bamboo roots in the valley we're in are stubborn, thick and deep. But they're always thick and deep, start spreading wild and fast as soon as the rains start. Guys have to dig on both sides of the roots and sink their trenches into the middle. Joseph was almost serious when he suggested we use a grenade but we kept digging away with our E-tools until we cut that bamboo down as far as we could see. From there, it was easy going to throw the dirt over our shoulders and form the trench. He remembered Joseph being philosophic but trying to make them laugh saying, "Hey, you know this is just what they did in World War One? Seems to me things haven't changed much."

"What the hell you think this is, Tadz?" Frosch said, as he picked off whoever ran by.

"The best sneak-attack I ever saw." He stopped, then added grimly, as if he didn't want to say the words out loud. "They want this landing strip, plan to put all of our helios out of commission." He turned to Frosch.

"We must've made 'em mad when we got out that day." The four of them were quiet as the rhythmic rounds of a machine gun peppered the ground above their hole. There was a hill Tadziu could see, a small elevation of land to the right about 200 meters away. He could see the glint of sun on metal and hear more than one machine gun, an ack-ack-ack that traveled through the air like a bad smell. The valley that separated them from the hill was like a music hall with perfect acoustics so they could hear the high pitch of Vietnamese voices as if the yellow faces were next to them. It was impossible to tell, unnerving. Maybe there were more beneath the elevation, dug into the earth. They did that so well. A man screamed the scream of death and they heard his body hit the dirt. Frosch had made a bull's eye but Tadziu didn't know if it mattered. There were so many of them.

The kid who jumped in with Frosch had freckles and red hair on his head and his arms. His name was Dave. The four of them lay as low as they could, listening to the sound of shells exploding, and hearing frightened curses from every direction. Bullets whizzed by like huge mosquitoes, seeking a patch of skin they could land on. Dust and falling debris filled the air like a tornado. Tadziu lifted his head for a quick minute and spotted more of their own guys in trenches about a hundred meters away.

They agreed it would be better to be eight or nine rather than four and made a run for it, alternating between running a few steps and falling to the ground and crawling. According to Tadziu's watch, they did that for thirty minutes or so. And shot and killed all the way. VC seemed to be behind every tree, popped up out of the ground like rabbits reproducing in spring. And fought like hell. How the hell could they do this so suddenly? Plan so well? Overrun our air base? They don't care if they all die. Just so they take us and our planes with them. At times, Tadziu lost track of the other two guys but felt Frosch right behind him. And the bullets got close enough to move their asses right to where they wanted to be, into that trench that suddenly seemed as sweet as home. "Wasn't it good of the farmers in this vil' digging all this bamboo so's we'd have trenches?" he said to the guys. Nobody laughed.

The animated faces they had seen from their trench were gone except for one, plastered onto the dirt like a blanket, his limp body blocking the stream of muddy water that ran along the bottom of the trench. They must have decided to take their chances and make a run for it. Tadziu turned the guy lying in the water. Somehow Tadziu's poncho, folded the way it was in his pack, was still pretty clean. He unfolded it and covered the guy. Frosch and the other two guys said nothing but Frosch blessed himself with the sign of the cross.

Even the muddy wall of a trench could feel comfortable if you could lay your head back. Tadziu told the guys to relax for a minute.

They're not guys, just kids.

I guess we just sit here for a while. Maybe I'll get a brilliant thought. Maybe Frosch blessing himself was the smartest move right about now. I wish to hell I knew something. They think I know something because I'm old. Almost thirty. An old man in the middle of these eighteen and nineteen year olds.

Tadziu heard himself saying to Dave, the red-haired, freckled guy who'd jumped in the trench with Frosch , "hey Dave, I always wondered. You Polish?" and knew what he never knew before, that he laughed and made jokes to cover up other things. Like fear. Helplessness.

Aw shit. Everybody does that, don't they?

They laughed a little, then talked about the guys in the perimeter further away, the grunts assigned to protect the air strip and its crew.

"There's another whole unit of marines out on that perimeter. Even if they were caught by surprise, they're awake now an' rememberin' it's their job to keep those bastards from getting' this far. Ya gotta know they're fightin' their asses off to keep 'em from reaching us" Frosch waved his arms around with excitement. "Those guys are less than 1000 meters away. They've even got tanks, for Christ's sake. More than the stuff an airstrip's got." For a minute, things felt better.

Then they had the shit scared out of them. Two more guys climbed into the trench—a Lieutenant looking blown-up and strange until Tadziu realized he was trying to wear two flak jackets. Some poor bastard with him carried a radio on his back and looked like a tag-along who didn't want to be there. The Lieutenant didn't bother with small talk.

"Jesus," he said, his eyes wild with what Tadziu recognized as fear.

This guy's a pilot. Not a troop commander

"There's a nest of those bastards hidden somewhere in that hill. We gotta clean 'em out." He looked around at the four whose trench he had invaded, his eyes stopping at each face.

Must be the radioman's excluded.

"They're picking us off from their little rabbit-hole. We're gonna charge and flush out them cocksuckers." Tadziu stared at the Lieutenant, felt his own mud and sweat and thirst like he was feeling them for the first time. He couldn't believe what the asshole was saying but he knew he was saying it to them. They'd be killed for sure. The Lieutenant must know it.

"C'mon, you guys, get goin.' That nest's costin' us. Every minute those Charlies are firin', we lose someone. You gotta get 'em."

It's true. The guy's nuts. He wants me and Frosch and these two guys to make a suicide journey to that friggin' anthill those guys have dug, are nice and comfortable in. What he's saying is just stupid. We don't stand a chance, won't even reach the nest of those yellow bastards before we're picked off like dogs in an open field.

A part of his mind traveled back to another day, the day he had talked with Lieutenant Colonel Whiting. To what he'd always known, but if he got back, would never take for granted again—what a good leader was, how he cared abut his men. Everything this guy wasn't. He tried not to scream.

"That ain't no good, sir. We gotta go around. Get them from the rear." The officer's face curled into an ugly sneer.

"Who's givin' the orders here?" Tadz was quiet. His head was fog and mud and fire. It was useless. The asshole couldn't see. He looked at the Lieutenant's face again.

No. He sees. He knows. He doesn't care.

"C'mon, c'mon," the Lieutenant screamed, "move it, you guys." His hard combat boots kicked Tadziu and he raised his arm, motioning for all of them to move. Frosch and the two soldiers looked at Tadziu. Tadziu looked at the officer. He was just like every blown-up asshole he saw back home.

"No," he said, feeling his muscles tighten. Something white and still sat inside him. His mind moved to a place away from here. Where he didn't hear the thin screams of the bullets, didn't hear the manic voice of the lieutenant.

"I'm tellin' ya, sir," he said, "we can't do it that way. Maybe if a couple of us could get around. It's the only way."

The Lieutenant lifted his rifle and pointed it at Tadziu, his voice wild with hatred and anger and his own fear.

"I'm givin' you an order. Move. Or I'll shoot you." Frosh and the other two stared at Tadziu.

This is the kind of shit I hate. Shit that makes no sense.

"Go ahead," he said, calmly. "Either way I'm dead. The minute I pick my head up from this hole, I get shot. Makes no difference if you shoot me now, does it?" The Lieutenant glared at him, then turned to Frosch and the other guys.

"You get started," he yelled, waving his gun. The two guys didn't move and Tadziu knew they were okay. He put his hands on Frosch's shoulders, held him down.

"No. Don't listen to him," he yelled. Frosch looked from the Lieutenant to Tadziu and back again. His eyes were bright, like an excited or terrified child.

"I can't," he said, as if apologizing to Tadziu, "I gotta listen." He sunk his heel unto the mud and pushed himself a half-foot up the side of the trench. Tadziu lunged, tried to grab him, to hold him back, to keep him from trying to climb the sliding mud, then felt himself sliding and falling back. With a bird's eye view, he saw the kid's boots slipping and prayed they'd keep slipping, watched in horror as the kid's boots scrambled and caught hold, so that he raised himself up, making not even three steps before he fell back to lay still in the muddy trench, his face opened down the middle like a melon. Tadziu knew he died quick, with no long hurting, but he felt himself weak with sorrow, wanted to howl his sorrow, to throw the Lieutenant to the ground and trample his face. He could only scream.

"You son of a bitch! You satisfied now?" The guys behind him were crying. The Lieutenant grabbed the radio from his man's backpack, blared into it that they were trapped by he didn't know how many VC who had worked their way this far and dug themselves a fighting hole.

While he was talkin' Tadziu and Dave crawled on their bellies, their packs loaded with grenades. The yellow bastards saw movement and set up a barrage of machine-gun fire. He didn't know if Dave got it but he kept crawling until he was as close as he wanted to get, close enough to pull the pin and throw it at the incessant ack-ack-ack. He knew he was probably being reckless. He didn't care. His head was filled with thoughts of Frosch. An explosion he didn't expect threw him violently backward. Then it was quiet. "Jeez, good shot, Tadz," Dave whispered and Tadziu realized how glad he was to hear his voice

Something inside Tadziu changed. Even before Frosch's death, he wasn't sure what they were accomplishing in this place, this war where the grunts barely knew who the enemy was, where girls with innocent faces threw grenades and half the prisoners they took seemed like children. He played with the trigger on his rifle and stared at the back of the Lieutenant's head.

Easy to blow his face open. Never be a better time. See him die. Without caring. He didn't care about Frosch. I could do it. Who'm I kiddin'? I think about it. But I won't do it. Just go on hating the fucking son-of-a-bitch. Maybe I owe it to those grunts dyin' out there to try. Okay, okay, Maybe. Maybe. If we ever get back to normal. Nothin's normal now. Nobody knows what's happenin' except we're getting the shit kicked out of us.

Tadziu looked at his watch and saw that only three quarters of an hour had passed from the beginning of the attack until now. Seemed like days. He stopped thinking about the Lieutenant, stored the thought of him in his gut, and concentrated on the stuff that wouldn't ever, he knew, go away——the dirt, the fatigue and now, the waiting to get hit.

He fell asleep for a minute and woke with a start to see the Lieutenant's man, who looked exhausted, trying, without success, to bring in transmissions. Tadziu realized that the Lieutenant, who looked disinterested in them, was moving away and climbing out of their bunker. "Let me try," Tadziu said to the radioman, whose face filled with gratitude. After a while he did get something. The sounds of fighting and confusion. Explosions. Rapid gunfire. Shouting. Swearing. One word over and over again, "Incoming. Incoming, and then, a desperate voice from the other end. "Sit-rep. Sit-rep."

The voice fluctuated between the sound of explosions and screams, but when Tadziu could, he told the guy on the other end what their story was, that there were five of them pinned down, that they'd seen many casualties and were the only ones left in their section of the field. He gave the guy their coordinates as well as he could. Somebody sounding important but harassed came on.

Between static and battle sounds, he heard a question. "This is Lieutenant Colonel Michaels. Who's your Actual, son? Give me your Actual."

The Lieutenant was all but gone.

"That's me, sir," Tadziu heard himself saying. "Corporal Tadziu Wreblewski, sir." There was a pause at the other end. "Okay, son." Then he learned what he already knew. The entire squadron had been caught in a well-planned and executed attack. Commanders were trying to revamp but it was slow going. It was uncertain how many casualties had been taken. Radio communication with many companies had been lost. Tadziu could tell what the Lieutenant Colonel didn't say, that they were lucky to be alive, so close to the airstrip. He handed the radio back to the guy who fastened it to his back again and began following the Lieutenant who was stumbling away.

Where the hell's he think he's goin'? He's gone bonkers.

"You're better off here, sir," he heard himself say, but the Lieutenant made no response, kept walking as if he were in a daze. Tadziu saw Frosch's face, the face that didn't exist anymore, knew he would never stop seeing it. He said nothing more to the Lieutenant.

He'll be killed. I won't have to do it. No one here will have to do anything.

He thought about the radioman but knew he couldn't help him.

As he watched the departing figures, two other Marines jumped into the trench. "Jeez, don't wait to be invited or anything," Tadziu said. One of the guys was an NCO but the insignia on his shirt had been bloodied so Tadziu couldn't tell what he was. The grunt with him called him "Sergeant Hood." The Sergeant also had a radio, and Tadziu watched him operate the dials in his effort to make contact. There was only another round of static.

The Sergeant had looked pale when he jumped into the trench but Tadziu had not thought much of that considering the mess they were in. Now he saw the shoulder wound that dripped blood slowly down the front of the Sergeant's shirt. "Good work," he said to Tadziu as he wiped the sweat from his brow. "Keeping these guys together." He pointed to the two on the bottom of the trench, one of whom was Frosch. "We'll get these two Medevaced as soon as possible."

Tadziu wondered how he could do this but he liked this sergeant. He made no reference to his injury and sensing that he didn't want to be asked, Tadziu kept quiet. Neither he nor Tadziu could make radio contact with the CP. Sergeant Hood's face betrayed his pain when he reached into his shirt pocket and pulled out a frayed piece of paper. "The last time we had contact these were the coordinates for the location of company Bravo, part of the Marine defensive force on the outer perimeter. About 150 meters north." Tadziu examined the paper and nodded his head. The Sergeant winced as he reached into his pocket for the pen and small pad of paper he handed Tadziu. He told him to write down the coordinates and that he wanted him and two of the other three, including Pete, the grunt he had brought with him, to head toward Bravo.

"To those who are left," he said. "God knows how many died trying to keep these sapppers from getting through. If their communication lines are open, their CO can advise headquarters about the mess we're in here, tell them we need air and ground reinforcements ASAP. My pilots, all my personnel, are scattered, holed up in different places Maybe some of Bravo will be ordered to work their way here. I don't know." He winced again. "In any case, we need help." Joseph, Tadziu's mechanic, would stay with the Sergeant. They would keep picking off sappers as they could, trying to keep as many as they could from reaching the airstrip and ravaging it further, It was only a matter of time, he felt sure, before he himself would renew contact with the CP.

Tadziu knew there was another issue—-how long their ammunition would hold out. The Marine unit must have heavy artillery weapons, even tanks, as David had reminded him. That hope would keep him and Dave fighting to reach Bravo, the Marines out on the perimeter.

Tadziu knew the Sergeant didn't like the mission he was sending them on, was doing it in the hope that one of them would get through.

One of us. Out of me and two kids. I can't stand to see kids shot up. We gotta try or whatever's left of the airfield and the squadrons will be lost.

Before they left, Tadziu pulled Joseph on the side and told him the sergeant was injured.

Not that the kid's a corpsman, but at least he'll know. He's a good kid. He'll do what he can.

After they scrambled out of the hole and were moving, David and Pete stayed close to Tadziu. David was light on his feet and quiet but Pete, despite Tadziu's frantic signals, was not. The earth came alive with clods traveling through the air as bullets chewed the ground. The air was pierced by the sound of rocket and mortar fire, fire that seemed like it was following them. Tadziu thought the beating of his own heart could be heard across the stretches of brush and open land.

I must be batty, worrying about the noise we make in the midst of this deafening barrage. I should be worrying about us not being seen.

These god-damned charlies were tough to outsmart. For such a bunch of little creeps, it was amazing. But they came out of underground bunkers, Tadziu knew. Even used candles at night to see. Probably heard everything we were saying. And those crazy guys in Washington thought they'd be easy. A bunch of asshole farmers not even trained.

Yeah. Well these farmers know their land, and how to zigzag through all its holes and secret hiding places. Especially the jungle. Maybe they weren't all trained. But somebody, the Chinese, he guessed, were training some of them. And providing them with weapons. They fight like bulldogs that won't let go once their teeth sink in. Like they don't care about dying. As long as they take some of us with them. Westmoreland and those guys in Washington should come down here and try 'em out. See how they like getting their asses blown off.

A grenade came whistling through the air and landed at Pete's feet like it had his name on it. The Sergeant's man was lost and they had to leave his body. Tadziu knew that after all this was over, their guys would want to know where the bodies were. He had lost his bearings but tried to spot signposts.

Mama, mama, I'm a rabbit about to be caught and skinned. And I can't do nothin' for the kid who just died or the one who's still alive.

Bullets continued to fly. Tadziu pushed David's head down until they were flat on their bellies. He knew that every tree, every rock they passed could be hiding one of those sappers.

There was persistent direct fire coming at them from the rear. "Them's snipers, Tadziu," Dave whispered and Tadziu realized they were trapped between a sniper's nest behind them and at least a half dozen VC in the front. The snipers had them in their range but he didn't know if the VC in front had spotted them yet.

What the hell do I do now? There's no way for us to get through that crew. Those yellow bastards are like worms hiding in the mud, coming out to shoot, then disappearing. For everyone you get down, ten more take their place.

They had traveled about sixty meters. Tadziu thought about the guys back at the bunker, guys who were so exhausted they almost welcomed a bullet in the head. He thought about how the sergeant would feel knowing they couldn't reach Bravo. But the sergeant might have reached the CP by now.

God-damn. I hate letting them down. But I got the kid. He makes me think of my brothers. The sergeant should have sent me alone.

He sat down with Dave against a tree so skinny no one could be behind it. And as luck would have it, the foliage around it, mostly elephant grass, was so thick and high no one would see them.

As if he had been reading Tadziu's thoughts, David spoke. "Look Tadz, it's just like you said to the Lieutenant that time, wither way, we're dead. We gotta keep tryin' to reach the Marines." Tadziu nodded.

He had to try doing something about the snipers behind them. He'd been good with a grenade last time. Crawling on his belly, he came within a grenade's throw of the sniper's fighting hole, saw the barrels of two rifles protruding from the hole like steel eyes. Holding his breath, he threw. And got lucky. He knew he made a bull's eye when he heard the screams. He motioned to David. They hovered in the grass as the VC who were about five meters in front of them scampered away. For that one moment it seemed there was hope. When the men disappeared, they began to crouch and crawl toward an outer perimeter and a company of Marines that seemed more real, less like a mirage. It was tough going, tough to make any progress, tough to stop thinking about the truth of their situation.

No matter which way we turn, we're cut off. About half-way between our bunker and the outer perimeter. The kid knows the shit we're in. Doesn't have to be told. I hope to hell officers realize how much their men know. The guys I know always know the score.

Slowly, they covered some ground. Sweat streamed down Tadziu's face and into his eyes, kept coming so that he couldn't see. He tried to wipe it away with his hand, the one that was not wound around his rifle, but couldn't raise his arm while crawling on his belly. The sweat wouldn't stop, dripped off his nose and into his mouth, its taste like salt. His sleeves and his chest were soaked.

The air presses down on you so your breath sounds like my mother's did when she was in the hospital, dying.

His helmet seemed made of lead. Each turn of his head took more effort than the one before. His fatigue turned into a lightheadedness that made him feel numb.

I gotta keep moving, gotta push myself, gotta place one knee in front of the other and crawl, one foot in front of the other and run.

He stumbled and tripped, fell into the mud, picked himself up and fell again.

Shit. This is just like being drunk.

David was almost at his side, a little behind, trying to lift his body or pick up his feet, looking like Tadziu felt—-as if he was wrapped in mud and weighed a thousand pounds.

Aw shit, he's just a kid, nineteen years old, from someplace out West. Talked a little about his brothers and sisters. Now he wants to quit, wants to lie down and let the mud cover him.

"C'mon, Dave, c'mon, we're almost there," he said, his voice like a robot, words without thought, just sound. "We gotta keep going, gotta get to the Marines." Bullets from somewhere started to ping off the edge of his helmet.

He thought they'd covered ten or fifteen more meters. That felt good. Until they ran into the yellow devils they thought had moved away. The bastards had tricked them, hadn't disappeared at all, just gone into hiding, waiting with anticipation until they could make their move. They wasted no time jumping on Tadziu and the kid. Screaming crazy chants. Like they were mad with hunger or hot and heavy with drugs. Tadziu downed at least six. The kid got filled with some kind of rage. Fought like a crazy man. He was crazy. They were all crazy. Playing a crazy game.

It was no use. Tadziu heard the kid screech like a tortured animal as bullets entered him and he fell. Bullets sliced through Tadziu like rods cracking through bone. As he lay, bayonets eased through him like butter and in a screen he couldn't close, he saw the yellow bastards laughing with glee as they thrust bayonets into David. He must still be alive. Every nerve in Tadziu's body felt exposed and raw. He felt pain he'd never known existed, opened his mouth to scream but nothing came out. As the slow-motion movie he was living continued to play, he tried to lift his M-14, again felt bayonets entering in places he didn't know he had, fell and watched them march away. Their party's over. They know we're finished. Usually they shoot again at every guy who's down before they leave. But we're not worth bothering with. They're running, screaming victory. Sons-of-bitches. Without looking at their own guys. To see if any are alive, can be helped.

We're all useless. Bleeding to death together. Under this sky with no color. Red blood mixing with mud. Turning brown.

Tadziu saw one soldier run to him, a soldier with a child's face and the beginning of a beard. The soldier bent down to see if Tadziu was dead. For a moment they looked into each other's eyes, like children in school seeing each other for the first time. The boy knew he was alive. He raised his rifle and Tadziu waited to hear it kick, to release its explosion. A look like regret, fear for what he had done and thought to do came into the boy's eyes. Silent and white, he turned away, as if he could no longer look at Tadziu, and hurried to catch up with his comrades. Tadziu knew that if he lived, made it out of here alive, he could never forget that moment, that Vietnamese kid.

Tadziu moved in and out of consciousness. The dream came back. Like a movie reel that had been interrupted, it started where it had stopped that afternoon, pulled him so that he wanted to give in.

But I can't. There's the kid. David.

The cold returned. He was lying on ice. Was it Vietnamese ice? Or ice on the street outside Marys's grandmother's house? Stars burned overhead, turned cold in the black sky. He saw Mary in the window again. And waved. She waved back. He had the sensation that he was expanding, growing larger, becoming warmer. He wanted to lose himself in the warmth in which he was floating, a warmth that erased all his words yet answered all his questions. Everything answered him now. The world. The night. The sky.

Mary kept waving. And then she was next to him. Wiping his brow. Like his mother used to do. Brushing his hair back from his forehead. He didn't want to leave the dream. He could keep himself there.

But what about the kid?

Thinking about the kid brought him back to where he did not want to be, filled his head with pain. Until he fell into the dream again. Mary moved closer, close enough to touch, for him to reach out and hold. The throbbing in his head began to disappear. He was floating, looking down at himself and her.

His mother came in from somewhere, her eyes filled with brightness. His father was behind her, holding his jacket open, tugging at it repeatedly. Tadziu realized his father wanted to show him something, a bullet wound in his side. A wound that he held with his hand because, Tadziu could see, it caused him pain. "Let me see pa," Tadziu said and his father showed him the blood running freely down his side except for the places where it had hardened into dark scabs. "Don't close your jacket, pa", he said. "Open it wide. The sun will dry the blood and make it feel better." He knew the sun would heal the wound. His father looked at him with doubt in his eyes but held the jacket open and turned so the sun would reach the bullet hole. *Moj syn. Moj syn* [50] he said, and smiled with surprise at the words. Tadziu knew the sun's warmth was reaching into his father's pain, relieving it. Making it disappear. They gazed at each other until his father's face grew dim. Tadziu couldn't say the name of what he was feeling because it was made of so many feelings, but he knew part of it was contentment and part of it was forgiveness.

His contentment changed to fright. He knew he was dying. Then he was angry. It wasn't right that he should be afraid. He told himself he wouldn't be afraid. He watched with interest as his body moved slowly, erratically, like a car motor losing its power, then receiving a jolt from somewhere so that it shot forward and shrieked before settling into a slow and steady rhythm.

He had never thought about this moment. Didn't want to think about it now. Why should he? It would take care of itself. The headache returned, then lifted again, drifted upward like pieces of cloud, small tornadoes spiraling dark and ugly at the base, then disappearing into light.

He saw other men lying close to him, saw they didn't move, knew they were VC, felt pity and sorrow, wanted to reach out and stroke them but pulled back in horror, as if touching them would drag him into what they were. He pulled himself along the ground on his elbows, tried to avoid the pools of blood, the legs and arms that were attached the wrong way. He had to get to the kid. He could see the kid's chest heaving up and down like a pump working overtime, could see he was aware and had a terrified look in his eyes, the terror of being torn apart, suffocated like an animal possessing no mind, no reason. Tadziu couldn't stand to see the kid's fright. It made him move faster along the field littered with bodies and sharp with debris, made him forget the raw flesh of his own legs, flesh no longer covered by skin. He stretched out his arm, touched the kid's face and watched as some inner switch turned off the kid's fear.

Amazing. Because I'm here. With him. With him. Being with someone is the most important thing there is. The only thing that matters.

"Just hang on," Tadziu told him. "The corpsmen are comin' for us. We'll be lifted out of here." Knowing it was a lie, that no one could reach them in this fuckin' hole.

He felt himself beginning to fall into the place where he could be with Mary and Jimmy and his mother when her hair was filled with sun. He had to fight himself.

It's so easy. To just let go. If I go there it'll be quiet. The explosions will be gone. The dead guys will be gone. I want to see Ma. I gotta fight what's pullin' me. I can't leave the kid.

"It's okay, Dave. They're comin'," he said again, and saw the kid's eyes begin to relax. But he couldn't tell if the crooked turn of the kid's mouth was a faint smile or a grimace of pain. Until his eyes settled on Tadziu's face. And Tadziu saw the kid no longer smelled the muck he was lying in or tasted the blood in his mouth. His eyes held words from a place Tadziu now knew existed, the place where life takes refuge from what seeks to destroy it. Words the kid would never say, words Tadziu would never answer—-"I love you, buddy"—— silently crossed the narrow space between them. Tadziu had difficulty holding up his head but he had to in order to keep looking into the kid's eyes.

Keeping him safe. I'm keeping the kid safe. The kid feels safe because of me.

He managed to free his arm from whatever was holding it. He found the kid's hand with his hand and held it like an expensive present someone had given him. He kept holding tight and looking into David's eyes, keeping him safe. He held tight while the silence began to surround him and the kid's chest pumped slower and slower until he closed his eyes. Then Tadziu knew it was okay. He turned his eyes toward his mother. He never understood. But it didn't matter.

I love you ma.

He saw Mary and placed his hand on the pocket where he carried her letter, muddy and wrinkled from reading it so many times and now soaked in blood. *I love you. I've always loved you.* That's what she wrote. She was a child again. He was a child. He felt himself moving through air that cushioned him, insulated him against the pain. Still holding the kid's hand, he closed his eyes and let the waves of silence wash over him.

Day is Done

The funeral was crowded. After the Mass, people stood three rows deep at the cemetery. Jimmy clung to his mother's hand, crying uncontrollably. Martha wiped away her own tears, blew her nose and bent down to him. "Your father was a brave man," she whispered in his ear. "He knew you were brave too." Michael held Mary's arm. So far back that she was almost invisible, Amanda stood alone.

Jimmy's two uncles, Albert and Tom and four other marines in uniform carried the coffin draped with an American flag, placed it on the bier that stood on the canvas tarp covering the grass, then moved to the crowd and stood silently, hands crossed, eyes cast before them, as if avoiding the sight of the burden they had borne. The priest swung the censer and sprinkled holy water around the casket, pausing to bow his head on each side of the elongated box. He spoke about Tadziu's bravery at the Tet Offensive, a very difficult battle of the war.

The Polish Hymn *Serdeczna Matko* rang out, hobbled at first, and then gained momentum, straining to reach the sky. It was the hymn Mary's grandmother often sang to herself as she worked, the hymn they sang at her funeral, and the hymn that ended all Polish funerals. *Serdeczna Matko, opiekunko Ludzi. Niech cie placz Sierut. Do litosci zbudzi. Wygnancy Ewy, do ciebie wolamy. Zmiluj sie zmiluj. Niech sie niech tulamy.* The chorus reached its apex, then drifted back to earth where it dissolved into grievous sobs.

Another contingent of eight Marines stood motionless, their eyes focused on some invisible object, the barrels of their rifles polished and gleaming, the brass buttons of their caps and dress blues reflecting the morning light. The priest nodded his head slightly to the corporal in charge of the detail. Above the attempts to stifle the cries and moans, the words "attention" and "firing party prepare to fire volleys" could be heard. As if it had been instructed, the crowd was hushed.

As members of a single body, the eight Marines turned, the heels of their shoes hitting the pavement and echoing as one sound as they held their rifles against their sides in the gun salute, then pointed them upward in firing position, the click of firing mechanisms again breaking the hushed silence. The commands "aim" and "fire" were followed by the thunder of arms exploding three times. After the command to "present arms" was spoken, their white-gloved hands were raised to their foreheads in a synchronized salute. As the sound of buglers playing Taps floated a final farewell, the gathering became universal, a single body of inconsolable sorrow, carrying people into time immemorial, honoring each warrior ever slain in honor. The detail resumed its arms, faced to the right and marched away. As the Marines left the field, like the descent of a darkened cloud, only weeping remained.

Again a unity was formed. Jimmy's uncles stepped forward. In slow motion they removed the flag from their brother's casket, folded it into its triangular form and passed it to the officer who stepped forward, approached Jimmy and placed it into his open arms. Jimmy held the flag like a treasure entrusted to his care. His eyes were large as he listened to the words, "On behalf of the President of the United States, the Commandant of the Marine Corps, and a grateful nation, please accept this flag as a symbol of our appreciation for your loved one's service to our country and corps. God bless you and this family and God bless the United States of America."

Michael held Mary's elbow, trying to keep her steady. Through the mist before her eyes, a thought kept returning. She had trouble holding it, keeping it from slipping away. She began sinking into the flood of words and people surrounding her. But the thought wouldn't leave. Although she couldn't grasp what it was, she knew its importance. It was something she must do for Tadziu, something he wanted from her. Like a secret revealing itself, the picture came. The picture of Amanda. Mary looked around and saw her standing, inconsolable, confused, as if, like Jimmy, she didn't understand what had occurred. Tadziu's sisters and brothers stood behind her, not knowing who she was but with that unexplainable human instinct, knowing she'd been close to Tadziu. Mary turned around and walked to Amanda, took her hand, and drew her into the circle of herself and Jimmy and Tadziu's brothers and sisters. She'd explain later, at the breakfast, that this was the girl Tadziu had intended to marry. She knew they'd love her, would accept her as the woman Tadziu loved.

That was later. Now she and Jimmy walked back to Michael's car, the car they'd come in, that would take them to the restaurant and back home.

Michael, Martha, Aunt Irene, Barbara, Uncle Ben, Jimmy, please help me get through this. Just let it be over. Let me think of him the way I thought of grandma. The way I still think of her. I'll hold up, grandma. I'll hold up.

She saw another face, a younger version of her grandmother. It was Elizabeth, her mother.

She knew, at that moment, that Elizabeth would know her sorrow, a sorrow so deep, it was death, her death. She knew, at that moment, how much she loved her mother.

Please, grandma. let it be over. Finished. Let the singing and the crying be finished. Let the priest stop walking around the casket, sprinkling holy water on it, blessing it, praying over it with folded hands. Hide the open ground, the fresh earth overturned and trying to hide beneath a piece of canvas, the flowers on the casket saturating the air.

Despite Jimmy's holding her hand so tightly that it hurt, revealing his fear, his lack of understanding at what he suspected, of what she would have, in some way, to help him understand —-the certain, harsh, and merciless finality of death—-she felt the warmth of Tadziu's skin against her own, the urgency, always the urgency of his mouth upon hers, the firm yet tender movement of his hands caressing, caressing, until she could bear no more. She felt her body respond to the thought of him and his fierce love, felt the protest of the flesh that longed, its hunger never satisfied. She felt the incompletion of the self she was, the missing limbs never to be restored, the heart stolen, never to be returned.

People moved back to their cars in a quiet parade, heels hitting the ground in slow motion, the only sound that of sobs being repressed. Mary felt herself held close, wrapped in arms that threatened to suffocate her. Helen held her face and kissed it, whispering in her ear, "He loved you so much, Mary. We all know he did." Mary cast down her eyes, remembering Tadziu's attempts to reunite, the attempts she'd denied and wondered if they knew, wondering if he'd ever told them. Then it was Gina kissing her, her face pale and washed clean by tears. Tadziu had told Mary how gentle she was. "Helen, Gina," she tried to say but no words left her, only the sound of the anguish filling her stomach, trying to crack her and bend her to the ground. Other people came, and each time her voice refused to sound. Until Elizabeth. Rushing to put her arms around Mary, holding her, supporting her. And Mary's voice was freed.

"Mama, mama, I loved him so much."

"I know, I know."

No further words were spoken.

But Mary's cries left her like a river gone wild, overrunning its banks. Jimmy, holding her hand, was swept along and joined her until David came and lifted him into his arms. "It's all right, young fella, it's all right," he crooned as Jimmy sobbed into his shoulder.

Mary's mother continued to hold her. The sky was quiet, watchful, shedding its light on lifetimes of sorrow.

People moved back to their cars in a quiet parade, heels hitting the ground in slow motion. Cars began moving, a ghost drive to the restaurant and Mary held tightly to her mother's hand.

Thoughts came, settled.

If Tadziu had come home, we'd lie on the bed together as we did in our first apartment, sleeping and waking, moving away and moving back to each other until dawn.

And I'd tell him things—everything ——and he'd smile with eyes bright from the reflection of our bedroom window. "I know," he'd say, "I understand" and kiss my mouth again.

I'd tell him what it had been like for me all those years without him and he'd tell me about himself, all the things I wanted to know,

I would explain to him about the different parts of me, the ways in which I was torn, the things I didn't understand about myself, the two persons I am, and he would understand and silence me with his fingers gently on my mouth.

And the part of me, all the parts of me that forever belong to him. And that I can't face life without him, this too, he'd understand.

And hold me and stroke my head on his shoulder while I cried.

She looked out the car window. It was winter and the ground was turning into ice. For a second she knew was delirium but couldn't relinquish, she saw herself and Tadziu, children walking together in wintertime. She wore layers of clothing and he wore a jacket that was too big and his leather pilot's cap. She tried to see them running and laughing together, to feel him behind and ahead, beneath and above. She tried to feel him, his hand in her own, the always warm hand on her own that was always cold. She tried and tried to see and to feel. Despite the truth, the reality she would know each day.

Tadziu, Tadziu, my Tadziu is gone.

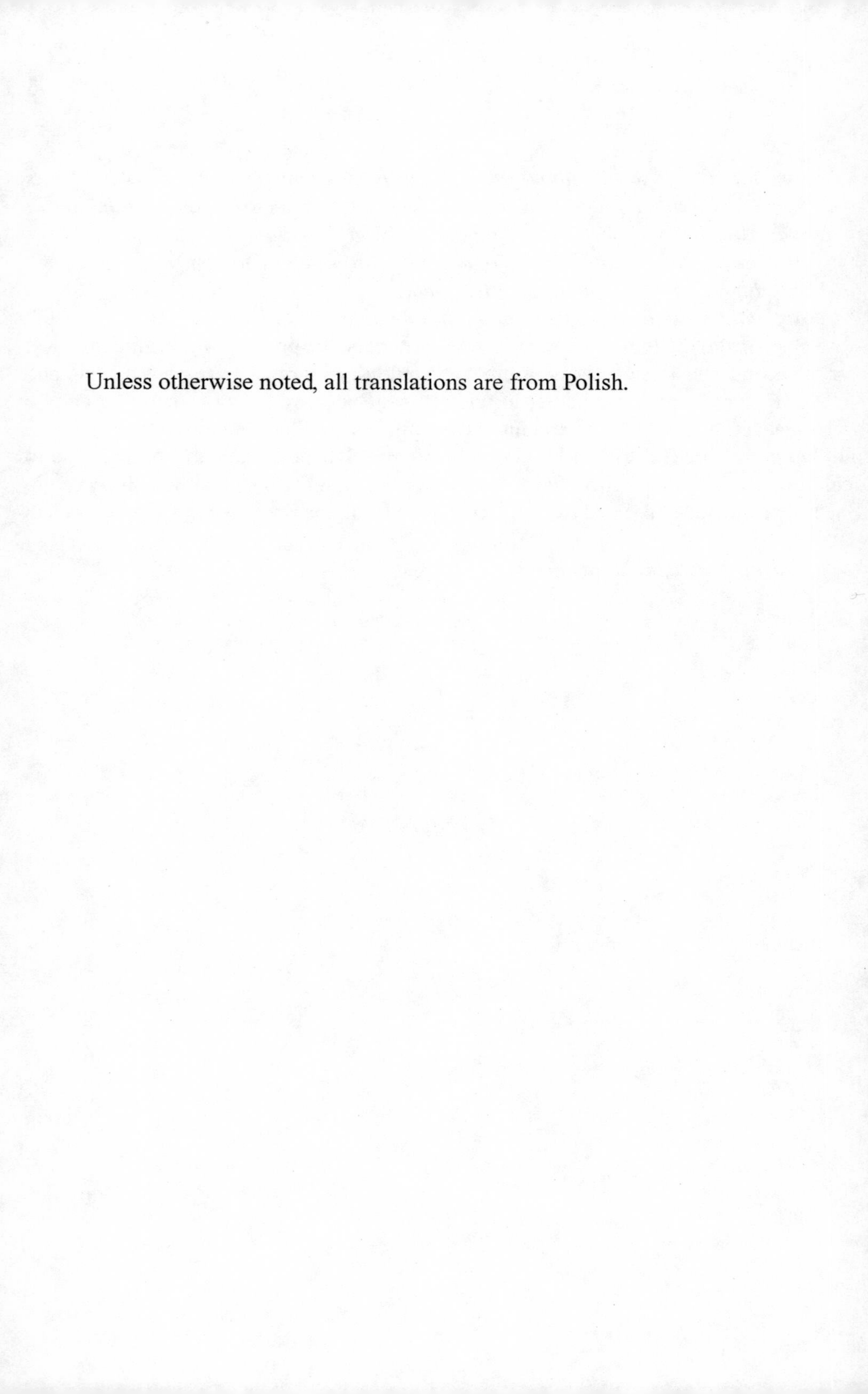

Unless otherwise noted, all translations are from Polish.

EndNotes

[1] Translation: Comforter or quilt made from the feathers and down of geese or ducks. Down is the highest quality of filler, the warmest and most luxurious. If the down is not stripped carefully from the feather, a quill can penetrate the cover. Feathers are also used as a filler but the quality is inferior.

[2] Translation: “Oh Jesus, oh Jesus.”

[3] Translation from Latin: “Pray for us.”

[4] Traditional Polish hymn sung at funerals. One of the translations: “Beloved Mother, guardian of our nation, / Have pity on the cries of orphans, / Rejected Eve, to you we call, / Care for us, care for us. Don’t let us wander.”

[5] Polish dances, filled with spirit and life, also folk dances performed on stage.

[6] Translation: “What a beautiful wedding!”

[7] Translation: ”Mountain-boy, aren’t you sad?” Folk-song in which a mountaineer is asked if he is sad to be leaving the mountain and won’t he please return.

[8] Translation: “Silent Night.”

[9] Translation: “Lullaby sweet baby Jesus.” As a group, Polish Christmas carols are termed “koledy”, and are all joyful, containing an innate poetry. ”Silent Night” is known to have originated in Germany, its author Franz Gruber, but most traditional Polish carols are anonymous. They are essential to the Polish celebration of Christmas.

[10] Translation: “Our Father, Hail Mary, Glory be to the Father.”

[11] Translation: “No, that’s too much.”

[12] Traditional Polish soup made from the blood and meat of ducks, sometimes referred to as “chocolate soup”. The soup was tangy and rich with dried fruits such as plums and raisins.

[13] Translation: Derogatory Polish word for “Jew.”

[14] Translation: “The Lord Jesus.”

[15] Translation: "Everyone. All mankind."

[16] Translation: Derogatory term for "Polish person".

[17] Translation: "so beautiful."

[18] Translation : "May God repay you" Traditional Polish "thank-you".

[19] Translation: "Go with God". Traditional Polish good-bye.

[20] Translation: "Where were you? Out on the streets?"

[21] Translation: "Egg noodles in milk." a soup-like dish made by beating an egg in flour, simmering the resulting clusters in milk and serving warm.

[22] Translation: Polish custom of taking food to be blessed before Easter, foods that have been limited during the fast days of Lent, such as ham and butter and sweetbread, or "placek". Church rules for Lent were stricter at the time in which this story takes place, regulating the size of meals for adults as well as the omission of meat on Friday. The *swiecone* basket helped mark the liturgical end of Lent and the beginning of the Easter cycle. The butter that is lamb-shaped symbollzes Christ, the "lamb" of God who, Catholics believe, has been sacrificed for the redemption of mankind. Colored eggs symbolize the new life of grace that Christ has won for all men, the grace that allows them to be the children of God and entitles them to eternal life. Pierogi are a traditional Polish holiday food. A flour dough is rolled, cut into half-moon shape and stuffed with various fillings such as farmer's cheese, sauerkraut, raisins, prunes or potatoes.

[23] At the opening of the Mass, the priest speaks the words: "Introibo ad altare Dei", Latin for "I will go in to the altar of God." The altar server answers: "Ad deum qui laetificat juventutem meam," Latin for: "To God who is the joy of my youth." At the time of this story, these words and all the words of the Mass were spoken in Latin.

[24] Translation, Latin: The priest intones "Gloria Patri, et Filio, et Spiritui Sancto", "Glory be to the Father, and to the Son, and to the Holy Chost", to which the server replies: "Sicut erat in principio, et nunc, et semper, et in saecula saeculorum. Amen. As it was in the beginning is now, and ever shall be, world without end. Amen"

[25] Translation, Latin: The opening words of the Confession, formerly spoken by priest and server, currently by the entire congregation as well. "I confess to Almighty God…."

[26] Genuflecting. Act of kneeling. In Catholic worship, accompanied by folding of the hands as in prayer and bowing toward the altar in respect.

[27] Cassock. Long black gown worn by priests and altar servers, comprising the first layer of clerical garb.

[28] One of the seven sacraments in the Roman Catholic Church, in which the penitent, after an examination of conscience, tells his sins to a priest. The priest acting in Christ's place, assigns a penance to be performed and absolves the penitent of his sins. The penitent's contrition and resolve to sin no more are necessary for this absolution. This sacrament is now called the "sacrament of reconciliation", and is based on Christ's words to the apostle Peter: "Thou art Peter, and upon this rock, I will build my Church. Whose sins you shall forgive, they are forgiven them. Whose sins you shall retain, they are retained" John: 20:22-23.

[29] The surplice is the garment worn over the cassock, usually knee-length and having wide, open sleeves.

[30] Song traditionally sung at Polish funerals, dedicated to the Blessed Virgin Mary. Another translation: Beloved Mother, guardian of our nation / O hearken to our supplication / Your loyal children kneeling we beseech you / Grant us the grace to be loyal to you. Where shall we seek our solace in distress? /Where shall we turn, whom guilt and sin oppress? Thine open heart, our refuge e'er shall be./ When trials assail us on life's stormy sea.

[31] Sacred cup that holds the wine to be transubstantiated, changed, into the blood of Christ. Transubstantiation is the heart of Roman Catholic belief . After the consecration, when the bread and water is turned into the body and blood of Christ, Catholics receive Holy Communion, as the priest distributes the wafers and offers the cup of wine to the communicants. Partaking of Christ's body and blood, according to Catholic belief, is a sacrament, as is confession, an outward sign of a sacred event taking place in the soul of the recipient.

[32] Act by which the priest, acting as Christ at the Last Supper, changes the water and wine into Christ's body and blood, saying the words, "This is my Body, This is my Blood" Mark 16: 22-23.

[33] Translation: "Enough, enough."

[34] Translation: "I love you."

[35] Translation: "my little angel."

[36] Baptism is the first sacrament a Catholics receives, a ceremony in which the priest pours water on the child's forehead, anoints the child's forehead, feet and hands with the sign of the Cross using oil consecrated at the Easter vigil, a feast linked to Resurrection and new life. The water symbolizes the infusion of the supernatural life of grace which the child receives through the merits of Christ's passion and death. The new life of Christ implies the death of an old one, the life under original sin in which the soul was unable to attain the life of grace through its own efforts. Original sin refers to the belief that Adam and Eve, the first parents of the human race, through their disobedience, lost sanctifying grace and life in Paradise for themselves and their descendants. The child's godparents, in his name, renounce Satan, his temptations and his works.

[37] Translation: "In the name of the Father and of the Son and of the Holy Ghost. Amen."

[38] Translation: "my son."

[39] A gold vessel that covers burning incense and releases the scent into the air during significant Catholic celebrations.

[40] Translation: "beautiful".

[41] Translation: "innocent".

[42] Translation: a sweet bread containing raisins and coated on the top and sides with a crumbly mixture of butter, flour and sugar.

[43] Translation: A prostitute, a streetwalker.

[44] Translation: "Oh Jesus, oh Jesus."

[45] Translation: "my"

[46] Translation: " His stepfather wasn't good."

[47] Translation: "No. no."

[48] Translation: "My son, my son."

[49] Translation: "Thank you."

[50] Translation: "My son, my son."

LaVergne, TN USA
17 November 2009

164483LV00001B/7/P